CASTING STONES

Published by Mindstir Media, LLC
45 Lafayette Rd | Suite 181| North Hampton, NH 03862 | USA
1.800.767.0531 | www.mindstirmedia.com

Printed in the United States of America
ISBN-13: 978-0-9600237-5-2
Library of Congress Control Number: 2018965000

CASTING STONES

A NOVEL ABOUT THE 1985 ELECTION IN GREECE.

JAY BECK

MINDSTIR MEDIA

INTRODUCTION

"*Casting Stones*" continues the adventures that began in "*Panama's Rusty Lock – A novel of the 1984 Presidential Election*" with the fictional character American political consultant, Mark Young, discovering more about the intrigue and danger of managing an international election.

Set in Greece, the historical political thriller pits the United States against the Soviet Union in a battle over Greece's political and economic future, and also traces my experiences during the 1985 Greek national election when I worked as a political consultant.

"*Casting Stones*" gives the reader, not only an inside view of an international election, but it also takes place in the middle of the fight between the Unites States and the Soviet Union over which economic system would direct the world's economy near the end of the Cold War.

Greece's current financial troubles were apparent during the election over 30 years ago and have continued to cause increasing problems for its economy. My experiences during the visit to Arta are a real examples of the kinds of problems that lead to its financial decline. The book also looks at the false promises of socialism and draws uncomfortable parallels between Greece in the mid 1980's and the United States today in its rapid accumulation of debt, political dysfunction and rigid ideology. I have tried to use those issues to suggest similar problems other democratic societies face in creating balanced and debt free economies.

Unfortunately for Greece, the mid 1980's was also a time that saw the beginning of many hijackings and bombings, primarily by Arab terrorists. Similar bombings, assassinations and terrorist attacks by both Greek and Arab extremists targeting US citizens have continued to plague Greece up until the present day. The terrorist incidents described in this book did actually happen, fortunately not to me.

One of the novel's main characters, Maria Beckett, who unfortunately

V

died in 2012, was a woman I worked with while in Greece, and her efforts in the national resistance to the military junta are from my memories of the many stories she told me. She remains the most fascinating woman I have ever met, and my fictional version of her could never do justice to the real adventures in her life or to her heroic character.

Several of the people mentioned here are also part of the public record of that campaign as well as thie history of those times. Although there are events described in this story which actually happened: the conversations, intentions, personalities, motivations, as well as many of the characters, are fictional. Actual names and events were used to add realism to the story, not to suggest any historical or accurate intentions. Many of the scenes and the intrigue are enhanced and exaggerated for dramatic effect. Any offense to those living or deceased is unintended.

During my time in Greece, Igor Andropov was the Soviet Ambassador and Sergei Bokhan was his deputy. Although the references to them in the book are fiction, all of the newspaper references to them included in the story are quoted exactly. The actual fate of the son of the former Soviet Premier, who was the mentor to Vladimir Putin, provides another aspect to the novel's contemporary story.

I am grateful to Virginia Apperson and Pete Williams two gifted Jungian therapists, for assistance with the Mark and Vicki relationship. Thanks also to Claire May for her reading and suggestions. In particular, thanks again to Rosalind Thomas for her patient teaching and perceptive editing as well as a lifetime of friendship and taking the place of the sister I never had.

PRINCIPAL CHARACTERS

AMERICAN

<u>Mark Young</u> – Political consultant, 36 years old, tall, attractive, competent, but nervous about leaving his girlfriend for another overseas job as campaign consultant in a Greek presidential election. He feels the empty space where a family should have been.

<u>Vicki DuVall</u> – late 20's, serious, likable, intuitive, and attractive girlfriend of Mark. She has a job as a researcher on Capitol Hill and they live together in a Washington condo.

<u>Angus Whelan</u> – late 30's, steady leader of team of the New York consulting firm that is providing advice to the campaign and making the commercials. Feels some pressure for bottom line and to make money for firm. Sees international campaigns as something of a serious game.

<u>Bruce</u> – late 40's, shadowy CIA operative, profane, arrogant, unlikable, but competent and useful to know.

GREEK

<u>Maria Beckett</u> – 60, with a stellar past as dissident to the Greek Junta and a leader of the New Democracy party. She manages the campaign and has a past of international intrigue.

<u>Stanos Petkas</u> – early 40's - An academic and intellectual who is one of the world's authorities on Greek culture and art. He is the field manager and event organizer for the campaign. Friendly and athletic. Devoted family man with wife, Cyrilla, and two children.

Sophie Speros – 23 - Beautiful but dissolute girlfriend of Igor Andropov. Socialite whose uncle, Milos Dedacus, 60, is one of the cabinet ministers and a leader of the ruling Socialist PASOK political party.

Andreas Papandreou – Mid 60's - Devout socialist and Prime Minister of Greece who is running for reelection.

Eudora Patmos – 30, and attractive with flowing dark hair and eyes and a striking figure. She is a spy in the New Democracy campaign for the opposition PASOK party.

SOVIET

Igor Andropov – Mid-forties, dashing and handsome playboy son of the late fourth General Secretary of the Communist Party of the Soviet Union, Yuri Andropov. Recently assigned as Soviet Union Ambassador to Greece. Inexperienced but aggressive and arrogant.

Tatiana Andropov – 40 - wife of Igor, beautiful, blue-eyed, blond-haired and manipulative.

Valentine Gubanov – 65 - Tatiana's uncle who works at the Soviet Oil ministry, demanding and crooked.

Tito Petrovia – 45 - Gubanov's fixer and bodyguard – shadow character - ex-KGB, dangerous.

Sergei Bokhan – 45 - Deputy Assistant to Igor Andropov. Career bureaucrat in the Soviet diplomatic corps. Assigned to be the detail man to keep the dashing son of the former Soviet Premier on track for greater things in what promises to be an illustrious career. Family man with wife and two children. Devout member of the Russian Orthodox Church.

TABLE OF CONTENTS

CHAPTER 1

Once again, this morning the goats were out of sorts. The rattling of the fence awoke Anatos and he saw in the dim light that they were agitated and gathered pressed to the far side of the little pen, anxious to leave the overhanging mountainside, and find the gentle, sunny hills up the valley from the stone hut. Likely, they were also anxious to move away from the unusual odor that sometimes came up from the cracks in the nearby rocks and the tremors which had been coming more frequently. He could not smell it today, but sometimes there was something different in the air, not unpleasant, but definitely an unusual odor, not unlike rotten eggs.

After clearing the ash from last night's fire and banking in a little new wood, he finished eating his bread and milk and put down his chipped bowl. When he looked out now, he saw in the brighter light that the goats had pushed open the gate by themselves and were wandering up into his small valley, chewing on the spring leaves starting to grow on the twigs of hillside bushes, and the weeds or grass … anything foolish enough to thrive in the presence of hungry goats.

He then got his wife up, smoothed her hair, put a tattered robe about her shoulders and sat her in the wobbly chair, that he had been intending to fix, by the one window in the house. There she could watch the goats and feel the sun coming down the valley to warm her while he did his chores.

The sky was clear and he could tell from the flies rising in the humidity that it would be another hot day. As he walked slowly toward the goats, out away from the shadow of the tall and menacing hillside behind him, he could see down the narrow valley to the tops of the stones from his first house that had been built near the olive grove. That was years ago though, when he had first brought his family from Macedonia to the area of Delphi at the time when there were more tourists and he had his store by the road with food and the trinkets his wife made. Down toward the foot of the small valley where he had lived before, there was more water from the thin mountain stream and his trees and garden had grown much better closer to the road than the patch he tended up here in this dry soil.

He had lived below in the time before the king came and brought with him the son of Anatos who was a solder in the king's army. He remembered the stories told to him about the monarch by his son who had gone to school with the future king in Macedonia years before. Alexander had rewarded his son by making him an officer in his army and part of his personal guard. When Alexander came to see the Oracle, his son had proudly led the personal guard, and they decided to make camp in this valley, which at that time was a great honor for Anatos.

He had been disappointed that many of the soldiers in the camp guard did not behave well, and his garden and most of the trees were destroyed and burned in campfires by the time they left. Later, he grew tired of people coming to see where the king had made his tent and slept, so after his son returned from Athens and the secret mission to which Alexander had sent him, he moved his wife back up to this higher place along the side of the mountain and built this smaller, one-room house where they were no longer disturbed. Here he could do his duty by watching over what his son had brought back from the stone factory. He was glad their other children were back in Macedonia and were not in this place where life was becoming more difficult.

After checking that his goats were safely grazing and giving his wife some fresh water, Anatos entered the nearby cave with the humility and awe he always felt when he was among such a powerful presence. His slid his hand along the dusty rock to guide his entrance, and he wondered why after so many years there was still no word from his son or the people who worked for King Alexander in Macedonia. He was worried. They had been too long in Persia and in other places he had never heard of where they had their battles. Rumors of great victories came back to him, and he knew they must be attributed to the gods he stood before now. He had the local scribe send message after message to his son and to friends he had known in Macedonia, and even to Alexander's mother, Queen Olympias. When would his son return?

Nothing had come back to him. No instructions on what he should to do. When he asked the oracle about when his son and Alexander would return, nothing.

Yet he was glad that he had moved with his wife back up the quiet valley to be closer to the hillside by the entrance of the cave because he felt so vulnerable here in this empty valley. It was better that people were not coming by the road near his place as much as in past years, and now no one could see his house from the road. He felt he had to hide here back up the valley because he had no idea what he would do if thieves came and tried to take the treasure. Here he felt more isolated with his secret and better shielded from inquisitive eyes.

Years earlier the soldiers had cleared out the cave to serve as a protected place for Alexander to sleep when he was there, which may have given Alexander the idea. Before they had gone to Athens to fetch the treasure, the soldiers had further cleared the floor of debris, leveled the dirt, and carefully prepared each place to receive every large container in the cave. He remembered when his son later brought all the items back, each in its own cart with a great deal of straw and boards and cloth wrapped around them.

It had taken much longer than usual to come from Athens because they were very careful to avoid any bumps in the road. Once they returned, the group of more than 20 soldiers took three full days to pack them carefully into the cave for safekeeping, using the wood, metal and leather from the wagons which they disassembled to add as additional support to protect the crates. They also placed stones and large blocks of wood around each one to secure them. Those were the last days he saw his son before he left with his troop of soldiers, their armor and weapons clanking in haste to catch up to Alexander and prepare for his conquest of Persia. Anatos was told that after the wars in Persia were over they would come back here and then have the time and resources to finish moving the treasure to the king's palace in Macedonia.

Anatos was proud of himself that after the soldiers left, he had put extra rocks around the large containers to protect them further from shifting when the tremors came. Sometimes smaller stones did fall from the top of the cave ceiling, but the boxes protected the great secrets inside. And here in this space he could pray to the gods and feel that they were so close to him that they would hear his message. Still no one came to move them to their final home in Macedonia.

He was perplexed that he had the greatest treasure in the world in this small space, and only he and his wife knew about it and were entrusted with its protection. The people of Greece needed the statues of the gods to be out of their confinement and put in a place open to the world so they could be worshiped properly. He felt that perhaps they had become angry at not being sent to the king's palace in Macedonia where the world would come to see them, marvel at them, and receive their grace and benefits.

Anatos carefully climbed up on a rock and from there onto a small ledge he had made, and moved aside the extra protective limbs from the trees he had put there. Now being several feet off the floor he could move the packaging and straw just a bit so he could peer into the one box he had pried open last year. From this position, he could look down onto the young face of the swift Hermes. His hair was blowing back from his forehead as if caught in the wind, and the expression in his eyes had the look of intelligence and wisdom needed to carry the important messages that his father Zeus and the other gods needed him to relay. His noble head was in the act of turning to one side, as if he had spotted his fellow gods and had begun to move quickly toward them to deliver the dispatches. You could see the sinews and veins in his strong neck as the head turned. There was a god inside this stone aching to emerge and impatient to communicate the news that could change the world.

He could not imagine how powerful they all would look when at last they were placed together, free from these rocks and wooden cases in the dusty cave, and once again assembled and seen in all their glory. All twelve statues again standing proud in the sun and ready to receive their honor and to be worshiped as the gods of Olympus.

Anatos had no way to know that the treasure he protected in this dark, rock room would have the potential to shake the modern world over 2,400 years later.

4

CHAPTER 2

It was two days after Soviet leader Leonid Brezhnev's death, on November 12, 1982, when Yuri Andropov was elected to lead the Communist Party of the Soviet Union. His election was an unusual honor because he was the first former head of the KGB to become General Secretary. After many intense years of service, he had finally gained the power to follow Brezhnev, and now he would run the Soviet Union his way.

He had enjoyed an historic career after fifteen years as the chairman of the KGB, during which time he purged many of those who challenged the ideals of the Soviet Union. Early in his career Andropov had many successes including convincing a reluctant Nikita Khrushchev that military intervention was necessary to crush the Hungarian Revolution. He was considered even more of a hero by leading a campaign of disinformation, intimidation and imprisonment that effectively strangled the voice of dissidents in the Soviet Union, such as the upstart intellectuals Andrei Sakharov and Alexander Solzhenitsyn. He felt he had not received enough credit when he gave the correct advice to Leonid Brezhnev not to invade Poland after the rise of those Solidarity movement people, and he thought that he had displayed a keen insight when he promoted that reform leader, Mikhail Gorbachev, to begin his rise through the ranks. Those moves proved him to be a man of subtlety and reason, and not just a hammer.

Yuri Andropov told the staff to wait outside and entered his palatial new office alone after the long ceremony to think and clear his head from all the noise and commotion. He had so much to do and now he needed to plan how to put his personal stamp on the Soviet Union. He knew where the bones were buried because he had buried many of them himself through his years directing the KGB.

As he started to walk across the expansive space highlighted by the beams of the afternoon sun shining through the great windows, he felt the familiar urge, so he went to his private bathroom, only to see the pink urine that had been coming out of him more frequently lately. Back in the main room, it required many steps to cross the large empty floor to reach the area configured for his office, and as he looked around he thought, 'In the early days we could have housed six families in this space.'

As he approached the enormous desk he could smell the oil his administrative staff had used to bring the wood to an illustrious shine. He put one hand on the corner of the desk and the other on the arm of the large chair and let himself down wearily onto the special pillow that took away some of the pain from his back. Getting old was no fun.

Increasingly, he felt a lingering weariness from his long struggle and recent maneuverings to become the General Secretary, and his back had been hurting more than usual. But he didn't crush all those people to get here in order just to be a caretaker. He rested one elbow on each arm of the massive chair, steepled his rough hands, and thought that if his health would only hold out, he could accomplish much of what he wished to do, but as that was not a certainly, he'd start by cleaning house.

He took out paper and pen and began to write a list of names which he would soon give to his able subordinates to start an anti-corruption campaign against many of Brezhnev's cronies. They'd clear out the old guard and anyone who had treated him with the slightest disrespect or could be a threat. The register that he started that day grew to 18 ministers, and 37 first secretaries of party and government units. He selected others in his entourage to begin criminal proceedings against several high-ranking party and state officials. That gave him a good beginning to put his own brand on the Soviet Union.

His country needed more people like the young Vladimir Putin, who had only been in the security services for ten years, but was already showing signs of promise and leadership. Andropov had recommended that the crafty Putin be sent to Dresden in East Germany, clandestinely labeled as a translator to give him broader experience for his career. He knew Putin would make the most of this assignment. He had seen the determination in his young protégé that Putin knew what to do with power. He was a man Andropov would have been proud to call his son.

Later, despite his best efforts to manage the nation, the discomfort in his bladder continued to affect Andropov's abilities. Not only was his health a concern, but while his purges took place, several events occurred that increased his blood pressure.

The most distracting was the ongoing disastrous war in Afghanistan which was made doubly disconcerting because he had inherited a war with no end in sight and which he had opposed from the beginning. He remembered how aggressively he had counseled Brezhnev and the others that going into Afghanistan was a bad mistake. Then came the blunder of shooting down the Korean Air Flight KAL-007 that carried 269 passengers and crew, including a United States congressman from Georgia. After that his country was labeled an "evil empire" by the new U.S. President, Ronald Reagan.

In an aggressive chess move to regain some initiative between the two superpowers in the international public relations battle, he publically declared that the Soviet Union would stop all work on space-based weapons. Andropov thought that would give him a geopolitical victory over Reagan and show that he was a reasonable leader as well as cut back on the outrageous expenses of the arms race. Unfortunately, that sneaky bastard Reagan announced his Star Wars research program into a ballistic missile defense system that made Andropov look like a fool and caused him to reverse himself. He had to ratchet up a continuation of research and building more weapons in what became an escalation of the cold war that Russia could not afford. In addition to his declining health, it seemed to him that he had brought bad luck with him to run the Soviet Union. However prepared and committed to a good plan for governing, he knew that national leaders are most often judged by things that happen on their watch over which they have little or no control.

The Moskva River slithers through Moscow like an angry serpent contracting to strike. On the western side, it gathers its waters into a head-shaped lake near the western auto ring called the Moscow Oblast. Not far away beside a small, dense forest is the Central Clinical Hospital guarded by the Federal Protective Service, a place that is considered one of the best hospitals in the world. In August of 1983, Yuri Andropov entered the renowned hospital where he would spend the last six months of his life. Ironically, he only had assumed the job of Chairman of the Soviet Union nine months earlier at the pinnacle of his career.

Eventually his struggles with diabetes had wrecked his kidneys and that brought on total renal failure over a six-month period earlier in February of 1983. His increased pain and discomfort were evidence of the last stage in his long history of chronic kidney disease.

When he began his final decline, Yuri Andropov knew the end was near, and he called his top assistant to him for a private conversation. "You must promise to help me this one last time. I have been too busy with my career to do much with my son. Find him a job in the diplomatic corps. He has no experience there, but he has a kind of charm that is often useful in that line of work. He needs to be groomed, and unfortunately, I have not invested enough of my attention to do that. He will need a competent advisor as his number two. Find someone smart who has character and morals and not some obsequious, toady apparatchik. After I'm gone, I can't have my son descending into some depressing Kremlin limbo.

"Get him a posting someplace where he can learn and grow. I want my son to have a chance to develop and move up in the rankings of the Duma into the Politburo. The Party owes me that. They're going to replace me with Konstantin Chernenko, and he's sicker than I am. Who knows who they'll put in after he is dead and gone."

In late January, 1984, due to the growing toxicity in his blood, Andropov's health deteriorated sharply and included periods of unconsciousness. Sensing the end was near, Andropov's staff called his family to come to his bedside.

As is sometimes the case with the children of notable public figures, his son, Igor, now in his early 40's, had become a playboy who favored sporting Western clothes, had decadent habits, and for public events gained additional, unsavory notoriety when he was often accompanied by his glamorous wife. It was unfortunate that Igor Andropov had few skills related to a real job, and the little authority he exercised was slyly linked to the rise of his father's fearsome power. He had learned to chill people's frivolity and rivet their attention by dropping phrases into conversations like, "I wonder what my father will think about what you are suggesting?" or "I may need to run your idea past my father first." In the lower realms of Soviet society, this crass associative demeanor got Igor the acquiescence he desired, brought him any favors he wanted and also enabled him to avoid undesirable tasks. When he was called to his father's bedside two days before Yuri Andropov's death, Igor was serving as the number two Soviet representative at the Madrid Security Conference meeting in Stockholm, a gathering that resembled a hog call of well-dressed flunkies.

Soviet Premier Yuri Andropov died at age 69 on February 9, 1984 at 4:50 p.m. in his hospital room after only fifteen months in office.

Promises were made and promises were kept. Eight months later the handsome Igor Andropov was named the Ambassador to Greece and arrived in Athens with his wife, the beautiful blue-eyed, blond-haired Tatiana. The couple wore the latest in Western styled clothing and each spoke several languages. They were dashing and immediately became the most desirable guests in the Athens social circuit among the diplomatic corps. People often said the couple looked like the top of a wedding cake. Tatiana began to appear in fashion magazines, attended runway shows, and Greek designers begged her to wear their latest creations. Igor Andropov arrived in Greece right at the time when Prime Minister Andreas Papandreou's government was sharply attacking U.S. foreign policy, fawning over the Soviet Union, and getting ready for his important reelection campaign. The Greeks saw the young Andropov as an important and welcomed ally, and it seemed Igor Andropov's stars were finally aligned and his new career in diplomacy would lead him to greater things.

CHAPTER 3

Mark Young had just drifted off to take a nap, scrunching his 6'2"
frame into a semi-fetal position because he was too long for the couch,
when the phone began to ring. It was unusual for him to get calls late on
a Sunday morning in Washington, D.C., and as he rolled over to look for
the noisy phone, several sections of the Sunday *New York Times* fell off his
chest to join the *Washington Post* in a big pile on the floor.

His freshly opened eyes now focused, and he looked around the condo
where clothes and magazines were scattered all about. He caught the but-
tery smell from the empty popcorn bowl still sitting there under the table
after last night's movie. The TV was on but with the Sunday morning
talk shows over, the sound was way down and playing softly in the background. As his consciousness slowly registered, he heard his girlfriend,
Vicki DuVall, shouting from the master bedroom towards the den where
Mark struggled to wake. "Mark, honey, will you get that please, I'm in the
middle of something here."

Her words now fully awakened him and he was reminded how much
comfort he got in hearing the way the murmur of her voice washed over
him, even from a distance. Then he realized that he had never told her that.
Mark picked up the remote and fully quieted the TV, then picked up the
princess phone balanced on the edge of the coffee table and heard, "Mark,
it's Angus. How are you doing? Have you fully recovered from Panama?"
His friend, the highly competent and gregarious Angus Whelan, directed
the international campaigns for the Duncan Rogers political firm head-
quartered in New York, and together they had worked a presidential campaign in Panama that had ended two months before. They met when they
both worked for the administration of Jimmy Carter a few years earlier.

"Yeah. We're doing great here." Now he was fully awake, and as this
was business, he hunched himself up into a sitting position. The remains

of the paper hit the floor. "I've been doing some consulting on a couple of ballot initiatives and enjoying the slower pace." Mark, who ran his own political consulting firm in Washington, D.C., had learned a great deal by working in his first international campaign. When Angus hired Mark for the Panama job, that campaign gave Mark additional credentials for his political consulting business.

In Panama, he had worked his heart out for over six months in an election whose only result was the continuation of support for a system of power propped up by corruption and greed. He had lost his idealism. Now he saw one philosophy of government over another as the means to the end of achieving power and although he did not like that hardened cynicism in himself, it was there now. Despite the fact that he still believed democracy was the best hope for the world, its flaws depressed him even as he worked toward its incremental improvements in Washington. He still recognized and admired idealism in others, like a child who has found out about Santa Claus, but silently enjoys the fantasies of his younger siblings.

Angus continued, "Well, I'm calling to see if you want to pick up the pace. We've got an election in Greece and it's not like Panama in that this time we're just giving some oversight and advice. The pay is actually better than before, and you'd be doing something similar to what you did in Panama to train the staff to organize events, scheduling and some field operations."

By this time Mark was fully sitting up. "Yeah, you mentioned that something might be coming up, and it does sound interesting. Can you send me a care package of material on the project? What's the timetable?"

"We would be going over in two to three weeks. Likely be going in and out of Greece over several months. But this would be really more training them to do their own campaign and much less hands-on than Panama. The hours would be shorter, and we would not have the pressure of having to be responsible for so much of the campaign results."

"Well that does sound much more appealing, but, Angus, your description sounds like a sales job for a political cruise line. I've known you for almost 20 years, and I know there is more to it than your rosy sounding BS, remember I've seen you operate. Just send me the stuff and I'll call you later this week and find a time to come up to New York." He hung up to Angus's laughter on the other end of the phone.

Three days later Mark walked into Washington's botanical garden building carrying two brown bag lunches and was immediately enveloped by the warm, humid air and combination of odors from flowering plants and decay. In the humid space, he smelled the accumulation of floral accents unfurling, bright and new, searching in the filtered sunlight for their zenith, ironically just above the decay from those dropped petals exhausted from hanging on too long.

He and Vicki often met in the beautiful, lush, crystal palace with the glass-domed ceiling during these cold winter months because it gave them both a feeling of having an instant tropical vacation, and it was also close to her job as a researcher on nearby Capitol Hill. As he waited for her while looking at all the colorful foliage, he was reminded of his mother's habit of always having fresh flowers in her kitchen. She had read in one of those etiquette-conscious women's magazines about self-improvement, that flowers in a home were a sign of upper middle-class prosperity. His mother really did not care so much for the flowers, but she craved respectability.

His parents' careful rigidity and fear of public criticism made them loyal to a firm work ethic which also acted as their social life preserver. They were uncurious, orderly and they restricted their affection as they presented a proper front to the communal propriety they desired. He grew up in the 50's when uniformity was a desirable thing.

They sought out friends of similar values and they reinforced each other's conservative attitudes. For them authority was never questioned. For them their place in society represented the desire to belong to a federation of privilege which was the place to display a polite decorum practiced in their public appearances, and returned to storage after use. They loved predictability.

His parents had been dead now for over two years after a drunk driver hit them returning from their club. As an only child, he had to take off from campaign duties for several months to oversee the cleaning out of the house and the settling of the estate. He had met Vicki shortly after returning to Washington. Rejecting his parents' lifestyle, Mark made it a point to find his own way.

Despite his efforts he saw their patterns emerging in his own appreciation of order and loyalty. Vicki told him that this attribute was why he could be detached and clinical in his job, which was a good trait for political consulting, but not so good for their relationship. Often, she could see him more clearly than he could see himself, but he rarely wanted to discuss these personal inner feelings and, after her analysis, he just said, "Yeah. Interesting."

When Vicki arrived, they sat down under a huge fern foliage canopy on a bench near one of the fountains to eat and talk in a place where they would not be bothered by the intermittent external street noise or chatter from groups of tourists walking the pathways in the nearby gardens.

Vicki was one of those people who seemed to have been born an adult and grew up quickly through the chaos of her parents' fighting and eventual divorce. The serious circumstances of her childhood did not prohibit her from experiencing youthful joy, laughter and happiness, but instead helped her to develop an intuitive understanding of their importance and fragility in a complicated world. She was an anchor of reason and everyone liked her, the kind of person who was often chosen for class offices in school, attractive but with the kind of non-threatening beauty that avoided the jealousy of others. As she became a woman, she made her own way toward achieving her goals in both her career and her relationships.

After polishing off the sandwiches, Mark lay back on the bench with his head in her lap and looked up at her beautiful, show-stopping face. He said half in jest, "You're so much better than ninety-nine percent of the career-grubbing leeches up here. You deserve better than me."

Vicki smiled down at him. "I'd like to think I've got better." She stroked his hair, "I like to think what we have together is a fortunate thing, that's sometimes hard to come by in a one-company town like this, where people seem to be interested only in what you can do for their careers."

Mark rolled toward Vicki, propped himself up on one elbow across the other side of her body and leaned closer to her, looking deeply into her eyes. "How can we make all this," he waved his free hand about, "go away and be on our own deserted island, wearing," he looked up and down her trim, fit body, "wearing that satin thing you got from Victoria's Secret, and block everything else out? I'd like to get you away from this crazy city and this rapid pace in our lives."

Vicki leaned towards him and put her hand on his cheek "We can do that tonight at home or after my two o'clock meeting in the broom closet down the hall from my office, or pretend no one is watching or do it here, at least until we get arrested. Although . . . "

Mark leaned closer until their lips almost touched and said, "Yes, baby."

"Mark, we can hang out together like this anytime we feel like it, but we can't look at each other like this if you're several thousand miles away and wrapped up in another international campaign. Let's enjoy what we have now, but let's know what we will be giving up." She gave him a soft kiss.

Mark looked at her with his face still close to hers and said, "God! I hate it when you talk that way. You're always so, so . . ."

"Right?" She gave him another peck.

Mark continued his thought as she kissed him. ". . . aware. You see things better than I do, and you're smarter than most twenty-seven year olds."

Vicki nodded, "I try to see things as they are. And, I don't want to lose you and I don't want to miss you for nights on end. I've gotten used to your messy papers and your slurping water at night, and your puffy eyes in the morning. I'm not sure about how smart I am, but maybe you are just a late bloomer?"

Mark looked away for a moment realizing the larger implications of what she had just said, and then looked back at her, "Is this one of those career versus relationship choices I've heard so much about?"

Vicki looked at him, "It doesn't have to be an either-or choice, but it is a choice that's gonna have consequences one way or the other."

Mark said, "I love you."

"I know. Me too."

They kissed.

Now past his mid-thirties, Mark had been wondering what he was going to do with himself when he grew up. He was successful and becoming nationally known as an effective political consultant, both as a technician and as a strategist in political campaigns. Lately he was becoming a bit bored with the drudgery of Senate and governor's races, by the petty jealousies he often felt from the staffs who had been with candidates for a long time, and sly manipulations by family and friends who wished to have their half-baked ideas accepted as campaign dogma. Shepherding a group of nervous and frightened people through the political traps and public exposure of a statewide campaign increasingly tested his patience. The new avenue for international campaigns gave him both excitement and a nice paycheck, but the travel wore him down and was an anathema to his tendency to putter around the house and be a homebody on the weekends with a woman, and in particular with Vicki, who he cared about and appreciated more each day. That kind of travel also ran counter to an instinct that only recently he had admitted to himself, that he felt in the empty space where a wife and family should have been.

CHAPTER 4

Tatiana, the wife of Igor Andropov, shivered looking out through the quivering window.

The freezing cold rushed the stooped pedestrians bound in heavy clothes, struggling along icy streets seeking any nearby shelter as the howling wind battered the glass and stirred the outside air containing the grey snow along the gray streets next to the gray buildings.

She thought, 'Moscow in the winter has to be the worst place on earth', and then she began to smile as she anticipated the warm sun, water and beaches of Greece. The new assignment of her husband, Igor, was a promising first diplomatic posting, and she felt she had paid her dues standing by him as he floundered in the backwaters of the Soviet hierarchy. Now maybe he could give her something of the life she really wanted.

Tatiana Gubanov Andropov had only heard the news of her husband's posting as the new Soviet Ambassador to Greece when her powerful Uncle Valentine Gubanov called with congratulations. She knew that her uncle, the disciplined and sometimes frightening official in the Soviet Union's Ministry for Oil and Gas, wielded much greater power than it would appear just by comparing his title and position to the others in the list of the 37 ministries that comprised the unwieldy bureaucracy governing the day-to-day operations of the Soviet Union.

In addition to being in the oil ministry, he was also a deputy member of the Duma. His area was one of the few offices that actually created the revenue the Soviet Union needed to run its vast, cumbersome operations and keep its largely outdated army functioning. The need for additional funding was made all the more important in the past six years since the ill-advised invasion of Afghanistan in 1989, that had bled their country of resources, and now more of their young men were coming home in body bags or bitter, angry and drug addicted from that rock-infested hell hole.

She had recently been receiving rather specific requests from her uncle, Valentine, who had risen through the ranks of the Soviet oil and gas ministry, not by an understanding or competence in petroleum production, but by supplying his superiors with what they wanted. Her uncle prided himself as a student of human desires, personal not professional, and he knew that fulfilling the shadowed needs of his colleagues would ingratiate him with those receiving his gifts far more than producing studious memos on oil rig proficiency. He saw his niece Tatiana and her husband, the son of the former Soviet General Secretary, as now being in a position to help him further his career with their new Greek posting, and he thought, it was about time.

Valentine Gubanov had become the man to procure western technology and culture, who found the young ladies to come to the dacha for the weekend, who got the errant children off from illegal indiscretions. Valentine anticipated the trends for human greed and assembled a staff with the skills and international contacts to reach far beyond the iron curtain to obtain the impossible to acquire. He was always looking for new outlets and backdoor channels to secure illicit goods or services to keep his friends happy. Having access to the supplies of an entire nation through his niece and her husband offered the attractive potential for additional patronage to bestow on his colleagues in the oil ministry.

Gubanov's secret was that he knew that most of the fumbling herd of sub-managers in his agency did not actually do much except pretend that they were important. He saw his role as supporting this large group by continuing to uphold their misperceived value and by keeping them happy in their illusion. Many of them got their jobs through government relations or as a payoff for a past service to a more powerful official. Some were placed there as sleepers to comply with their benefactor's request for support at the appropriate time in the future. Gubanov's work was necessary to keep this crowd's vanity placated and away from the handful of men who actually made things function. He knew his role in appeasement and distraction was a value to the real bosses, and they appreciated him mollifying the dilettantes and hangers-on. The Soviet Union needed men like him. In fact, his role was essential to keep the nation on an even keel while the enormous bureaucracy underneath - dawdling and uncomplaining - let the big boys do their work.

But the festivities, comprised of the drinks, the girls and the weekends at his or other dachas, were getting too familiar and predictable, and he feared his act was going flat and needed new spice. He felt the need to step up his game and to bring in something new and interesting. If not, his value to the real working men would diminish and that was a prospect he did not wish to imagine.

Now, if the truth be known, much of Valentine's overinflated appraisal of his job and value to the Soviet Union was only relevant in his head, and he assumed an ostentatious attitude to confirm his own self-esteem. All the same, there was enough of an element of truth to his fantasy, that the game he played was serious and there were dangerous consequences to those who crossed him.

Valentine felt important by being the man in the spotlight, the one to offer the pleasures of the flesh and other distractions to his colleagues. He never questioned whether the gaggle of hedonistic bureaucrats that he entertained fit a profile uncomfortably like himself. For Valentine truly believed he was the valued ringmaster and social director necessary to keep the critical oil ministry functioning as the key element in the Soviet government's economy.

In 1985 the Soviet Union was fast becoming the world's largest producer of crude oil and natural gas. He could see that the pressure to increase production would demand new investments to boost the technology and infrastructure in the current Soviet oil and gas industry. The critical need to keep the commerce flowing was exacerbated because of the funds diverted to support the disastrous war in Afghanistan and the cumbersome Soviet management system. The oil and gas production was further tainted because prices were strictly controlled, and domestic producers and exporters were unhappy that much of the profits were diverted into state revenues for the war. They all realized that the building crisis was unsustainable for the Soviet economy.

A few years ago, Gubanov had encouraged the marriage of Tatiana to the handsome Igor when his father was the head of the KGB, and Valentine was delighted when Yuri Andropov became premier. But until now Igor and his niece were in danger of descending into the mundane backwater of Soviet officials destined for lesser duties and gradually forgotten by the bureaucracy.

Now as the new Greek Ambassador, Igor needed to prove to Gubanov that his marriage to Tatiana would be the vehicle to help him increase his influence in the oil ministry. Gubanov was determined the posting in Greece would prove to be the ideal vehicle to sustain his ambitions.

Valentine considered that perhaps at this opportune moment he could also get credit for increasing shipping for the Soviet fleet and counter the influence of Greek or Western shipping businesses. So, he had reminded his niece that she and her family owed him their status and place in society. He planned to push her to accommodate his needs through her husband who, so far, had appeared to be something of a lightweight. Despite Igor's own weaknesses, which seemed to outweigh his strengths, Gubanov was hell-bent to milk Andropov's job as ambassador to Greece for all it was worth.

The beautiful, young woman slowly packed her bags and admired the new lingerie and soft and revealing clothes she had been given. She loved the way they clung to her exceptional figure. This was in part her reward for undergoing the past month of strenuous training in the PASOK political camp. She had worked hard and graduated well ahead of the others, who may have been better at picking locks or working the listening devices or planting bugs. Eudora Patmos smiled as she knew that her beauty was the secret ingredient that gave her the edge over the other young women who were her competitors for the prize of infiltrating the New Democracy campaign. She also excelled at office work and knew how to operate some of the more recent pieces of equipment, such as sophisticated copy machines.

In addition to her old day job in a corporate office, she had worked for the PASOK party in a local and regional capacity and learned about the political benefits of socialism and the dangers and treachery of capitalism. Now they were sending her to meet a person who would give her final instructions on what to do and how to live in her nation's capital, get her a place to live and show her how to apply for a job with the New Democracy party represented by the business elite. Once she was hired there she would be on her own to find ways to sabotage the capitalist party and ensure the reelection win for her prime minister.

She was excited and felt she was up to the challenge and that this job would set her career on a path to much greater success. She knew that she might be required to do some things that were considered distasteful, but for her they would be a pleasure as they were the keys to open the locks to her success. Eudora Patmos was motivated, dedicated, trained and more than ready as she boarded the bus for Athens carrying her suitcase of skimpy clothes.

CHAPTER 5

On the return flight from New York, Mark reviewed the documents Angus had provided on Greece, some of which had been redacted by the source, which indicated to Mark that they had been classified at some point. The material showed that since WWII, Greece had increasingly been under the influence of the Soviet Union. The New Democracy Party had emerged over the last 10 years after the fall of the Greek junta, with a commitment to counter the rise of the Soviet Union and socialism, which had become a dominant influence over most of the governments in Eastern Europe after World War II. New Democracy was anchored by a group of wealthy business leaders and cargo shipping owners who became best known to the U.S. public when shipping magnate, Aristotle Onassis, dumped the great opera singer, Maria Callas, in 1968 to marry the much younger, Jacqueline Kennedy, the widow of the assassinated American President.

The pro-business New Democracy political party was designed to be more like the moderate U.S. Republican party from the 1960's and 1970's, but without all the social activists and warmongers. New Democracy advocated a free market economy and was opposed to the existing government that represented a philosophy more like textbook socialism or communism. These two sides in the Greek political conflict were much more extreme and better defined than the left and right, as they were known in the U.S.

Greece's drift toward Soviet influence increased in 1981 when the socialist government of Andreas Papandreou came to power and took the country in a radically left direction. The new bureaucracy of patronage and government monopolies employed over 20 percent of the population and had quadrupled the national debt while providing most Greeks with generous benefits from the government. The socialists under Papandreou were allied with the Greek communist parties and controlled much of the media with a decidedly anti-American message. The Soviet government employed their international secret police, the KGB, to look for any way to discredit the U.S. in the Cold War environment of that time, and the Soviets actively supported the Greek government's socialist intentions.

The political dynamics of the coming election were characterized by that increasing international polarization that put Greece dead center in the target of the Cold War. The past decades of frequent conflicts and bloodshed had hardened loyalties, and the political divisions were recognizably rigid. Recent national polling indicated the socialists had almost 50 percent in public support, the New Democrats, who employed Mark and Angus, almost 35 percent, and the Communists about 15 percent. The nation had a total population of under 10 million people, which was the size of metropolitan Chicago; that meant most of the national leadership knew each other. So, it would take a dramatic event to cause big changes in the voting patterns, although the poor economy, quirky personalities, and the incompetence of a smattering of leaders had begun to cause some erosion of support from the left toward the New Democracy party.

To Mark, the Greek election represented another clear opportunity to help democracy and the U.S. government with its free market, democratic philosophy. He thought this campaign seemed like a much greater way to help the United States and its interests than getting involved in another domestic campaign where the views of the various candidates, once you discounted the theatrical propaganda, did not vary much from one to the other.

He saw Greece as likely being his last campaign abroad and decided to absorb as much of the environment as he could. He was not looking forward to being overseas for stretches of several weeks at a time, but this seemed like a good cause and worth the sacrifice. Plus, the money was going allow him to put aside significant savings for whatever he decided to do in the future. Mark smiled as he recalled Angus in his enthusiasm for intrigue saying their job was like being political spies. He came back to Washington excited and motivated, but was torn because he knew that this would also cause stress in his relationship with Vicky, as extensive traveling had for previous girlfriends.

That night they were both clearing the dinner dishes when Vicki began the conversation he had been avoiding since his return earlier from New York.

"You're getting sucked into this thing."

Mark had been trying to find the right time to tell her that he had agreed to go, and had been equivocating in earlier conversations as though he were still deciding. "Well, that's what I'm going to try to find out. This campaign could be about history. It is enticing and intoxicating, so I'm trying to see what things look like. We can deal with whatever we have to after that."

Vicki, gave a knowing smile to herself, looked down and then back up at Mark, with a serious face. "Don't kid yourself, or me. You're going. I just hope it will be worth it. You're moving into a midpoint in your career and you don't want to look foolish by jumping into the unknown. You're known in politics here as being stable and having common sense. Don't risk the reputation you've built unnecessarily. From what you've told me there is no chance of winning this election in Greece."

"Thanks, Mom."

Vicki put down the dishtowel, "There's something else Mark…"

He looked at her, and realized she was really serious, and he sat down to listen.

"I need to say up front that I'm conflicted in what I'm about to say. I believe in what you are about to do, maybe not in the person or candidate whoever they are, but in the idea of

making the world a better place. I believe for a lack of a better word that it's important. Okay. I have two 'buts.' First, I did some research, and Americans are not so popular in Greece. Westerners and soldiers are being attacked. People die. Second, you are approaching, if you're not already in, the time of life we call middle age."

Mark blinked, a little shocked to hear himself defined that way.

"You've been running off from one campaign to another for going on twenty years, and it's time to find out if the chase is more important than

23

catching whatever you are after. You need to find out if the glory of being a Senate staffer or a White House staffer or an Assistant Under Secretary of whatever is your ultimate goal. Or are you just caught up in the chase and competition of one campaign after the other. What is your end game here?" She looked down and sighed and then looked back up. "I'm twenty-seven. I want a husband and a family. I believe we can have a good life together, but not if you're going to charge after every windmill that comes by."

He started to say something, and she raised her hand to stop him. "My biological clock is ticking. I'll wait this one out, Mark, but no more. I want a husband who comes home at night, who's going to be there for the kids. I believe you could be unbelievably good at that, but you've gotta be willing to give up the chase. I don't care if you are a shoe salesman or if we live in a trailer, or if we live in North Dakota, but I want you home with us."

She stopped, "Okay, you can speak."

Mark paused a minute to let that sink in, "I heard all that and I caught the nuances; and you know how I feel about you. I'm not so excited about running off, and I'm not sure I want to do this again. Although if... there is a chance to make a difference and I feel something inside, I ..."

Vicki interrupted, "How much of it is ego, Mark?"

He blinked and was again surprised at how well she knew him and could see through him. When she used his name in a conversation directed at him, it was not good news. He stammered. "I don't really know. I do feel that whatever it is, it is not worth losing you. Let me do this. I'll be thinking and I know you will, about what we do with our relationship afterwards. I promise not to screw this up. Screw us up."

She closed the dishwasher with a little bit of a bang. "So, you're going to Greece for more money than you have made in any two or three campaigns combined and also a chance to make history, and gain a little glory?"

Mark grimaced, "It's not just that. I've been thinking about all the ways I could really help these people. Vic, this is really kind of an opportunity of a lifetime. After all, Greece is where democracy started. It's a chance to make a difference. We could change things for the better. I know it sounds kind of naïve or lame, but this campaign is an opportunity to actually work against the bad guys, the damn Russians."

Vicki sighed again. "One more thing. Don't get your back up, this is constructive criticism. Around here when you sound naïve, most people recognize it is your way to ingratiate yourself and be friendly. That can also make you sound, well … not as smart as you really are, and it can give a bad first impression. Also, you can be a smartass sometimes with your wisecracks. Here in this town we all get it. In another culture with language issues, I'm not so sure those traits, which you sometimes think are endearing, well … they may not come off as smoothly as you think. Just sharing."

"You make me sound like a jerk. Am I that bad?"

"You are the man I love and one of the smartest, kindest and most well-directed people I've ever known. It's just that sometimes you have a way of obfuscating what you're after. I've seen you in meetings act all friendly and uninformed like a puppy dog, and then at the next meeting people find out that you know more than they do, that you've already gotten your way behind the scenes, and that you have set them up. It works here with Capitol Hill staffs and some lobbyists, because so many people here are playing games. I'm just suggesting in another culture the people there might find that disingenuous and offensive. You might need to be more aware of some of your little habits."

"Okay. Thanks. I'll try to be aware. That's good advice." Mark leaned against the counter, folded his arms and stared at the floor in thought.

Vicki realized the conversation was over, punched the settings into the dishwasher, and realizing Mark needed a break from what she considered good advice, said, "Well, at least then you'll be earning enough to keep paying your share of the rent while you're gone."

Mark, still staring at the floor, turned his head to the side and gave her a "give-me-a-break" look.

Eudora Patmos sat on a bench with her control officer from the PASOK political party on a quiet side of Syntagma Square, the central square of Athens near the Old Royal Palace, that now housed the Greek

Parliament. She reported to him her success at becoming a trusted staffer on the New Democracy political team and that because of her office proficiency and fluency in English she was designated to be the support staff for the Americans who were coming to help on the campaign. Eudora was congratulated for her skills at achieving this milestone as a key part of the plans PASOK had to disgrace the New Democracy party and send the Americans home in defeat.

She and her handler discussed several potential traps for the Americans, and Eudora was instructed to investigate the viability of each and select the one with the greatest potential. She was reminded that a significant portion of the success of the presidential campaign depended on her ability to create a scandal that proved the debauchery and treachery of the West. Her handler looked up and down her body and at the tight dress she wore as an example of the type of clothing she would wear at the campaign. He liked what he saw and looked at her with undisguised lust and he found her perfume intoxicating. She smiled back at him, appreciating his approval as it gave sanction and anticipated her accomplishment.

She knew her success in this mission would advance her career with the PASOK party and ensure her the gratitude of the socialist government, and although the top party leaders did not know of her specific assignment, they would fully appreciate the result. Since she had been tasked with this job, she had been dreaming of her triumph and inside she purred with anticipation.

After this meeting, she would be on her own and fully imbedded in the New Democracy campaign until she executed her plan. She assured her control she was ready and dedicated to the destruction of the Americans. He detected her raw ambition and felt she would not rest until she had achieved success, and smiled as he imagined the shame the Americans would receive in world opinion.

In preparation for his trip abroad, Mark began to invest his time in more research of Greek history and politics and to read books on recent activities in the country. He found that Greece had been in turmoil and overrun by many conflicts over hundreds and even thousands of years, and in decline for many centuries since around 300 BC. At the height of its power in antiquity, it essentially created both democracy and Western civilization.

He stopped getting his hair cut by expensive Washington hair stylists and started to grow it longer and found ways to let it look more unkempt. As his time was limited, he could not do much more because he had to let his few clients know that he would not be available for a while, and one client with more pressing needs had to be turned over to someone else.

Mark knew it was important to dress like working-class people to blend into the Greek streets where he would likely need to travel. He began packing by pulling out several very old shirts with frayed collars and cuffs and got out his older thick sweaters with turtle or crew necks and old black pants. There were some spots where he had forgotten to have the sweaters dry-cleaned before he'd put them up at the end of last winter, and was actually glad as he felt they added to the rumpled impression he needed to create.

Nothing was selected for the trip that contained western logos. No polo riders, or swishes, or any American logo symbols of a brand. Nothing to be noticed or remembered or that suggested USA. He'd get shoes in Greece but would start out with an old pair of Doc Martens that looked clunky enough. He put in two old Adidas tracksuits and shoes as exercise clothes into the bag, also because Adidas was a German brand. He topped that off with a stocking cap that could be rolled up or down and an old-fashioned flat newsboy hat. The headgear he washed, stepped on and twisted enough to make them look old. He would take two bland wool sport coats and other better clothes for certain meetings, and one good suit.

Mark and Vicki began to eat out more in Greek restaurants so he could learn the names and tastes of various kinds of food. They attended services in the Saint Sophia Greek Orthodox Cathedral on 36th Street not far from the home of the Vice President on Massachusetts Avenue, and Mark found the church services gave him a better feel for the ambiance of being in a Greek culture.

He liked the methodical old-world atmosphere given by the sing-song chanting, shaking bells, incense and candles, and long black cassocks in a congregational space decorated with icons, church saints, and deceased leaders from long ago. He was curious about the Orthodox Cross with its three-bared cross, one at a slant, and discovered that the slant cross was supposed to represent the foot rest kicked out of place; and on the top, a short bar was where supposedly a sign was placed reading "King of the Jews." Mark remembered the more traditional images of the smiling Jesus finding lost lambs from pictures on the church fans lying on the pews from his youthful Sundays in South Georgia. More than a religious significance, Mark felt he was in the presence of centuries old traditions that gave the parishioners a sense of belonging and collective comfort.

About week before he was to leave, Vicki sat him down for another cautionary conversation. "I know you've been learning a lot about Greece's politics, but I've also been doing some more research. There is this left-wing group of revolutionaries called N-17 in Greece who were started because of the ultra-conservative Regime of the Colonels and they are very violent and bloody. They are targeting Americans, particularly American soldiers, and may have been responsible for several of the recent killings. They and a lot of the socialists and communists want our military bases out of Greece and are killing people to prove their point. You are going in there to work against them. Mark, this is dangerous."

Mark started to say something but Vicki stopped him. "Four years ago, one of the people in the political bureau of our embassy was killed in a car bomb. Three years ago, there were two bombs at our ambassador's home. A month later a CIA agent's car was burned. A couple of months after that there were multiple attacks on American companies, banks and the Greek ship owners. Two years ago, one of our admirals was shot to death and last year an army sergeant was shot." She leaned back and looked at him.

Mark slowly shook his head, held her hands and waited a moment for both of them to feel calmer. "I also looked up the references that you just mentioned, but what we have seen recently over there is the terrorism of the Arabs, mostly Palestinians, who are pissed off at Israel. What I'm going to be doing is far away from all that. Vicki, we're trying to get people elected who can help settle down the violence. I'm not going to do anything to call attention to myself. I am not a military person wearing a uniform nor an embassy employee. It may be that I never even go to the American embassy. Part of doing my job is to be invisible and I am not looking for trouble or to be noticed. You know my role in international politics is about trying to get the best governments elected out there, and hopefully ones who will be friendly with the U.S." She leaned over to be closer to his face, "Mark, you can't change what's been happening there for thousands of years, much less the past year or two. You're just being arrogant. Angus can find someone else to go do what you do. You may be in real danger there. He doesn't need you. They don't need you. You are only irreplaceable to me."

They left the discussion with no clear solution or any changes to Mark's plans, and again found themselves in the familiar territory of many of their discussions where no one won or changed the other's view. Vicki however seemed particularly needy and more emotional than normal. As a piece offering they both agreed to meet in Paris to celebrate their anniversary of moving in together in the coming spring three months after Mark had been in Greece and was settled into the campaign. A Paris vacation together had been a dream of theirs and it gave them something to look forward to. April in Paris, what could go wrong?

The conservative banker and publisher Nikolaos Momferatos, walked out of the expensive jewelry store on Voukourestiou Street pleased with his purchase. As he held the small box in his hand, he looked up at the nearby towering Lycabettus hill and thought how fortunate he was to live in such a beautiful and historic city. He wondered if he had time to walk across nearby Vasilissis Sofias Avenue for a quick visit to the Byzantine Museum but decided he needed to move on before the traffic got any heavier.

He needed to get his wife to wrap the bracelet he had just purchased as a gift for Maria Beckett in gratitude for her agreeing to manage the New Democracy campaign. The gift was to be a surprise for the campaign manager from a group of financial donors to the party. They would need to arrange for a dinner to present it to her because he knew Beckett would soon be so intensely involved in the campaign, they would not see her again for many months.

He looked for his driver, Panagiotis Rousetis, and waved him to bring the car. As the car pulled up to the curb, a motorcycle that had been parked in an alley cruised up at the same time and the man on the back of the bike began to fire a gun and bullets hit both Nikolaos and Panagiotis. The man then calmly got off the bike and shot them again with the .45 cal. pistol before remounting the back of the motorcycle which then zigzagged quickly, but not incautiously through the traffic and disappeared. Later the Marxist terror group N-17 would claim credit for the assassination. The bracelet which had been in Nikolaos's hand now lay nearby on the street, and was picked up as an expensive souvenir by one of the crowd which soon gathered to observe the aftermath of the attack.

CHAPTER 6

Mark met Angus at the ever-grimy LaGuardia Airport in New York and together they boarded the flight to Athens. Angus carried his trademark rectangular typewriter-sized briefcase stuffed heavy with books, ideas, intrigue and invoices. After the flight was underway and the announcements were over, Angus began to brief Mark more about the campaign as they sat together in the comfortable business class compartment. As he started to talk, Mark noticed that Angus had gained a little weight, and then noticed the same thing about himself. He made a mental note to get more exercise in Greece than he had done in Panama.

Angus spoke in a low voice, "In this election, we will be setting up for the next one, so it will not be as involved as Panama but maybe more important because of the U.S. and Soviet elements. This election is not just about grabbing power like in Panama or in the U.S.; this is a philosophical confrontation. In Greece, we will be facing our main international political competitor for the last 60 years. Greece is kind of like a swing state, but between democracy and communism.

"Our candidate, Konstantinos Mitsotakis, is a former old lefty environmentalist from Crete where he has a large collection of ancient Minoan art. He once worked with our opponent Andreas Papandreou, but broke from him in the mid 1960's, which helped to cause the fall of Papandreou's father who was in power in Greece at the time. So, there is bad blood there. Over time Mitsotakis worked his way up to become the New Democracy leader last year and he's probably considered more of a centrist than hard right ideologue.

"What we need to do is to help them get organized, to show them how to have a visible presence, and to put a strong effort into this upcoming election that leaves our candidate and his party looking like a reasonable and responsible option with a good plan to improve the future of Greece.

There may be a different candidate for the new Democracy in four years, so this is more about making the party institution look good. You need to teach them how to set up the rallies properly like you did in Panama, but you don't have to manage them up to the election. Give instructions on how to do advance and scheduling and also how to make the political decisions so when they do have to make a speech they give consideration to who else speaks, who else is on the stage, backdrops and stuff like that. It's a political teaching job. I may be in and out of the country as I was in Panama and I need you to be there for me to hold their hands. The leadership of the New Democracy party thinks the socialists will screw the economy up so much that they don't need to take too strong a position on any issues just now. They just want to be ready and to appear reasonable for the next election.

"You'll be working directly with a professor who is from one of the universities, so a smart guy. He'll train the others on what you teach him.

"I'll be working with their media people and we'll write some spots in our office that give them a message that can position them for the next time, and maybe if the other guys somehow screw it up significantly, we can win now, but more likely this election will just set us up for the next go around.

"You've got a treat in store because the campaign manager for Mitsotakis is Maria Beckett, a woman of about 60, who is a legitimate political super hero. She has led an incredibly active political life that began as a child during the Nazi occupation in WWII when she carried resistance leaflets around Athens in her doll carriage. She told me that she remembered once finding a dead girl her own age huddled on her front step. She also remembered a time not long after that of fleeing Greece on a ship that was strafed by the Nazi Luftwaffe while she huddled on the deck with her family. When she described that memory, she said that she felt the water splashing up on the deck from the bullets in the water and heard them banging into the side of the boat."

Angus covered the recent history of Greece, including the Greek military junta which overthrew democracy and began a rule that included censorship, mass arrests, and torture. "Maria was on the side of those who wanted to restore civilian rule and were against the military. She married an American law professor in the early 1960's, lived in Boston for a time, and had two daughters. She's divorced now and the daughters are grown, but while she was in the U.S. she became a familiar figure at the United Nations where she worked tirelessly against their recognizing the Greek dictatorship. In 1969, she produced evidence of torture from the testimony of victims she had smuggled out of Greece, and she got Greece dislodged from the Council of Europe. Despite her efforts, the junta survived and so she came back to Greece and continued to fight them through the resistance movement and for a time she became what would be described today as a terrorist.

"She's been in the background of most of the political upheaval in that area for many years. Maria was in Damascus in July, 1974, when she learned that the junta tried a disastrous coup in Cyprus, that caused Archbishop Makarios, the head of the Greek Orthodox Church to run for his life. That led to the Turkish seizure of half the island and finally the collapse of the junta itself. With the help of some Palestinians, Maria set up Radio Free Cyprus in an olive grove near Beirut and broadcast messages from Makarios to reassure his followers that he was still alive. Not long after that, she came back to Cyprus to organize international aid for all the Greek refugees fleeing the Turks. So, it's a tough neighborhood. Democracy returned, but Maria turned down an offer to become Greece's ambassador to the United States. Instead, she used resources left over from the anti-junta campaign to rescue Turkish dissidents opposing their own government. In short she is the most fascinating woman I have ever met."

Back in Washington, Vicki began to feel like she was getting sick and felt a pain in her lower abdomen area. She noticed spotting in her underwear and went to see her gynecologist. After an examination, her doctor told her that she was experiencing some side effects from her body's being on the pill for several years and recommended she switch to an IUD after the inflammation subsided. She told Vicki to stop the pills and come back later for a fitting.

CHAPTER 7

The first morning in Greece they walked out of the hotel into noisy, rambling, narrow streets jammed with a mixture of restaurants, shops, sidewalk vendors, offices, trucks, cabs, and banners swirling with color. As soon as they hit the pavement, Mark adopted a look he had been cultivating and had practiced last year in Panama of making his eyes inattentive and face lackluster. He had learned that using this 'dull eyes' technique along with his drab clothing made people assume he was not worthy of consideration. His subdued physical presence was particularly important on a crowded sidewalk because when people passed they looked for the faces that stood out and his washed-out look was the mask that made him appear as someone with a dull mind going through the motions of life.

At the same time, he began to see fresh details through the dull eyes he might have missed before when acknowledging and responding to people's faces. He was like a vacuum sucking up visual details of his surroundings through the slack-faced mask.

He and Angus tried to find their way to the office on foot following a street map, but the Greek words were incomprehensible to them and soon they got lost, gave it up and hailed a taxi which took them only a few blocks to the New Democracy campaign, housed in an office building packed into the oldest and densest part of Athens.

At first glance along its sidewalks Athens looked like many European cities, with ornate midsize structures or newer Bauhaus-styled buildings, narrow streets and sidewalk cafes. However, sticking out in the middle of the old town on a small steep hill, was the Acropolis, with an ancient temple on top called the Parthenon, a structure which definitely made Athens nothing like other European cities. The distinguishing columns of the mausoleum defined Athens, made it an image known worldwide to its tourism industry, and kept it anchored in its past. Mark could see it both from the office and also from the nearby hotel where he and Angus stayed, and he soon found he could use the famous Acropolis as a landmark to guide his walk to through the crowded streets and souvenir shops, back to his hotel or to the nearby Greek Parliament and many other historic landmarks. He was enchanted by the atmosphere of the birthplace of democracy, surrounded by 2500-year-old architecture.

More importantly for his work and his personal gratification, at the campaign office he was introduced to Maria Becket, the woman Angus had told him about, and she soon pulled Mark into her vast circle of admirers who were fascinated with her personal history, her unwavering integrity and quiet charisma. She was the liaison to the Duncan Rogers firm for the New Democracy Party in the upcoming election and a campaign manager who was idealistic, determined, diplomatic, and uncomplicated in her communications. Over time Mark would find that she was so orderly and precise that she somehow found occasion to chart every move of the campaign as well as develop a system to grade the proficiency of each assigned task and its outcome. She used the system to catalogue each rally, each speech, and the names and abilities of all the local leaders of the New Democracy party for future reference.

She was a member of the Greek Parliament in her own right and must have been well over 60, but carried herself as a fit, trim person of 40, Mark guessed from all the walking. She always had her wiry hair done up in a loose bun resembling a Brillo pad and he imagined it would be quite unruly in a down coif. She had dark piercing eyes that usually radiated seriousness with little patience for small talk, but implausibly she could also, on occasion, unexpectedly switch to telling humorous stories and laugh with her head thrown back and mouth wide open.

Mark learned that after the defeat of the junta, she had led a mostly quiet life for ten years until her old friend Constantine Mitsotakis had asked her to become the manager for his campaign for Prime Minister. Soon Mark met many of the other campaign leaders from the regions around Greece and was impressed that most of them were skilled individuals who had business and family contacts in many of the nations in the region. He saw that their intimacy with other nations in Europe and the old Ottoman Empire parts of west Asia was like the familiarity Americans in the U.S. have with neighboring states. The campaign staff all spoke English and most spoke several other languages as well. Being a part of an international campaign reminded Mark how insular most people were in the U.S. and how ill equipped to relate to other cultures. Whereas Mark had worked to improve his Spanish while he was in Panama for the last campaign, the Greek language looked and sounded so difficult he did not even try.

Mark and Angus were assigned a young woman named Eudora Patmos to assist them with clerical and other needs pertaining to the campaign. She was thirty and attractive with flowing dark hair and eyes and a striking figure. Eudora was from Patras, Greece's third-largest city located west of Athens, overlooking the Gulf of Patras. Because Mark and Angus did not create enough for her to do, she also handled other clerical and filing duties in the campaign office. She did, however, translate for them and was a skilled typist.

The staff were pleasant and the campaign appeared to be well-organized and professionally managed. Eudora Patmos seemed to be overly friendly in a flirty way as she made her way around in the administrative offices. Under other circumstances in earlier years, Mark would have followed up with her lingering eyes and sly smiles, but all he could think of now was Vicki.

In one of the early meetings he met the key staff and particularly the Greek scholar, Stanos Petkas, who was to be the person he would be working with most often. On a break from the first meeting Petkas came up to Mark in the hallway, "So you have worked in these elections before and some campaigns in the United States as well?" Petkas seemed curious about Mark as though Mark somehow might have the answers to any campaign problems. It was not the first time campaign people had acted that way toward Mark, but Petkas seemed particularly curious, and Mark at first felt flattered and then decided this man was just trying to soak up all the campaign knowledge he could and treating the campaign like an academic seminar.

"Yes. I've been doing this kind of work for over 20 years, but mostly in the US. Greece is only my second international campaign."

"You must still know a lot of people in the United States in politics and I would love to hear more about how your government works when you have time." Although the interest Petkas showed seemed genuine if not excessive, he promised himself that he would do his best to help this man in any way he could.

On the first night, they all went to dinner together with Maria, Stanos Petkas, and several others who managed different aspects of the campaign. Maria was encouraged to tell stories as they drank wine and enjoyed the wonderful meal. Group dinner meetings became a pattern for them in the evenings, and Mark never tired of listening to the stories of her past adventures, over the incredible Greek food. On this first night, once they had ordered and had their wine, they all sat back, and she told of her early involvement in the Greek Resistance and how she became one of the leaders.

She explained that the early Greek opposition leaders to the junta were not trained for military action. They were an eclectic group of academics, business people and labor supervisors, many of whom had not been political before. The lack of martial skills among the rag-tag rebels resulted in several people being killed trying to devise explosives and planning attacks through ineffective small group tactics, using a hodgepodge of imported firearms and hunting weapons. Then they learned that Archbishop Makarios III of Cyprus knew some people in the Middle East who were training irregular soldiers in the desert, and he offered to help them with introductions.

She smiled and leaned in towards the center of the table conspiratorially, "A large meeting of the resistance leaders was called to discuss the need for training, and I was invited. At first, I just sat there listening to the men's discussion and wondered how we would ever become efficient enough with our lack of skills to fight the military junta. Finally, the main speaker asked for volunteers to go into the desert and receive the military training that Makarios could arrange so they could come back and educate the Greek fighters in the art of war, and the room got very quiet." Mark was enthralled as Maria made a sour face and explained, "This was the first meeting when the resistance was faced with the real sacrifice of arduous travel to an unknown country. When presented with the prospect of training for a guerrilla war under dangerous and unfamiliar circumstances, the men who made up the leadership of the underground began to make sheepish excuses about having to run businesses or needing to take care of their families." She still retained the disgust from those many years ago when she told the campaign staff leaning forward in their seats, captured by her intensity, that after an uncomfortable period of quiet, she stood and declared that, "If none of you men will go, then I will leave my two young daughters and go into the desert, learn the military skills, and come back and teach them to all of you."

Maria continued to spin details into her story by describing how she left for her training and after secretly changing airplanes and vehicles several times, she finally arrived in Damascus and met the Palestinian leader, Yasser Arafat. "He was a nervous man who seemed to relish the power he had. He told me they would train me to make bombs, but I would have to go through the entire course of instruction and live in the Syrian Desert, and they would not give me any breaks regarding the difficulty and danger of military training. I would be treated like a man, live with the men, and do all the same work they did and accept the same risks. When he said these things to me he leaned back and smiled with a hint of cruelty. I think he believed I would run out of that room in terror and go back to Athens, and I think he was a little disappointed that I stayed. Maybe he lost a bet."

Mark tried to imagine this small, cultured Greek lady siting across the restaurant table going to live by herself in a tent next to dozens of Arab men in a desolate desert outpost where she learned to shoot guns and rockets, toss hand grenades, and make bombs. Maria told them that the recoil from shooting the rifles at targets in the sand, which they did every day, caused a large, deep bruise on her shoulder. She would be in agony at night, and have to go back the next day to practice all over again and place the butt of the weapon over the injured, painful spot. The Arab men in the camp treated her like their slave, with disdain and contempt. They gave her every dirty, demeaning job they could imagine and made her clean their toilets.

Mark cringed while listening to her give examples of the horrible conditions just to gain the knowledge to train the men back home how to make bombs. When she finished her story, he asked her, of all the primitive, difficult conditions in the desert, which was the worst, and she looked up at him and said without hesitation, "the roaches." She finished her military education and came home to train others, bringing with her a scar on her leg from a grenade explosion during training. After she returned, she persuaded Yasser Arafat to offer other Greek partisans weapons training in his Syrian camps and her experiences shamed the other Greek men into action.

Petkas leaned over to Mark as the others continued with their conversation, coffee and cigarettes. "Mark, another thing it would be good for you to remember is that modern Greece is not such a large and powerful country. We are in a neighborhood filled with other more powerful nations who have been very aggressive with each other and we have often been caught in the middle, resulting in some very bad consequences for our people. In the past hundred years or so we have had to find refuge by picking sides and making alliances with more powerful countries just to protect ourselves. Sometimes we have chosen wisely, other times not so. Often, we have been split by choosing multiple godfathers at the same time, which complicates our national identity and our need to feel independent as a sovereign country. Right now, we are being pulled toward the west by the U.S. and east by the Soviet Union. We don't like to admit it to ourselves, but that's where we are."

Mark thought to himself that Petkas was very clear-eyed and practical for a novice politician, and that he could admit so easily to this national weakness showed that he was honest and wise. He thought that working with an international authority on history and culture as well as a savvy political man would be a pleasure during this campaign. What a welcome change from the political liaison he had had in Panama with a sleazy party hack.

That same night at the Soviet Embassy, Sergei Bokhan, the deputy to Ambassador Andropov, thumbed through the dossiers of the people who were assigned to work in the New Democracy campaign for the capitalist bosses. He had been assigned to support the novice diplomat, Igor Andropov, by the party leaders in Moscow several months before because of his well-rounded experience and calm demeanor. Now he wanted to get a better understanding of the Greek political campaign to brief the ambassador and in case he was asked questions by any of the men back in Moscow.

Bokhan saw himself as the perfect number two. He did not have the ego, looks or presence of a leader, but he did have the knowledge to tell a leader how to behave, what to say, and how to explain the sometimes complex positions that should be taken by Soviet leaders. He had long been in the diplomatic trenches, and had worked almost every job an embassy could offer for the last 25 years; and his unblemished record satisfied him that he was qualified and experienced to be the man behind the man.

The New Democracy dossiers had been prepared by the Soviet and Greek staffs at the embassy with input from the KGB intelligence department in Moscow. He had heard that two Americans had arrived the day before from New York to help with the campaign, and he wanted to know his enemy. Bokhan picked one of the Greek staff profiles at random, glanced at it, and turned to the embassy intelligence staffer. "Tell me about this man who manages the campaign in the various areas around Greece."

The young man stood proudly to give his report. "He is a teacher of antiquities who is the manager with the scheduling and advance for the campaign named Stanos Petkas. The professor has a master's degree from Stanford University in California and a doctorate from Oxford University in England. He is the head of archeology at the National Technical University of Athens, but he also has lectured and taught courses at the Aristotle University of Thessaloniki.

Bokhan wrinkled his brow, frowned and leaned to look closer at the paper in front of him and then towards a map on the wall, "Where is...?"

Anticipating his boss, "It is near Macedonia. Thessaloniki is north of Athens by about a 6-hour drive, but only less than 50 miles from the Macedonian border. Before the campaign he used to travel there at least once a week for his teaching.

"He is to be the liaison to work with the American, Mark Young, who

40

arrived yesterday. Mr. Petkas is highly respected as an authority on Greek history and art, and one of the world's experts in Greek Archeology. However, we have questions about whether he will be very effective as a field organizer."

Bokhan mused, "I don't know why you would say that. He will know the terrain of Greece and likely have former students he can call on for help?"

The staffer stood taller. "Yes. But he has no experience in campaigns and only became involved with the New Democracy party a few years ago. He is married and has two young school age children, but is somewhat new to politics, so we are not sure he will have the time or experience for the campaign."

Not wishing to take too strong a position that could come back to haunt him if his opinion was wrong, the aide added, "But on his behalf, he is a very smart man. He knows Greek history, geography, and has a good feel for the dispositions of people in the various areas of Greece. And for all his ability and education he is also very well organized, a humble man and is reported to get along with everyone."

Bokhan looked back at the folder containing the information and a photo of Stanos Petkas, and said in a low voice more to himself than the young staffer, "Competent but inexperienced." Then he looked up at the young man. "So, all the same, you will keep him under surveillance and this person from America, Mr. Young, as well as the other top people. We do not want any surprises for the election. It could put a bad light on our efforts here."

"Yes. Comrade Secretary."

"How many people have we placed inside the campaign?"

"We have one there now, but another will start on Monday. They are in the clerical positions so they will have access to many papers and most of the filing. We assume the Greeks also have placed one or more people there."

"That is good for a start. Have them volunteer to do any unpleasant task that will keep them around the office, things like cleaning up or taking out the trash. Make sure they have those small cameras to make photos of anything that might be useful to us. Now let me see the dossiers on the other campaign workers. I know something of the manager…Beckett, but I want to see what we have on her in these files. And also, I want to see transcripts of the phone conversations once they are translated. Make sure we have taps in place in the homes of the key workers and in the Americans' hotel by next week."

Bokhan closed that folder and before opening another asked, "Now, do we have anyone in contact with the left-wing terror group N-17? I know our intelligence services gave them financial support about 10 years ago. Find out how we have kept up with their leadership and if they will take assignments from us."

The assistant who had been at the embassy for the past three years nodded and was happy to be able to answer his new boss. "Yes. Although they mainly finance themselves through bank robbing today. Not long ago about the time you arrived they executed a conservative newspaper owner and his bodyguard. They claimed that the men were agents of the American CIA, though they say that about many of the people they kill. Two years ago, they killed the deputy chief of the Joint United States Military Aid Group to Greece. They use .45 cal. handguns so it is very messy, and that makes them useful to keep things stirred up and to frighten the capitalists, but our friends in the Greek intelligence say to let them alone or just encourage them to attack the capitalists' targets. They are so volatile that if we tried to get too close to them, they could see us as the establishment and …."

Bokhan raised his eyebrows while listening to that comment and nodded. "Okay, I don't want them coming after me, but keep close tabs on them through the Greeks in case we need to get them involved against the Americans."

CHAPTER 8

Tatiana Andropov handed her son, Kostya, over to his nanny as she finished getting herself ready for the Embassy party. She hoped that the embassy outing would make up for Igor's unwillingness to make the courtesy calls on the other consulates, as she had asked him to do earlier when they first arrived. She felt that because of his reluctance to spend more time on the social circuit, she was falling behind on finding the correct contacts to fulfill the request that had become more of a demand by her uncle to find some Greek sculpture and art for him. Her uncle had remembered that her college training included several classes in ancient Greek art and felt it would give her the background to spot good items for him. Then she could use Igor's job as Ambassador to obtain those materials and arrange for them to be shipped back to her uncle's Black Sea dacha or to his elaborate home in Moscow.

Her uncle had no intention of actually paying for the art, but figured that the Soviet Ambassador could find a way to procure it out the back door of a museum or bully the Greeks to loan the art to him and then never return it. One of his ideas was to enable the pilferage of Greek treasure by asking Igor to arrange a contract on favorable terms for the Greek government to supply maintenance and repair to Russian ships in Mediterranean waters and to discount fees for Russian ships docking in Greek harbors. That financial transaction would provide the opportunity for a payoff to Greek government officials and open the door for the government to look the other way when Igor carried off some of their old relics.

He had bragged to his friends in the oil ministry and now they were pressuring him to get them some ancient Greek artifacts. He had reminded Tatiana that he was the most influential member of her family and her own father owed him his job. He also claimed that it was his influence that had helped her to marry the son of the former prime minister. She was obligated to him, as was her husband, and she knew with the pressure from her uncle's demands that she had to deliver and pull her weight in the family.

He told Tatiana to remind Igor that his father was no longer alive and he needed to have other powerful friends in the Soviet Union to watch over his career now. Her uncle thought Igor was spoiled and too much of a pretty boy. He needed to be pushed to do what was required and use his new position to benefit his friends and relatives. Igor needed to learn that his career was dependent on key friendships and receiving favors from those in power as well as his ability to return the favors.

As she dressed, she looked in the mirror, stopped and pouted. She could never forgive her parents for conceiving her with a large and noticeable birthmark on one of her thighs which prevented her from having the courage to wear bikinis or certain types of revealing clothing on her otherwise flawless body. Since she had been in her early teen years, only her lovers had seen it, and she quickly let them know the birthmark was not a subject for discussion. Ever.

She finished dressing and made plans to push Igor later that evening after the party to live up to his responsibilities. Tatiana smiled as she remembered the ways she had found to speak to Igor that would raise his anger and inflame his insecurities. She felt pleased at having the power to make him squirm when she reminded him of the influence her uncle had and how he could either help or harm Igor's fledging diplomatic career.

Sergei Bokhan had driven his staff with many checklists and endless meetings for several days to prepare the embassy to receive the diplomatic corps of Athens. The decorations, food and drinks were all perfect. He had agonized over where people were to stand, the kind of music to play, the invitations and the press coverage. He had arranged for just the right people to introduce the ambassador and his wife to the other members of the diplomatic corps, journalists, military, business leaders, and other dilettantes. These first few weeks it had been difficult to encourage the new ambassador to familiarize himself with the necessities of political social interaction. Now, finally he had the day planned, the room dressed and had prepared the ambassador with background biographies on the people he would be meeting, their pet interests, national needs and other tidbits to be used in polite conversation. As he watched the space fill and the people mill around enjoying the imported vodka, caviar and sturgeon, he felt he had done everything possible to make the embassy coming-out party for the ambassador a success.

However, the newly ensconced Ambassador seemed to be bored as he meandered through the reception. He went through the motions of smiling and nodding at various diplomats and military officers, as secretly he thought how pedestrian they all were and he made jokes about them in his mind.

He also watched his wife, Tatiana, circulate through the room and thought how often she tried to act like the man in their marriage. Igor resented her influence over him through her bastard of an uncle, and he was forced to accept much more of her haughtiness than he would under other circumstances.

Now as they worked the room together, he was disgusted to be moving about, only to be introduced to one overweight clod after the other. Just then he looked further across the room, and there was, oh yes, there across the room was a very pleasant distraction, looking at him with a smile on her face.

Earlier in the evening as she dressed, Sophie Speros had looked at herself in the mirror and twisted this way and that as she decided how best to present herself at the embassy party. These events had become the most interesting thing in her life. She believed her uncle, Marcellus Dedacus, who was in that group of political leaders who supported the boring Prime Minister Papandreou, invited her to these embassy receptions because of the attention her looks brought to him. She thought her beauty helped people notice her tedious uncle, remember his governmental position, and wish to come up and speak to him, simply because she was with him and somehow that elevated his importance.

The political parties, particularly at the embassies, were also a good place to meet other young and exciting people who could help her get the cocaine which she was becoming increasingly fond of using almost every day. She looked at herself in the mirror in the tight low-cut dress and then took off her underwear which was noticeable through the fabric, and she knew her well-rounded bottom would be more enticing through a smooth dress line. Today's party would be interesting for her as she would meet the new Russian Ambassador, Igor Andropov, who was good-looking in his pictures. She was sorry that she had not had the chance to meet him attending some of the earlier parties, but had seen his photo in the newspaper and on the television. She wondered what kind of a reaction she could get from him as she practiced making alluring faces in the mirror and moving from side to side to show off her figure. At 23 her looks were at their peak and she had learned to use them to disarm or attract as she chose.

She remembered what she had read about Igor Andropov, who was supposed to be a rising star in the Soviet Foreign Service and she had cut out the article in the newspaper with his photo that described him when he came to Greece as the Soviet Ambassador in February. The paper said he was an immediate celebrity on the Greek social circuit. A Greek government official stated, "Andropov's appearance here is a flattering sign that Greece is being taken more seriously by the Kremlin – and a regard for the socialist government's expressions of support for Soviet positions on a number of international issues." Papandreou praised the Soviet Union as "a force that prevents the spread of capitalism." How these old men could gush over something as boring as a government made no sense to Sophie.

Now at the edge of the sprawling ballroom she hung back at first and watched as the dashing Russian worked the room, seemingly being led and encouraged by his beautiful wife. She measured the pace he was taking and figured she had time, so she left her uncle for a few minutes to sniff some cocaine in the bathroom and then came back into the ballroom to watch as he circulated from one group of fawning diplomats to the other, many from the Soviet block of nations and some from central Europe. His wife looked interested in some of the other ambassadors and

Greek officials, but she was also reserved. She had classic looks and was dressed in the latest fashion, but appeared to have a cold personality and seemed to be at least 15 years older than Sophie. However, she appeared to be adept at making the correct comments and gestures as she lightly touched the arms and kissed cheeks with just the correct level of attention. She carried herself like someone in an arranged marriage who had moved on with her life from the romantic, to the social, to the maintenance. She did not look like someone who would stick around for the nursemaid phase of a relationship; and she did not look like someone who would be a competitor for Igor's affections; but, she could see his wife was also not someone to cross.

He on the other hand was exciting and definitely handsome with an air of danger about him. She liked that in a man. He was calculating and smooth, tall, and looked delicious over there on the other side of the room, and while working his way around to her, he seemed to be the male embodiment of power. He had an air of command about him as he whispered demands to others who jumped to please him. He noticed her from across the room and nodded in her direction. Bingo. She knew now that he would quickly make his way to her and they would make a connection. He gave perfunctory greetings and moved quickly past the Swedes and the Germans, now over to Spain. As he got closer, being led by the Greek minister who was making the introductions, she shifted her weight and stepped so her legs were further apart to tighten the thin dress and she felt the air circulate to cool the inner skin of her upper thighs and gently touch her above like a lover. She knew right then that they would be together. Here across the room and headed in her direction was a man that could open doors to the exciting places in Europe and the Soviet Union. He was strong and powerful and had the air and cool detachment of someone who knew exactly want he wanted, and at this moment, it was her. As far as Sophie Speros was concerned, the welcome party for Igor Andropov was turning out to be a great success.

Mark and Petkas waited in the office for Maria Beckett to return from the Embassy party. If the circumstances permitted, she was going to approach the new Soviet Ambassador and find out how informed he was about the economic problems in Greece and see how committed and motivated he was at helping Papandreou with his campaign. While they waited, Petkas gave Mark another lesson about Greek history and art. "Art is a curious thing. It is defined by what remains of art. Imagine how fragile some ideas and subjects are. Think of all the items on parchment, velum or paper that have been lost over the years. Think of the loss when the Library of Alexandria was burned in Egypt. Look at the books of the Bible such as James, Mary and Timothy which were not included in the Council of Nicaea, but still remain as fringe elements of Christianity and could have easily been omitted or lost. Look at 'On the Nature of Things' by Lucretius. What if it had not been rediscovered 500 years ago by Poggio Bracciolini in the Benedictine monastery in Fulda, Italy? He helped to define the Renaissance. And what about wood or cloth or other fragile items used to convey art. So much of it just does not last. It is gone and who knows what information or inspiration that could be useful to us today was lost and how really valuable it could have been if we still had it today?

"You are here for this election, and there remains a scene of Greeks voting by casting stones, on the side of a broken but repaired wine cup from 490 BC. So even the early evidence of democracy is fragile.

"And in sculpture. The next time you are on the street, look up at the Parthenon. It is one of the most recognizable structures in history, but much was destroyed in the explosion during a war in 1687. All we know of the progress of sculpture is the evidence of what was not broken or lost. The greatest wonders of antiquity and even the genius of individual artists greater than anything we know about or which history could have produced may now be lying in architectural landfills.

"What about all the ships that sank to the bottom of the sea carrying priceless treasures. Only about one percent of all shipwrecks have ever been inspected. Our knowledge of art, my friend, is defined by what remains, and it's likely that what remains is not the best time had to offer.

Our taste in art has been defined by what we've seen. What if we had available the choice of everything that was lost or everything that has ever existed? How would that affect our concept of knowledge, art and history? I can show you some beautiful things while you are in Greece, but I wish I could show both of us the prime examples of the best art ever produced that are no longer available. We no longer have the artisans who worked with their hands all their lives, most of it learning as apprentices to ones who were better than them. Today we have science and technology. Today we create gadgets of entertainment, not art. With all our so-called progress, we have not been able to produce anyone today who can create what people thousands of years ago made with a hammer and chisel. No one can make a marble sculpture today that looks like it can actually talk to you and then walk off down the street."

They heard Maria coming in from the Embassy party. "So how did it go? Was he receptive?"

Maria put down her purse and took off her shawl. Then she stopped to pat her large wad of hair while looking in the mirror in the hallway and made a frown. "I am afraid the Soviet Ambassador is a bit of a lightweight. Other than a polite hello, I didn't get a chance to talk to him as he was surrounded by admirers who seemed to like him just for his movie star looks. He seemed content with their attention and small talk. I watched him from across the room. In some ways, he was even reticent, and he was awkward for an Ambassador and somewhat haughty. His wife worked the room well even although she was also formal, but he did not engage in much conversation after a few introductory banalities. That is an unfortunate thing. I had hoped to find an ally in Mr. Andropov who could work the other side of the street, so to speak, to get Papandreou under control. The only thing he seemed to concentrate on was the niece of Marcellus Dedacus, who is young and beautiful and vain, and has been making the embassy circuit with her uncle as a kind of added attraction the past couple of years. All around, it was a disappointing evening."

As the three of them split up, Petkas began to clear his desk to leave when he realized they had only a little over three months before the election, and he knew he would have to act soon if he was to expose his secret in a timetable with the possibility of success.

Since his amazing discovery four years before, the focus of Stanos Petkas had slowly shifted from a respected international scholar to a subtly motivated modern-day, real-life Indiana Jones with the accompanying intrigues, paranoia and passion to preserve ancient hidden treasure of immeasurable value. His hidden reverence for what he found had now become the primary motivation of his life that he had not shared even with his wife, Cyrilla. Over the months and years, he felt that he had become adept at hiding his secret even though the fear of its discovery crept into him as an ever-present and foreboding cloud.

He began to worry that his involvement in the New Democracy party and the campaign might bring him more unhealthy attention that could result in government audits to his academic budgets, grants and field activities. He assumed the Papandreou government could be punitive and take steps to put him and his family at risk, which led him to think about one of his sons who had a learning disability. Petkas felt it was too late to turn back and that he was so far into the campaign and his other activities now that he was already exposed to criticism and scrutiny. The clear risk of discovery argued for him to escalate his plans.

A few weeks later Sophie was still attracted to Igor's power and felt it rub off on her as she could see that people were differential to her when she was with him, and even without him when she came into the presence of others who knew she was his girlfriend. She liked it when he complimented her on her beauty and he had taken her with him to tour a Soviet Warship in the harbor where she felt he had paraded her in front of the sailors. He had talked about taking her with him to St. Petersburg and to other places that Sophie could only dream of, and she prattled on about him with her girlfriends when they discussed their "prince charming" fantasies.

Still, she wondered if she would get used to the unusual sexual needs he had and how he squeezed her until it hurt and sometimes left bruises. She hoped his strange enthusiasm was just the first part of passion and would lessen over time.

Anyway, the quantity of cocaine he got for her let her forget her sore spots when he came over to see her in the apartment he had given her. She felt very independent and in control as she lounged in her apartment or went shopping for new nightgowns that he liked to rip off her as she did her sexy dance in front of him. Gradually she began to dodge her old friends because she didn't want to answer their questions about her bruises. She started to withdraw from her family as well because she hated their nagging about her seeking a job, developing a career, or finding an eligible Greek man to marry. She was also afraid they would notice her red nose from the increased cocaine use or might also see the bruises. Sophie considered her current behavior as something that was just a passing phase in her young life. She could become more responsible later; but now was the time for her to enjoy herself. She could control the drugs if she wished, and over time the Russian would learn to be gentler with her. The fast road ahead was bound to become smoother as well as more exciting.

CHAPTER 9

Mark had started to work exclusively with Stanos Petkas and they spent several hours every day planning the candidate's time and setting up campaign events. Although Petkas was an academic and one of the world's authorities on Greek culture and art, he was also charming and gregarious and much less intimidating than Mark had anticipated. He was six inches shorter than Mark, but they balanced each other well in the more important areas of work ethic and enthusiasm to achieve their assigned areas of responsibility in the campaign. Mark noticed that Petkas had a thin pencil line moustache that he must have to spend time on each day or during each shave to get just right. It reminded him of old 1940's movie stars, and it gave the professor a look of distinction and was an indication of his precision. Mark also had a moustache, but his was bushy like a 1970's folk musician.

They hit it off immediately and had a mutual respect for each other's talents and experience. Petkas possessed a natural inclination for orderly process and approached everything methodically which rather than slowing him down, gave a solid foundation to his efforts. Mark had a feeling that Petkas crunched the key possibilities in his head before he spoke about an issue or took any action, but he masked what might have appeared tedious by being self-deprecating and generous. He volunteered never-ending stories about his own academic career, and he communicated openly like a colleague and an old friend. When he explained something, he spoke in an easy, relaxed manner instead of using big words and complicated phrases like some highly intelligent people did when they wished to grandstand.

As Mark walked to the office each morning, he passed streets with vendors selling woven baskets, food, trinkets and colorful clothes of all kinds, and restaurants that spilled onto the street with small tables and two chairs tucked next to the buildings on the sidewalk. Mark had to dodge some of these tables that butted out near the flow of traffic on his way to work. Some shops had street-side windows or half doors that opened to form a kind of shelf or counter to sell goods to passersby. It presented an atmosphere that Mark liked and made him feel welcomed by the fanciful hustle and bustle. The smells of cooked bread, garlic and olives permeated the air.

On his walk to the office the next morning Mark was stopped by a half-hearted rally for their opponent Papandreou, with about two hundred people carrying signs down one of the streets he had to cross to get to the office. They were headed towards the legislative buildings. As he waited politely for the people to pass, Mark could tell this effort was poorly organized and disjointed. He assumed it was because it was still early in the campaign and hoped that he and Petkas could manage their public gatherings more effectively.

He and Angus worked at the campaign office and went to meetings with other campaign staff, but there was a lot of spare time, and sometimes they waited a day or two for participants to come from distant areas of the country for a particular meeting or training. With his extra time, Mark got to know the campaign staff who were at ease and unruffled by the pace of campaign activity and were competent in their jobs.

As his friendship with Petkas developed, Mark noticed that his colleague seemed particularly curious about how the U.S. government worked and he asked if Mark still had contacts at high levels there. He frequently posed questions about Mark's background, family, and his experiences in the U.S. government and other campaigns. Mark admired Petkas for his inquisitiveness and candor as well as the commitment and integrity with which he took on tasks, but his questions led Mark to assume that decisions and promotions in the Greek government were made more from inside an old boy network than based on merit or experience.

In his insatiable thirst for knowledge, Petkas asked, "So in the U.S. when one administration leaves the government, do the staff people stay over? Do you still know people in the various departments and agencies from the time you were in the Carter Administration? I would like to know more about how your government works so that might help me to understand better why ours is so inefficient."

Mark tried to be as specific as he could to the broad inquiries. "Some of the people I know from that time are still in Washington, and they tend to go into the next administration of the same political party where they can serve again or hang around Washington to go back into government later when their party comes back into power. Nevertheless, as it is here, if you represent the other political party and lose an election, you are usually out. The career institutional staffs are the backbone that makes the government function from the one president to the other. There are inefficiencies in both systems."

Petkas furrowed his brow, "But the government workers and people who make the wheels turn are still there and you still know some of them? So, if you have a government problem to solve you would know who to talk to in Washington?"

"Maybe. Depending on what the problem was. I'd likely have to network into it instead of knowing the correct person directly."

Petkas smiled, "That is good. So, if we needed help there you could get us in touch with the right person?"

"I think you may not appreciate that in the U.S. we try to keep the political part of running for office and setting the policies separate from the part that actually makes the various offices function from day to day. That separation of efforts does not always work as successfully as it was designed, but that is our theory of how we try to operate. Plus, the size of our government is massive compared to Greece's."

Petkas nodded, "I look forward to working with you and learning more about how we might make our system function better here in Greece. I will study this scheduling manual you gave me and I have already sent it to get translated for the people in the field so they will know how to do things correctly when we ramp up the campaign. I agree it is important to have as much standardized as possible and the operational guidelines you suggested will make the campaign run more smoothly." He mused for a while, and then said, "Perhaps while you are here, I can tell you a bit about Greek history and archeology, which is my field." Mark smiled, "I'd like that very much."

Petkas spread his arms wide, "To understand Greece in its politics or anything about Greece, one must first understand our love of art and architecture. When we look at the Acropolis we see ourselves, not only our history, but ourselves today and our future. We cannot give up our dreams of grandeur and power. Understanding how we are influenced by our history is the key to winning elections here and the key to winning the hearts of the people. From the most conservative businessperson to the most ardent communist, we all suffer from ancient pride, and we are ashamed of our current diminished state in world opinion, and so, we seek others to blame."

While Petkas was having the campaign's guidelines and checklists translated, they got to know each other by taking walks through Athens, with Petkas giving Mark history and art lessons, and Mark explaining to Petkas the logic and practicality of political event organizing. On these walks, they discovered in each other the mutual enjoyment of hiking, general exercise, and exploration. On their first climb up the steep-sided Mt. Lycabettus, Mark felt the burn in his quadriceps and before he made it to the top was breathing as hard as he had when he took up jogging years before. Mark soon became a fan of Petkas's wife's fantastic cooking and his efforts to augment the children's education through creative projects, that made it clear he was a good family man.

Angus was working more closely with Maria on the advertising and budget, so Mark mostly saw him at dinner, and as the days and weeks went by, it was Petkas who became his friend and close confidant.

Mark tried to call Vicki at least once a week, and he gave her glowing reviews of the city and its history. She kidded him that he was fast becoming a philhellene, which she explained meant a lover of Greece and Greek culture, to which Mark pled guilty.

After a few weeks, he went back to Washington for a week's visit. It was wonderful to be with Vicki, but he had to tell her that it was looking like Angus would not be in Greece as much as he had thought, and he would have to anchor the project and spend more time there, which meant that visits home such as this one would be infrequent, if at all. This led to a serious discussion and a promise from Mark that Greece would be his last international campaign.

Near the end of the visit to Washington, they both knew the final day could be the last time together for several months and they wanted to make it special because Mark left early the next morning. That afternoon they attended a matinee concert near the Watergate of the National Philharmonic playing the Third Orchestral Suite by Johann Sebastian Bach. The Adagio or "Air" in the suite was one of the favorite pieces of music to both of them. Afterwards they walked back from the Kennedy Center through Georgetown to their favorite restaurant for their favorite meal there. Earlier today than usual.

They came back home and then changed into more casual clothes for one of their favorite walks under the tree canopy on the C&O canal, an area that rented canoes and kayaks where there was a dirt-topped bridge over the canal to get on the bank between the canal and the Potomac River. As night fell they meandered along on the packed earth of the canal tow path where 150 years before barges were pulled by mules to haul the coal, produce and other supplies from the west to support the needs of the Nation's capital.

When they came back to the condominium Mark showered first and finished packing as he was to leave early the next morning for Greece. When Vicki came out of the bathroom in a short nightgown with spaghetti straps, Mark saw her standing backlit from the light from the vanity which showed through the fabric and outlined all of her curves. She stood still in that light at the foot of the bed. He walked over to her and reached for her with his hands on both sides of her shoulders and looked deeply into her eyes. His fingers slowly and gently massaged her ears, which he knew Vicki liked, and then he moved to kiss her forehead, cheeks, neck and shoulder. His hands then slowly moved up and down her back softly just feeling the skin through the thin fabric of the satin. He slowly reached and then slid one and then the other strap over her shoulders and down her arms and then lightly touching the sides slid the nightgown over her breasts and down to the floor.

Later there was an awakening that the world had returned. They were in the room that had walls and carpeting and certainly a sturdy bed. Vicki rolled over and reached to hold Mark's sweaty face in her hands and leaned into him, then moved even closer so their eyes were only inches apart. She looked deep into his eyes and said, "Come back to me soon."

One afternoon while Mark was in Washington, Petkas sat at his desk with his office door locked. He pulled four old photos from his briefcase and looked at them carefully as he had done many times over the past several years. Because Petkas did not trust a film developer to see the photos, he had used a Polaroid camera, the kind that instantly printed out photo prints which slid out from a groove at the bottom of the camera. The lighting was very dim in the cave so the prints were dark. He had sacrificed quality for secrecy.

As he looked at them lovingly and carefully with a magnifying glass, he could to see the perfect, smooth skin pulsing with thin veins just below the surface and the curls of hair falling softly over the head and neck. He restrained himself from rubbing his finger over the faces because the delicate prints were already starting to degrade, and he wondered if they had been exposed to the light too often. As he put them back in the envelope and then into the sleeve of his briefcase, he thought to himself, was this American, Mark, a person who would appreciate this secret? Could he trust him enough to share it with him?

CHAPTER 10

When he returned to Greece, Mark found it strangely interesting to be living and working in a society where there was almost constant awareness that their best days had ended over 2000 years ago. The glorious past created a national consciousness where the collective desire was not so much for pursuing greater achievements, but a thin hope to recapture a sliver of former glory. To Mark, this historical drag gave a kind of weight that complicated suggestions of how to improve the economy and move the country forward into a better future. Petkas had been right about the allure and attraction of the mythological past filled with historical significance.

During the early days in the campaign, he saw to it that the mechanical elements such as the material distribution of brochures and signs to the provinces were handled efficiently, and he made sure that the lists for mailings and phone contacts were complete. He discussed with Petkas the infrastructure of campaign organization and staffing. Maria and Petkas had known each other for many years and had an easy and friendly relationship. There was trust between them and Mark never saw them quarrel.

Mark did occasionally meet with the candidate, Constantine Mitsotakis, but he almost never came to the campaign office and was at his home or law office when he was not out on the campaign trail. He seemed boring and rumpled to Mark and an example of party politics where internecine longevity instead of talent was the path to leadership.

Once the training was done and the candidate's schedule was put in place, Mark only had to think about setting the atmospherics for the rallies. He was grateful that he did not have to worry about the candidate's time of arrival, mode of transportation or any of the technical details he normally fussed over at a political rally.

Eudora Patmos began to bring a daily English summary of the news in Greece to Mark and Angus, when he was in town. Unsolicited, the initiative on her part and her ability to spot their unspoken needs was appreciated. She also offered to drop documents off at their hotel, but after she did that once or twice and found excuses to linger, her continued presence in her revealing clothing made Mark uncomfortable. She kept up the alluring glances and smiles, but when Mark did not encourage her, she was left without any significant personal interaction and found herself only appreciated for her efficiency and putting long hours into the campaign. Mark kept Vicki at the forefront of his consciousness, but with Eudora's consistent flirting, sometimes that required more effort.

Angus, Maria and the other top half dozen campaign operatives decided to concentrate their television and radio commercials with a message that was critical of Papandreou's moving the government to a rigid form of socialism that was tilted too sharply to the left and hurt the economy. Mark asked for the inside story on the opposition because he felt he needed to better understand Papandreou as a candidate to be comfortable with the message of the New Democracy.

The briefing on Papandreou happened over a dinner at Maria Beckett's house with Mark, Maria, Angus and Petkas. After they finished the baklava and sat with their coffee, Maria folded her napkin and gave Mark a serious look. "To give you a better idea about this election," she said, "you need to understand that in today's world, Greece is in a kind of international middle ground. We are part of NATO and rely on a lot of trade with the U. S. and other western democracies, while philosophically the current government has moved to the left and is greatly influenced by the Soviet Union. In addition, you need to think about everything in terms of Greek history. Because we have been invaded and overrun so much in the past, we Greeks became adept at deceit and hiding our thoughts and intentions just to survive. It has put a stamp on our national character just like in the United States the propensity for violence has become imbedded in your culture.

"The conflict here is a microcosm of what is going on in the world, and that makes this Greek election a proxy fight between the U.S. and the Soviet Union. We are in a time of change regarding the influence of capitalism or communism, two competing approaches to governing, which have been fighting each other for the past 40 years. Both of those philosophical arguments are getting tired and running out of gas. Most countries have already chosen a side or had their choices made for them. Both the East and the West are spending money and military influence to outdo each other internationally, and the control of Greece is a reflection in the contest of who's ahead. We're one of the few places remaining where a clear choice is still up in the air. If Papandreou makes the mistake of moving too fast to total socialism and fails, the West will look good by comparison. If we can win the next election, then it will be our turn to try to make some sense out of what is becoming an economic disaster.

"The terms liberal and conservative here do not mean the same as in your country. In America, Democrats and Republicans are almost the same thing. Here, there can be life or death differences in the political parties. Here decisions can wreck our country's future or try to make us relevant again in Europe. We delude ourselves by thinking we can be grand again, when what we actually need to do is to survive. In your country, you are so rich that if you elect a leader who makes a mess of it and your economy gets out of balance, in four or eight years some other person can come along and reset the apple cart. Here, the swing of the pendulum is so dramatic it can shatter the cart and leave all the apples to rot.

"Now let's look at the prime minister, and our opponent. Our current national leader, Andreas Papandreou, covers all aspects of international politics. He's been banished, and he's been a traitor. He's been moderate and extremely liberal. He's sucked up to the United States and to the Soviets. He's been down and out on the floor of despair and he's now the prime minister of the cradle of democracy. And in any of those situations I just described he was in it whole hog. He is the quintessential politician in that he has been an opportunist for all his political life and has taken advantage of every situation, even misfortune. You need to understand that Papandreou's history mirrors the deceit and treachery as well as success that have been a part of Greek history for thousands of years.

"Papandreou has been trying to move the country toward socialism and communism, but does not have a clue how to pay for all the giveaways. He tries to market his socialism like it is actually going back to the early Greek idea of democracy, but it is a distorted message to anyone who can

JAY BECK

get past the bluster and thinks about it seriously. Unfortunately, populist figures oftentimes are effective at peddling these dreams to people, and it takes some time for them to realize the dreams are really nightmares. To understand modern Greek political history, which is like a ping-pong game, let me take you back a few years." Mark was now excited to finally learn of Greece's recent past from Maria Beckett, a woman who had made much of it.

"Almost twenty years ago in June of 1967, a bunch of colonels in the Greek military staged a coup and took over. It shook up everything here. The Johnson administration in the USA let it happen, and then the Nixon administration with its Greek-American vice-president, Spiro Agnew, encouraged it. And there was a cozy relationship between the Greek and American military and the CIA. Soon the colonels in the junta were sitting pretty. The junta tortured and imprisoned opponents such as Papandreou, purged the armed forces of any opposition, subjugated the civil service, dominated the church, dismissed the country's most noted judges, and eliminated civil rights. Police budgets went up and social programs were cut. They moved the government to the right and began to encourage foreign investment that transferred sections of the Greek economy off shore, much of which was snapped up by wealthy Greek-Americans and Greek businessmen operating from New York and London. These are some of the same people who are now funding our campaign. So, you see the loyalties here can be complicated.

"People like Papandreou, Mitsotakis, me and lots of others were outraged and plotted how to overthrow the colonels. I have known him for many years and in his youth Papandreou was like your New York liberal red from the 1940's and 50's. Early on Papandreou was run out of Greece for Trotskyism and came to the U.S., where he earned a PhD degree in economics from Harvard University and he got involved in the 1952 presidential campaign of Adlai Stevenson. Immediately after getting his doctorate, he joined America's war effort and volunteered for the US Navy, was a hospital corpsman at the Bethesda Naval Hospital and he also became a United States citizen."

Mark laughed, "How about that. A socialist in the U.S. Navy!"

61

Maria gave him a look that quieted Mark into remembering the briefing is serious and he should not pop off with his smart quips. She continued, "When the Greek colonels took over in April 1967, Papandreou was thrown in jail. He held the Central Intelligence Agency responsible for the coup and became increasingly critical of the United States government. We worked together then to liberate Greece from the colonels. I tried to move the U.S. away from the colonels by talking to your diplomats and pointing out the junta's human rights violations. Papandreou, however, was much more radical and idealistic and did not see the need to work with the moderates in the West who had the power and resources to overthrow the totalitarian and oppressive junta."

Maria recalled working on the US state department's Greek desk and with Gustav Lascaris "Gust" Avrakotos, a high-ranking CIA officer in Greece who was close to the colonels who led the coup, and who did not like Papandreou. She smiled when remembering her old colleague, Gust, and said that earlier when the CIA was looking at the rise of Papandreou and his move to the left, they were wondering if he would be a problem in the future, and Avrakotos had advised them to "shoot the motherfucker now because he's going to come back to haunt you". Maria laughed, "Gust always talked like that. I'm not sure they make them like that anymore.

"Then Papandreou went into exile, taught at Stockholm University, and later traveled around plotting opposition to the Greek military regime. He saw the obvious political opening from the left, and after the junta fell, came back here and formed, the Panhellenic Socialist Movement or PASOK. He renounced his American citizenship, was elected to the Greek Parliament and in effect, became the chief economic advisor to his father who was prime minister after the overthrow of the junta. Papandreou wanted Greece to be more independent from the United States and criticized the American military and intelligence. He accused the Americans of extending their Latin American quasi-colonial policies to Europe.

"He became more passionate as his socialist movement grew and found purchase in the Greek legislative elections. In 1974, PASOK received 13.5% of the vote, but by 1977 he almost doubled that to 25%, and Papandreou became known as the leader of the opposition. Then in the

Greek legislative election, 1981, PASOK had a significant win over our party as we were making the case to be more moderate and to resist radical change. Papandreou became Greece's first socialist prime minister under his party's main slogan, *Allagi,* which means change.

"However, once in office, just like we see in a lot of politicians after they are elected, he

reneged from many of his campaign promises and became a conventional leader. Political duplicity is international. The relationship with the U.S., NATO and the rest of Europe remained largely static.

"He began to borrow money from both the East and the West and was effective in playing everyone off each other to promote his theories of socialism. His government became so steeped in socialism that he began a program of wealth redistribution that created a welfare state. Although he implemented a textbook form of socialism, he made it sound on the surface like the motive of the early Greek democracy. Socialism was, however, an effort to level the distance between rich and poor, and he made it seem more equitable than it was.

"He increased state funds devoted to social welfare and health, and tried to close the gap between the highest and lowest paid workers. He instituted more progressive taxes to affect the wealthy.

"I believe he thought if he could get past the growing pains of his changes and to the other side of the transition, then his idealistic socialism would work and he would be seen as the new intellectual head of the world's left. It is in that delusion of grandeur that he saw his link to the past greatness of Greece. And though it may sound crazy to us, he still believes it, and no one has been able to dissuade him so far from this quest. The problem is that he is deceiving half of our country with his BS and they are buying his theory. Makes it hard to argue that a guy needs to go back to some mundane low-paying job when they hear that the government's going take care of everything if they will just be patient.

"So, his 'change' was directed at reducing the influence of the oligarchs, who were largely the ship owners and other business leaders who dominated Greek politics and the economy and belonged to the traditional Greek right. They are the bedrock of our New Democracy party. He did this so quickly that it shocked the system and caused a radical decrease in wealth and also the influence of business leaders.

"Rather than wait to see how these new economic changes would affect the government, he came up with his 'Contract with the People,' that was a set of new liberal laws that implemented things like expanded health care coverage through a National Health System, increased entitlement aid to the unemployed and the poor, increased pensions and set up a minimum wage. He made it harder to fire workers, promoted state-subsidized tourism, set up recreational areas for the elderly, community health centers, and increased support for artistic and cultural programs. These constant announcements were smart on his part because he discovered that if you keep on making headlines, it will be harder to examine what you have done or proposed to do and find the flaws.

"Still, perhaps his biggest efforts were toward women. He established parental leave for both parents, set up childcare centers and gave out maternity allowances. His creativity in social engineering presented new options for women and put them in competition with men. He improved the legal status of women in part by decriminalizing adultery, abolishing the dowry system, and simplifying divorce. Only just last year women were guaranteed equal pay for equal work. Something you do not have in your country.

"He also introduced reforms in our educational system, and gave significant administrative rights to students and abolished tenure. But the effect of these reforms was limited by a lack of resources, and inefficient administrators. That change was such a disaster that it died from its own lack of leadership. His educational reform was yet another example of being strong in public relations and economic theory but weak in implementation."

Mark interrupted her monologue, "You know, coming from a Democratic Party background in the U.S., those programs sound like a kind of utopian dream. Papandreou sounds like any Democrat in the U.S. but on steroids. You would have a hard time finding a U.S. progressive candidate or party leader who was not for most if not all of the programs you said he is implementing."

Maria patiently explained to Mark, "But that's the same problem Russia is having. You can't just give everybody everything they want.

Somebody's got to do the work. Somebody's got to pay enough in taxes to have the money to run the government. If you don't take in more money than you spend, your government is going to get in trouble. There is a cost for good government, but Greece has gotten lazy and unappreciative. That's the problem with communism and socialism.

"It's the same problem a conservative government has if it spends money it does not have in the budget to prop up or expand military or businesses desires. Sometimes that is done in the form of tax cuts or financial grants to businesses. That also results in deficit spending.

"Your State Department is very familiar with this. Angus and I met with them last week in a briefing. I have dual citizenship so am afforded a certain level of security. They follow this East vs. West situation closely as your President Reagan called the Soviet Union an 'Evil Empire' a couple of years ago when Ambassador Andropov's father was in charge. That characterization kind of pushed everyone's buttons."

Mark, understanding the situation better now, agreed but still offered a caveat, "Yeah, but the problem with capitalism is that greed overcomes empathy, and the inevitable inequities breed discontent."

Petkas now interjected, "Most politics is bullshit. You don't get elected on one hand by preaching conservative economics and denying benefits, but on the other hand people don't appreciate it if you just give them what they have not worked for and don't deserve. They start to resent the giver and assume they are being patronized, which in some ways they are. Democracy needs a middle ground to be successful."

Mark shook his head, "Well I'm not an economist, and those things Papandreou tried to do sound good to me, but I guess if you can't afford it and it bankrupts the country, then you're right. It does not make sense. I guess whatever government you have comes down to finding a balance among all those conflicting ideas somewhere."

Petkas replied, "Those might be noble goals for a government to provide for its people. The problem comes in considering the word 'utopian.' The government here is going into great debt. Businesses are pulling out and going elsewhere because of where the tax burden is here in Greece.

"The theory of socialism sounds good until you try to put it into practice. Somebody has to set priorities and pay the bills. Papandreou is trying to do everything at once with no way to pay for it. You can't make the business environment so people are not motivated to work, and you can't make it so businesses are not motivated to exist. The function of a government, any government, it to find the sweet spot in the middle. Here we are far past that, and we are headed downhill and I'm afraid have already used up the brakes. People never seem to learn that it upsets a society to change it too rapidly. You'd think the Soviets would have remembered that from the chaos after 1917. And here in Greece where our ancient history is so ingrained, it makes that kind of radical change even more impactful."

Sensing the end of the night was near, Petkas folded his napkin and laid it on the table by his plate. "The Soviets finally learned that long ago, so their top one percent who control everything just take what they want and find someone to blame for the problems of the other 99 percent. Well, the Soviets do beat up the dissidents and throw them in jail, which does help to keep down the complaints. So, they figured that out for the short term. That's not so different from the USA where the top one per cent calls the shots.

"But you see, Mark, the main reason I am here and the reason I got into political work is that it will take some time to completely wreck the Greece economy and for Papandreou to kill what was once a great society. My hope is to turn it around or to at least hold off the disaster that I fear is coming."

Mark said, "I am sorry about the economic decline in your country. Let's hope we can begin to correct those problems in this election. It would be a shame if all the great art and history, economics and politics you have shown me and told me about were to be destroyed by such idealistic naiveté." Mark then looked around the room, "Tell me, though, how are we the good guys in this?"

Maria who had been listening to Petkas with undisguised appreciation jumped back into the conversation. "Over the years I've worked both for and against the oligarchs. They don't have utopian answers any more than we do. They want to make money and yet this group we are working with now... well they understand that as much as they like money, they need to have a stable society in order to keep it. It does no one any good if the large mass of people at the bottom become panicked or abused. They need to be comfortable, have a path to move up in society and feel some sense of security for their families. Capitalism, if it does not get out of hand, offers the best chance at that. They see Papandreou and his rush to socialism as a recipe for disaster and they see it happening right in front of their eyes. They're scared and their fear has tempered their greed.

"We understand that the Soviets are also worried about Papandreou. It is in their interest to have a stable Greece, and these policies have the potential to wreck the economy in the next few years. It's something the old-line Russians came to understand. I don't have a good feeling for our dashing, young Mr. Andropov as yet. When I do get to know him better, I'll try to talk him into helping us subdue Papandreou's more radical impulses. The Americans agree with me that we and the Soviets all need to work together to keep the socialists here from taking the initiative out of our society. If things really get worse, then people will get desperate and our society will develop a mindset to disintegrate. That's when bad things can happen like the military takeover here 15 years ago, or we might have a Soviet putsch.

"To avoid that we need to come to a place where the liberal and conservative sides can meet somewhere near the middle and still save face. We need to find that neutral zone soon before it is too late to save the Greek economy. It does not matter so much who is president or premier now, it matters that we don't wreck the place. So, I'm not sure how to address your 'good guys' issue. Many of us see that we need to help Greece to survive first, and then later we can figure out who gets credit and who are the good guys. It may be that the Soviets are the only ones who can convince Papandreou to slow down. I'm just hopeful that the new Mr. Andropov is up to the challenge. I'm also hopeful that Ambassador Andropov understands what the challenge is and can see his role in it. He is very young and handsome and may not be a serious enough person to handle the responsibility. I just hope he is not one of these young Eurotrash dilettantes."

Mark sat back feeling soberer now, and looked from Maria to Petkas.

"To hear how you explain this situation is enlightening and also frightening. I'm just here for the campaign, but whatever I can do to help, please let me know and count on my support."

Maria smiled at Mark in a condescending way. "I know that compared to your country's wealth and political stability we must seem very provincial. But here we are trying to stay afloat. Sometimes we have these discussions with each other, like tonight, in the hope that we may find solid ground. To your ears it may sound alarmist and overly dramatic, but we need to keep looking for a formula that gives us a better future. Thank you for your offer to help. We may need it."

As they were leaving for home after a long and fruitful night, Petkas realized that with each passing day he had begun to feel more that Mark Young just might be the person that he could trust to help him with another issue that had been worrying him for several years.

CHAPTER 11

Igor regretted that it was too late for him to receive the approval he had always wanted from his deceased father, who when he lived was aloof, distant and highly critical on the rare occasions when the father and son had dealings with each other. There was also an unsaid strain with his mother and her relationship with his father, but his mother doted on him and although he resented her babying him and thought her infirmities of age were humorous, he still felt some obligation to please her. Because he had spent most of his childhood with his mother and only rare times alone with his father, it was his mother who had encouraged him in school and early in his career. It was his mother who encouraged him to marry Tatiana as she saw it as a good match that would help him with the Soviet party and the Duma. Igor felt that, however well intentioned, his mother had been wrong, and his wife had turned into more of a nightmare than a dream. His wife was frivolous and demanding and her uncle, who he had to admit had been helpful to his career, liked to give Igor orders as though he was his boss, and at times could be very abrupt and unpleasant.

Igor remembered a recent phone conversation with the uncle who had said to him, "What have you done about getting me the contracts for ship maintenance? Tatiana says you are not being social with the Greek government officials. You need to get to know them well enough so you can make a deal and pay them off to get them to do the business we need. You have leverage over them before the election, not after. Leverage is the basic part of making a deal. What did they teach you in the ambassador school? That is common sense. You are worried about the election. You should be worried about making deals for me and others in the Soviet Union. That is the role of an ambassador. I thought you knew that." The man was demanding and always made Igor feel small and insignificant. However, Valentine Gubanov now seemed to have given up on the shipping contracts and was only concentrating on getting some Greek sculpture any way he could.

Only recently the uncle had told Igor to offer the Greek museum managers some money to sneak artifacts and sculptures out of the museums; and if that didn't work to frighten them. Gubanov gave these and other patronizing directions as though Igor had not already thought about them himself. Then he offered, or almost threatened, to send a henchman he had in his employ to Greece. That was the last thing Igor wanted. That man was intimidating. He had seen him two or three times around the uncle and Tatiana. The man was not really big, but very solidly built, and he had a face that seldom smiled and had a look of cruelty. His wife had told him that this was the man who could make people do things they were reluctant to do. He did not say much, but there was a low noise coming from him almost constantly, a slight rumble. Tatiana, who was also afraid of him and had been around him much more than Igor called him, "the hummer."

Despite these offers or almost threats of assistance from Tatiana's uncle, Igor felt now it was his time to figure things out and to be a man. He cursed his father for not getting him a position like this ambassador's job when he was alive and could have done more to help ease the path for him. Now he felt alone and he would have to show the memory of his father what he could do. He could only rely on himself make his career a success and to please his mother back in the small town in Russia where she lived. As he thought of her, he pictured this formerly dignified woman rejected by her husband turning into an old babushka, going deaf, and waiting by the window for the mailman to bring *Pravda* which she carefully read every day looking for stories of her son. She never had anyone's respect. He'd show everyone who doubted him, whispered rumors and made jokes behind his back; and he'd show her as well. One day she would pick up the paper and there he would be wearing medals, a hero of the Soviet Union.

Now he absentmindedly watched the broad shoulders tapering down to a slim waist of one of the guards as he walked away down the hall. Coming out of his daydream he thought to himself, he needed to stop thinking those thoughts, someone might notice. Those thoughts could get him killed. He needed to concentrate on his job and knew that he was much smarter than these lackeys on the Embassy staff and also the other ambassadors he met from the Soviet bloc countries who were obsequious to him in the hopes that he would carry them along with him on his rise to power.

Igor found most of the Embassy tasks boring, and he did not feel it worth his time to learn the details of all the issues which he had a staff to do for him. He would concentrate on the big picture, on how to improve the public posture of the Soviet Union and himself. His wife was helpful in these publicity settings, which he found distasteful, but which seemed to be necessary. As long as she could take her shopping trips to Paris, London and Milan, she would do her job to be seen as an attractive figure in public settings and leave him to his pleasures. She was only a problem when she lectured him on his job and reminded him that he needed to please her family to keep his job and their marriage secure. He'd just have to put up with her, for now.

He found that he was becoming interested in the intrigue of politics and knew that he had a gift for understanding collusion and the motivations of corruptible people. He'd spent some time studying that aspect of diplomacy and what he could do to help win the upcoming Greek election for Papandreou. He planned to find things to do that put a bigger spotlight on himself and he would leave the agricultural and trade contracts to his staff, like Bokhan. He began to consider ways he might further influence local politics and what reflection that would have on his image back in Moscow as he walked down the hall and then entered the staff meeting on the upcoming Greek election.

In the meeting, it seemed everyone on the embassy staff was nervous and uncertain about the results of the upcoming voting and what the fallout might be for the Soviet Union. The new Soviet leader Mikhail Gorbachev had only been in office for three months after his predecessor Konstantin Chernenko died after less than a year in office. No one knew what kind of a leader Gorbachev would be as yet. They speculated that he might actually be around for a few years because he was much younger than the other leaders that the Soviet Union had known recently. On the other hand, Gorbachev was more than 20 years older than Igor. Igor had only met him once and therefore did not know him well. He was unsure if Gorbachev had any past conflicts with his father, which was another worry.

Igor contemplated these factors and he also wondered if the way the new leader governed would be as predictable or more reactionary compared to those who had come before him. Would this new man think it was time to be more open and friendly with the West? If so, Igor's social skills to fit in there would come in handy. Igor began to think how he might become more visible and do something to gain Gorbachev's trust and prove his loyalty. He felt pressure building to do something soon that would give him credit in his job with the new leaders in Moscow. He needed both a way to have good news to report about his performance as well as a way to overcome any unexpected bad news from Greece.

So, as he looked around the room at his staff gathered to do his bidding, he asked them to report on all the clandestine operations and to give him a review of the people they were watching. Perhaps they could find a traitor or make an embarrassing example of a corruptible American military person. He told them to look at every possible avenue for something they could enhance or manufacture that would bring Igor more credit in Moscow and make the powers back home forget about any unpleasant news that might come from slippage in the coming election.

He decided to make security one of the issues he did pay attention to and began asking for transcripts of phone intercepts and made plans to attend the First Chief Directorate, the

FCD, meetings in the Embassy. He also had Bokhan arrange for him to watch a demonstration of Spetsnaz commando training the next time he was in the Soviet Union. As he gave that order it made Igor once again wish that his father had involved him more in the past 20 years. Right now, he could use some of the knowledge his father had learned as the head of the KGB. However, as it was his time now, he'd have to make it on his own terms to show everyone that he was not only his father's son, but his better.

For a start, he looked at the reports of surveillance on the New Democracy campaign, including reports from the Greek security. There were 20 people assigned to watch the campaign working in shifts and with different responsibilities. Most of these were with the Greek security because they could blend in easier and some who had greater technical proficiency were in the Soviet embassy. They also had some people who were imbedded as volunteers or paid clerical workers in the campaign itself. He suspected that more suspicious activity would be uncovered watching the New Democracy organization and its activities around the country, and told Bokhan to make arrangements to shift the distribution of surveillance so that four to six people were assigned to monitor the professor Petkas and the tall American who was often seen with him. After making the assignments, he felt confident that he had a sixth sense for this kind of work, no doubt passed on to him genetically from the successes of his father years before in the Soviet Union.

Bokhan went back to his desk after the meeting with Ambassador Andropov to finish reviewing the clandestine photos taken by the Greek woman his staff had installed in the New Democracy campaign. Most were photos of staff lists, phone numbers, and calendars of upcoming events and schedules. But included there were these square-shaped images taken of other photos that were curious. They looked like those instant Polaroid photos. The quality of the prints he had was not good but they seemed to be of people perhaps taken at night and perhaps at some kind of a party. They looked to be wearing old Greek costumes, pasty makeup and posing strangely. He'd have to send them to the technical experts for their opinion. You never knew what you might get from gathering surreptitious information, but it needed to be vetted first for accuracy and tricks by the opposition to put you on a false path. There was no point in involving Andropov until these had been thoroughly analyzed as the ambassador was likely to jump to an unverified conclusion.

CHAPTER 12

One evening Mark and Angus were having dinner with some campaign friends and the meal went on late with drinks and conversation long after the dishes had been cleared. There was a rainstorm outside and no one was anxious to leave. One of the women they worked with who was in the media department was giving her clearly stated, liberal views about politics in the United States. Her comments did not make sense to Mark as he thought of the New Democracy party as more like Republicans in the U.S. With his assumptions grounded in American-style politics, he asked her why she supported the conservative, pro-business party and not the more liberal socialists or communists. She looked up shocked, jammed out her cigarette in one of the overflowing ashtrays, and said, "Because they killed my family!"

Petkas, feeling an edge entering the conversation, tried to explain. "We have become good at that over the years. We Greeks have been in wars and been overrun and have been both conquerors and slaves for several thousand years. War and killing, deceit, and other despicable notions are in this soil of ours. They are like a balance in our history to our beautiful art and architecture. We have known constant loss from ancient wars up until the most recent war, and this gives us a different perspective than you in the Unites States, who have not had civil war in your country for over a hundred and twenty years. We remember from just a few years back the names and faces of people who were on the other side and who came and took our family members out in the night and shot them.

"What we are doing now and what you are doing here in the campaign represents just another form of combat between the left and the right. I'm being facetious, but only a little bit, in saying it is our hope to dispatch our opponents, who seem determined to destroy our economy and send us all into poverty, but perhaps in subtler and even more humane ways. I fear if we continue on the path of the socialists, we will be begging everyone else in the world for bread, and we will kill each other over getting the biggest slices. The stakes here in this election for the continuation of our nation are great."

Petkas sat up straighter and patted the woman on the leg who had said her family had been murdered. He took a breath and there was anger in his words, not directed at Mark specifically, but at the Greek situation in general. "This conversation must seem maudlin to an American. You are more used to happy talk and with your place in the world you can afford to do just that. Believe me, if we were as rich a place as America, we would be doing just the same. So, you should feel no guilt at hearing my babbling or be embarrassed if I find problems with everybody and every philosophy and every government. Our problem is we have lived under them all and we know the truth that none of them work in the long run. They all disappoint. They all fail. Our job in this campaign is to find a way to prolong the inevitable, and despite the fact that it will eventually be a catastrophe here, for us it is a noble enough goal to carry our banner with pride for the time we have.

"There are a lot of political parties and philosophies that draw passionate followers just as there are a lot of religions and churches in the world. Both have dogma and faith in what they believe and they both try to ingratiate that into their supporters, but in both cases, there is no proof or an absolute arbitrator of truth. At the end of the day you believe and support something that you hope is the best thing, and you claim somewhat defensively to others that what you have chosen is the absolutely best choice. The god we choose is the dogma of the most familiar and convincing argument.

"Much of our society has found that we need to hang onto a political or a religious faith to keep us safe from the fear of the unknown, the enemy, the devil in our dreams. That choice gives us comfort and direction even if we barely believe it."

Angus clanked down his drink on a side table covered in books stained with water rings. "Wow! Stanos Petkas! You are a party animal. Thanks for pulling the rug out from under everyone. However, I think I'll stick with believing in something rather than your idea that there is a void under the floor of faith and politics. I think believing in a form of politics and religion rather than rejecting them and accepting anarchy is what keeps humanity moving forward. Without some form of faith, we'd have no inspiration, no belief that the future could get better. I think that faith was the catalyst that got us out of the caves and onto the moon. Faith in something is what produces order in living things. My dog has faith that I will give him a treat if he does not pee on the floor or deny him one if he does. That belief is the inducement and the glue that forms relationships. At the end of the day we are motivated by passion and the hope of reward, not intellect. That's why we pull the lever in the voting booth and that is why we follow a moral compass.

"You've just got to find a way to develop a Scandinavian model of high productivity and worker motivation in a sort of semi-socialism. There is depression and alcoholism and shit to deal with everywhere. Teenagers don't listen to their parents anywhere. Yet in most places they still get up in the morning and go to school or to work. You've got to find that key to motivation and it has to be from self-promise rather than fear of retaliation. You've got to believe in what you are doing in life and get over yourself."

Petkas nodded and smiled. "We thank you for being here and for your help." Then he used his liquor glass as an imaginary sword and thrust it into the air. "We will smite our enemy with renewed vigor and purpose." Then he looked down. "But, prolonging the inevitable disaster is a good enough cause for me." He then tossed back the last swallow of his ouzo.

One of the other people across the room slurred, "Capitalism is a less excessive form of socialism. Same problems, different solutions. More pay as you go."

Mark started to respond and then stopped, realizing that the late hour and the many drinks created a situation where it was better to let Petkas and the others vent their frustration. He felt it better to listen and try to remember anything the next day that would give him more grounding in the politics of Greece.

Petkas continued, "Papandreou is your text book liberal academic. Look, I'm an academic, so I know the type. But these academic theorists, particularly in economics, have had to defend their ideas for so long without any confirmation that if they get the chance to prove their theories, they go wild. When he became prime minster, he introduced pretty much every social conjecture that the left wing in the United States and the Soviet Union had been preaching for many years. All of them sounded like great humanitarian principals. Papandreou found a way in the beginning to keep everyone happy by giving them things from the government. It was like a national pyramid scheme. To be fair to Papandreou, Greece has had a history of taking on debt since the Ottoman Empire, so we've been at for a while and it is not new behavior.

"Now, under his ideal of socialism he's tried to do it all in a few years without any way to pay for it. He's sugar coated the changes by giving a sudden dose of egalitarianism to a people who were mainly hard-working, blue-collar workers and farmers. These were people who in recent history were basically advocates of free enterprise. Now they suddenly have all these government programs just handed to them with little required in return, and that has created a lazy society with little work ethic. There are no business or income-producing groups large enough to tax that will cover all the costs he has created in his government. One does not have to be a great economist to see that this will end in disaster and his largesse will likely bankrupt the country.

"The coming Greek election is the chance for the Socialists and Communists to show they can still win a competition with the West. They've been getting beat by the West, by the money, by the capitalists, for years and now they have a shot at proving why they are still relevant. The rest of us who don't really like the hardline conservative capitalists, still must be on their side, because it's the only counterbalance available to the disaster of socialism."

He looked down morosely. "The West will just use us and take the best we have to offer, like defiling a young virgin and leaving her for the rest of her life branded by her shame to work in the kitchen of the castle. In the West you cover greed subtly by supporting charitable organizations where the suffering has been partially caused by a financial caste system. Like my friend over there said earlier, they killed her family and she has kept a grudge, fearing that it will happen again, if not now, probably later.

"There is no incentive to try to make things better here or to have passion or be creative about your work. Angus and Mark," he nodded at them both, "you're right in that we need to find the middle ground between capitalism and communism. We want a Greek democracy that has peace, bread, music, laughter and being safe with our children, but the philosophy of government always disappoints. At the end of the day it is not important what you want, but that you appreciate what you have.

"Our party wants to see a nation where the government is based more on meritocracy and less on patronage, sort of like the basic and undistorted idea of your moderate Republican party in the United States, or even moderate Democrats, but right now we lack a clear enough political message to win national elections. Candidates in the New Democracy party filter up from a long time of service in the party trenches. Please don't repeat this, but our seniority system has resulted in the New Democracy now nominating a long serving loyalist but, not necessarily the best messenger.

"This election is our hope to change that trend and by next time be ready to win. We've got to find a way to stop the lunacy of our current Prime Minister. It does not matter so much about liberal or conservative. At the end of the day this is about the death of our country."

The rain had stopped and the room had gotten quiet as Petkas finished his long speech. Mark suddenly became aware that he was emotionally and physically drained, and that the room smelled of garlic, olives, stale cigarette smoke, and ouzo. He wanted to get away and go to bed.

Walking unsteadily back to the hotel on the shining slick streets, Angus said to Mark, "So tonight was an education on how the stakes in elections are clearly different here. It was good for you to hear that, and for me too. I can get so caught up in the business sometimes that I forget the very human needs people have. Elections can bring hope that they can avoid wars like those that have ravaged this country forever. It puts everyone in a tough and sometimes unforgiving situation to have neighbors fighting neighbors and then having to live next to each other after the fighting stops. Makes the politics bitter and the sides rigid. We both need to keep this lesson in mind.

"By the way, I'm going to have to spend more time away in the next few weeks. Our work here is kind of in place, but it would be best if you were to stay here, particularly with me gone. It would be a big help if you can look for problems in the systems we've set up for the campaign and alert all of us if there are big changes in the election or in what the PASOK people or the communists are doing. Go to the Embassy briefings for me. Manage things for me like you did in Panama while I'm gone. I'll make an adjustment in your compensation that will be well worth it."

Hearing Angus, Mark understood it meant that more trips back to Washington to spend time with Vicki were not going to happen.

CHAPTER 13

Angus took Mark to the suburb of Glyfada near one of the four military bases the U.S. had in Greece. They got out of the taxi near the sea on Poseidon Avenue to look at the last of the setting sun on the water. Mark tried to imagine this place with the ancient little stubby Greek ships powered by slave rowers and small sails bobbing in the harbor. He was standing on the same ground where thousands of years of history had taken place.

They meandered slowly into the little village, sometimes doubling back on their path or taking a sharp turn while looking into storefront shops and purposefully wandering for just under an hour until they found a place called Bobby's Bar on the main square to meet with the local military liaison. They did not see anyone following. The neighborhood with the bar had a look Mark was familiar with from his days in the military away from the US mainland of English signs in the stores in an attempt at attracting the ready cash of American soldiers. He could also see in the eyes of the locals wandering the streets, a resentment and distaste for overactive and often drunken G.I.'s who assumed the sidewalks of their hometown were a playground for any sudden whims and hormonal excesses.

The bar was on a corner not far off Poseidon Avenue and had a rundown wooden front plastered in English signage and Greek beer advertisements. The place looked more American than Greek and was packed inside with over 200 GI's from the nearby airfield, where elements of the 7206th Air Force Support Group were stationed a little over six miles south of Athens. It reeked of beer and was impossibly loud from the thumping music and with the noise of scores of soldiers competing for alcohol consumption, encouraged by some of the local girls hired to be there for stimulation. The military liaison officer steered them out to a table on the street side, where the noise of the evening traffic was peaceful comparted to the cacophony of sound inside. He gave them an update on the growing harassment of American soldiers in Athens despite efforts to keep the military calm and respectful when visiting the main part of town and encouraging them to restrict their activities to hanging out at these kinds of bars closer to their bases. The harassment and acts of violence had been increasing over the past few years and the Major did not think there was anything that could be done to make the situation any better.

He reported that the people on the nearby airfield were almost oblivious to the local elections and led rather contained lives near the bases. He offered no suggestions or actions they could take to improve the circumstances with the current government or to support the chances of the New Democracy campaign. They shared some beers and as the liaison offered little information that was useful, they left about 10:30 to find a taxi to take them back to the hotel in Athens.

About midnight a large blast occurred just outside the tavern, Bobby's Bar, that destroyed the wooden front of the building and wrecked much of the inside bar. Miraculously no one was killed although about 50 people were injured, 34 of them Americans. Mark called the military liaison the next day who told him they were sure it was a bomb, perhaps dropped off in a package by a pedestrian on the front sidewalk of the bar or tossed from a car passing nearby where they had been sitting a couple of hours earlier. He thought it was just a coincidence that the bomb happened the night they had been there and told Mark that the Greek authorities investigating the scene supposed it might have been a gas container that exploded. The local police's ludicrous speculation about the blast was made despite the base hospital pulling more than 20 nails out of the legs of injured GI's, after several hours of emergency surgeries. No one was ever captured or charged with the bombing, but Mark and Angus decided in the future to stick close to the hotel and only go out to dinner with their Greek friends.

CHAPTER 14

It was another cold, dark night in Athens and the streets were still damp from a late afternoon shower. Maria took Angus and Mark to a local restaurant and told them that this was where many of the local political people dined. Once they had passed the outside door, the restaurant threshold had a thick blanket hung to the ground over the inside entrance area which had to be negotiated to enter. She told them that the heavy cloth was to keep out the penetration of the damp, late winter weather.

So far, the gastronomic adventures of this campaign were turning out to be the most enjoyable part. Tonight, they were looking forward to what surprises they would find in a new dish that Maria would order for them each time they went to dinner with her.

Usually when they went out in the evening for a meal with Maria, Mark could pass at a distance for a native with his swarthy skin and dark hair that blended with his Greek attire. He looked pretty much like a New York delicatessen worker in a 'Saturday Night Live' skit. Angus, however, was big, ruddy, and Scottish, and it was hard for him to blend into the Mediterranean culture. They did their best to dress like the locals and not speak loudly around the waiters or other customers. In fact, however, they were both as awkward as 12-year olds taking their first dance steps.

Due to the close proximity of the small nation states, many people in this part of Europe were involved one way or another in diplomatic services and knew each other or had dealings with one another. After placing the order for a spicy chicken and rice dish, Maria left the two of them to cross the restaurant and speak to some ministers from other European countries she had recognized when they entered. Those diplomats told her that there was a big dinner meeting going on that evening in one of the private dining rooms with many of the Soviet Block ministers.

After Maria returned, she leaned into the table and they did the same.

Then in a low voice told them another of the amazing stories of her resistance to the Greek Junta 30 years before. As Mark and Angus leaned over the table, they listened carefully as her stories were a close second to the food in what they enjoyed the most about Greece.

She smiled as she picked up the pace of the anecdote and seemed to have great satisfaction in telling about the false bravado of the male resistance guerillas in Greece in the 1960's and early 1970's when they were faced with real life situations. Although her account was funny now, it related to the partisans' attempts to rid the country of the government taken over and then ruled by the brutal military.

Many of her stories began at a meeting. Mark guessed that even in a guerilla-led revolution people met and talked endlessly to decide what to do. He tried to picture a room filled with middle aged and young people all arguing and smoking with someone constantly looking out of shaded windows, worried that the military storm troopers might arrive at any moment and burst through the door from the streets to arrest them, or worse.

In this story Maria told of her efforts to acquire a large shipment of arms which she planned to deliver to an isolated airstrip on one of the sparsely inhabited Greek islands. The local partisans planned to meet the aircraft and retrieve the weapons as soon as the plane landed.

She had paid the arms merchants for a shipment of the much-needed weapons and watched them loaded onto the aircraft on a small airstrip just outside Izmir, Turkey. Because Izmir was near the coast on the Aegean Sea, the aircraft would only have to fly approximately 150 miles across the water to the small island where the rendezvous with the Greek rebels would take place.

On the night of the delivery Maria boarded the mid-sized propeller driven freight aircraft to shepherd the delivery and after humming and bumping along the rough air over the sea for about an hour, they reached the appropriate coordinates, approached the island from a course low over the water, and then began to signal the people on the ground using an agreed upon radio frequency. The men were there near the landing strip and had the trucks to haul away the weapons. Now they just needed to put lights on the small deserted runway so the cargo plane could land and offload the merchandise. A night landing on a dirt runway would be the most dangerous part of the trip for the aircraft, and the strip would have to be lit by a row of torches stuck into the ground and headlights from the vehicles on site. The dark dirt strip was not an ideal environment for a cargo plane heavily loaded with munitions.

As they were waiting for the runway to be lit there was continuous chatter over the radio from the men on the ground. Once they thought they had heard something and a few minutes later they thought they saw someone coming. At first this appropriate caution was welcomed, but after over an hour of hesitation and delay by the men on the ground with one imagined threat after another, the fuel on the aircraft was getting low for the return trip, and it became apparent that the men on the ground were just afraid of getting caught if they lit up the runway. Now, Maria tried to shame the local partisans into doing their duty, berating them over the radio, telling them how much the armaments on the aircraft cost and how much they were needed. It would have taken at most 20 minutes to land, unload the aircraft, and take off again. Even trying as hard as she could, nothing worked to motivate the men on the ground to take on the small risk to do their part of lighting the runway.

After circling the area for another half hour while waiting for cowering men on the ground to find their courage, the aircraft finally ran critically short of fuel. Two of the men on the aircraft pushed open a cargo door and dumped the expensive and much needed load of weapons into the ocean. Unfortunately, the nighttime landing story was just one of several egregious examples Maria had that showed the failure of partisan courage in the battle against the junta.

She completed her story about the time they were finishing the meal and were waiting for the check to arrive. From the back of the restaurant two sliding French doors opened and about a dozen men came out of a smoke-thickened room. As all the men from the room headed in a tight group for the exit door, one of them, a tall, dark, handsome man in his forties, looked around the restaurant and spotted Maria and her dinner companions. He peeled off from the others, crossed the room and passed by their table. As he strolled by, he said in English, "I hope you enjoyed your meal."

Mark and Angus froze at the man's comments but gave no reply as they tried unsuccessfully to deny their understanding of English. Maria nodded and replied to the man in Russian. When he had left she turned to them and said, "That gentleman was Igor Andropov, Soviet Ambassador to Greece and the son of the late Soviet President Yuri Andropov." Mark turned to take took another look. Igor was dressed in what looked like Armani and was trim and suave. He definitely was the new generation of Russian – more Western and looking more French or English than the heavyset block-shaped figures of the May Day newsreels. He was also one of their chief opponents in the political game they were playing.

In Greece, once again as it had been in Panama, they always assumed that they were being followed and that their phones were tapped, which was a common circumstance for most people working politics abroad. Sometimes on night walks or on returning from dinner, Mark and Angus spotted someone trailing them. On the cold streets of Athens, that night returning to their hotel they heard the asynchronous echo of footfalls on the cobblestones and turned to see an undistinguished, meandering old man acting unconcerned and inattentive in the dark. They had no way of knowing if it was someone taking an innocent walk, or if it was someone whose job it was to follow them.

As they continued their walk back to their hotel, Mark and Angus discussed in whispers that at the next New Democracy staff meeting they would propose the need to have a safe room at the campaign office with limited access that would be kept locked when not in use and could be swept often for bugs. They also needed a place to store secure files of sensitive information, likely in Maria's office. With that as a plan to discuss at their morning meeting, they felt better about whoever may have been following them.

Back up the narrow street in a shadowed doorway, Eudora Patmos watched, still and quiet, as the final phases of a plot slowly formed in her mind. Before she started at the campaign, Eudora had heard from her handler about Maria Beckett's many skills and was deferential to her, head down, asking permission, offering to volunteer for any unpleasant task.

Now that she was well entrenched as a spy with her good command of English and excellent office skills, she felt she was moving beyond providing services to the American consultants and making copies of sensitive documents.

Now she was now ready to move forward, to cause a scandal and then reveal the Americans as an embedded part of the Greek campaign. She felt the plan she was considering would be just the thing.

CHAPTER 15

Mark was excited to speak to Vicki and he decided not to mention the Bobby's Bar bombing as it would just upset her and fuel her imagination. He felt it had been too long since he had heard her voice. She jumped on the line and was as positive and full of enthusiasm as he had expected, "Well, tell me about it. Does Athens continue to be what you had hoped? Do you miss me?"

God, had he missed her.

As they spoke it was almost midnight in Washington and seven hours later in Athens, where Mark was looking out the window of his hotel at the sunrise of the next day casting a rosy glow on the rocks and columns of the Acropolis about a quarter of a mile away. He had cracked a window to feel the cool fresh air before the city smells of the day would change that into something urban and less pleasant. "It's beautiful. Like I told you when I was home, I like the people I'm working with, and I take a really good hike almost every day with a friend from the office to work off the incredible food they have here. How are things in DC, and how are you?"

"Oh, you know how it is here. Everyone is pointing fingers and blaming everyone else, as usual. I had a friend who left her job the other day after her congressman tried to pin her in his office and kiss her. The guy was like about 60. Barf. Anyway, I want to know about what's going on there. What is the candidate like? What about your opposition? Do you guys have a chance? And how are you holding up? And most importantly, and once again, how much do you miss me?"

Mark wanted to be forthcoming with Vicki and was concerned that he could not answer her fully on an open phone, but at the same time he did not want to be dismissive of her questions. "You know it's a strange feeling because in Panama we had the benefit of government support and all the power sources, and here in Greece it's the opposite; we're without any support from the government and in fact, active opposition. It's still kind of too early to tell how things will turn out. Our candidate is not as important as the party strength and structure. I'll figure out more about how all that works as I go along. And the only thing that is still the same is that I do miss you like crazy. I wish you could come over here so I could see you again and show you everything, and we could be together."

Vicki laughed, "Well, I want to know everything. Are there any issues going on there that could affect the research work I do here on the hill? Are the Greek socialists and communists sort of like the stereotypical characters seen in old movies like 'Zorba the Greek' or 'Never on Sunday.' Or are they more like the Soviet bureaucratic blockheads in the May Day newsreels?"

Mark was becoming more uncomfortable, but laughed at Vicki's characterization. "Well the content of those movies aside, sort of like that, at least the scenery. I haven't gotten a good read on the bureaucrats as yet. Some of the fashion I've seen out walking around is like out of the 1940's or 50's and the technology is not up to what we are used to, but Vicki, you'd love the streets. Life is kind of on display here with all sorts of open shops and sidewalk cafes and everybody seems to love just being out and walking around together. You smell baking bread and spices everywhere. Well, that along with the exhaust from traffic and sometimes trash that does not get picked up very quickly. The scenery and history are amazing and the traffic, though the mufflers are not very effective, is nothing like the crazy bustle we have at home. It actually feels so much safer here, a slower pace. I wish you could be here too, and we could see it all together."

"Mark, you're being your old stiff Washington self. Holding the cards close to your chest and talking to me formally. Lighten up. The scenery and baking bread are okay, but I would think you should be more enthusiastic to be involved in an election in the birthplace of democracy. You don't seem to be too excited to be there though, and I will just attribute that to how much you miss me. I'm disappointed that you can't share more, even if...." Before Mark left Washington, the two of them had discussed the limitations on how much he might be able to say on the phone, and Vicki, remembering that caught herself and toned down her inquisition. "Well, I'm not going to probe you now, but get ready the next time we are together. When we get a chance, I want to hear more details about what are you doing over there. Plus, I don't buy that it is safer. You need to be careful."

"Well, you know it's hard to talk on the phone here," he said. "I am excited because I hope

to be coming home soon while they finish translating some documents I gave them. Maybe by that time I'll have some answers to all your questions, and I want to tell you about this woman, Maria Beckett, I'm working with. She is amazing and you'd be so much in love with her just to be around her for a few minutes and see her strength. She is a real hero. She makes some of those women in Washington who talk all the time about women's rights seem like kids, but she has actually lived through tremendous danger to secure rights for everybody here."

"I'm sure I'd love to meet her, but don't go knocking my friends here who are working for equal rights."

"No offense intended. It is just that it is so genuine here where people's rights and safety have been in such jeopardy. When we meet, I'll tell you some of the stories I've heard and you'll be surprised."

"Okay, I hear you, but let's talk more about you and me now. Here's an order. Think of something colorful and traditional you can bring me when you come for your visit. Something like those clunky earrings made of old Greek coins or bold patterns on a dress like a Medusa head or something cool like that. Make it a surprise. And take some pictures! I want to see some of the things you are telling me about. When you get back, I really want us to think about redoing our condo or getting a real house. I want us to have something to live in that feels more like a genuine home."

He heard the part of the conversation she didn't verbalize. He hoped she heard his too.

When the transcript of the phone conversation was delivered to Bokhan a day later, two things interested him. The first was the hike the American was making every day. It would be hard to cover him with surveillance when he was walking about, so what was he actually doing on that hike? The hike could be an ideal opportunity for the American and the other person from the office to pursue espionage? Who was his 'friend from work?' Was it Petkas? He'd need to get the surveillance people to check on that and report to him.

He also wondered why the American allowed a woman to ask such probing and personal questions. What kind of man would not have better control over his woman … or any woman for that matter? It sounded like she was giving him orders. And he wondered, because the Americans were all so open, why did this American hedge on answering his girlfriend's questions about what he was doing and about the election. It seemed he had more to hide than just being worried about phone surveillance. He made notes and would put these two concerns into a file for follow up.

He directed someone to find out where the hike was taking place, at what time, and who it was with. They needed to make sure people followed this American and to be certain he and whoever was with him from the campaign were both under surveillance. Bokhan needed to know if the hiking activity represented a pattern, because patterns could be important. He would also have someone compare all the conversations with the girlfriend and look for patterns there and ask for a tap to be put on her phone in Washington by the embassy staff there. Once the information was gathered and analyzed, he planned to check the profile more frequently in the future on the two Americans his office was preparing, because that material could be useful as evidence to back up claims of espionage if they did anything suspicious.

It would be good to find a way to embarrass the New Democracy party. For now, he would direct the surveillance team to stay back and observe and listen. He put his notes in the folder and tapped it with his finger. He did not need to share the dossier with Igor now. Igor might jump to the wrong conclusion, but once it was gathered, if he could find enough significant material, he would bring it to his attention later.

He leaned back in his chair and closed his eyes. Initially Sergei Bokhan thought his appointment as the Deputy Assistant to Igor Andropov was a dream job. He assumed he was to be the detail man to keep the dashing son of the former Soviet Premier on track for greater things in what promised to be an illustrious career. He had wagered his own career that Andropov would be a shooting star to attach himself to, and moving to Athens, Greece, with his young family would be such a thrilling change from the noise, dirt, and poor weather of Moscow. He felt the weather in Moscow contributed to the gloom and oppressive feelings of suspicion and surveillance that permeated the government. In Greece, he was glad to be away from the hordes of bureaucratic watchers and he enjoyed the sunny, warmer weather and the history he loved to read about in his spare time.

He had begun to look for a Greek Orthodox Church here which would be a good substitute for his beloved Russian Orthodox Church. After all, Greece was an influential force in the world during the growth of Christianity. He had grown up loving the solemn traditions and ceremonies of the church and wanted his children to know the value of those religious festivals, the responsive readings and chants. The church provided guidance that prepared one to have a good and purposeful life. Bokhan felt that the patterns of order in the church mirrored the order and patterns needed in his job. Other than some jokes from non-believers, he had never felt any direct contradiction or official pressure from the Soviet Union for his beliefs, and he felt they were compatible. There were the undertones, and stated Soviet policy that discouraged organized religion, but the old church was still a part of the Russian culture. Here they could worship at the Greek Church and not receive the subtle disapproval he sometimes saw in the eyes of his colleagues in Moscow. The Greek posting could prove to be the ideal place to enhance his career and allow his family to bloom in a less repressive environment, surrounded by history.

His new boss, Igor was certainly flamboyant. His wife looked like a model and acted like a movie star. She dressed and carried herself with self-assurance as though she would be comfortable in any of the drawing rooms, balls, and fashion shows in the big cities of Europe. She often traveled to Paris and Milan and even to London. Perhaps that was just what was needed as the wife of a Soviet Ambassador. Away from the gossip of Moscow, she could open doors and gain access that would be valuable for her husband and for him as well. These Westerners were so casual and open they did not know when the things they said were overheard by calculating ears which could prove to be valuable to the Soviet Union. With care and precision, a dossier of these casual comments could prove quite useful to the party. Bokhan would see to that.

But Igor was not measured and careful like most diplomats he had known. He and his wife often went their separate ways. It was only a few weeks after they were settled in their jobs at the embassy in the Greek capital that Igor would come in looking very tired as though he had been burning the candle at both ends, and he seemed to appreciate the more attractive women in the office and at meetings around Athens than Bokhan thought was proper. It was not his place to bring this up to Igor, but he kept notes in his diary on his observations. Perhaps the behavior of Igor was just the nervousness of settling into the job and trying to be friendly with everyone. Time would tell.

Igor was also a demanding boss. Being difficult was not an unusual trait for Soviet leaders, so Bokhan was careful to anticipate Igor's needs and to be quick to respond and to have the correct answer or produce the requested information. He did not wish to anger the young Andropov or give him reason to be disappointed in his job performance.

He expected that the socialist government of Papandreou would easily win the upcoming election and the transition to a more complete communist state would continue with appropriate speed, thereby showing faith to the communist dogma needed by the people. His new job was not without concerns, but certainly it held promise. Yet, he thought, his new boss, Igor, was certainly flamboyant.

Eudora Patmos left the orphanage confident that she had paid enough money to secure the support of the person there she needed for her scheme and she was glad to be away from the unpleasant smell of institutional disinfectant. The twelve-year-old girl resident was obviously retarded, but Eudora could see with the demonstration of the clinic helper she had hired, that the small girl was compliant and obedient to adults and mobile enough for her purposes. She was also pretty enough to be photogenic and that would help to make the media stories all the more impactful. Her contact at the orphanage would let her pick up the girl when the rest of the plan was in place. Eudora had agreed to call the woman at least two days ahead with a warning when to get the girl ready. Her plan was going to work and it would be sensational.

CHAPTER 16

Mark had been pleased when he discovered that both he and Stanos Petkas liked to walk to get some exercise almost every day. He was fascinated by being in the birthplace of democracy and suggested they have many of their conversations on a hike out of the office. He became excited to be able to discuss business while moving about in an atmosphere that enabled him to see more of the ancient city and he felt lucky to have a job that allowed him to have extended conversations with a colleague who was also a world authority on Greek culture while on a meandering tour through the historic sites. Mark was staying at the Achilleas Hotel on Praxitelis Street, which was in the center of the old part of town and near the campaign office, so on some days, they began the trek from Mark's hotel.

Although it started as an opportunity to be outside getting exercise, both men thought the hike to the top of a nearby mountain would allow them to pick selective spots with less chance of observation when they wished to discuss any confidential information. So, for a vigorous workout, most days they climbed Mount Lykavittus, the highest hill in Athens, which was visible from all over the city and less than a mile and a half from the Acropolis. From the top of the 900-foot hill, Mark and Petkas always stopped to catch their breath from a place where they could see over to the Acropolis and the sprawling city of Athens spreading into the distance on all sides as far as the eye could see.

On most days once they reached the top, after they paused to rest, they walked around the bright exterior of the whitewashed St. George Chapel perched on top of the pine tree covered hill. Mark read in a brochure he found of an ancient local legend that Lykavittus had been inhabited by wolves. The pamphlet interpreted the name "Lykavittus" to mean 'Mountain of Wolves'. The hill was too steep for many structures and Mark could imagine a pack of wolves finding many places to

94

hide in the trees and brush halfway up the precipice thousands of years earlier. Near the St. Georges Chapel was an open-air playhouse called the Lykavittus Theater where in the summer months they held plays and concerts. Sometimes instead of the steep hill they would cut through the Athens National Garden near his hotel and abutting the Greek parliament building. No matter which way they walked there was history, incredible architecture and beautiful scenery to see.

He was on his way to meet with Petkas for a walk when Eudora Patmos happened to step into the hallway as he was passing and they almost crashed into each other. He excused himself, although the encounter did not seem to be his fault or entirely accidental. She was dressed in a fabric of soft cloth that clung to her curves and her blouse was unbuttoned to the center of her chest that made it hard for his eyes not to want to take a peek. Eudora pouted, "So you go to walk with Stanos? Maybe sometime you will have time to walk with others in the office and get a different tour of Athens. Many of us also have stories to tell." She held her hands clasped behind her back, smiled and shifted her weight moving her chest from left to right and then back. "You are such a serious man, maybe it would be better for the campaign if you relaxed sometime?"

Mark forced his eyes to stay on hers. "Miss Patmos, you are probably right. We are all so busy now, it's too bad there is not more time to tour Greece and see all the sights." He smiled and nodded at her. "Please excuse me." He hurried on to meet Petkas, but the alluring Eudora had once again caught him off-guard.

Eudora looked at herself in the mirror in the women's bathroom. What was wrong with the American? She knew she was still beautiful and could have been a model, particularly in the lingerie magazine advertisements. She had been so sure that she could have made him her lover by this time. No matter. The plan she had devised would work well even without her being the bait. She just had a few more things to do. The fact that he had resisted her would make springing the trap on him that much more satisfying.

After many of the elements of the campaign had already been put into place, the conversations Mark had with his new friend and colleague became more about the history of Greece rather than current politics or campaign logistics. He found that Stanos Petkas was happy to be his teacher and was also good at it.

Petkas started by asking Mark, "What do you know about Greek history?"

"Just what I remember from my school days. Nothing special or concentrated. I looked at some modern history to prepare for this campaign. I've seen some of the old costume dramas and sword fighting movies and of course 'Zorba,' the political movie 'Z' and 'Never on Sunday'."

Petkas smiled politely as they turned the corner toward the Acropolis, "Well, let me give you an overview of where we are and how we got here. Of course, much of what I'll be talking about will be before the birth of Christ which you likely know as B.C., but will also have relevance to today's politics. You see, early Greece was just a collection of many small villages or city-states. Even though some of those people thought of themselves as Greek, back then they were not formally connected by a national identity or government. Instead, they identified with their city-state and local or regional leader. That tradition of regional independence and affiliation has continued up to today. Ironically, we consider Greece to be the cradle of Western civilization, but for much of its history it has been a widely scattered diaspora. Most people would be surprised to learn that until 1832, the nation of Greece as we know it legally didn't exist as a single state.

"Usually a strong man ran the show in each of these districts, and over time these people and fiefdoms fought each other and combined or split up almost like chemical reactions. The territories grew larger through these combinations, and a nation evolved as the regions were joined or forced to support each other through mutual interests. A standard set of rules and trade guidelines also evolved, and methods of governing these provinces were tried and changed as needed. Greek palaces became structures of complex, highly centralized economies featuring regional networks for the collection and distribution of wealth. Gradually a form of what we consider democracy came into being, and for a time in history, Greece became the leader of the known Western world.

"Along the way, recordkeeping, writing, art, architecture, and other achievements useful to civilization evolved and became more proficient. Interestingly enough, most written records of early history were tax records and accounting. Be that as it may, it was still the strong man at the center of Greek and other cultures who most influenced history.

"There was a golden age known as the Classical period where for about 200 years between 500 and 300 BC, Greece controlled much of the Mediterranean area, and through Alexander the Great much of western Asia as well. By that conquest they had dominion over great natural resources and wealth, and the historic influence of that period in ancient Greece has continued up to modern times.

"Near the beginning of this period a leader called Pericles came to rule in Athens. He was the greatest statesman of ancient Greece, and he consolidated power. The period during which he led Athens, roughly from 460 to 430 BC, is sometimes known as the 'Age of Pericles.'

He made Athens the educational and cultural center of the ancient Greek world, which is to say the ancient Western world. His rule was sandwiched between the end of the Persian Wars to the beginning of a series of wars largely between Athens and Sparta known as the Peloponnesian War that lasted for almost 30 years, sort of between 430 and 400 BC. Pericles' time period marked the height of ancient Greece's riches in political stability, art, and culture. But in addition to being sandwiched between the two great wars of Classical Greece, he was better known because he promoted arts and literature.

"Greece today, as you may have discovered in our campaign, has been chasing an ideal of its past and its political, literary culture and art have created a kind of resilience... in the Greek brand so to speak. However, the ragged peninsula of Greece has often been conquered and ruled by many other nations. To make it more complicated, those controlling governments have often been in conflict with each other, dragging our country along in these struggles. So, our country has been linked to other nations while trying to hold on to its own historical identity."

They stopped and got a coffee and sat on a bench for a break from the uphill walking. In front of them perched on a small rise at the end of an uneven walkway was the remains of the Acropolis. Petkas explained, "Over there is the Parthenon, which was a temple to Athena. We are on the slope of the Acropolis. Acropolis is a contraction of two words, one meaning 'highest point' and the other 'city.' The Greek language as you may know often combines the meanings of things to express different ideas. It is not the highest point in Athens, but it is the highest point around here. And this whole area was a place of many important government buildings and temples."

They finished their coffee and walked up the winding steps through crumbling houses and rubble-filled lanes to get to the hilltop that housed the Parthenon. Then Petkas resumed his teaching as he pointed out the restoration scaffolding on one side of the Parthenon. "It's actually a miracle that it still stands at all. It took about eight years to build and has survived for 2,500 years of earthquakes and conflict. The temple was damaged during the 1687 war with the Venetians when some genius decided to store gunpowder there, and it was hit by a cannonball and exploded. We now have long range plans to restore and preserve that temple to Athena over there, which is the most iconic of Greek images, but thanks to the waste in our current Greek government, and its policies that have diverted funds for Papandreou's pet projects, it may never happen."

Petkas looked around, "We can thank Pericles for this area. He started to rescue and refurbish the structures here on the mountain of the Acropolis in the center of Athens and paid particular attention to the Parthenon. He gave the people of Athens renewed beauty, pride and reflected glory. These public works projects also gave jobs to many people in the city and that was greatly appreciated and contributed to a booming economy. He massively expanded the business of stone carvers and sculpture artisans.

"The statues have been moved long ago. Some are here in our museums but many are in museums around Europe like the Vatican and the British

Museum." He shrugged, "At least they are safe. Here they would not get the attention and care needed, and some might even be sold or carted off by the oligarchs in Russia or the rich Arabs."

As they walked around the towering columns, Petkas continued as he looked up at the structure with undisguised admiration, "There were no building plans and yet this complex is so precise, and there is tremendous architectural creativity here." He stopped and looked at the stones lovingly. "It has been called 'the supreme effort of genius in pursuit of beauty.'" Pointing to the Parthenon he continued, "To the outside world this construction represents the historic achievement of Greece. But what once was the envy of the world is now unfortunately a bad joke. We're looking at a place that represents the contrast between the beauty and the intellectual achievements of the ancient Greeks and the clumsy folly of expediency in this new group of leaders. That contrast is what got me involved in politics. We have lost the appreciation for greatness, and Greece can never regain a seat at the world table unless it can find a modern-day Pericles with the vision to bring us back to the glory of that time." He stopped and shook his head. "Greece is at a sad place, my friend."

Two dozen blocks away, Eudora Patmos put the passkey for Mark's room in the Achilleas Hotel into her purse and timed how long it took for her to go from the restaurant next to the hotel along the sidewalk, through the lobby, up the elevator and to his door. She had confirmed with the contacts she had in friendly media who would show up when called to cover the story. Of course, she did not tell them what it was about, only that it would be sensational. Now that everything was in place, she'd execute her plan the next week.

Early the next morning Bokhan received the transcript from the surveillance of Mark and Petkas the previous day. He questioned the team member who brought him the document. "This security report does not make any sense. They are talking about Greek history and art, but not the campaign."

"Yes, sir. We thought it was strange also, and as you can tell from the gaps in the translation, we could not pick everything up as they were walking about, but this transcript is what we were able to get."

"Okay, call our code people. Send this to Moscow. We need to have the KGB people go over it. I can certainly understand admiring Greek history and art, but there should be more happening here than talking about old history and sculpture. It may be that some of these people or the sculptures they refer to in these conversations are code for other things. See to it."

"Right away, sir."

The next day Petkas led Mark on a different walk, this time through the Athens National Garden which was located behind the Greek Parliament building. It was a large open area like central park in New York and situated between and a little to the west of the Acropolis and Lycabettus hills. These three geographic locations formed a squished triangle and each was a good place for a long walk. The National Garden was also a good place to talk while walking, because the Greek legislators and their staffs who were also walking there on a break from their lawmaking made it harder for the Papandreou government or the Russians to wiggle secretly between the Greek officials to conduct espionage on Mark and Petkas without being noticed.

After a few quick thoughts on the campaign, Petkas again picked up on his history lesson. "Let's go back in time about 2500 years. Near the end of the conflicts with Persia, Pericles rose to be the leader of Greece. He's the guy I spoke to you about yesterday and is known as the greatest statesman of ancient Greece. It was Pericles who laid the foundation for one strong central ruler. During his time, Athens set the level of taxes or tributes from the member city-states, which were now subject to its dictates. The wealth gave the Athenians great power and influence. They kept gathering other city-states under their wing until they had about 175 of them paying Athens tribute or taxes. Now flush with cash and man-power, Athens and Pericles controlled much of the area around the Aegean Sea. The enormous wealth entering Athens from subject states financed the flourishing of democratic institutions, literature, art, and architecture that contributed to the golden age of Athens. Pericles now became better known because he promoted the arts and literature and the four greatest Greek playwrights: Aeschylus, Aristophanes, Euripides, and Sophocles, all wrote during this golden time.

"Now let me tell you about Greek sculpture. Early on, the Greeks decided that human beings were the most important subject for art. In the early Classical works the human forms were sort of like a column, stiff and rigid with the hands held down by the sides. The art and the artists continued to evolve by concentrating on human forms that showed the accuracy of human anatomy and proportion. Then they began to show musculature and skeletal structure and art modernized around 500 BC to become more natural, and figures carved in stone began to relax and rep-licate normal human motions and became more fluid.

"As with pottery, Greek statues were commissioned either by aristo-cratic individuals or by the state for artistic display but also as a way to show off wealth and to appreciate the gods at the same time. Not many of the actual artisans from that time are known, however Phidias, a friend of Pericles, oversaw the design and building of the Parthenon and is consid-ered the greatest Classical sculptor. A man named, Praxiteles, was known for his nude female sculptures. And another man, named Lysippos of Sicyon, was said to have made over 1500 statues, mostly castings. Greek art became increasingly diverse, influenced by the cultures of the people drawn into the Greek orbit and later by the conquests of Alexander the Great, but many of the sculptures that are known by references to them in history books are lost.

"Some images appear in copies or replicas, and popular images like the gods were reproduced over and over, but usually with a diminution of artistic skill. Nevertheless, we do know that the transition from the Classical to the Hellenistic period was at its height during the 5th and 4th

Centuries BC. To distinguish between the two eras, think of the more modern Hellenistic as Helen of Troy, the wild child beauty dancing in flowing robes to represent the more fluid forms. The technical ability of the Hellenistic sculptors is clearly in evidence in such major works as the Winged Victory of Samothrace, and the reliefs in the Pergamon Altar. The newer statues still depicted Classical themes such as deities and mythical legends, but their treatment is far more sensuous and emotional than the austere taste of the Classical period would have allowed or its technical skills permitted." He stopped and smiled at Mark. "Remember, Helen of Troy was hot."

"Pericles was the man who changed the face of Athens and how Greek sculpture was created from that time forward. It really was a magical era with the inclination to encourage this artistic creativity, the availability of a collection of talented artisans from all over the known world, and the money to finance it. The Greek people are enormously proud of the influence its arts, history, and politics have had on the rest of the world. You will see evidence of their pride everywhere you look in this country."

CHAPTER 17

Sergei Bokhan drove himself to pick up Igor Andropov at an apartment the Embassy kept as a safe house because he did not want his Embassy driver to see the place where the ambassador kept his Greek mistress. It had not taken long for the handsome Igor to influence a naive and willing young woman impressed by his looks and power. As he waited in the big front room with a musty smell he could hear Igor moving about in the back getting his clothes and papers together to leave. The bedroom door opened and Sergei saw the woman who Igor had ensconced in the apartment move slowly from the bedroom to the bath in the hallway. She did not notice him but kept her eyes down on the floor, as though she was afraid of tripping on something. She clutched a robe tightly about her, and he could see even at a distance where her neck had a large bruise. The ear above the bruise had a tinge of red, and as she shuffled along, she trailed one hand along the wall as a guide to the bathroom. She never looked up, but steadied herself through the bathroom door and closed it slowly behind her.

Although he felt sympathy and concern for the well-being of the woman, Bokhan, as the assistant to Andropov, had an obligation to protect his boss. He began by making some discreet inquiries into who the woman was and how involved she was with Igor. His research found that she was the daughter of an influential PASOK government official and had met Igor at one of the receptions in the early months he had been in Greece. She was young, impressionable, and beautiful, in her early 20's and she was slightly estranged from her family. Igor with his advance publicity, dash, and predatory instincts, swept her off her feet and installed her as his mistress in the apartment.

That fact, in and of itself, was no problem. But Sergei had not known of Igor's need to sometimes punish his women physically. It disgusted

Bokhan personally, and he was unsure how to approach Igor about the problems his indiscretion could bring. When he returned to the office, he decided to keep a watch on the situation and assigned someone to put a monitor on the entrance to the apartment and on the phones. The surveillance information would be sent directly to him and he would know of the girl's movements and when to act on the girl or to help his boss. As a backup plan, he found a low-level but ambitious young woman in the security office and had her take an apartment nearby in the same building. Her directions were to meet this Greek woman casually and to befriend her. She was not to let on where she worked, but to alert Bokhan to any signs that the woman had ill intentions toward Igor or if the relationship was getting further out of control. Sergei knew from his experience in Moscow that these communist party princes often did not know how far they could take a situation, and he felt that it was part of his job to stay ahead of trouble.

Then he began to think of his own family. He worried that the Greek schools and the Soviet Embassy schools in Greece together were not nearly as good as the teaching they had received in Moscow. He knew that Soviet children had to test well to advance in the system and be considered for certain higher education that would define how their later lives would unfold. He made plans to hire tutors to keep his children's studies ahead of the classes here so that when they returned to Moscow they would not be behind their classmates there.

He then thought more about his boss, Igor, and his new-found interest in security. That was not a bad place for the ambassador to concentrate, because it was always the defining issue in Soviet advancement. God help the career of an apparatchik who only had expertise in raising pigs or cattle. No, security was a good place for Igor to concentrate. Nevertheless, Bokhan had a reservation, that with Igor's lack of experience, he could get too enamored with the guns and uniforms and not learn the importance of good intelligence, strategy, and patience when seeking to understand and analyze an issue.

He was also concerned that Igor's swagger might not be a good fit with the need for anonymity in intelligence, and he realized he would have to work on this problem slowly and release bite size chunks of information and suggestions to Igor in order to educate the ambassador without offending him. He had noticed that as long as Igor felt that people were deferring to him, he was satisfied. However, his boss seemed thin-skinned and he had already found that trying to educate the ambassador was a time-consuming and often frustrating process. He would need to provide subtle direction to help the ambassador grow into his job.

Later that afternoon, he received the report detailing the analysis of the photos someone had taken at the New Democracy campaign office from the briefcase of the man, Petkas. The review said the pictures were of stone, likely marble sculptures. They certainly looked like real people to Bokhan so he asked the analysts to make additional inquiries and use the stone faces and match them with museum data to find out where the originals were. If they were here in Athens, which was likely, he wanted to see this incredible art for himself. He guessed the historian had many pictures like this, since art and archeology were his passion as well as his work when he was not stirring up trouble in politics. He also needed to be thorough in finding where these real sculptures were and more importantly, was there somehow a connection between them and the campaign of the New Democracy.

Eudora disrobed the young girl while speaking softly and explaining that they were playing a big game that would be so much fun. She carefully tied her hands to the top of the bed frame in Mark's room and told her to stay quiet and wait for the big surprise which would come soon.

She checked her watch and then looked around the room to see that everything was set just as she had planned and told the girl she would be back soon and shut the door as she left. Then she walked down to meet the media pool of television reporters and those from the newspapers with flash cameras. She had told them to gather quietly and out of sight in the back-room bar of a restaurant next door to the hotel. She told them to stay calm and have a drink as she peeked through the restaurant's window until she saw Mark sauntering down the street towards his hotel after a long day of work. Then she gathered the reporters and brought them into the front room but still kept them away from the window.

She had concocted a tale for the Athens media who loved salacious stories and had arranged for two television stations and three photographers to be on call for her trap that she would spring when Mark came home from work. She would burst in with the media just after he entered to find him with the girl tied naked to Mark's bed posts. The visuals would be so stunning that, along with the tale she would provide, the visuals would drive the story of a perverted American Capitalist trying to corrupt a young virgin in Greece. The fact that the girl was mentally handicapped would only embellish the salacious story and make the American seem that much more depraved.

She counted the moments and figured that now enough time had passed that Mark would be approaching his room with the nude girl. Then she quietly led the gaggle of the media out and through the lobby into the elevator, up and off onto the third floor and down the hall to Mark's room where he was not to be seen and the door to his room was closed. Eudora positioned everyone and held the television cameras and flash cameras at bay while she quietly fitted the pass key she had gotten a week before into the lock. When she was ready she nodded, and they turned on the powerful television lights as she flung open the door. The gang of reporters and cameras pushed Eudora into the room with the momentum of the door opening and the dim space was suddenly filled with blinding light.

Inside, an elderly Italian couple were hovering near the bed in their underclothes. The woman screamed and the man indigently shouted "What the hell is going on? What are you doing in our room?" The circus stopped as the woman and man threw bed sheets around them and called the front desk. Confused Eudora quickly checked the room number and oriented herself to confirm that this was the location of Mark's room. The media turned off their bright lights and started shouting at Eudora along with the partially clothed Italians.

Eudora and the now very disappointed group of the Athens press corps were wondering what had happened and the media started peppering her with questions, while at the same time all of them were apologizing to the shouting Italians screaming for them to leave the room. Then the hotel manager and two policemen arrived and took charge. The officers detained everyone for questioning until the problem could be sorted out.

Next door to Mark's old room the 12-year-old retarded girl, now clothed, was enjoying ice-cream with two social workers who told her they would take her back to her care facility once the television program she was watching finished and in time for her usual dinner. At times, they had to listen carefully to the cartoon due to the commotion and shouting from the room next door. At the same time, Mark, accompanied by two of Maria Beckett's friends in the New Democracy security forces, was down at the end of the hall unpacking and getting acclimated to his new room.

The next day in the operations meeting Maria explained to her full staff that unfortunately Eudora Patmos had to resign suddenly from the campaign and return to her hometown for personal and family reasons. After the meeting, she kept Mark and Angus for a shorter, second conference and turned on the radio to a modest volume. Mark looked inquisitively at Maria, "How did you do all that yesterday? One of your security guys whisked me to a new room when I arrived at my hotel and another was in the hall with all my stuff he had grabbed from the room. Why didn't you tell me what the hell was going on?"

Maria, smiled and nodded, "We were on a tight schedule. When I learned of the plot to embarrass you and the campaign by having you caught in your room by the television cameras with a naked, retarded 12-year-old girl, I had to act fast to put together a counter story and gather the people to pull it off. I didn't tell you because I don't know you well enough to know how you would react and keep the secret. I was afraid you would reveal that we were on to her and I needed to make sure you would act natural. I've used the Italian couple in something before and I knew they would play their part well. I've been waiting for several days for this plot to eventually be executed."

"But how did you find out about her?"

"I had a tap on the home and office phones of Miss Patmos. I found out that something was going on when she called the mental hospital where she found the girl."

"Had you suspected her before?"

"Not particularly. She was good at her job."

"How did you know it was her?"

Maria smiled, "She did seem a little too good to be true, but I had a tap on the phones of everyone here. Including you two. For me that is standard procedure. I'm surprised that the PASOK people would not have figured that out. Just because we are not in the government, does not mean we can't have surveillance." She smiled at the two men who were looking at her open-mouthed.

Maria continued. "So, the opposition may have shot their wad with her as their main plan to discredit us, but we need to stay vigilant. I feel sure they still have one or more people in our office, listening and watching, as well as electronic surveillance. Use common sense. Go back and do an inventory of what she may have handled for you two and let's decide if we need to build any back fires or change anything we had planned that her stealing our intel could have hurt."

Angus smiled at her. He loved this kind of intrigue and admired Maria's attention to detail and he asked, "Do you have someone inside their campaign?"

Maria smiled back at Angus and answered, "I'm not going to speak about that right now. However, Miss Patmos has left Athens and we have disrupted this set of PASOK's clandestine operations in our campaign for the time being. Likely there will be more attempts to damage us. It's their style. It does argue that we should increase our security precautions at the campaign, and I've started to work on that. You two be alert. They'll be watching you more closely now."

Mark asked, "What about her?"

Maria let out a bubble of a laugh and shook her head at Mark. "Your little friend, who seemed to take quite a liking to you, failed to destroy you. That is not a good result for advancement in the PASOK organization. The fact she got caught with the media present and by police, went hard for her. I'm sure it was an expensive embarrassment for PASOK to cover up. She is gone into some backwater village now and likely will not be given any responsibility in the future. That is actually a good thing for us, because she was fairly good at what she was doing. Too bad she was not one of ours. And by the way, kudos to you, Mark, for resisting her ample charms."

Angus leaned forward, anticipating her answer, "So, have you identified the others in our campaign office working for the opposition?"

"If I did I'll keep that a secret for now. I've found that disinformation can be a good tool and if there is a chance to let our opponents think they know some secret of ours that is false, it can be very useful and misleading. Also, if I fired anyone I knew to be spying on us, they might be replaced with someone more capable and dangerous. I like that old saying, 'keep your friends close, but your enemies closer.' I'll certainly let you two know if something comes up that affects you."

In the next weeks Mark, now more aware, began to notice familiar people showing up in public as he was out walking someplace, buying souvenirs, or going to lunch. It was not always the same person, but he remembered two or three faces that were frequently hanging about and seemed to have nothing to do but show up in his vicinity.

The potential surveillance was on his mind as he left his hotel for a meeting at the campaign office, and walked into a nearby souvenir store. The store was more upscale than the street vendors and had none of the plastic knockoffs or tin replicas people hocked on the street corners. Stashed in various areas of this store were piles of sandals, leather pouches, busts of forgotten deities, wraparound cloth clothing, knives, flashy necklaces and earrings, and Mark felt that with a little imagination he could feel himself transported back 2000 years to a similar shop in the same location that would have looked and felt much the same. The busts of Greek gods were in real marble or porcelain and the coin replicas were real silver. He browsed and picked up a couple of items to take home as mementos and gifts. As he was paying at the counter he stopped to look at some other items in the window display, when across the street he caught the eye of a man leaning against a building and staring at him, who immediately looked away. Mark noticed the pattern on the man's coat and thought he remembered seeing the same man in the lobby when he exited his hotel.

With the visual proof that he was being observed, Mark began to think of ways to lose his pursuers. He decided to start by visiting a more diverse variety of retail stores and restaurants. He would ask the clerks for the location of the restroom or the backdoor and over the next two weeks he acquired a complex list of ways in and out of places near his hotel and the campaign office. He also found the back alleys, gaps in fences and other ways to get lost on the boulevards. He figured that when he was in a crowd it was most important to change what a follower could see of his head and shoulders and he concentrated his disguises in that area. He began to bring an extra sweater or coat to the office and leave it there and would swap clothing after lunch some days just to get the feel of how it would change his appearance. He purchased several hats and caps, different pairs of cheap sunglasses, different colored scarves, some bright to be easily noticed and others muted, and had them at the office or his hotel and began to carry one or more changes with him under his coat, although never using them. He'd have them ready to change his appearance if needed.

He remembered scenes from detective and spy movies, and began using window glass reflections to see behind him and across the street. He tried to be subtle at keeping track of his watchers, and gradually he felt he could spot them without their seeming to notice him doing it. He also noticed places where taxis loitered, so he could jump into one quickly as an additional way to distance himself from the followers if he thought it became necessary.

Over time he started remembering the habits and patterns of the tails. He knew who was fast or slow, how far behind him they would usually be. He could tell who was fit and who had trouble keeping up when he increased his pace. He noticed when they swapped the people trailing him or changed their clothes to throw him off. For Mark the awareness of his followers remained a kind of game, and as an American citizen, he doubted they would do anything to him. He decided they were just keeping tabs on him and it turned into a kind of diversion from the boredom of the slow pace in the campaign. His new-found awareness gave him the confidence that he was becoming more on a par with the surveillance skills of the followers. He knew he was developing the ability to give them the slip if he needed to; however, he continued to keep that move to himself in case he needed it.

On his walks with Petkas he mentioned the tails and pointed out the person who was following them at that moment. They talked about the surveillance and Petkas, who was more concerned about the trackers than Mark, began to develop his own means of being alert to the unwanted company and decided which steps he could take to lose them if needed. They gave the tails names like "Scarface," "Baldy," or "Mussolini" so they would be easier to remember and share references to the watchers in a simple code with each other. In discussions with Maria and others in the campaign, they had all noticed the tails, but just accepted them as part of life and speculated on how much money the socialists and communists spent on these pastimes rather than doing something that was useful for the government.

They soon learned which of these men could keep up with them as they climbed the steep trails of Mt. Lycabettus and could adjust the speed of their walk if they wanted to gain some real privacy and talk about something they absolutely wanted to remain a secret. Sometimes, however, at Marias's suggestion, they would say things purposefully to throw the escorts off such as talk about a media buy or a message they were crafting for the candidate to use in some upcoming speech that was absolutely false. Later they would laugh when imagining the PASOK people makings plans to counter the false information they had let them overhear.

Because she had a room in the center of the campaign office area that had no windows, they decided to use Maria's office as the safe room. The incident with Eudora Patmos had made her more aware of the need for increased security. She hand-pickled the workers who installed a heavier frame and door and added special locks that were changed every week or two and that were only accessible for a very few trusted staff. The electrical was rewired on a special circuit. Additional lead-based acoustical padding provided by a source Maria had in Iraq was put in the walls in the hope that it would prevent listening devices from outside the room overhearing conversations, and they installed a plug-in white noise motor, in addition to a television and radio. Maria arranged for the room including for the floor and ceiling to be swept for listening devices and cameras every few days in a random pattern, so they thought they were relatively safe. Her room became the depository for the most sensitive documents and where they had their top-level meetings.

In one of the first gatherings in the secure space they discussed the recent public assassination of a prosecutor who was suspected by leftist radicals in the N-17 organization for being too restrictive in the government giveaway programs. Maria and the security people from the New Democracy Party expressed concern that the extremists on the far left could increase their active terror attacks and use the approaching election to make a statement. They cautioned everyone to be extra vigilant when in public.

In the next conversation with Vicki, after talking about how much they missed each other, and a possible visit in the future, they turned to politics. Mark decided to omit any references to the attempted scandal that Maria had uncovered involving the comely Miss Patmos. It seemed too complicated to explain on the phone. He did tell Vicki about the long drunken dinner and the subsequent conversation about democracy and communism. He did not think it would matter if anyone listening to their conversation heard that. He repeated an argument Petkas had made about the danger of socialism wrecking the nation, and made comparisons to Democrats and Republicans in the United States. Mark speculated about liberal and conservative values and the need for a government to pay for things when they were purchased, and subsequent dangers in not balancing budgets and the gamble created by having deficits. He had become concerned as the Reagan administration had been building up large deficits and already from the time the Reagan administration entered office, after only a few years, it had doubled the national debt the United States had amassed in over 200 years. They were on a course to triple the national debt if Reagan remained in office for the full eight years. The discussions about Greece, which were a microcosm of what the United States was experiencing, had alarmed Mark.

Vicki pointed out that the debt and deficits under Reagan were to build up the United States military and cut taxes, which they claimed would improve the economy. Mark still had his doubts given the conversations he had been having with the Greeks. To him it did not matter the reason a country went into debt, it was still debt. He felt government should pay for what they bought at the same time and then rebalance their budgets. When he expressed this sentiment to Vicki, she teased him that he was becoming a conservative Republican by hanging out with the Greeks. He replied that the Reagan people were shooting holes in that stereotype by their reckless deficit spending. Her comments reminded Mark of his time in Panama last year and the U.S. foreign policy that was supplying covert military assistance to rebel groups in Central America.

Vicki changed the subject as she had heard about the recent assassination of a Greek court official, and once again expressed her concern over the potential danger, which Mark downplayed as not involving him. She could tell he did not want to talk about it and being sensitive about the likelihood of people listening in on the conversation, let it drop.

At the meeting inside the PASOK offices, the socialist and communist political leaders and members of the Soviet delegation sat quietly around a large table. Several polls commissioned by each group lay on the table and they all contradicted Papandreou's research that was more positive toward the candidate. In addition, they had a poll from the New Democracy party received from one of their spies that also acknowledged the decline in public support for PASOK. The Papandreou polls predicted success and public enthusiasm for Papandreou's programs. Bokhan assumed these must be local pollsters who wanted to curry favor with Papandreou and tell him what he wanted to hear.

All the other polls showed him losing public support and still winning, but by a modest margin. The local communist party members were concerned that Papandreou would cut into their loyal following and both Bokhan and Andropov were worried the election was moving in a negative direction.

Papandreou leaned back in his chair and insisted that he would not say or do anything to curtail his social programs or the debt that was accumulating to finance it. He insisted that once the programs were implemented, the economy would improve, the deficit would be wiped out and prosperity would be shared all over Greece. He dismissed the polls that did not agree with him as well as the predictions of the economists.

He felt that any short-term disruption of his plans just for the sake of the election would hurt the country in the long term. He did not care so much about the margin of victory, just that he won and could continue to implement his social programs. He said he wanted to do more, not less, to make the Greek economy like a pure socialist utopia and promised that over time his vision of a world where everyone would have their fair share was on the horizon. The communists kept relatively quiet but they did suggest that Papandreou could say that he would slow the reforms and pay for them from a practical budget and then he could break the promise after the election. He dismissed that idea as dishonorable.

Igor, watching quietly, believed Papandreou was protecting his ego by being so rigid about not backing down from his social programs. He did not understand many of the economic arguments and was afraid to offer a foolish suggestion, so he just sat smiling and doodling on his legal pad.

Bokhan had hoped that having Igor in meetings like this one, where substance and politics were discussed, would give him the knowledge to make him more interested in governance. However, he could look at the doodles and see that was not happening. At least Igor was being quiet and had not insulted anyone. The meeting ended much as it had begun, and the efforts to dissuade Papandreou from his sweeping pronouncements had failed. Bokhan knew the socialist leader's intransigence meant that he would have to force the local communists to provide votes to Papandreou's PASOK political party and that would alienate them more from Moscow, but that was less important than making sure the socialists won with as big a margin as possible.

Back at the embassy Sergei Bokhan reviewed the polling results discussed earlier with Igor and also looked at those he had commissioned independently. He explained to Igor the trending decline for Papandreou, attributed to a dwindling Greek economy and the successful campaign message of the New Democrats and how the details of the polls proved that the socialist and communist parties were much too optimistic about the upcoming election.

Small shopkeepers as well as larger businesses that had been supporting PASOK were alarmed at the increased taxes and had expressed their displeasure to the pollsters. Also, teachers and students, even those who were very liberal in their views, were questioning how Papandreou could continue to recommend new social programs without having the money in the budget to pay for them. Bokhan could remember hearing the undertones of these complaints when he went to services at the Greek Orthodox Church with his family and mingled with the crowds.

After Bokhan's patient explanation, Igor now had a better idea of what the polls represented and he was alarmed as he exclaimed, "We have to do something here and now and do it fast. The dissatisfaction with Papandreou's politics will reflect poorly on me and could hurt my career if he loses support in the election the same year I came into Greece. Can't the Greeks just have a heavy hand on the scale when they are counting the votes?"

Bokhan answered, "I have talked to them about that and they can count some extra votes for Papandreou, but that will only be one or two percent at most. They are worried they will be caught by international observers if they do more than that. The only thing that will have a significant impact would be to order the Communist party to have some of their voters actually to vote for Papandreou and the socialist party rather than for their communist slate of candidates. It would risk cutting down on their legislative seats, but could keep Papandreou where he is in popular support. I have already heard from the Greek Communist Party and they are against reducing their power at all and promise to be very critical of us if we ask them to make such a sacrifice."

Igor was up and pacing now, "Why have we not seen these kinds of polling results from the PASOK party people before? Don't they know about this decline or are they lying to us and to Papandreou that there is a terrible reaction to what he is doing? We can't have these stupid Greeks wrecking my career." He stopped pacing and looked at Bokhan. "Order the Communist party to shift votes to Papandreou. At least give him another three to five percent. They can take the votes from places where they have safe legislative seats. If their leaders balk at your request, send them to me. I'll remind them where they get their budgets funded. We also have to think how to redirect Papandreou after this election is over to slow down what he is doing." Bokhan demurred in his role to give balanced advice to his Ambassador, "I will do as you requested; but, Mr. Ambassador, what he is doing is in accordance with the philosophy of the Soviet Union. Greece is a perfect experiment of instituting communist principals into a largely peasant society on a scale that can be measured for its outcomes. We could be criticized by the Moscow party intellectuals and people who monitor communist dogma for stopping or slowing down that movement."

Igor sighed and tossed his fountain pen on the boardroom table where it rolled all the way across the smooth, shining surface and dropped to the floor with a metallic clunk. "Sergei, you are here to handle those kinds of things. I must consider how my ambassadorship here will set me up for career advancement later. If these Greeks are beginning to resist social changes, it is because of the incompetence of Papandreou, not because of the philosophy of our Soviet system. We cannot let the leaders in Moscow think our agenda is faltering in Greece. I can't be tainted by this election. Figure a way to blame some of this on the Americans. Start some rumors and arrange for protests that claim the Americans are trying to undermine the Greek economy. Say the American capitalists are trying to win the election for the right-wing ship owners. Say the Americans want to expand their bases here. People will believe that. But whatever you do, Sergei, fix this!"

CHAPTER 18

Stanos Petkas and Mark were now working smoothly together on the campaign, and Petkas was convinced that Mark was the person he needed to trust with his great secret. He decided before having such an important conversation, that traveling with Mark for two days on an upcoming journey would convince him if Mark was as honest and sincere as he seemed. So, he approached Mark at his desk. "Mark, I've got to go on a short trip later this week to see about a rally we are going to have in a town that is northwest of here. We will be using the plans you wrote and we had translated. Now this trip is just a set-up meeting for a rally with Mitsotakis to happen later, but I think you ought to come."

Mark was thinking of what he had to do in the office, "Well, I don't know."

Petkas shook his head and smiled at Mark, "Look, you've been stuck here in Athens all this time. We've only got about seven weeks left before the election and you should get a feel for what the other parts of the country are like; you need to see life in the villages. It will give you a much better perspective of Greece and may sharpen the methods you suggest for how we attract people to come to our final events."

Mark still was not sure, "That sounds like it could be . . ."

"And listen, you will see the countryside. You will see how beautiful this country is. I'll drive and give you a travelogue of Greek history. The best part is that the food in these small villages is twice as good as the restaurants here in town. There it is fresh. Not a day old. We will only be gone a couple of days ... three at the most."

Mark smiled, "Okay. I'm sold. You had me when you started talking about the food. So, when do we leave, and what kind of clothes should I take?"

"We'll go Thursday morning ... early. Take your casual, peasant clothes. No coats and ties where we are going, and don't shave for the next few days. From a distance, you will need to appear like a Greek in these villages. We don't want too many people thinking we need an American to teach us about democracy."

Mark soon took care of most of his other duties because he was unsure he could get much telephone work done from the hotel phones in the little mountain villages. He called Angus to tell him where he was going. Angus thought it was a great idea and lamented he could not go on the trip, but he was leaving Greece to begin the planning for another campaign.

Thursday morning Petkas picked Mark up at his Athens hotel before light at 5 a.m. and they left for a drive toward the northwest, diagonally across much of Greece, to Arta near the Albanian border. It was a trip that for Mark turned into a travelogue of Greek history as they crossed the Isthmus of Corinth which separated the area of Athens from Sparta, then later they took a ferry over the Gulf of Corinth. They made their way toward the Romanian border and the land of the gypsies, past centuries-old rock walls and olive groves and places with names from antiquity. Mark was reminded from his recent dinner conversation that betrayal and deceit were common behavior for survival here and were seared into the souls of the people. That knowledge, along with recent terrorist violence and the attempt by Eudora Patmos to embarrass him, made him a little uncomfortable.

As they left the sprawling city and headed northwest, Petkas stopped for more coffee at a roadside filling station and convenience store. Refreshed and fortified with the steaming coffee and some incredible sweet, flavored rolls, they watched the sun come up through the rear-view window as they continued the trip, and Petkas picked up his ongoing lecture about Greece. He explained that he was taking Mark on the scenic route to Arta so he could show him more of the countryside and give him a show-and-tell about ancient Greece as they passed the dusty landmarks on the trip. Mark thought that was a splendid plan.

Petkas was an amazing guide and kept up a rolling narrative that make the trip go faster as he pointed out the milestones and gave historical perspective on the areas they passed. From his recitation of the antiquity and the cluttered landscape, Mark surmised that the story of southeastern Europe was littered with the defeats and suffering of those who tilled its soil and marched in its armies and then scratched civilization from the refuse of those efforts. Regardless of the results in the upcoming voting, this election would not be worthy as a footnote to the thousands of years of history that surrounded them in the rocky fields with the scraggly trees and colorful flowers that somehow found purchase and nourishment in the tarnished soil.

They travelled over roads that took them past vineyards of olives, herds of sheep, and remnants of historic settlements. Mark was surprised that there was not very much traffic. Just a few cars now and then and some flatbed trucks hauling what looked like construction materials, with two or three men on top hugging close to the back of the cab to avoid the chilly wind.

As they neared Delphi, Petkas cut off road and drove up to the ruins on a hill thought by ancient Greeks to be the middle of the Earth. He picked his way carefully through the terraces that set the grade up the slope of Mount Parnassus, which included the Sanctuary of Apollo and the site of the ancient Oracle that overlooks the Pleistos Valley. Petkas explained that the Delphi region was also the area of the Pan-Hellenic games that was the precursor of the modern Olympics.

As Mark listened he became more impressed with what had been accomplished in a place that was so bumpy and hilly. Moving around in ancient Greece must have been hard, and that made the history and economics of the particular areas they passed even more impressive. Mark tried to imagine thousands of people traveling to this rocky and remote place for athletics and what it must have been like jammed with naked athletes, and cheering crowds of dignitaries, servants and common citizens.

Toward mid-day Petkas pulled off the main road for a light picnic from a hamper he had in the back. They laid a blanket on the grass and sat in the shade of a cliff to pick at the lunch of olives, cheese, sausage, bread, water and wine. Over lunch Petkas continued his education. He described the allure that Delphi had in ancient times as a pilgrimage and how the area grew prosperous with many small villages and scattered family settlements to accommodate the tourists' needs for lodging and food, as well as the trinkets and other items amazingly similar to what tourists still buy today.

Petkas continued, "There are a couple of things you should know about the Oracle at Delphi. The first is that there have always been rumors that the place had a strange smell and there were sulfur dioxide and hydrocarbon fumes and water bubbling out of the ground in various places around here, especially in periods after seismic and tectonic agitation. That is the same kind of gas that was used by surgeons for anesthesia until about a hundred years ago. When inhaled, a rapid and slightly pleasant mental clouding occurred. In other words, the Oracle got a little high. Although I don't want to be misleading or to pile shame onto the poor old Oracle, but there are some theories that she chewed Cannabis or oleander leaves that may have provided some additional toxicity.

"And the second major thing is that the gas fissures and water rising out of the ground and through the rocks made the area very unstable. There were many slides and rock shifts and earthquakes over the years in this area in what later came to be known as the Delphi rift. The earthquakes may have resulted from a release of rocks strained by too much pressure or a kind of tectonic slip along the Delphi fault zone, and may have been responsible for the release of gases from the underlying bituminous limestone formation."

Petkas looked closely at Mark then said, "You know back in the day when many tourists came here attracted by the atmosphere of the fortune-telling and the many springs in the area, various settlements were formed near the actual oracle and temple, and others likely within 10 miles or so, which would have been an easy day's travel. Gifts and commerce from those who consulted the oracle and visited there made the mountain village of Delphi one of the richest sites in Greece, and for a time that trickled down to other nearby settlements.

"Over that way a few miles," he pointed to the east, "are some fairly imposing ruins of the temple of Apollo that are scattered on the Southern slopes of the Parnassos mountain where we were earlier. A large temple lasted there in one form or another from about the 7th century B.C. to about the 4th century B.C. It was a big deal and people came from all over to see it and the nearby oracle. The carvings that adorned its pediment were the creation of Athenian stone workers Praxias and Androsthenes, who were the leading sculptors of that time. People around here set up inns and restaurants. Delphi was like your Disneyland, and the surrounding areas of entertainment, lodging and dining you see today surrounding Orlando, Florida. For a period of time 2500 years ago, Delphi had become a pilgrimage destination for those who could afford it, just like in later years at Santiago de Compostela in Spain or Mecca in Saudi Arabia.

Down to the end of the fifth century BC, the oracle was consulted for just about everything including before new colonies were founded, wars were declared, or changes of government made. There were several elaborate temples near here, now all destroyed, mostly by earthquakes and landslides, and some by wars. These earthquakes not only destroyed the temples, but villages and homes in all the little valleys with steep walls in the area. After a while, when the oracle's allure faded and as the structures were destroyed, people moved on and the whole area reverted back to subsistence farming."

As they left, Mark was worn out from trying to absorb all the history and nodded off as they continued their drive to Arta. They checked into a local hotel and got a good night's rest in preparation for several meetings the next day. As he was drifting off, Mark found himself wondering if there was any particular reason that Petkas was telling him so much about this area of Greece.

After breakfast, they drove another 30 miles on a dirt and gravel road up to a small hillside village near the Albanian border, and had to stop along the way to allow for the passage of goat herds. It was cooler in the hills and there was a light dusting of snow from the night before. Petkas told Mark that likely he was the first American to be there since World War II. Along the road they stopped briefly, visiting farms and other places, and meeting with other local leaders to encourage them to attend a regional meeting. For these short stops Mark waited in the car while Petkas ran into one house or store at a time to encourage the residents to participate. They passed a local bus grunting up the slope packed with people Petkas said were headed to the meeting.

At one stop two men took Mark on a tour of a farm nearby while Petkas met in private with the regional New Democracy leaders so they could talk in Greek freely and not have to stop to translate for Mark. Mark was encouraged to walk about the farm and one of the men was sent along as his guide. Although hilly and with many more rocks on the ground than Mark was accustomed to from his days in South Georgia, much of the farm equipment looked familiar with tractors, plows, disc harrows, and wagons. But other than a few animals, the farm largely grew oranges. As they walked through the large orchards, Mark was at first startled and then alarmed to see so many oranges on the ground and others looking very ripe on the trees.

He picked up one and when he bit into it he found that it was delicious, juicy, and sweet, and he was surprised to see these were the orange oranges and not the red oranges he had often had in restaurants elsewhere in Europe. After his walk on the slightly chilly ridge, he went back into the stone farmhouse for a coffee and sat by the fire.

When the meeting broke up and the others joined him, he asked about the oranges on the ground. The farm manager said that they could not find people to hire to help bring in the harvest. He explained that the government policies covered many of the modest survival needs of the local people, who were content to live on that basic subsistence and had lost the desire and ambition to work for more money to buy better things for themselves and their families, because the Papandreou government kept promising more support. Picking up oranges on a rocky incline was difficult work which required real motivation and he could not afford to hire them or pay enough to entice them to come to his farm to do the work.

There were some restrictions and considerable expenses to bring in migrant workers from elsewhere and those measures did nothing to help the Greek population. The local workers' lethargy had been accompanied by increased taxes on the farm to help support the government's programs, which also incongruously promised subsidies and crop loss guarantees.

The man went on to explain that because he couldn't get his crops picked to sell, he did not know how he would pay the increase in taxes. He said his family had been there for many generations, but he might be forced to sell the farm or just shut it down because he could not afford to continue to replace the dead trees and fertilize when there was no labor to bring in the harvest. It was a problem that had been getting worse over the past two to three years with the government's subsistence programs.

Those suicidal economic moves sounded extreme to Mark, and although he was not sure whether to believe that a government would be so foolish as to tear down its economic base, he did not have the financial background to know. He thought if this kind of thing was happening even in a more limited way elsewhere and in other economic sectors, he could see where it would have long-term devastating consequences for Greece. He reflected back on Petkas's somewhat drunken rant a week ago about how Papandreou was wrecking the country. The group mostly spoke English for his benefit, and then they went together to eat the best lamb stew ever made at a sidewalk café on the square of a little nearby village.

After about two hours of encouraging attendance at other brief stops they arrived at the village where the regional meeting was to be held. On the sloping hillsides, the houses and shops were scattered about like a child had haphazardly placed the structures there from a Monopoly game instead of being linked together in neat rows on connected streets like most small American towns. The village was divided between political parties, and they did not trade with each other, but rigidly held to their political loyalties after many generations of conflict.

One of the locals pointed out where the communists and socialists lived in the town and described how they all stayed to themselves. "As people moved in here over many centuries, there was always neighbor against neighbor. Each side encouraged the lies, the deception. They split families apart with false promises of utopian worlds under their system, and that has led to Greeks taking a position in the many wars when we have been invaded. It seems war has happened every 10 years or so and people still smell the blood. They remember the neighbors who were against them and the scars and the hatred are still just under the scabs of memory."

They stopped at the town hall the size of a moderate American house, and inside there must have been 250 people jammed into the meeting room no larger than 3000 square feet. The temperature was cooler in the mountains, but all these people sandwiched together made the place toasty inside. Petkas told Mark not to speak in the large meeting space and to pretend to be a Greek because they did not want the average locals to know an American was helping with the campaign. The room had a public-address system consisting of a microphone wired to three small speakers that looked like they had been ripped off a U.S. drive-in theatre. Everyone sat on a rough jumble of furniture: stools, benches and chairs and tables of various sizes that had been dragged into the place from neighboring houses and pulled together in makeshift rows for the gathering. There was thick Turkish coffee being served in the small adjoining room, and almost everyone was smoking. It was the most democratic meeting Mark had ever attended.

He studied the craggy faces that seemed to come from a movie's central casting, women wearing long black dresses, men with no-collar shirts buttoned to the neck, black hair with flecks of grey and two-week-old beards. Anyone who had something to say could go up to the microphone, and speak their minds. The verbal scrum of enthusiastic peasants went on for at least two hours, and there were many heated and hand-waving presentations. Though most speakers were passionate in their delivery, there was no tension in the room, and everyone was treated with respect. Mark did not understand a word but just sat packed shoulder-to-shoulder and staring across a small table at the backs of the heads of others in attendance. Occasionally someone would look at him and whisper a comment. He'd shrug his shoulders, or quickly drink a swallow of coffee and wave them off with a choking facial expression. Finally, the meeting ended, and they moved to a small nearby house with some of the local leaders. At last one of the locals pulled Petkas into a separate room and asked, "Who is the tall, silent guy with you who does not understand Greek?"

When Mark's presence was explained, he became a curiosity for the small group of local officials. Mark found out that during the meeting much of the conversation was to let everyone express their opinions on what their candidate, Constantin Mitsotakis, needed to say when he was in their area and what local issues needed to be addressed in his speech. Petkas would assimilate the information and suggest it to the candidate's speechwriter as an important section of the speech for the upcoming rally. After the meeting, they returned to Arta to inspect the plaza where the political rally would be held.

The next day when they started their return trip to Athens, Mark commented to Petkas how impressive the meeting had been and how much he had learned by coming on the trip. Petkas smiled and said, "What you have seen is what we must fight to preserve. That meeting was an example of open democracy, and it is as imbedded in our politics as it is in our art and in our history. Democracy and the desire to improve our lives are part of who we are through individuality and hard work, and Papandreou and the communists are wrecking it." Petkas smiled, gave a glance northward and added, "You know, you are likely the first American to have been in the place where we had the meeting yesterday since World War Two. Another time and another example of fighting for democracy."

After they had been on the road for a few hours and neared the Delphi region, Petkas again pulled off the road into a field for a rest stop and another afternoon picnic. He had been describing the exploits of Alexander the Great and explained that Alexander inherited a sophisticated kingdom and a modern, well-trained army from his father Philip of Macedonia. Philip had consolidated his rule over many city-states in that kingdom just north of the current borders of Greece where he developed the powerful army which had also conquered Greece a few years before. One ingenious thing Philip did was to bring the sons of all the warlords and wealthy people in his kingdom to one place for a terrific education. There these children met and bonded together with other children of promise, solidifying the kingdom. His own son, Alexander, went to the same school and formed alliances with all his contemporaries.

This was the time that Greek arts, literature, philosophy, and science flourished, and King Philip hired a brilliant young philosopher and teacher from Athens named Aristotle, to come to the school for several years and become a teacher and mentor to Alexander. When Alexander went on to conquer most of the known world, he was filled with the ideas and knowledge of Aristotle and the Greek culture and civilization. Soon after beginning his rule after his father's death, the ever-ambitious Alexander came to visit the Delphic Oracle, wishing to hear a prophecy that he would soon conquer Persia and perhaps the entire ancient world.

The family of one of Alexander's classmates had earlier moved to a place near Delphi to take advantage of the flourishing economy, and when Alexander decided to see the Oracle at Delphi, he camped near there at the small homestead where the family of his Macedonian classmate lived. It was in a small valley less than a day's ride from the oracle, and he had known the family from his childhood before they moved to the south. The family had a son who was an officer in Alexander's army and came to see the Oracle with him so he could visit with his family.

To Alexander's surprise the oracle refused a direct prediction and asked him to come back later. Furious, Alexander dragged the oracle, Pythia, by the hair out of her chamber until she screamed "You are invincible, my son!"

The moment he heard these words he dropped her, saying, "Now I have my answer."

Mark laughed and joked, "I guess the oracle had not sniffed enough of the fumes that morning."

Petkas noted Mark's polite attention and glib reply, but he could tell that Mark was getting a little bored with the history lesson. So, he leaned toward Mark, "But, you see, Mark, on Alexander's visit to Delphi where he stayed with that Macedonian family is the same valley where we are now having our picnic."

"What!" Mark looked around as though with this news he might expect to see Greek soldiers or remnants of armor. The field where they were sitting just off the two-lane road, stretched upwards into a narrow valley rising toward cliffs behind them. "Stanos, if Alexander the Great really did stay here when he came to see the oracle, I'm surprised there is not a plaque somewhere to let people know. I would bet there would be tourists wanting to see that or even stay in a campground or a hotel where they could spend the night in the same place where he did." Mark looked around and shielded his eyes with his hand to see further up into the small valley.

Petkas continued, now that he had captured Mark's full attention, "Well, I found this place, sort of by accident. As you know I teach at a school in Thessaloniki which was founded by Macedonians and has always had strong ties to Macedonia because it is near the border. Alexander the Great became a natural interest to the school's students because our campus was so close to his homeland. To engage my students further, I started a project to search very old records both in Greece and in Macedonia for more historical information on the young king. The availability of computers made it possible to collect and sort many pieces of history, and based on the bits of records we gathered, we built the puzzle into a kind of story of Alexander's travels. In one of his journeys, we found that here in Greece and in Delphi there was reference to the taxes paid by a family named Anatos from Macedonia for use of the lands. The information did not give a specific location but referred to the land as a small valley being west of the Temple of Athena by less than a day's journey. Anatos was also the name of one of Alexander's military entourage.

"So that information sparked my interest because the former Macedonian family must have lived here about the time Alexander came to Delphi at the beginning of his journey to conqueror Persia. One thing led to another and the speculation grew. We began to search for this place on field trips over several years, narrowed down the choices, and later I finally found it."

Stanos Petkas smiled and began to gather the plates and napkins to return them to the hamper. "But there are very few people who know that story. It is one of the advantages of being an historian that one can know these things. Fortunately for me, I can enjoy places like this without them becoming a Disneyland. I like it that only I and one or two of my former students know of this little secret, and only I and now you know of this location. I'd appreciate it if you would help us to keep it that way." Petkas remembered how he had constantly used new students in his search, never keeping one on the project longer than one semester so they would not become too enchanted with the prospect or suspect his long-term motive.

Mark looked around, still amazed at the history here, "Oh, sure. I'd likely never find this again on my own anyway. Sorry... sometimes we Americans try to figure out how to market everything we see. I do understand why it is a good thing to know the story you just revealed to me and yet also know that it is a secret. I appreciate your having faith in me to tell me about it." Mark looked around. "To me, this looks like most of the other valleys we have passed. Can you tell me more about how you found this place?"

Petkas put the cork on the wine bottle and remembering his fuzzy Polaroid photos, looked up onto the valley again. "History is often made of unrelated pieces of information. It is a mystery that has to be sorted to make the story of history. We first found those references from Macedonian history about the family of one of Alexander's classmates moving here. As I said yesterday, there were many booming businesses here 2400 years ago when this was a place where people came looking for answers, and merchants were providing, food, shelter and other things for the visitors. Remember what I said about the vapors and hot spring waters. In those days, it wasn't only just the oracle that attracted people to come here. They had the games and temples. It was a kind of pilgrimage site. Delphi was one of the most famous places in the world during Alexander's lifetime. Because of all the activity here, there were many bits of records that we found that had to be assembled.

"Archaeological history is like a great puzzle. We have to find the pieces and interpret them to make the solution appear. For this job, the invention of the modern computer has been a great help. The clues we found in northeastern Greece, Macedonia and over at Delphi led us to this valley."

Mark was curious, "But the oracle and the Delphi settlements here ... it all stopped?"

Petkas nodded and continued, "The ground here near Delphi was unstable and there were landslides and tremors. People often thought those were omens that the gods might be angry or were danger signs not to be here.

After the earthquake that destroyed the temple and other landslides, many of the people moved on, and over time the place became less hospitable. Just a few years ago we had a 6.3 earthquake not far from here. As you can see, it is rocky and hilly and hot and dry. These are not enticing amenities for a holiday vacation."

After the meetings, planning the Arta rally, and Petkas's history lessons, they continued the long drive back. In a state of numbing weariness on the highway, Mark watched the sunset reflected off the car's back windows just as he had watched it rise out of the windows of the small car traveling back through history two days before. They could see the glow of the lights of Athens from almost 40 miles away as they approached the comfort and long-awaited rest that lay ahead.

CHAPTER 19

In the security meeting, Sergei Bokhan reviewed the surveillance report with disgust and tossed it on the table. Both Stanos Petkas and the American, Mark Young, had not been seen for two days. The surveillance teams had gotten in a habit of beginning the first shift at 8:00 a.m. when the New Democracy people left for work or arrived at the office and had not been physically monitoring their homes or the hotel in the evenings after midnight. No one had any idea what had happened to the two field staff workers until they showed up back at the hotel and in the case of Petkas at his home in the evening two days after their disappearance. Bokhan thought the embassy security staff here outside of the Soviet Union were definitely second rate and he worried that these changes in the daily patterns of those under surveillance could be important.

To top off the incompetence of the surveillance team, the forensic analysts had reported that they could not find the location of the sculpture that he had seen in the grainy photos that had been taken in the office of Dr. Petkas. Bokhan had given them specific instructions to look in the files of museum archives all over the world, not just in Greece and in published art books; but after two weeks, they came back to say they still had not found them. They had even looked at the records of private collections. His research staff's inability to find the sculpture even after working through the home office in Moscow was very curious. Bokhan could tell the quality of the stone carving was superb. How could this Dr. Petkas have the photos, and his Soviet staff including those in Moscow could not find where they came from? Then the analysts came back again a few days later and said their enhanced photo analysis methods felt that the photos were taken in a dark room with rock walls. Could these pieces be some private collection here or on one of the Greek islands that was unknown to the historians and archeologists?

Bokhan called his contact person in the Papandreou government and got him to agree to have his surveillance people monitor the hotel and the Petkas home along with other New Democracy staff, such as Maria Beckett, at night. The security teams would work out a hand-off time together and set up procedures for relief of the watchers. Round the clock surveillance would look better in his report and Bokhan would cover himself from criticism if something went wrong. He also planned to check with the person in the Greek government who had placed the electronic surveillance in the campaign office of the New Democracy Party. He needed to make sure he got to see the Greek transcripts as well as his own, make sure all the areas were covered and eliminate duplication with the Greek surveillance. There was no need to tell Ambassador Andropov about this oversight as he had made the correct adjustments, but he was already late to escort Igor to another meeting, and he quickly went to the family quarters to meet him.

Tatiana Andropov slowly replayed the recent conversation with her uncle in her mind. She knew he could be demanding and that he knew how to apply pressure, but this was the first time it had been so severely directed at her. He was so accomplished at displaying his anger that she sometimes was not sure if it was manufactured for her benefit or for real. He had fumed, "You have been in that rock pile of a country for months now and I have heard nothing about my sculpture. Where's my ancient Greek treasure? What the hell have you and that excuse for a husband been doing? My comrades at the oil ministry have been asking me over and over, 'What about the Greek sculpture?' What am I to tell them? I don't want excuses. Only two weeks ago I hung one of the paintings I took away from the Hermitage museum in my home. It's not so hard to get what you want if you just act. I'm getting tired of waiting. Don't make me send someone down there to help you get it done. Do it yourself and show me you have what it takes to be my niece. I don't want to have to do something unpleasant to members of my own family. Do I have to send

Tito Petrovia down there? You know, the one you call, 'the hummer'?"

She had been shaken by the tone of his voice as much as with the words. Of all the people she had ever met, Tito was the most frightening. After she made excuses to her uncle she picked up her son from the nanny and went to see Igor who was in their embassy residence chambers.

Now she railed at Igor, using the same attitude and emphasis in her voice her uncle had used with her and she made similar threats. She had learned from her uncle how to get things done, so to ensure success for this discussion she wanted Igor and their son to be together. She had found that if she could shame Igor in front of their child, he would not talk back too much and would have to knuckle under to her demands. He would recognize that she and her family held all the cards in this game of Igor's career, and her son would learn at an early age that she was the one who mattered in their family. She was right. Igor tried to stop her demands by agreeing early in the conversation, sneaking side glances at their son.

She continued however to walk back and forth in front of him and their son, demanding a timetable for him to produce some ancient Greek treasure, thumping on a nearby table as she added additional requests just to see him cower and agree. She recalled a recent newspaper article and repeated the story to Igor that some smugglers had been caught with Greek artifacts. She berated him that the coins and bits of old pots he had given her were not enough and that her uncle wanted a whole sculpture. Her last demand was that he had better be dressed and ready and in a good mood for the reception they were supposed to attend later that evening. After she finished, he looked thoroughly beaten and sulked out back toward his embassy offices. She looked over at her son who was watching her with his young mouth opened in amazement, and she felt a warmth just below her stomach.

As she watched Igor leaving to stew over the demands she had just made, she saw the toad, Bokhan, standing with his head down in the entrance hall to the family quarters, obviously embarrassed to have overheard while waiting to accompany the ambassador to a meeting. Good, she thought, "his underlings need to see who's the real boss here."

Maria Beckett made polite conversation as she watched the diplomats circulate though the French Embassy reception. She was looking for signs of support for the New Democracy party, but knew most of these people, being diplomats, would remain polite and distant. But then across the room she noticed Igor Andropov and his wife, wearing the latest in French fashion. As his wife charmed the Embassy courtiers and seemed to be thoroughly enjoying herself, Igor appeared more removed. He hung behind his wife as though he did not want to engage in conversation, and Maria got the impression that he was only interested in cultivating people who could help him, which did not include most of these sycophants. He was also sulking and appeared to be unhappy about something.

She noticed that he stayed away from Milos Dedacus who was a high official in the Papandreou government. She thought this behavior strange as she had heard that Igor had made the Dedacus niece, Sophie Speros, his mistress. Maria wondered why Igor was not using that connection to Dedacus to further advance the Soviet Embassy policies in Greek affairs. She had noticed the young and impetuous niece of Dedacus for the past two years at embassy parties, and she had seen her latch onto the handsome Igor at one of the early receptions when he came to Greece. Then Maria realized that she had not seen the beautiful Sophie recently at any function. She wondered if the affair was going smoothly, and she made plans to look into that entanglement in case it offered some political advantage.

Across the room, she could see that when he was approached by someone, Igor had a habit of not initiating any conversation and giving brief answers to the people who came up to him so that without any stimulus they would soon feel awkward at having a one-sided conversation and move on. She saw another undiplomatic gesture that seemed to be characteristic of his behavior, that when he was in a conversation he would pull his head and shoulders back and seem to scowl at others, which also encouraged people to move on from talking to him and circulate in another direction.

She could understand not having respect for many of these third level diplomats, but to show even the slightest disdain in public, was a sign of immaturity and arrogance on Igor's part. She continued to watch him from a distance and could see that the relationship with his wife also seemed strained and contrived, which was another thing to remember and perhaps use later. She had watched him looking at one of the male waiters longer than would have been appropriate, wondered about his hidden proclivities here in his first diplomatic posting, and decided to have some research done to find out more about his character and desires. She knew unconventional desires could be a grave danger to those in the Soviet hierarchy, so she had made a career out of unmasking men who were keeping secrets, and all personal information was important.

Years of being on the social circuit had given her the skills to extract information subtly from people, and Maria moved over to Sophie's uncle, Milos Dedacus, whom she had known since the junta, to see if he would reveal any animosity or stress related to the affair. One never knew when bits of knowledge gathered at random might coalesce into something useful later on. Unfortunately, Dedacus, never the sharpest knife on the shelf, was more interested in promoting himself than talking about his niece, and it was difficult to have much of a conversation in the crowded room with different people coming up to speak every few moments. Maria did not have a chance to get into any details that would give her more information about the Sophie–Igor relationship, but the flame to her suspicion was lit.

CHAPTER 20

Sitting with the executive staff at the New Democracy campaign meeting, Angus looked over the latest polling from the Greek firm hired to support the campaign and smiled as he lowered the paper onto the table next to Maria Beckett. "If this is true, there's been a shift in the electorate in the past few weeks that we can exploit. You told me that the campaign operatives in the various provinces have been reporting more enthusiasm for our party than we had expected." He looked back at the poll results and tapped them with his finger. "It looks like our criticism has caused unrest and dissatisfaction about Papandreou's changes on the Greek economy. This poll shows a growing number of people are concerned over Greece spending money it doesn't have on social programs they didn't know they needed. We've got about a month left. Let's shift some money into negative ads and maybe we can move more undecided votes toward New Democracy. Use ads that concentrate on wasteful spending by the current government that hurt the average worker and small business. Don't attack him directly or aggressively. You don't want to look mean-spirited and have it backfire. Make the tone of the ads more like 'Isn't it sad what has happened to our nation.' It's worth a try and may actually peel off more of their supporters this time, which will help you to win the next election."

Maria nodded. "I agree. We'll make the shift to negative ads and hammer them on putting Greece into debt...politely as you say." She looked around the table and others on the campaign staff concurred. "Also, Mark and Stanos, you need to shift the speeches for Mitsotakis into more of a critical attack. Use the talking points the polling found that will blend with the message of the new ads." Both Mark and Petkas nodded.

It had been over six weeks since Mark had been home and Vicki had buried herself in her job so she would not miss him so much. Between work and long runs out to Hains Point with some of her girlfriends, she had kept so busy it was a week after she normally had her period that she remembered it had not come. She waited another week and then realized it was really late. She had not gotten fitted with the IUD as yet because she did not see any need to since Mark was gone, but because she usually was very regular, she got a pregnancy test from the drug store and now she sat there looking at the changed color on the swab. She remembered how closely she felt connected to Mark after that last night before Mark left to return to Greece and the remarkable time they had. If ever there was an occasion to get pregnant, that was it, and those few weeks after she got off the pill were the only time she had not had protection.

She sat there considering all the potential paths before her. Abortion was not an option. Most women had only a few opportunities to have a child and she was not going to pass this up.

They had not really discussed what the next steps were in their relationship and they certainly had not considered having a baby right away. Yet, their relationship was such that getting married seemed like the next logical step they both wanted.

She started to pick up the phone and call him, but then since they were meeting in Paris in a couple of weeks, for their anniversary weekend, she thought what a good opportunity it would be to tell him then. Paris was their dream vacation together, and sharing the news about her pregnancy would be the perfect way to make it even more memorable. She thought that they could get married at some quaint French chapel and later have something of a ceremony with friends and family back in Washington when Mark returned. She called her gynecologist to confirm the pregnancy test and verify everything was okay with her and the baby before the Paris trip. Yes, Paris was it, and then she thought that they'd need to get married for sure before she started to show.

Vicki had grown up in a home where her parents wrote second shelf critiques for art and music magazines in New York. They and their friends in similar positions often met to encourage each other's work and would

136

sit together listening to the phrasing of sentences that would go into articles describing the latest recordings of artists like Glen Gould. They'd
shout out ways to describe the Bach as they played the records over
and over while writing the articles, and Vicki listened as the music was
described with Gould's hands flying over the piano, his head bent over
the keyboards, the stool creaking and him humming over the recording's
best efforts to capture the passion and the art. She was infused with the
descriptions as the adults around her got more excited and she felt herself
transmigrated to the recording studio, sitting by the master, humming with
him and being carried away by the Goldberg Variations. Separated from
her parent's chaotic world, she found in the fantasy world of Bach the
peace and order she lacked at home.

Sometimes the writing sessions fueled by the adults' drinking that went
with them lasted from one day to the next, and the young Vicki would
awaken in the morning alone on the couch in the den that was littered with
empty bottles and containers full of the ashes and stubbed paper of dead
cigarettes. Even with the stale smell in the room, she was glad, as she
knew this meant that her parents had finally gotten the article to be the best
they could, after arguing over each word and the length of each sentence.
The war zone of the bohemian apartment showed the effort to achieve a
temporary truce negotiated along with the article by her parents and their
friends who had fought valiantly to make the best of a description that
might seem second rate to others, but was their pride and joy.

There was a calm and finality to those mornings that gave cover to the
other arguments that continued after the article was put to bed, proving
that the passions of creative writing did not stop with the last period. The
bickering over the article was actually the diplomatic side of her parents'
relationship. They must have been in love, but with it came incessant arguments over everything. Vicki felt like a sandstone in the desert being worn
down by constantly swirling winds, an obstacle to be circumvented by
chaos. So, for a time she relished those quiet mornings lying in the detritus
of the session's aftermath before she sensed the unhealthy energy that still
existed elsewhere in the home building momentum in the quiet. It was this
tension she felt in her stomach that no amount of creativity could soothe

and she carried in her gut her parents' inability to let anything go and their incessant anger.

Now inside her was a baby. Hers and Mark's baby was living inside her and growing and she knew starting a family would change both of their lives. She leaned back and imagined them as parents sharing the care of the infant and then seeing the boy or girl grow and become a wonderful adult. What for a few moments had been shock and uncertainty now began to build as a joy and anticipation of something that would now define their lives. My God. She was going to have a baby. They were going to have a baby. She could hardly wait to see Mark.

Her parents again flashed in her mind. No. She and Mark were better than that. They would not make those mistakes. Not her child or theirs. No matter what it took she was determined that their child would be loved and protected and nurtured and not put in the vulnerable position she remembered all too well. She and Mark would make this child the center of the universe. History would not be repeated here. Her hands rubbed over her belly and she wondered if the small growing seed inside could know how much she already loved it.

CHAPTER 21

About a week after the trip to Arta, Stanos Petkas joined Mark for a late morning hike up Mount Lycabettus and at the top they sat to enjoy a lunch of lamb sandwiches laced with cranberries. Earlier, when they left the campaign office, they tried an experiment and went to an area where there was a political rally for Papandreou and blended into the crowds. Ever moving, and separating they meandered their way through the tightly packed throngs and gradually edged over to the entrance of a large department store across the street. They entered and quickly moved through several areas of the store separately, then rejoined each other, exited out to a back alley and headed to the Mountain. There was no sign of the short, bald-headed man who had been following them whom they had named Mussolini.

Now peacefully enjoying their lunch near the top and confident they knew how to lose those tailing them, they talked between bites. Then Mark discreetly pointed out a man with close cropped ruddy hair who Mark had almost bumped into a few moments before loitering near the Temple on the top of the hill. The man, who Mark had appropriately named "Red," turned when he saw Mark and acted like he had mistakenly taken a wrong path and then looked at a map in his hands before moving away from Mark. They speculated he had been stationed there earlier in the morning to wait for them because they often came to this mountain over lunch.

Petkas also remembered seeing the man before, and they began to discuss how far away the observers would have to be to overhear what they were saying, and they wondered if the spies had microphones. Petkas said, "I think we should hold up a piece of paper or a sandwich in front of our mouths when we want to say something about the campaign or anything we don't want them to know in case he reads lips."

Mark agreed, "Yeah. We can also bend our heads down and kind of talk into our chest. I think we should not let on that we know who they are, because they might change the trackers and then we might not spot them as easily as these guys. Let's each update a separate list of the people we've seen near us or following us recently on the street or on these hikes, and then compare the lists with each other. We need to be in agreement on who these guys are."

Petkas then asked, "Mark can you come over to dinner tomorrow night? I'd like you to get to know my kids better and there are some things I'd like to go over with you that might take longer than a hike or grabbing a few minutes around the office. Say about 6:30 so you can have some time with the kids before they have to go to bed. Why don't you walk out like you're going to dinner someplace near the hotel and then just impulsively grab a taxi on the street?"

Igor soaked in the tub of his girlfriend's apartment with his third drink of the afternoon on the nearby ledge. The more he thought about his situation, the more upset he became. His wife criticized him for the size of the apartment that served as their home in the Embassy, and she was also disappointed that they were not appearing in the newspapers as much as when they arrived. She was going to go to Paris the next week to shop and see a certain French gentleman she knew very well there. Theirs was a kind of arranged marriage not uncommon among high-ranking party members. She and Igor got together when his father was head of the KGB and still rising in his power.

She knew her family's influence kept her husband in check, and that Igor was afraid to beat her as he wished to do or even complain too much, or she would go running to her uncle. Because she was spoiled and protected, she sometimes made him miserable by belittling his achievements and complaining of the interest he had in other women, which was the only practical release he had for his fantasies and desires.

For his part, he dared not pursue his other more exotic sexual instincts and had to be content with the Greek woman, Sophie. He did have to admit that his wife's tastes for Western clothing and fashion had benefitted him in his career and actually helped him in his conquest of many women. She gave him good advice on how he needed to dress and wear his hair, although she did it in her condescending tone of voice. He had asked her to bring him back a new sport coat and some casual shirts, and he knew that she would do well in her selections for him from the most expensive Paris boutiques.

Igor also had to admit that her looks and pedigree did give him another opportunity to please the Kremlin bosses, and it was worth putting up with her criticism and nagging for that benefit alone. He would have to be more careful with her now that his father was dead. He knew she and her family could do him more harm than good if they decided to turn on him. It seemed that he was always looking for newer ways to express his value to the bosses in Moscow. Now that damn uncle kept pushing him to steal some Greek sculpture. But how? He could not just back up a truck to the museum and haul it out. It was tiring and it seemed almost a full-time job for Igor just to imagine what things he might do next to show leaders in Moscow that he was worthy of their consideration for continued advancement. Where was he going to find the time or the means to find out how to steal Greek sculpture?

Then there was his assistant, Sergei Bokhan. He was due to come here soon on some business about diplomacy. He was helpful in most things, but he had this priggish way about him. He could always predict that Sergei would pick the solution to any problem that most benefitted the Soviet Union's dogma of the ideal communist. He was the ultimate straight arrow in a world where one needed to shoot around corners. He took another swallow of his drink. Bokhan was loyal to his wife and those urchins, boring in his dress and language, and predictably efficient in presenting Igor with boring memos and timely reminders. When he was lost in thought he often fingered that obnoxious Russian Orthodox Cross. What advantage could anyone see in that? No one in the Soviet Politburo orthodoxy cared about religion anymore.

He was here in the semi-backwater posting with these stupid Greeks who were screwing up the coming election by their own incompetence. It did not seem fair, and he felt like he was being forced to help them. If he went all out to support the prime minister in winning his reelection, it would make his Communist party friends here mad at him, and if he did not, he feared the Communist party leaders in Moscow would somehow hold him responsible. Even if he was successful now, there did not seem to be any way to correct the decline of Papandreou. He missed the simpler days when he just had to go to parties and smile and make jokes with diplomats, even though he found that demeaning and distasteful. He was finding the ambassador's job was hard and had stressful consequences. He needed to find an easier way to improve his prospects back home.

After Sergei Bokhan had finished the other embassy work which the ambassador had neglected, he packed the two fragile pieces of art in a special suitcase and as he had promised, took the gifts with him to show them to Andropov. He was red-faced with shame that Igor did not think the Greek delegation was important enough for him to stay in the office to receive these priceless gifts in person.

Igor had made excuses when leaders of the Greek Orthodox Church and officials from the ministry of culture came to present the icons to him, and he left before the ceremony and delegated the job to Bokhan, who was gracious to the Greeks as he received the icons and made additional excuses for Andropov. Now Bokhan was determined to show them to Igor and make him appreciate their significance and make him understand the importance of the church leaders and how having a good relationship with them was a benefit to the friendship of Greece and the Soviet Union.

This time he had an embassy driver take him to the apartment where Igor was with his mistress. As he sat in the front room of the apartment waiting for Igor to get dressed, he wondered what more he could do to make Andropov understand the niceties of protocol required to be an ambassador and the importance given by the host cultures when their emissaries gave these kinds of gifts to the representative of a foreign government.

He looked lovingly at one of the treasures he had brought with him, the ancient icon of Saint Leonitus, the Bishop of Rostov, who 900 years earlier had become a saint in Russia after many years of converting pagans, destroying idols, and serving as a monk in the caves of Kiev. Bokhan knew of the saint from his worship in the Russian Orthodox Church.

The gift of the Russian icon was also pared with another iconographic image, Leonidas of Corinth, painted on a similarly sized wooden board. The saint, martyred in Greece, had lived 1700 years before and was drowned for his faith.

Bokhan had been told that both images had been made over 300 years before, and the Greek political leaders and leaders of the Greek Orthodox Church thought that Igor would appreciate how the similarity of the names and the circumstances of the religious leaders' difficult lives provided a bond of faith for their two countries.

As he sat in the apartment while the subdued beauty, Sophie Speros, made him coffee, he noticed that she and kept a robe drawn tightly over her clothes. Sergei worried about this as he remembered seeing the young woman with bruises before, and he was concerned that her fragile condition was caused by an apparent pattern of abuse by Igor. As he waited for Andropov to come out of the back bedroom he pondered how to approach Igor about the way he was treating Sophie and to remind him that this woman was related to a Greek political leader, no matter how drug-addled she might appear.

In her small talk, Sophie rambled somewhat incoherently as though she lacked the capacity to organize her conversation. Bokhan listened carefully when she began to babble about keeping a journal of her reflections and a diary of her daily activities. He thought that the befuddled girl before him had no idea of how dangerous that was. Her diary likely included unattractive references to the Soviet Ambassador, however incoherent they might read. But for now, he did not want to raise that issue with Igor or Sophie, and he tucked the knowledge away for a later day. Sophie brought the tepid coffee from the kitchen that smelled of spoiled garbage from the stained plates piled in the sink, and then shuffled to another room in the back of the apartment and closed the door.

When Igor appeared, Bokhan could tell he had already been drinking even though it was still midafternoon. He thought to himself, this was yet another problem for him to address.

The Ambassador asked for a summary report about a meeting that he had missed and after giving him the report, which Igor largely ignored,

Bokhan opened the case to show him the icons. He was just starting to explain to Igor about the history of each one and why the Greek delegation wanted him to have them when Igor grabbed one, smirked, and threw it across the room where it skipped like a rock twice, three times on the floor and slid into the wall with a loud thud.

Andropov was cocky as he also often was when drinking, "What the fuck do I care about an old piece of wood with that ugly face on it? Don't these stupid Greeks know that Russians don't believe in this religious crap. What I want from them is to win this damn election and not to spend their valuable time in finding this old shit to give to me. What they can give to me is a victory." The ambassador leaned back and took a long swallow that finished off his drink.

Bokhan nodded and hid the pain he felt at the dismissive way he was often treated by his boss. He forced himself to say calmly, "I'll keep these church icons out of sight and only put them up if the Greek leaders come to visit you again. It is often helpful to let them see the gifts they have given you when they come to call. Please remember it is traditional for host countries to give this type of gift to a new ambassador." Bokhan then walked over to pick up the icon and rubbed his finger slowly over a corner where the wood had been chipped when it hit the baseboard. The wooden plank was now cracked down the middle and hung loosely connected. He could not look at Igor or his true feelings would show. Instead he carried the two icons over to the case, looking down at them and not over at Igor as he carefully put them away. All the while he was thinking to himself that Igor had no respect for art or history or diplomacy or religion.

He had to control his emotions so when he looked back at Igor his disdain would not show. Slow deep breaths. He continued to keep his head down and only glanced up when Igor went into the kitchen to get another drink.

Andropov had calmed down when he returned to the room because Bokhan had not given him any resistance to confront. He sat in a chair across from Bokhan and stirred his drink with his finger, then sucked the tip. "You do what you think best. Have someone in the protocol office write a thank-you note from me and put this crap away some place. You are right that we do need to maintain good relations, but I want another meeting to see the polling results on where this election stands. Our problems in Afghanistan continue to get worse and we cannot look like a failure here as well." He rubbed his wet fingers and then wiped them on his pants leg. "Greece is so dusty. Next time I will ask for a civilized posting where there is more to do than deal with these problems," he nodded his head toward the rear of the apartment, "and be around stupid people like that lazy fool in the back.

"Set up a meeting to look at the election tomorrow. And I want more reports from the people we have placed inside the New Democracy campaign. I want to know what those pigs are doing." Igor lay back again on the couch and rested his head on the pillow until Bokhan reminded him they were late for a meeting.

After the men left, Sophie Speros sat at her dresser looking at her face in the mirror and thinking about her relationship with Igor. To get her started, she first snorted another line of cocaine and then dabbed makeup over her latest bruise. She was confused and at a loss about what to do with her life and her current situation.

The Russian, Igor, had turned into something of an ogre who sometimes seemed not to respect her and was very rough in bed. If it was not for the free place to live and an endless quantity of drugs, she would have left the Soviet ambassador and continued to find something else to do with her life. He could be so nice and friendly sometimes, but often lately he had been mean and not only said hurtful things to her, but he pushed her and squeezed her arms, and when they had sex, he would leave her with bruises and sore places that did not have anything to do with lovemaking.

However, he had made it hard for her to make a change. She was embarrassed to tell her family how she was being treated and kept almost like a prisoner in the apartment where he had put her. When they did go out together it was usually with some of his Russian friends, and she did not understand the language well enough to know what they talked about except what she could guess when they looked at her and laughed.

Her situation was made more complicated because sometimes when they were together, just the two of them, she could talk to him and he would talk back to her in a regular conversation just like a real couple. She felt that was their special time when he would let her know all about how hard his job was or how much he really did not like his wife. In those times, she felt a connection to him and she felt he needed her, but then he would get into another mood and be quiet or sometimes rage at her for the slightest thing.

Her relationship with the Soviet ambassador was the first time she had spent so much time with a man almost twice her age. Their situation must be what married life is like and men must be moody when they had important jobs. The boys and younger men of her experience were all just for fun and looking for the next thrill. Sometimes when Igor got quiet after drinking, he looked so needy and clearly required a friend as well as a lover. In those special times, she felt she had found her place in this world of deep drama and important things which she did not understand, but she sensed that being with Igor put her into an important world in which she had a special place. She could be the person he came to when he had to get away from the pressure of his work and distance himself from all those who did not understand him. She was the one he came to when he needed a friend or to be quiet or to drink away his troubles.

Her relationship with Igor, however unusual, gave her a sense of importance that she was the one the Soviet ambassador really cared about, and she could be his friend when the problems of the world got too great to handle alone. What were a few bruises compared to his burdens and her ability to help such an important man in the affairs of the world?

However, everything seemed to upset him more than it should. Igor reminded her of her younger brother, who when adults did not pay attention to him and flatter him, sulked and was inconsolable even though he tried to hide his feelings and did not want them to know he was upset; and he put on an act as though it didn't matter.

If she could only help Igor get over these difficult times, they could be a real couple and live a good life. Then he would be kinder to her. For now, supporting Igor was her calling, and she could imagine herself in a year or two after he divorced his wife as a woman in an international environment with him. Perhaps her old friends and her family would never fully understand her being with Igor, but they might really admire her as the new wife of an Ambassador. When she felt better she would write down her ideas about how to talk to him and make him see a way to improve their relationship. If she could be successful in this, he would truly love her and see her value to him, and then he would make her his wife.

She brushed makeup over the ouchy places to blend as best she could the discolored parts to meet the unblemished freshness of her skin, that prior to her time with Igor looked to have been soaked in milk. She recalled how her family had always wanted her to be in the front row of family portraits.

She knew that she was taking way too many drugs, but it was just so easy when he or one of his men brought them to her so frequently. She hardly had the motivation to leave the apartment and when she did, her mind was so confused she barely knew how to talk to her old friends anymore. When they called, she ended the conversations hurriedly because she could not think what to say or keep up with the complicated things they said to her. Sometimes Sophie found her mind making plans to leave Igor and do other things, but she always seemed to decide to make those moves before she took some more drugs. She had been staying away from her family because she knew they would be able to tell that she was not her old self. It took more makeup all the time now to cover up the red edges around her nose. She had to make a change from this situation, but how? Igor was so commanding when he was there and she was afraid what he might do if she told him she was going to leave. She put down the makeup container and laid out another line of coke.

Still, she felt she knew him and understood his moods and why he needed sometimes to be angry and to shout. She just wished he would not be so violent with her, but she kept thinking that was temporary and would change with time. If he were to leave his wife and make her the wife of the ambassador, she could just imagine herself dressed up in those fine clothes going to all the parties and being seen by everyone and making grand entrances on the arm of such a handsome and powerful man.

Well, if she decided to move on, she could just do it. She'd take all the cocaine in the apartment to tide her over, and then leave.

CHAPTER 22

Waiting for Mark to arrive, Petkas brooded over the same problem he had been worrying about for several years. He felt that this American, Mark, now seemed to offer the best possible answer, but then his other familiar concern arose over his family's safety. After all, one of his children had special needs. What kind of a husband and father would he be if he did not put his family first, and yet what kind of a human being would he be if he did not do everything he could to preserve the treasures he had found for all of humanity to appreciate? None of his academic training or other life experiences had prepared him to make this kind of a choice or endure the stress caused by the intrigue and paranoia his secret had created.

When Mark entered Petkas's home for dinner, he found his friend with his children in a back room where they were undertaking an art project. He'd been there several times before and was always amazed at the ways Petkas found to work with his kids and teach them about the history of their country. This evening Petkas was showing them how to make tempura paint by mixing gypsum, glue, eggs, paint pigment, and water. There was a sheet of plaster for use as a canvas and a photo of Greek art on the wall to use as a model and the kids seemed excited about the project. Nearby he saw evidence of wood carvings and molded clay that emulated Greek sculpture. Petkas was patient and gave simple instructions that tied the art to Greek history.

The two boys were ages six and nine, and after seeing Mark again they rushed to hug him like he was an old, familiar uncle. This caught Mark off balance and pleased him enormously. He got down on the floor and played with the boys as though they were his own. They pulled him by his arms into their room to show him, once again, all their toys, including tin Greek armor and tools which they used to prospect for imaginary buried Greek treasures. On the walls Petkas proudly displayed awards from their grade schools.

He listened over a wonderful dinner to the stories of the times that Petkas and his wife had taken his children to museums, sailing, and to venues that gave them a better sense of the history of their country, and Mark could see with Petkas as a father they were learning the history of Greece from a world authority. Around the house he saw plaster of Paris molds of their hands and feet from various ages. Here was a man who not only was a good academic and a competent political manager, but also was a good man in his personal life.

Petkas watched Mark play with his kids and be cordial to his wife, Cyrilla. Mark seemed genuinely interested in his family, and was open and kind. He thought that at last here was a person with the ability and contacts who he could trust to help him with his secret. But he knew he would have to be careful how he held the conversation with Mark so his story would be revealed slowly, and that each additional bit of information would be supported by the facts laid down before. He had been setting this night up by laying the groundwork of history almost from the moment he met Mark, and now that they had become friends and a trust had grown between them, he felt it was time to let Mark in on the secret and solicit his help. After dinner, as Cyrilla and the kids stayed in the house, Petkas invited Mark to walk out into the backyard garden with their coffee. There they sat next to each other on a swing set that was taking up space in the yard and offered seats just big enough to fit them.

"Mark, there is something I need to tell you, but I must have your promise that you will not reveal it to anyone unless we both agree for you to do so. What I have to say is very important to me, and I need your help. So please indulge me for a few minutes while I say what I need to."

Mark promised him.

Petkas put his coffee cup down on the ground and made gestures with both of his hands in front of him as he talked. "Remember back when we had the picnic in the valley where I said Alexander had camped on the way to see the Oracle at Delphi? Well, I only told you half the story. In the more complete story, Pericles, remember the preeminent builder in Greece history, gave a commission to Phidias, the foremost manager of early sculptors.

"Phidias ran the largest sculpture business in Athens employing many of the best sculptors of that time, and he was asked to create the largest and most important series of sculptures ever made, called the Gods of Olympus. It would be a collection of the twelve most important Greek gods, made in a setting fashioned in an imaginary kingdom of the gods, Olympus, or what you might call heaven. Because they were so careful with the carving, it took the best sculptors alive more than twenty years to quarry the stone and then sculpt and finish all twelve of them, and the statues were kept at Phidias's studios where they had been created. The twelve gods were made to look as if they were together in Olympus, standing around as in a group. These sculptures were referred to in the ancient tax records of Phidias we found here in Athens.

"Pericles ordered the sculptures but unfortunately died not many years later at about the start of the Peloponnesian Wars in 429 BC. And though the 12 sculptures were finished before the end of these wars, they stayed in the stone carving studios which were now managed by the successors to Phidias. There they stayed semi-forgotten as a jaw-dropping curiosity. They were visited and seen by the intellectuals of Greece, like Aristotle, as the marvels they were, but the centralized political leadership of Greece was diminished after 400 BC, and the city-states once again became the more established power of a divided government. There were no strong leaders for about 40 years until Philip of Macedonia in about 360 BC.

"Without a strong centralized leader like Pericles, there was no one to finish paying for them with the revenue from wars and taxes collected from the city-states. These carvings were expensive to create over the 20 or so years, and the balance of the expenses, minus a substantial deposit, were likely deferred and expected to be paid later with the treasure won in battle.

"Alexander heard about the gods of Olympus sculptures from his teacher Aristotle who knew about them because he lived in Athens and had actually seen them when he was studying at Plato's academy. After teaching Alexander in Macedonia and telling him of the sculptures, Aristotle returned to Athens to form his own school, the Lyceum.

"The main reason I was able to find all this out is that the bulk of

151

surviving ancient written records from this time are about ownership of valuables such as deeds and tax records.

"I briefly mentioned records to you in one of our early discussions, but I was throwing a lot out at you. Anyway, we found from the person who was the business manager of Phidias references from other ancient accounting records that included a rental contract for the space in the studio and grounds. We found documents indicating that a sizeable space at his facility had become available again, not long after Alexander had visited the Oracle - space that previously had been filled for several decades of use. The records also showed a significant up-front payment to the factory by Pericles almost a hundred years before, I'm guessing to purchase the materials and get them started. We also found a substantial loss of revenue to the sculpture factory because no one had ever paid for the finished commission to make the statues. Accounting records documented the sculptures being made, where they were warehoused, and then their being gone, and that space in the sculpture studio being opened for other uses. The dates of these things all coincided enough to give me a historical map."

Mark shook his head in disbelief, "A map to what?"

Petkas put out his hands to slow down the conversation, as he wanted to be precise, "In the military records of Alexander, I found part of a requisition order that sent a group of his soldiers to Athens. I matched that with records of the family of his classmate who lived near Delphi where Alexander stayed with them when he was there. I found that through a requisition order, actually another billing record that covered some of the food and drink for Alexander's camp. I was able to match the dates and made the story fit largely from that information.

"I was then able to use a scrap of some Macedonian documents from Alexander's mother's palace, that said a large space was to be prepared in the palace about the time Alexander went to Persia for several pieces of sculpture that would be brought from Athens. All that information made the story fall together.

"Computers allowed me to combine all these bits of information from history into a chronological puzzle and that became the germ of a story, and as more data appeared, I cross- referenced it too into a matrix. Some of it is unrelated to anything else except that it supported my theory of the story. That led me increasingly to believe what I found made sense and was true.

"I believe that while Alexander and his friend, were on the trip from Macedonia to visit the Oracle at Delphi, so near to Athens, it reminded him of the legend of the sculpture he had heard from his teacher, Aristotle. Alexander had the idea and decided to bring the Gods of Olympus collection to Macedonia and install them at his palace. Although he had never seen them, he was motivated because Aristotle told him stories of their beauty and superiority. And quite frankly, Alexander liked to own stuff that made him look more powerful. He was a grabber.

"I speculated that while they were camped there, Alexander sent someone, likely his childhood friend, the son of the Anatos family which had moved there, with a group of soldiers to start the journey by first bringing them from Athens to the family campsite. He wanted to take possession of them and then to start them on the trip back to Macedonia which would keep them from other potential poachers here in Athens.

"The family had a cave nearby which he decided to use to hold the sculptures as a stopping point on the transit. It was not uncommon for villagers or families to keep things in these small caves for preservation. They were to be sent on to Macedonia once they were packed more thoroughly for the journey into the hills. The distance from Athens to the valley we visited is only about 100 miles and even in those days the road was on relatively flat terrain, but it is another 350 miles to the capital of Macedonia and some of that journey is in the mountains, and the sculptures never made it.

"However, soon after this trip to Delphi, Alexander continued his journey to begin his conquest of the lands to the east that took over 10 years and he never returned, and so he never finished moving them and Alexander never even saw the sculptures. It would have taken a significant effort to move them to Macedonia and, without his direction and influence, the sculptures, safely packed away and awaiting the second part of the journey, remained in the possession of the Macedonian family near Delphi. My guess is that the sculpture went no further because nobody would have wanted to be the person to tell Alexander that they had dropped one of his priceless Gods of Olympus statues off a mountain pass.

"Then we were able to cross-reference that information leading to the cave with several accounts from the time when Alexander entered Persia and began his years of conquest. He sent back a great deal of gold, jewels and many other treasures to Macedonia because it was the seat of his kingdom, and these statues would have needed to be there. Because of the value of the merchandise, they made fairly good records of what had arrived and what was expected, which is where we found the references to reserve space for the sculptures. Alexander would have sent soldiers and movers to go and get them after he returned from his adventures in Persia and India, but as you know, he never made it back.

Mark blew out a deep breath, "But Stanos, there are so many ways that could be a wild goose chase. You would have to be guessing right on so many things for it to be possible."

Petkas picked up his cup and took the last swallow, then put it back down so he could again use both hands when he talked. "Yes, you are right, but just listen, there were many caves used like secure storage houses where items were packed for preservation over the years and only the items needed for daily life were retrieved. Food stuffs and the like. Other items that were not needed for ready access were put in what you might call cold storage back in the caves.

"So, a Macedonian family that moved to Delphi would likely have found a decent location to settle near a place with storage like a cave, and as there was a good bit of activity and travel near the famed Temple and oracle, and also the Pythian games and festivals held nearby, there would have been enough commerce to sustain the family.

"However, Delphi could have been a poor choice of a hiding place. Since these small villages were really clans of a few families or sometimes even only one or two families, they were isolated and after there was something like a flood or earthquake the population surviving these frequent natural disasters would not try to rearrange nature or clear out the debris from a landslide. They just accepted their situation and moved their settlement to another location where it was perhaps safer. With the complication of modern data, we can see that this pattern has some basis of proof. There are many references to earthquakes and tremors which did cause landslides and wipe out settlements.

"The sharp, hilly area near Delphi with many draws and small valleys would have been an ideal location for slides that would leave changes to the landscape. In those days people did not dig out those obstacles, they simply went around them. My theory evolved over time as more information was available and science was able to determine more about the evolution of Greece and in particular the area where the sculpture was lost from sight. It became practical to assume that geological changes could have hidden the treasure Alexander was sending to his palace, and because the area was remote, it was a safe assumption that the memory about the safekeeping of the 'Gods of Olympus' could have been lost.

"Covering up a cave caused by an earthquake, would make it a natural preservation chamber. Imagine a corner of that little valley where we had the picnic after a landslide had wiped it out. You could never tell anything had been there, but it would remain secured behind the rocks. And these life-size sculptures would withstand tremors better if they were sufficiently padded and stored. "University archeological and geological teams searching the area have found newly discovered caves in the area that had been covered from previous slides for many centuries, some containing artifacts put there for safekeeping. New technology and equipment allows excavation of these caves, but because of Greece's financial status, there is not enough funding to do it properly. Our government can neither afford random searches to find hidden historical objects or build new museums to house, protect and preserve them. Some of the way that research is prioritized is through academics like myself. As a professor of archeology, I have some control over this and could manage to direct the search, which I did. I never used the same students for more than a semester at a time so they would not become too interested in the research and would not become suspicious of my actual plan. Now I'm worried that my recent political involvement might bring an audit or call attention to my search. It looks like the clock is ticking on my secret.

"For six years I started traveling every chance I got to Delphi. I walked through and looked at many small valleys thinking that a rockslide had covered up the place where the sculpture was stored. So, I picked my way through several rock slides as well. I wrote papers on Delphi to cover my tracks and studied other phenomena of the area and I kept on looking for the small valley of the family from Macedonia.

"It became my obsession. I began to search for the cave about seven years ago and found it four years ago. But unfortunately, that was when Papandreou came to power and my confidence in the Greek government faded. It was at the time of the rise of the socialists and communists which put the sculpture in jeopardy. I realized I would need help to do anything with it, so I kept my discovery a secret and became heavily involved in the New Democracy party. I kept my research segregated so my students would not put the various pieces together. At any rate, I'm the only one who has all the assimilated facts, except now for you. I knew the New Democrats were most likely to have the financial clout of the business leaders to secure the help I needed, and now I am entrusting you and your contacts in the United States to help. The Gods of Olympus are the biggest secret in the world of art and antiquity, likely many times bigger than the King Tut discovery or anything else. There is no way to calculate their value. I'm just overwhelmed by trying to find the answer to how to move twelve pieces of sculpture likely weighing over a ton each and that are so fragile that they could easily be damaged."

"There is another problem in that there is a very active black market in antiquities. People from museums here as well as treasure hunters, and including our own government, are participating in the theft. They are selling items all the time to buyers both to the private collections as well as museums in more affluent countries. A little over 10 years ago the Metropolitan Museum of Art in New York purchased a terracotta bowl by one of our greatest ancient potters, Euphronios, considered one of the finest Greek vase artifacts in existence. There is a legal battle to try to get it back to Greece, but the fact that one of the greatest and most respected museums in the world could buy it shows that there is a thriving market for stolen relics. If it had been sold to an Arab Prince or a Russian oil baron it would never have been seen in public again.

"The fact is that the people who wish to acquire these kinds of works have more money than the people trying to protect them. My fear is that if the Greek Government gets control over them, these invaluable pieces of sculpture will disappear and never be seen again."

Cyrilla Petkas came out on the porch, "Stanos, I'm putting the children to bed. They want you and Mark to say goodnight to them." Petkas always said goodnight to his children and told them a story. They stopped the conversation and agreed to continue the next day. Petkas reengaged with his children, calm and focused, as though he had just been giving one of his lectures instead of the incredible story he had just told Mark.

Mark was amazed at Petkas's ability to suddenly shift his demeanor and detach from talking passionately about the treasure to telling bedtime stories to his kids. Mark did say goodnight to the kids but did not stay to hear the bedtime story. As he made his way back to the hotel, bouncing along in the dark taxi, he felt a tinge of fear rise in him that this intrigue was far more complicated and potentially more dangerous than the campaign. But it was also exciting, like the way he had felt eighteen years before in the airplane packed with other soldiers flying in the dark skies over the Pacific waters headed to Vietnam.

CHAPTER 23

The next day Mark and Angus sat with Maria Becket, Petkas and several of the other top staff of the campaign looking at the most recent commercials. Now was the time to make the final changes before the election. The commercials they watched had been designed as Angus had suggested to undermine the support of PASOK by lamenting that the socialist government had caused many problems including a shortage of products produced by Greek companies which had weakened the economy. The advertising campaign was aimed to build support toward the next election, and they all felt it would be effective at showing New Democracy as a more reasonable alternative to the current socialist government.

Their limited polling and anecdotal reports from the field offices continued to indicate that the earlier advertising with a similar message was having some effect. The polling also showed that a shift in voter opinion would be too slow and lack the scale to win this election, but would, as intended, set them up for four years from now. After a long morning stuck in the meeting, everyone needed a breather, so they agreed to split up for lunch and meet back in the office.

As the group was breaking up Maria motioned for Mark, Angus and Petkas to stay.

She turned on a radio with the volume at a medium level and asked the three to come in closer. "An old American colleague of mine from earlier days" she nodded over to Angus and Mark, "sent me something that we may wish to use." Maria then produced a small cassette player and clicked the play button. They listened to Maria translate a tape containing Papandreou's voice from a Moscow radio interview two years earlier talking about his plans for Greece. In the segment he told the interviewer that he planned 'to drive all the evil capitalism and big business out of Greece.'

Petkas leaned back in his chair. "What an idiot."

Angus smiled and said, "That's good. Have your people make it into a commercial, but only play it a few days before the election and get your production people to put a lead into it so it will sound like it is a current news broadcast. Don't give the other side time to respond and don't over-play it. Have it run just a few times on radio stations in news programs where we know there are undecideds like small business owners who may be listening. It will be better to have the spot start a word-of mouth rumor mill, like 'Did you hear what Papandreou said on the radio? What was he thinking?' Get copies to any radio commentators you think will use it and talk it up."

Before they left the building Petkas pulled Mark into his office and showed him the four small square photo images of the sculpture. He explained, "The camera was not very good, and the place was dark, so all the photos I made of wider shots of the cave and multiple sculptures were too dim to see. I could only make these close ups of the heads and shoulders using the flash. I keep them hidden here in my briefcase. You can see that there is no color on the stone. That was the clue that they were never paid for by Pericles. Finished sculptures in those days were always painted in bright colors.

"That made these fit the chronology, because Pericles had assumed he would get the rest of the money to pay for them with the war booty or profits after winning the Peloponnesian war, but he died before that hap-pened. I believe the completed stones were left at the stone yard at first because the managers and owners assumed someone from the government would eventually pay them and then put the sculpture in a palace or a cathedral. That was the assumption I made and it supported my idea of the sculpture being left there in the stone yard rather than being transferred to a museum or palace. The lack of color on the stone sealed the timetable of my theory."

Mark was amazed at the lifelike appearance of the faces, and from what he could see, of the incredible detail of hair, skin and expression. He was not very familiar with sculpture, but these images seemed far more sophisticated that what he remembered seeing previously in pictures or museums. Mark was still trying to get his head around the secret he had now become a part of, and he and Petkas whispered together in the small office about their options regarding what they could do to solve the dilemma of all these hidden enormous blocks of stone? Mark said, "So, many of our earlier conversations have been leading to this moment. The trip to Arta, hikes, and other things... you are a fairly sneaky guy for a history professor."

Petkas put the photos back in his briefcase, "My apologies if I misled you, but I had to know I could trust you. I hope you will forgive any deceit on my part."

Mark shrugged "No, I understand it all now, but it's a little mind-blowing. It must have been hard to hold onto this secret for several years."

"You have no idea."

Mark looked at Petkas evenly. "And you've got to know I'm not your ideal partner in this. I don't know if I have or could even get the answers you want or the contacts you are looking for."

"Yes, perhaps not now, but I'm hoping you will help me look for the answers and network through your contacts to find the right people to help. I'm stuck here in Greece and just do not have the resources you do as an American who has worked for the White House."

Petkas caught Mark pondering and instinctively knew Mark was thinking about the sculpture and not about the campaign, just as he himself had been doing for many months. He guided him out of the office and they walked to a place where they could sit on a wall and observe if anyone was nearby. Petkas picked up the conversation where he had left off the night before. "So, as I said, I came to the conclusion that a landslide likely had hidden the treasure, and with everyone's attention focused on Alexander's conquests all over Asia, records here on the mainland were limited. It was a safe assumption that the memory of the safekeeping of the Gods of Olympus back in the time of Alexander could had been lost.

"Other discoveries show caves being great storage facilities, including something as delicate as preserving the 15,000-year-old cave paintings in France or the Dead Sea Scrolls of Christianity which were preserved for many centuries. Stone carvings, as long as they were not crushed by shifting rock, would stay preserved forever just as they were when placed there for safekeeping 2400 years ago.

"Here." Petkas gave Mark a piece of paper that contained the Gods of Olympus. "I've included the Roman names as well because Rome adopted these gods, and much of Western civilization used the names interchangeably. Here is a list of what is in the cave."

Zeus / Jupiter - King of the gods, ruler of Mount Olympus
Hera / Juno - Queen of the gods and the goddess of marriage and family
Poseidon / Neptune - God of the seas, earthquakes, and tidal waves
Demeter / Ceres - Goddess of fertility, agriculture, nature, and the seasons
Athena / Minerva - Goddess of wisdom, reason, intelligent activity, literature, handicrafts and science, defense and strategic warfare
Apollo / Apollo - God of light, prophecy, inspiration, poetry, music and arts, medicine and healing
Artemis / Diana - Goddess of the hunt, virginity, archery, the moon, and animals
Ares / Mars - God of war, violence, and bloodshed
Aphrodite / Venus - Goddess of love, beauty, and desire
Hephaestus / Vulcan - Master Blacksmith and craftsman of the gods
Hermes / Mercury - Messenger of the gods; god of commerce, communication
Dionysus / Bacchus - God of wine, celebrations, and ecstasy

Now that Petkas had taken Mark into his confidence, it seemed all the secrets bottled up in him had to come out. He began to talk about the sculpture almost every time they were together. Though they continued to be careful of what they said and where they were, their earlier caution had begun to wane. The more information Petkas shared with Mark, the more nervous he became.

On their walk one particular day, Petkas described the sculptures and how passionate he was to have them preserved. "I have looked at parts of most of them and their beauty is indescribable. The place where they are buried is safe and hard to find, but I made a small opening to get into the cave. I have been careful not to go there too often and have covered up the hole again each time.

"But it is not just that they made all 12 of the major gods of Olympus together in one group meant to be displayed together. These were something of transition pieces. The techniques of the carving of sculpture in the work of Praxiteles and Phidias was evolving from the rather stiff positions of earlier times to the more fluid classical forms we see today, like the black figures on the amphora vases in many museums.

"Dionysus, or Bacchus as he is more commonly called, is carved with grapes mingled in his disheveled locks, and made like vines with budding fruit flowing from his scalp to mix with his real hair and hang inside and outside his shaggy head of hair on tiny stems, and his face and body show signs of excessive living like we see today in alcoholics and in some politicians.

"Hestia, the Goddess of Health, is shown with very fine skin of smooth marble and draped in a thin fabric that clings to her finely formed body. You can see the veins pulsing under her skin through the stone cloth.

"Aphrodite is similarly dressed, but her look shows a controlled lust. Her breasts are taught and nipples firm and she has a look on her face of one seeking a partner. Her passion is tangible. To look on this piece of rock is like watching a sexy movie star. "These were made in details that showed their Olympian functions carved into human-like characters. And yet we can see them turning one way or the other, posing slightly to be in communication with one another. If they were to be arranged as intended, the viewer would apprehend a scene of Ares holding what I assume would have been a bronze sword or spear looking at the muscular Hephaestus, the master blacksmith and craftsman, who would have made the weapons for Ares to carry into battle.

"It is not just the fact that they exist and would be one of the greatest archeological and artistic finds in history, but that they represent the missing link between earlier and later schools of Greek sculpture, and on top of that, not only were they were designed to show the highest artistic skill of their creators, but here we also have all twelve sculptures relating to each other in one setting. They are simply unique in their value and their beauty. It is as if the dozen best sculptures of all time were hanging out and talking to each other in a garden party.

"They were made by men whose fathers carved stone as taught to them by their fathers, who knew no other skill and talked of no other subject. They were made by men whose hands held the hammer and chisel almost from birth, whose muscles knew what to do almost better than the minds of the artist. These are skills now lost to history.

"The one thing that modernity has not done to improve on the ancients is the ability to carve marble, and these are the best-carved marbles the world has ever seen. They are the pinnacle of achievement in the ancient world and are equal to anything that Michelangelo did 2000 years later, but there are twelve of them, not just one. These pieces are so rare and so valuable that the world will have to rethink everything we know of ancient art and will be forced to assume that much of what we have today in our museums throughout the world are second rate leftovers that were fortunate to have survived the scourge of time and the violence we humans love to inflict on priceless works of art during the destruction of our wars.

"I'm at a loss how to protect them and have no confidence that the nation of Greece in its current circumstance could do them honor. They would be so beautiful in a museum - perhaps with a special room designed for the sculpture where a limited number of guests at a time could walk through an imagined setting of Olympus. I am so afraid of what the Greek government would do to them and I truly fear the Russians would get them and scatter them among the new government's oligarchs. Same with the Arabs and perhaps even the Japanese where recently there has been a large influx of new money. The statues deserve to be honored and appreciated together."

Mark put his hand on the arm of Petkas, causing him to stop walking. "Stanos, hold on… stop. I appreciate your telling me all about the sculpture and it must be as amazing as you say, but you need to quit talking about it…at all. I am afraid we will be overheard by someone who may have bad intentions, and all the effort and time you have put into protecting these works of art will be gone as soon as that happens. They will grab you and make you tell your secret. Agree with me now, the only time we talk about them is when we are sure we are safe. And that is not walking around the busy streets, in the office or anywhere else where other people are near."

"Yes. Yes. You are right." Petkas continued, "Now that the campaign is almost over and we have an important secret to keep, we need to be much more careful about our conversations. We have a lot to discuss and plans to make, and we must have absolute secrecy."

Mark leaned back, feeling somewhat overwhelmed, "I agree but I don't know anything about being a spy and neither do you. I accept that the campaign is not as important as the...the secret, but we need to have a long discussion about what to do, and I'm wondering if we should involve Maria Beckett. She has done some things like deal with secrets and intrigue, and she might be able to give us advice."

Petkas quickly responded, "Not now! Not yet. Let's talk it out between the two of us first, but right now we've got the campaign to finish." Petkas turned and started to walk, Mark followed and they both went back to the office.

CHAPTER 24

Tatiana was preparing to attend the May Day celebration of 'International Workers' Day' at the Embassy, a celebration of peasants which Tatiana disdained but understood she needed to acknowledge as one of the duties of an Ambassador's wife. She planned to honor the workers by wearing a hand-embroidered, tightfitting French gown she had recently purchased on her latest trip to Paris. She was almost ready when her husband carried in the disturbing facsimile transmission he had just received from her uncle, the impatient and demanding Valentine Gubanov. "Look at this." He handed her the stiff paper, coated with the special substance needed for the transmission.

She squinted at the type on the dark, grey paper as she read aloud, "He says he is tired of waiting for results and is sending one of his... oh no. Igor —"

He interrupted her with a haughty sneer, pointing at the paper in her hands, "So now your uncle is going to send one of his lackeys to help me, or more likely spy on me. I don't need this shit. I remember something of the man... Tito Petrovia. He looks like a bully. What can he know or do about running an embassy or winning an election?"

Tatiana, let the paper drop. "I know this man. Let me tell you and believe me, Igor, he is a man who takes care of serious problems for my uncle. Tito's mother was a prostitute from the Carpathian Mountains and she married a low-level Russian soldier who had been charged with war crimes just after the end of WWII. He never fit into any place when he was a child. He was always an outcast and picked on by others, until he learned how to pick back. He grew up alone in back streets and alleys. He is the guy you send to get people to do what they do not wish to do. He is not big like a bear, but is very strong and most importantly has the eyes of death. When he tells someone that he will hurt them, they always

165

believe it. He has this habit of making low noises that come from his chest. The other men who work for my uncle call him, 'the hummer.' I am very frightened by him. He's a man who scares me every time I see him."

Igor gave a derisive laugh trying to forget the menacing look on the face of Tito Petrovia the few times he had seen him. "We'll see. I spent time with the Spetsnaz commandos on my last trip to Moscow. Those are men who can really make one afraid." He had relished his time visiting the KGB offices and watching Spetsnaz commandoes at their training facility. He remembered the excitement of watching the commandoes run through the obstacle course while shooting at targets. No wonder his father had liked his job so much.

On his return to Greece, he felt a new sense of pride in his country, at what the soldiers were capable of doing, and also a greater appreciation for what his father had labored to build over many years in clandestine operations. He'd not trouble himself over this "hummer" person. He would become more dedicated to the security issues in Greece and, started by requesting a briefing from the security deputy in the embassy.

The security official was one of the staff who normally reported directly to Bokhan, and the man was apprehensive about going around behind the back of his boss to speak directly to the ambassador. But Igor Andropov had demanded to have a detailed, personal briefing on surveillance on the New Democracy campaign. As they met and talked, the security man thought the ambassador's questions indicated he was obsessed with finding a way to keep the Papandreou government in power and not to lose support in the upcoming election.

The man stood at attention and nervously cleared his throat as he continued his review. "We have a new report from one of the Greek surveillance team. The man was watching the American and the man, Petkas, from New Democracy as they were having a walk up the Mt. Lycabettus hill. They make this walk almost every day, but because they were moving it was not easy to get too close to them, but he did overhear something on his microphone. Back in the audio lab the technicians cleaned the tape as well as they could and edited it into the most relevant parts for the report." He nodded at the Ambassador. "They kept a full tape in case our leaders wanted to delve into it more closely later. The transcript they prepared contained select portions and was sent to our embassy to share with the ambassador's office... with you, sir."

"Get on with it! I don't care about those technical details. What did he hear?"

The security man cleared his throat again and swallowed. "The men kept moving about, and he could not get close enough or get a good angle to pick up the entire conversation. He could not get everything he wanted and it was frustrating but he did as well as he could with the equipment he had."

"What is it?"

"Mister Ambassador, sir, I'm trying to tell you, but it is important that you understand the details as they affect the veracity and quality of the report."

He laid a copy of the full report onto Igor's desk and flipped over to the page in the relevant section and pointed to the passage. "The document we have says that our man overheard the American ask Mr. Petkas about the quality of some sculpture, and Mr. Petkas said it was 'invaluable.' That was the exact word he used."

Igor Andropov frowned, "But that could mean anything. Any sculpture in any museum."

"I must confess Mr. Ambassador, his equipment was not the best and they were moving around so he could not pick up enough of what they said, but later in the conversation he heard Petkas say," the man reached over to the desk and flipped over to the next page and pointed to the relevant section, 'it must stay buried until we are ready to take it out.'"

That bit of information caught Igor off guard and he jerked, then leaned back in his chair and immediately smelled intrigue. He spoke to the assistant half in an actual order and half in an internal musing. "Call Sergei Bokhan in here to hear this. If we can catch the American and a Greek from New Democracy conspiring to steal the art of Greek history, it will make a very good propaganda story. If the American is planning to steal some artifacts from Greece with the help of this capitalist professor, we need to catch them at it. If we can catch them it will be a great intelligence coup for me in Moscow and will get Tatiana's uncle off my back."

He looked at the security aide who was still standing in front of his desk not sure of what to do, "Now! Go find Sergei Bokhan now, I need to discuss this with him. You have brought me good work. Keep up the surveillance. Everywhere this American goes I want him followed. Get more recordings. Also make sure there is a trace on the phone of this Petkas criminal and follow him as well. This discovery will be very good for us all."

Igor filled in his deputy, Sergei Bokhan, on his suspicions and gave him a copy of the report from the Greek security forces. "Sergei, I don't trust the Greeks to be able to handle this. We need to do it on our own. Call our KGB friend in the Kremlin. I want a team of our surveillance people sent here to supplement the people we have on staff. Also, if this works out, I want to have us make the arrests. Have some Spetsnaz soldiers be on call and ready, and get at least a squad or maybe a platoon. Have them prepared to come in quietly as civilians or tourists. Get their gear here as well. Have the commander come to see me for instructions once they are here. I will let you know when to implement this order, but I want them ready and waiting for me and not on an aircraft on the way to Afghanistan when I want them here." He pounded on the desk. "Do not say anything to Moscow about why I want them or what I suspect. The treasure needs to be our surprise. Those bastards will come here to claim credit for my discovery. We must wait until we have found out all their plans and we have captured the American and this Greek professor with the goods."

Bokhan bit his lip, "But, Mister Ambassador, don't you think this is premature? We don't really know what it means yet. I agree it could be very important, but in these kinds of cases we must have a full story and facts to make such serious charges. Let me work on this... at your direction, to put together a full dossier and make it a case that can hold up." Bokhan started to leave and then turned back on his heel, raising one finger, "And, do you not think our Greek colleagues should also get some credit? It is their country. They will look bad if they don't even know what we are doing.

Don't we at least owe them the courtesy of doing this together?"

As Igor listened he leaned back in his chair, "They are idiots! However, perhaps you have a point. A small point, but one nonetheless. Find a Spetsnaz group to stand by for my orders. Later on, at the same time I arrest these thieves and traitors, I will bring along some of the Greek political people and perhaps a policeman. Hear me on this, they must know nothing until I am ready. They are clumsy and cannot keep a secret. This arrest will be my glory, and I will not let them squander it with their petty bureaucracy. We're sending dead boys home every day from Afghanistan, and everyone in the Soviet Union is pissed off. We need to show Gorbachev a victory. That is what will get us attention in Moscow. These same Americans who are supporting the New Democracy are giving arms to the Afghanistan rebels that are killing our boys. We are not just fighting a political battle here, we are fighting a world war against the same enemy. Never doubt that these American consultants and advisors are our enemy."

Bokhan now remembered the conversation he overheard a few weeks earlier between Igor and his wife over Greek art. He decided this was the time to bring Igor up to date. "There may be something else you can use. I have been tracking a lead and waiting until we had sufficient evidence to bring it to you, and this latest information may play into that."

"Get on with it."

"One of our plants in the New Democracy office did take some photos of other photos she found in the history professor's briefcase. I had them analyzed and they are of some kind of sculpture. When I had other research done, it turns out that these are not known to exist in any public museum in the world. That could possibly be what the Greek surveillance team heard them discussing. With what we have picked up with our own research, it could be that these photos represent some Greek art that this professor knows about or actually has in his possession or under his control that is not known elsewhere. If that is the case and we can find it, you will have what you need, and this professor and the American spy will not be able to complain because they were going to steal it anyway. Greek statues that are unknown or not in some museum will be much easier to take."

Igor smiled, "Good work. Get me copies of the photos. I need to show them to Tatiana's uncle to keep him off my back."

He pointed at Bokhan, "From now on, the missing sculpture is your main job. You've got to solve the mystery. Get more information and find out what they are hiding, where it is, and let me know when we might expect the extra surveillance men here."

Bokhan returned to his office and sat thinking that when he first got this assignment, he thought it was a job which could have had the potential to enhance his chosen occupation. However, in the Soviet system, if a person was given a chance to prove they could handle greater responsibilities and they were not successful, no matter what the reason, it was the end of any progress for their career. Now it seemed that the job he had been given was to babysit an arrogant, unqualified, loud-mouthed showman. Igor would not listen to suggestions for on-the-job training and was proving too headstrong, which meant Bokhan's career and his family could be in jeopardy. He looked at the damaged religious icons in his desk drawer that Igor had so disdainfully thrown on the floor a few weeks earlier. For his family's sake and his own, he would try harder with Igor, but he feared the aberrant patterns of the ambassador's personality would be too difficult to overcome. He had to think of what to do.

A shadow crossed his door and along the glass looking out into the reception area, and he watched as a muscular man dressed in black passed the door. Bokhan could see the man wave off the ambassador's secretary, knock on the door to the Ambassador's office and then immediately enter.

Ambassador Andropov was sitting at his desk thinking about how the new information about some secret sculpture might solve his problems of the meddling uncle when he looked up to see a man with an expressionless face enter his office unannounced. The man continued to walk over to him confidently as though they knew each other. He recognized the man, but for appearances pretended that he had not seen him before. Igor leaned back indignantly. "Who the hell are you and what are you doing in my office?"

The man stopped a few feet away and smiled for the first time. "I am your new special advisor. I come with the blessings of the Honorable Valentine Gubanov. While I am here I will help you with your problems in security."

"I don't need any help. You can't just come in here and assign yourself a job." While he was speaking, Igor thought he heard a faint noise, sort of a low rumble coming from the man.

The man smiled again. "Do not concern yourself. I do not need an office, I will stay on one of the ships in the harbor belonging to the Soviet oil fleet. I will come and go as I wish. I will help your security people with some of their surveillance and you need not worry yourself with my activities." Tito did not tell Andropov that he felt safer on the Soviet ship than anywhere he could have been in Greece. The ship had good communications, guards, Russian food and little chance of phone or video intercepts from the opposition. Yes, he thought to himself, do not concern yourself, Mr. Ambassador. I know what I'm doing. Then he noticed the ambassador, who despite his arrogant appearance, looked nervous, and as he swallowed and fidgeted Tito could tell the man was working himself up to say something.

"I gave no orders for you to be here. You . . ."

"Mister Ambassador, I do not work for you. But I will help you in this problem of ... a failure of achievement."

"You can't . . ."

"I am Tito Petrovia. And I assure you that I can."

"But . . ."

"The election is almost here and you have to get my boss some sculpture for export. These two things will be settled very soon in a satisfactory way, and then I will return and leave you and the lovely Tatiana to your lives. Do not concern yourself over what I do or how I do it. Continue to do your job as you have been doing, but know I am here now and I see everything." The man touched the side of his head near the eyes.

"But . . ."

"Good day, Mr. Ambassador."

CHAPTER 25

Miraculously, Mark had managed to take enough time off the campaign to meet Vicki in Paris for a long weekend at a hotel on the Ile St. Louis and enjoy a much-anticipated one year anniversary of their relationship. It was the perfect time of the year to be in Paris: not too cool or too hot, no college kids crowding everything, and flowers everywhere. It was a magical atmosphere and they quickly became tourists swirling in and out of museums and cathedrals, hugging and kissing with abandon and with no concern of disapproval from the Parisians who relished signs of romantic affection. They enjoyed several hours in a bookstore called Shakespeare and Company where they perused towering stacks of books in narrow passageways with crowds of other booklovers. Mark had developed a new enthusiasm for Greek art and spent more time than normal in the Louvre museum, lingering over the Winged Victory at Samothrace, the Venus de Milo, and other magnificent pieces. He marveled over how the ancient artists with just a chisel and hammer could create the impression of draped fabrics to look so real on the beautiful bodies, and he pointed those attributes out to Vicki, speaking with the authority of one who felt as though he had in a short time become knowledgeable on ancient sculpture.

On the third evening, enjoying dinner at a sidewalk café in Montmartre after climbing to the top of the towering Sacre-Couer Basilica to watch the sunset over the city, Mark revealed to Vicki part of the secret he now carried. "Something has come up here that will require me to stay over in Greece for a little while longer."

"What? The campaign is almost over. What would detain you from coming home now?"

"Well, I've got this friend who I've mentioned to you, the one who is the professor of art and history. Anyway, he has discovered an archeological treasure of Greek sculptures that are like 2400 years old, and they have been buried in a cave for all that time.

"He wants to get them out of Greece, but he is afraid the current government and the Soviets will just steal it or sell it off to rich Russians or some other people who will just want to own it and have it their houses. These are not just some old trinkets. They are priceless art treasures. I gave him my word that I'd help him figure out how to protect them and get them out of Greece, and I'm the only person he has trusted with this great secret. I feel an obligation to try to do something because of his trust, and because of the value of the sculptures."

"But Mark, isn't that illegal? I thought if a historical treasure was found in a country, it belonged to that country. Greece must have had many of these kinds of finds and so isn't there a precedent regarding the legality? Why can't they just put it in a Greek museum? It seems like you are taking a big risk here."

"The Greek government is corrupt and it's broke. They hardly have the resources to take care of their existing treasures and some of them are being stolen and sold on the black market all the time. That is likely what would happen to this discovery. They may never even let the Greek public see it, but would just sell it off to the art underworld which would snap it up in an instant, and the Greek government would either be complicit or too incompetent to stop it."

Vicki frowned, "But they do have the power to arrest you and throw you in jail and do God knows what. Mark, it is very noble to try to help your friend and to save valuable artifacts, but you could be putting yourself at considerable risk here. Are you thinking about this idea rationally?"

"I hope so. I plan to make contact with our government to help. I'm going to turn all the intrigue over to other people as soon as possible and not try to smuggle anything out myself. I know my limitations and have no desire to take undue risk. The reason I'm telling you this is not only so you won't wonder what I'm doing or ask questions over the phone, which is likely being tapped, but also that I may need you to help at some point. I have a plan I'm working on. I'm sure they are listening in on my phone calls, so the next time I call, we will talk about another getaway weekend sort of like this one. That may be just the story I need to leave Greece for a clandestine meeting, and I need your help to sell it on the phone. When I call you about scheduling another weekend, I'd like you to call and book this same hotel and book your flight. On the same day we are supposed to leave, cancel both. If it ends up costing you, I'll make it up to you later."

Vicki shook her head, started to tear up and choked it down. "Mark, are you telling me you are not coming home soon, and on top of that that the Russians or other people are listening to my phone too?"

"I don't know, but I'm guessing it is likely. Sorry, but this will be over soon and I don't know about all the cloak and dagger stuff, but it's better to be safe than sorry. Don't worry. The only reason they might be listening to you is to hear what I have to say. But, just in case, we both need to be careful of what we're saying to each other until this is over. It won't take much longer than we had planned, maybe just another week or two. A month at the most."

Vicki looked over across the city toward the Eiffel tower lit against the night sky in the distance. She suddenly felt the crush of Mark being so wrapped up in this clandestine election and him being so far away, and now for an extended and undetermined time. Mark's new plans and his excitement abruptly changed the atmosphere of romance and joy she had expected and anticipated on the flight over. Mark's disclosure had spoiled all her plans and the mood for what she wanted and had planned to discuss here and now on an entirely more personal subject. She half whispered, "This is not good." She was quiet and bowed her head sullenly which was uncommon for her. She composed herself as best she could and looked back up at him. "Mark, one of the reasons I was so excited to be here with you in Paris, was to tell you that I'm pregnant."

Vicki looked down again and flashed a memory of her eagerness on the flight to France to find the perfect time to tell Mark how her enthusiasm had been building since she found out. She had been thinking about the special way she would tell Mark and how excited he would be. In her daydreams on the aircraft, everything went perfectly. Now it was all in a jumble and nothing had turned out as she had planned. She looked back up at Mark.

Mark's face was washed with a look of amazement without the joy. His body pulled back a few inches from her. "I... What?"

Vicki continued, "I am about eight or nine weeks in and I'll start to show soon. I'm sure this happened the last time you came home, and I've been to the doctor now. I am thinking we should get married, perhaps here, perhaps tomorrow. Damn, none of what I want to say is coming out like I had hoped. I didn't tell you earlier or on the phone because I did not want you worrying and not being able to do your job. I was thinking of you!

"Then I thought what a wonderful surprise it would be to tell you here in Paris. Now it seems you will not be coming home soon, like you said you would. Now it seems you are going to be stretched out in Greece indefinitely in this...." she waved her hand in the air, "...thing. We need to get married and I can't just be pregnant in my job alone in Washington and around all my friends and seeing my family and not be married." She threw her napkin on her plate and leaned back with both hands pushing against on the table and gave him a hard look. "I assume that is what you want too?"

Mark, still flabbergasted said, "Why didn't ... how could you keep this news from me? It's just not fair to drop this news on me like this."

"Fair! Fair has nothing to do with it. This is our lives we are talking about here. I did what I thought was for the best." She gave him a hard, angry look. "Whatever." She waved her hand. "We are here now, and we are going to have a child. I know this is not the way we both thought it would happened, but it has. We have to deal with what is happening with us now, not some ideal of ..." Vicki looked down again, realizing this conversation was getting further out of hand and nothing like as she had imagined. Flashes of her mother and father fighting filled her mind, the very fear she had been pushing away from her thoughts the past weeks rushed in.

Mark now leaned back towards her. "You know I want everything about us to work, but I'm in the middle of something here. I've given my word and ... can't we just wait until I get home. It will be no more than another few weeks, maybe less. If we wait until then, we can . . ."

Now with a combination of anger and fear, "You've not spoken of the child! Our child." Vicki's eyes filled with tears and they spilled and rolled down her cheeks. "My God. I just told you I'm pregnant. And you ...

How could I have been so wrong about you. Stay here. I need some time alone." She pushed herself up, rattling the glasses and a small vase of flowers tipped over on the table as she rushed away, as Mark, still shell-shocked, sat staring at his plate.

He looked up to call her back, but she was gone. He was numb. He finally got the waiter's attention, paid, and walked in the direction she had left, half expecting to find her any moment, wandering through the part of Montmartre behind the Basilica of Sacre-Coeur past streets lined with street vendor artists looking for tourists to paint. Finally, not finding her he sat down on a curb to think. It had been difficult enough to try to figure out what to do about the campaign and then the art treasure. Finding out he was to be a father so unexpectedly and then Vicki suddenly asking to get married was such a great shock and so much to process.

He remembered hearing that pregnant women had rushes of hormones that made them irrational and he decided to find her, and try to reason with her, to decide what to do that was a more orderly approach to the situation they were in. It made more sense to plan a marriage when he returned from Greece. He also realized that he needed to let her know he wanted to get married and become a father and that he was just stunned earlier, not that he wasn't pleased. He felt more comfortable with a plan to follow and he went back to the hotel, but when he got back to the hotel room he found that she had packed her things and was gone.

The next morning Mark returned to Greece and tried to call Vicki, but she did not pick up and did not return his calls or answer his messages. He then wrote to her, with no reply. He felt both guilt and anger: guilt over the unresolved marriage discussion and also his not being there to celebrate and support her in the pregnancy; but also anger over her dropping the news on him as she did. She had acknowledged though that he would have to finish out the campaign, and now she knew of the importance of the sculpture. He recognized the guilt he felt that he was not going to be with her during this important time in both of their lives was exacerbated because his parents were dead and she was somewhat estranged from hers. He felt like a soldier off in a war, but knew there was more to the choice he had made than that. For right now though, he needed to finish the business at hand in Greece.

Igor and Bokhan were listening to a report from the security staff about the mistake the security people made by not keeping a close watch on the American who had left the country. Bokhan decided to take charge to get ahead of Igor's anger and asked harshly, "That American went to Paris last week. Why did we not have people go with him?"

The man fidgeted, "It seemed he just went to the airport and then he left, and we did not have advance notice of it or have people who could follow him. It was too late for us to get someone on his flight. We found his destination at the airport and had our people in Paris find him and follow him, but he met some young woman there for a romantic weekend, and we have some photos of them walking about and kissing, but it did not seem like this was spying of any kind. They did the regular tourist things: museums, restaurants, walking in the Tuileries Garden. We could not get into the room to put a listening device there until the last night. We discovered the woman works for the United States Congress in a clerical research position, and we notified the Washington Embassy to put a track on her."

Bokhan said, "We haven't already done that?"

"I don't know sir. We did see that they did not stay for as long as they had rented the room. The woman left early and during the night. She came in, packed and then, poof. He came in about two or three hours later. Then he was gone the next morning. One of the people following them said she was crying or something, like a lover's quarrel. It did not seem like espionage to the people we had in Paris."

Igor now inserted himself. "I do not want you to fail me again. Put people on him who are prepared to go wherever he goes at a moment's notice. No more excuses."

Bokhan, embarrassed by the security lapse, pointed his finger at the security man. "Make sure our people in Washington follow up on the woman."

Tito sat in a corner of the room humming softly to himself as though he was not paying attention.

The next week Igor, Bokhan and several of the officials at the Soviet Embassy were beginning to panic about what else they could do to influence the declining fortunes of the Papandreou campaign. The Greeks around the prime minister seemed to believe in the rosy predictions of the local pollsters, which the Soviets knew to be playing to Papandreou's ego and not giving him accurate results. Even with the steps the Soviets had taken to provide some of the Communist votes for Papandreou, the election research still showed a decline in his support from the previous polling. As they asked around the room for ideas most of the suggestions were predictable and would have little effect. The intimidating Tito Petrovia, was sitting in a corner quietly humming to himself and not participating in the conversation.

Igor who was warming to his newly found love of intrigue, and in part to show the menacing Tito that he was a bold leader, posed a more radical idea. "What if we use our contacts in the media to suggest that the United States and NATO are planning an invasion of Greece to take it over by force, and they were disguising it as a NATO military exercise?"

Bokhan shook his head since he knew no one would actually believe an invasion scenario. "Why would they do such a thing? What would they need with Greece? Why would they want all of Greece's problems? No one will believe that."

Igor countered, "But the proposition would stir up the idea that the West was making imperialist plans and could not be trusted. That would spill over to the New Democracy. It does not matter if people actually believe it, the rumor would plant the seed of doubt and suspicion. And it might cause the Greeks to buy more Soviet arms. A new arms sale here would be good for us to deliver to our leaders in Moscow."

Bokhan, knowing the proposal was just another of Igor's off-the-wall ideas, and that he was not open to discussion nor could he be dissuaded from the idea nodded. "Yes, Ambassador. I will discuss this idea with our propaganda people and see how best to promote it. They will have ideas on what media to use and how to direct the story." Bokhan hoped that in a few days Igor would have forgotten about this conversation and the idea. He would protect his ambassador and not send such a ludicrous plan to Moscow where it would be seen as a bad reflection, not only for Igor but for him as well.

In the corner, Tito gathered his things as the meeting wound down. Unnoticed by any except Bokhan who was taking an increased interest in this imposing new man, the small crease of a smile moved across Tito's lips.

CHAPTER 26

While listening to the sounds of singing Cyrilla made in the kitchen, Petkas helped his boys get ready for school, finding one's lost sock and making sure the other had his last night's homework papers tucked away in his book sack. They laughed and he joked with them as he usually did, but inside he was worried because he was on a path that would change this idyllic life forever. He and his family were headed for a dramatic change because of the lost sculptures, but he knew he could not share his secret with his family yet, more for their protection than anything. His wife came in smiling and gathered the boys to go to school, pecked him on the cheek, and left.

He followed them outside and slowly looked up and down the street where they had lived with the same friends and neighbors since he and Cyrilla had married over 15 years earlier and which had been the only home his boys had ever known. The passion for his secret and the enthusiasm for his find had been bottled up in him for several years. Now that the time to act was fast approaching, the unforeseeable future frightened Petkas, and once again he thought through all the obvious options for a path to take with the sculpture.

Each idea he considered further bound him to the task ahead and each one was filled with considerable risk. On top of the danger, he felt like he was cheating his family. It was as though he was having an affair with the beauty of the smooth, vulnerable stone, and now that he had shared the confidence with someone who just a few months ago was a stranger, it made keeping the secret from his family feel like even more of a betrayal. He had to get this worry out of his head, and he left for work thinking that the activity at the office would be a welcome distraction for his constant fixation on the sculptures.

On May 15, with the election fast approaching, one of the wealthy Greeks financing the campaign wanted a status report. For much of the campaign, the financers had been content to let Maria Beckett handle things. But now some of the more nervous donors wanted a better understanding of the details and assurances they had bet their money on the right horse. In response, Maria asked Mark to give the man and some of his friends a briefing in his office located a few blocks south of Aeros Park and about a dozen blocks from the National Archeological Museum which he and Petkas had visited several times. She felt a briefing by the American who once had worked in the White House would give the financers confidence - the pros from Dover syndrome.

Mark put together a presentation of slides and charts that could be projected on the wall and with a small cassette tape of commercials took a taxi to the office building to meet with the man and several of his associates. He took an hour to give a thorough briefing that included showing the commercials, giving anecdotes from his trip to Arta, discussing the poling results, and providing a handout that was a summary of the campaign's activities. As he finished they began to discuss the promising improvements for the party in the upcoming vote and their future prospects when suddenly they heard the distinct bap, bap, bap sound of gunfire outside the building. A security man rushed in, carrying an Israeli made Uzi machine gun, and moved everyone away from the windows to an interior board room with no windows, but not before they heard many more gunshots and screams from outside, as well as shouts from people in nearby offices and the banging of upturned furniture and the slamming of doors.

They were kept in the room which was surrounded by armed guards all carrying Uzis for about an hour and could hear through the walls the faint sounds of the approach and departure of emergency sirens. Later the leader of the security detail came back into the room and told them that a gun battle had taken place right in front of their building and that several people had been killed or hurt. The ambulances and city police were clearing up the street and they had to stay indoors for another 30 minutes. The wealthy New Democracy man who was worried about being kidnapped or assassinated by radical forces before this incident, became increasingly afraid.

It was late afternoon before Mark got back to the campaign offices and shared the adventure with the campaign staff who had heard reports on the radio of the shootout on the street. They filled Mark in on the story that the police had seen a man on a stolen motorcycle and when they approached and asked him to stop, he opened fire. Everyone speculated how fortunate it was that Mark was in the meeting instead of back on the street or he could have been caught in the crossfire. Three policemen had been killed, along with the wanted man. Two others who participated in the gun battle escaped.

Mark considered what could have happened and was grateful that he had not been on the street. He remembered what it felt like after a mortar attack or distant skirmish on the borders of the bases when he had been in Vietnam and the luck of the draw when a rocket round missed or erratic scattershot bullets bypassing other buildings and bunkers sometimes would thud into nearby buildings where he worked or ping off close metal objects. Aside from those intense periods, he had generally felt safe from hostile contact even in that war zone. Today brought all those feelings back.

He decided not to write to tell Vicki about this incident as she already was worried about him and had mentioned something in one of their recent conversations before Paris about terrorists killing court officials. He also wondered after what happened in Paris if she still cared or even opened his letters, which still went unanswered. He had an unsettled feeling regarding how to talk to others in the office about the shooting incident since it had happened so close to him. He had that all too familiar awareness from his days in Vietnam that people had died near him, yet he remained unscathed. He had carried that perception and the feeling of nearby death since the war and it was like a phantom weight that was hard to shake.

Igor hung up the phone from the first positive conversation he had

had with Tatiana's uncle in some time. The uncle's voice had boomed, "I finally think I can see a leader in you. The pictures and research that showed the sculpture does not exist elsewhere shows me good detective work. The transcripts of the conversations of the Greek and the American tell me that they are hiding some big secret and your staff have done a good job of spying on them. You have impressed me. Use Tito if you need his help. He has special skills. So now you must go and get them for me. When you bring these things to me, you will pay me back for all I have done for you and my niece."

Igor now felt more accepted by Tatiana's uncle and had some assurance that his career path would be confirmed if he got these carved rocks for Tatiana's uncle and his friends. Her uncle seemed so pleased that he did not even ask for the details of how many sculptures there were or what shape they were in. Questions he could not have answered. Fortunately, Igor now felt he had some flexibility on when he delivered the goods, how many he had to provide to the uncle and how much of the remaining sculptures he could use as bargaining chips elsewhere. Maybe he could make some money out of the transaction as well. He then realized he was late for a campaign meeting.

Now, with the huge secret between them, Mark and Petkas often found it awkward to talk around others in the campaign. Whatever the subject of the conversation around the office or at dinner with friends, in the back of their minds they were always thinking of the sculptures. At last they got away for one of their regular walks. Because of what had almost happened to Mark, they were even more aware of the random danger in Greece and careful of eavesdroppers, and Petkas had become obsessed with his family's safety. Lately he had been distracted and began to repeat a dialogue with Mark, but which was mostly talking to himself, that he continued when they were alone together.

He spoke in an intense whisper, "Mark, I am so torn about what I have to do. How can I risk the lives of my family over this?"

When they stopped for a break to let a street vendor make them sandwiches, Petkas continued walking back and forth with his head down and speaking in a subdued tone of voice. Several times he crossed his arms over his chest and then wiped his hands on his pants legs while he paced. He would glance up at Mark to see if Mark was watching him, then with the sandwiches in hand Mark led him toward the park over by the Greek Parliament.

As they ate Petkas rocked back and forth. "I don't want to take my wife and my children away from the only home and only county they have ever known, but I see no other choice. I have not talked about what I found in the cave with my wife as yet, and I feel guilty about that as well, and as you can see Mark, I'm a mess.

"This collection of sculptures represents the best of my country's astonishing artistic history. These pieces show a momentum in technique, design, technology and artistry that was not apparent for many more centuries. Mark, there is no comparison to anything else in the world. It eats at my soul to think of these being separated and becoming hat racks in some Russian's home."

Mark let Petkas rant as he watched to see if anyone was close enough to overhear. He could understand the stress his friend might be feeling, but he also realized that if Petkas did not get a grip on himself and stop the rambling, he would soon have to get in the face of this gentle, intelligent man and straighten him out.

As he arrived back at the campaign office after the lunch walk with Petkas, Maria called Mark into her secure office that was soundproofed. He could see that she had a serious, almost pained look on her face. "Mark, I had a visit with a security official I've known for many years and whom I trust." She rapped her knuckles on her desk a few times with her head down and suddenly looked up at him with an intensity in her eyes. "What I need to say is an example of how naïve Americans are and how they don't understand the problems that can exist in a violent world. It is about the incident that happened a few days ago. What you did not know at the time was that the man on the motorcycle was a terrorist who two weeks before had killed a government prosecutor. He was wanted by the police and was spotted by them accidentally when they saw a motorcycle in an unauthorized area in front of the building where you were for the meeting. Three policemen were killed along with this guy, Tsoutsouvis, when he started to take off and would not stop at their command and they got into a gun battle."

Mark immediately put his mind back into that day and the secure room where he sat nervously with the other men waiting for the 'all-clear' message from the security people. He instinctively, almost by rote, repeated the same thing he had been saying for a couple of days to people who inquired about the incident. "Wow. I'm just glad they got that guy."

Maria nodded and pursed her lips. "What you don't know is what I learned from my friend in the security service, which is that Tsoutsouvis was likely there waiting for you to come out. He and his accomplices had no other reason to be in the area and should by all logic have been in hiding. He was carrying a note with your name and description on it. The chance to kill an American working with New Democracy must have been too much of a temptation. Those policemen who were killed in the shootout likely saved your life."

Mark felt something like ice water wash through him and then drain down leaving his upper body hollow as this news made him sink further into the chair. Everything in the room slowed down, and he felt a slight ringing in his ears. "You mean he came for me? But how did he know I was there?" He felt queasy as he thought about the random chance of those policemen stopping the man on the motorcycle, and then dying for it. He imagined himself walking out of the building into a hail of bullets.

Maria leaned over and touched him on his arm, "That's one of the reasons why you are followed all the time. The other side wants to find where you are in case they decide to act on something like this shooting. You folks from the U.S. have not had to consider this kind of surveillance, political terror and violence. You are lucky and you are naïve. The world we live in here in Europe has constant elements of political terror and a certain level of intrigue, things we have to address on a daily basis. You should hope it never finds its way to America."

She thought for a minute. "I don't think the PASOK people would have done this. I know many of them and this is not their style. I think this came from the Soviets. Maybe they are seeing how bad Papandreou is doing and thought your assassination would shake things up. It would have exposed you and Angus helping us here, and that would have hurt us in the election. The shooting was likely contracted out to N-17 who are wild men, and that way it would not lead back to the Soviets. Still, it's a bold move even for the Russians. I did not think that Andropov and his staff were this aggressive. You're damn lucky to be alive and need to keep a low profile. I've got to go to a meeting, but you sit here for a few minutes and absorb this. Start to think how you can vary your patterns of movement and make sure you know how to shake the tails at any time you feel a threat. You've got to become street smart and look out for trouble."

Mark did sit there and thought of the policemen who must have gone into the situation thinking they were in a traffic stop of a stolen motorbike and then had been caught in the gunfire of waiting assassins. It was likely he would never properly be able to thank the Athens police or the families of the dead men for saving his life. Although he understood the political dimension, it seemed so unreal that some people had decided to take a chance to kill him in order to benefit a political campaign. Maria was right, he was naïve and he did hope this kind of terror would never come to the United States.

Later that same week, Bokhan arranged for a meeting with Igor Andropov and his senior staff, during which Igor paced in front of the room, "I need to know more about what is happening in the political campaign. I had a call yesterday from Moscow, and they are worried that Papandreou is slipping and will not do well, and could even lose. They must be running their own polling without telling me. How many people do we have inside of the New Democracy party?"

The security liaison answered, "Three, Mr. Ambassador."

"Put more people on monitoring the phones, and have a couple more people put inside the campaign to tell us what they are doing. I want accounts from them with anything unusual happening every two days, even with mundane activity."

The security liaison covering any tracks that might imply he was not doing his job quickly answered. "We have sent in reports on the successful message of the television advertising by the capitalists. The polling that we are doing shows that unfortunately their lies are cutting into some of Papandreou's success."

Bokhan, making sure Igor's wishes were well known, said to the security men and political operatives present, "We need to go ahead with the plan to get some of the communist party voters to vote for the socialist party." He looked at the staffer. "Finish our planning and make sure that is set up to happen."

One of the other staff that had not been party to earlier conversations by Bokhan and Igor said, "But our communist party leaders would not want to do that."

Igor erupted, "I don't care what they want. We have a plan do to it if we need to. Moscow is more important than these backwater organizations here. We are losing prestige because of the damn Afghanistan situation. We cannot have the election here look like the philosophy of communism is becoming less attractive. Our leaders are looking for us to support them and have a strong result here.

"Another thing, use the people we have connected to the media here and in our political operation to start the rumors that there is a plan to move the U.S. Sixth fleet from Naples to Athens. Make the rumors simple. Have news people report they have seen documents saying they are making plans for the move. We must have people here thinking that they need to increase their strength in the Greek military and they need a new Soviet arms deal to protect Greece from the west. Make it a black and white socialism and communism vs. capitalism fight." He turned to Bokhan, "You should have thought of that! I should not have to come up with all the good ideas here." Bokhan realized that Igor had forgotten an earlier version of this same crazy idea which Bokhan had ignored.

Tito Petrovia hummed in the corner.

The meeting continued with Igor making demands and ordering his staff to carry them out. He kept his demands on what he thought was needed for their success clear and unambiguous, although he gave the staff no suggestions on methods of how to achieve the results he expected. Bokhan felt his attempts to educate and manage the ambassador were fast becoming unraveled.

A few days later as Mark walked to the campaign office for the morning meeting, he saw demonstrators on the streets carrying signs demanding the removal of U.S. military bases on Greek soil. He could tell that the demonstrators were led by well-organized managers, who got them to chant their slogans in unison with the use of bullhorns. The signs and banners had the look of being professionally produced. Some of them were slogans in English for the international television cameras supporting the Soviet Union's "rescue" of Afghanistan and criticizing the United States of "imperialism" against Greece. Mark could appreciate that the protest parade was well planned by the socialist or communist parties as an election ploy to stir up anti-Western sentiment. It was working. He had heard the day before that two United States sailors had been beaten outside a bar last week, and three days before one of the airmen from the Hellenikon Air Base had been stabbed near the entrance to the base.

He thought that if the situation in Greece did not turn around soon there would be more and perhaps insurmountable pressure to remove the U.S. bases and find another place to station American military forces in the eastern Mediterranean. He did not know how the pressure to remove the U.S. bases might affect the campaign, but if they were not asked to leave now, it would likely still be an issue by the time the next election rolled around in four years.

After the morning meeting, he and Petkas left for their mid-day walk. Mark noticed that Petkas was becoming even more unnerved. Time was running out and they had to come up with a plan to do something soon, and the needs of the campaign had been taking their attention away from deciding what to do about the statues. Petkas was distracted to the point he was becoming sloppier in the way he handled his communications and in the haphazard way he carried himself in the office and on the streets. Mark was growing concerned about him.

"The sculpture must be excavated carefully and surreptitiously, and moved to a place of safety. It will take people who know how to move heavy objects and significant equipment to transport them. They were each in their own wrapping for protection, but that has long since disintegrated. They are vulnerable in that rocky space and falling rocks and tremors have caused some minor damage that can be fixed, but if there was a significant tremor many more could be damaged.

"They will likely have to be moved in a hurry to keep them from being discovered and I just do not know how to handle that. We need experts… quick and quiet experts. So now we need to talk about what you can do to help me. You made sense when you said asking one of the Greek ship owners for help would not work. I agree that too many people would have to know of our plans working with the ship owners and word would get out. We need a plan now! I can't take the uncertainty anymore. You've got to do something."

Mark and Petkas were just two blocks from the National Garden on Leoforos Vasilissis Sofias Street walking through the Byzantine and Christian Museum. While Mark kept an eye out for the familiar faces of the watchers, he steered Petkas into a corner where they had been meandering from room to room. Remembering what Vicki had said to him before he left about his being too passive and misunderstood, he pushed Petkas against the corner of the wall and held him still with his forearm across Petkas's chest, then leaned close in his face. "Stanos, look at me." He grabbed his arm with his other hand and squeezed. "No, LOOK at me. You are coming unglued. You are ranting and not watching out for security. If you want to get caught and have the Soviets take these sculptures you have been protecting for so long, just keep up your mumbling in public. I told you I would help, and I'm ready to now, but not if you fall apart. If you continue to babble in public again, I'm done and will return to Washington. Now, we don't have a plan right now, but we need to talk about it in a secure place, which is not here! Do you understand, and do you agree?"

The color drained from Petkas's face and he seemed to crumble as he slumped against the wall and blinked his eyes a couple of times. "Yes. I'm sorry. I have not been sleeping and I've let my worry consume me. I will take a sleeping pill tonight and let's decide tomorrow where to meet and plan to move on to the final phase. I'm no good to anyone in the shape I'm in right now. I've not done any real campaign work in several days. I'm afraid I am having a panic attack. Thank you for putting up with me and trying to straighten me out. I'll be better tomorrow. I'm going to leave here now and catch a taxi and go home and get some rest before the boys get home from school. Please make excuses for me."

Mark let off some of the pressure on Petkas's chest. "You need to do that. If you don't get yourself together, I'm leaving right after the election and will not help you. I'm serious. No more of your whining, rambling bullshit. You've made a choice. Live with it."

"Sorry. You are right. I need to go home and get some sleep. I will be better tomorrow. I promise."

One of the secretaries in the New Democracy office was finishing up her work for the day. As she put the plastic covering over her typewriter and stacked the papers on her desk in neat piles to await the next morning's rush of activity, she also prepared a small paper bag that earlier had held her lunch. In it were some copies of advertising plans, polling, references to the New Democracy candidate's upcoming campaign stops and a brief transcript of part of a conversation …something she accidently overhead and wrote down about some objects belonging to Alexander the Great. She would pass it on to the man who waited by the bus stop, as she did every evening when she had something to share with the mysterious people who paid her.

CHAPTER 27

Mark met Maria Beckett in her home and she immediately turned up the music playing in the den. He then sat close to her so they could talk with some privacy. Maria could tell that Mark was worried and looked at him with concern that Mark's sudden visit might be some serious problem about the campaign. He began in a voice just above a whisper, "Stanos Petkas and I are in a situation that I cannot fully disclose to you, but it is serious and important. For now, you need to trust me and Petkas. He is under a lot of stress. I'm not here about the campaign, but we are involved in something that could prove to be far more important. You have a lot of experience in espionage matters, and Petkas and I have little to none. He's starting to come unraveled, but I think he has himself under control for now; however, we are both in over our heads. We need your advice and perhaps your direct help. I know that is a lot to ask without telling you exactly what the problem is, but we need . . ."

Maria held up her hand. "Don't over think or over talk about whatever you two are doing. I can see from your face that it is serious. I have seen you two in your quiet confidences and whispers around the office, and I have been in many situations where I could not disclose information to my colleagues. I understand." She looked around the room and then leaned even closer to Mark. "The election is almost here and we have done most of what we need to do. The election must come first and I don't want the little mystery you and Stanos are involved in to get in the way of your obligations to this campaign. That being said, what can I do?"

Mark explained that he and Petkas occasionally had to lose the surveillance following them, and they also wished to be able to take time away from the campaign without being asked any questions. He said he also needed to contact a person in the U.S. State Department or CIA familiar with Greece on a matter of international importance.

"Does your problem have anything to do with the attempt on your life?"

"No. Something else."

Maria leaned back and thought for a moment, "Well, I will do anything I can to help. I can take care of the campaign issues. It's almost over as it is. And I know a couple of people here in town I can trust if you need some muscle help. Come to me, but use practical measures so that the watchers don't suspecting anything. Both you and Petkas need to remember, there are people involved here with our opponents who can make you disappear. You just saw that because you are an American you are not somehow exempt from harm. You know now what they tried to do to you last week. The PASOK secret police are bad, but the Soviets are much more dangerous and more experienced. If you are doing something that is encroaching on their turf, and it sounds like you are, be very careful. I don't know people in the CIA much anymore but it sounds like you need the most devious, crafty, sneaky bastard in the universe, who will go to any lengths and stop at nothing to achieve his goal."

Mark leaned back and smiled, remembering a CIA agent he had met in Panama. "I know just the guy. He's in the CIA and likely does not know anything about Greece but he is a real son of a bitch."

Maria smiled at the characterization. "Well, if you do know someone with those qualities already, I suggest you get in touch with him. That's much easier than trying to establish a new relationship and develop trust. Go to the American Embassy, ask to speak to the man in the political office we met with a few weeks ago to brief on the campaign. Get him to let you use their secure phone. He can arrange for you to call this man you know, but that will only work if the guy in intelligence back at Langley remembers you. He would not take your call otherwise. Try to get to the embassy without being followed. Take two or three taxis and spend time going in and out of stores, hotels and such to lose the people who are almost certainly following you."

CHAPTER 28

Petkas sat down with his wife, Cyrilla, in the quiet of their backyard while the children were playing at a friend's house. He had planned this conversation and steeled himself for it over the past two days. He told her everything: from the first day he had understood the clues that took him on the journey to follow Alexander the Great's visit to Delphi, to the land belonging to the Anatos family, the parents of Alexander's friend from school, to finding the sculpture. Near the end he told her that soon they would have to leave Greece for their own safety. He concluded with, "The Greece that I love and the place where we had hoped to live at least for the near future does not exist anymore. It is gone and has been replaced by greed and incompetence and the rigid insanity of dogma that is leading the country into ruin. I am used to teaching students who want to learn about the glory of our history. Soon the government we have here will take steps to change that history. Soon they will make up lies like they tell in Russia. We must go to a place where our children can learn the truth in an atmosphere of freedom, a place where they can be whatever they wish to be. Here they will be pressed into the mush of a life dictated by a philosophy that wants everything to be distorted and controlled. Here there will not be anything exceptional, and our children need the chance to reach their full potential. Here that is not within the realm of possibility."

Cyrilla sat across from him, shocked at the news, "How can this have happened? What have you gotten yourself and us into? We are just a simple family living in the suburbs of Athens. You are a college professor. We are not spies. We have to live here. We have neighbors, friends and other relatives here. How can all that we know and have in our lives just change? Of course, I know how screwed up the government is, and I can see people out of work and complaining. But how can we just leave?"

Petkas took her hands, "The collection of sculptures is the most important find maybe in all of art history. It defines what Greeks are. It defines me…us. These pieces of stone have become the way to identify Greece's honor. If we stand for anything it is to rescue these treasures, and you may be right to blame me for not telling you sooner, but I'm in too deep now. I realized a few weeks ago that I no longer have a choice. I can't stay here after what I have done and also what I've hidden from the Papandreou government. They will find out whether I stay or go. If I'm here it will be the end of us.

"You and the boys speak fairly good English already. We can have a much better life in America. It is freer and they will have a superior environment for our kids. Our son with special needs will have a better life. Better care. Better schools. There will be more interesting things and activities for you and the boys to do. There are millions of Greeks there. We have friends there we know already. We will not be alone, and after a time, we can come back for visits. Please understand me. The secret I'm involved with goes to the bedrock of my life. I will be crushed and empty if I cannot go through with it. I love you and the boys more than anything, but the plan to rescue the sculpture is an absolutely necessary."

Cyrilla stood and paced back and forth in the yard, "But we cannot just move like normal people. From what you have told me, we will be like refugees carrying everything in our hands. What photos do we take? What relics from the past generations of our families? What will we tell our friends, our family, my aunt and cousins who live nearby. Do I take my father's war medals, my mother's skillet she used to raise us and feed us as her mother did before her? Do we take books in English or Greek? Our children only know this place here."

Petkas came over and hugged her. "It will be hard at first. I will see what we can do about getting more of our things out of Greece and shipped to us after we leave. Perhaps we can return in a few years. We can visit, and our friends and relatives can come see us where we are. They can send us things. It seems to be more traumatic now than it will be after we have moved. As you know the house is likely bugged. We should only talk about our plans to leave when we are here in the yard or on walks where they cannot hear. But I must warn you not to say anything to anyone or speak of this in the house or on a phone. We will get through the move okay, but I'm telling you now so you can start to think of what to take. We must be prepared to move on short notice. I'm afraid there is no other choice."

CHAPTER 29

Mark and Petkas sat back to back on the hillside of Mount Lycabettus largely hidden by trees and shrubs after they had outdistanced the followers on a fast climb. About halfway up they had cut to one side and into a thicket of woods where now they were catching their breath. Today, while they kept a careful lookout, was the important talk about what they were actually going to propose to get the sculpture out of Greece. They had both researched several options, all needing to consider the value, fragility, weight, remoteness, and the complex logistics of moving the heavy yet fragile objects stored in the cave. They knew that it was too big a job for them to handle, or even for them to manage with some hired help in Greece. They needed outside help and help with lots of logistical, technical and political muscle. That meant the U.S. or one of the European countries like England or Germany, and as they talked those options quickly narrowed down to the U.S. They discussed the international scandal it would cause if they were caught and how to pitch the idea to the U.S. to convince them to get involved.

Mark said to Petkas, that he knew now that very hard choices would be required, "I can't imagine anyone will come in here and invade the sovereign soil of Greece just for some ancient sculptures. We've got to make the sculpture a legitimate high priority for the U.S. to take such a risk. We've got to find a good reason and explain it, and we need something more than just the sculptures to motivate the action like greed, political dynamics … something. Plus, we've got to get them out of here soon."

Mark had been thinking of this moment since his talk with Maria a few days ago. He could feel now was the time he'd need to push Petkas and they both would have to develop a stiff spine to execute any plan. "To have a chance of getting my government involved I'm going to need measurements of the size of the statues. Are they all the same or are some different and how? I'm going to need the pictures you took before in the cave as well as new ones. Photos of all of them. I need a summary of your research about the sculpture, and a simple description of the story you have been telling me for the past several weeks. We must be able to make the reader see what we see about how it's all real. No one will believe me or you just because we tell this story. I will need photos and proof and we need to establish value."

Petkas frowned, "But that will mean that I have to go back into the cave again and it will be risky with the surveillance we've gotten." Mark nodded. "We cannot help it. The people I am thinking about will want every bit of evidence we can provide to believe as we do and then be motivated to act on it. Stealing a country's treasure is a very risky international project, and there would be serious implications if we were caught trying to get these things out of Greece. We will have to convince them that what we have is incredibly valuable for them to consider taking the huge risk of getting caught taking it out of Greece without your government's permission. You will have to make those arguments. I don't have the expertise.

"To convince them you will need to write up a sort of presentation that I will have to make. It will have to be no more than a few pages to go along with photos, measurements, and maps. If the sculptures are in a cave like you say, you may need a flash to get good photos. You've got to show more than those Polaroids did. You need to do the research on the kind of film and camera that will work in such a dark place so people can examine the detail on the sculptures and see where they are and how they are positioned in the cave. Get a better camera if that is needed. Starting tonight, practice taking photos in your basement in low light or with the light of some flashlights to make sure you can take good photos using whatever light is in that cave. You may need that high speed Ektachrome film that will do better in dark places.

"We have to make those people see what you see and need to document everything in the cave and the surrounding area outside the cave. Close ups and wide shots. We will need detailed maps on where it is. You've got to tell the story of the history of the treasure and how you found it in a few pages. I don't believe the people I'm thinking about will read much on the first pass. If they believe it, they will come back for lots more detail. Now, can you do all that?"

Petkas's shoulders sagged, "It's so much to do and I'm particularly afraid of going back to the cave at the height of the campaign, with both of us being watched and our phones and everything being listened to. The terrorist on the motorcycle getting shot in central Athens along with the three policemen bothers me. With everything happening to us, and the surveillance, how will you manage getting the help?"

Mark now felt some anger at Petkas suddenly becoming afraid. "That terrorist guy has nothing to do with us or the sculpture! Look, I've said I would help you and I'm someone whose word is good, but we're on a clock here. I've got to leave as soon as possible after the election. I've got personal things that I have to handle back in the U.S. and can't stay much longer after the election, which is just over a week from now. The people following us will likely drop off the surveillance after the vote so that is the best time to make our move. If I'm going to help you with your sculpture, it will have to be now."

He could see from the look on his face that Petkas now needed some positive reassurance. "With your proof, I'll have to arrange a meeting outside Greece to have a long conversation, and if they want to take the risk to help us, we'll see what they come up with as a plan. If we don't think their plan will work, we can both back out then. The key to making it happen will be to convince them that what you have found is real, that the sculptures are a missing link like you have told me, and that they are valuable enough to risk an international incident and major embarrassment to get them out. It's a tall order and I'm not sure they will go for it. First step is that you've got to write the descriptive document and get the photos. So, we need to have a way to make sure you can really lose our followers to go to Delphi."

Petkas seemed to be more positive now, "I know you're right; but, won't they be much more suspicious of me if they can tell I am purposefully losing the followers?"

"Your trip to Delphi is the last time it will really matter. From here on out if we don't get help it won't matter how many are chasing after us.

From now on we need to be super sneaky. And we have to plan to get the hell out of Greece quickly after that."

Petkas bowed his head. "It's likely I will have to leave Greece no matter what happens with the sculpture. I guess it's time to gird my loins as the warriors of old." He laughed. "Not something I've been looking forward to, but I can't be timid or hesitant any longer. I'm ready. Okay, let's talk about how to lose the followers," Petkas said, as he looked back at Mark with a firm and resigned face.

CHAPTER 30

Mark and Petkas came out of the campaign office, walked together down the street and quickened their pace when they noticed two people following them. They zigzagged through three smaller stores and exited out a back entrance in each one, which every time gained more space between them and the followers, then they entered a large department store, that was not crowded because of the bad economy, parted and then each of them took a separate elevator to the top floor.

Once they arrived, they hit all the down buttons on both of the elevators. Both Petkas and Mark switched to their back-up clothing in a corner by the exit steps. After listening for footsteps on the nearby stairs and being satisfied that the followers were not using them to come up, Petkas took off down the stairs. Mark moved to the other set of stairs and finished his disguise by putting on a coat identical to the one Petkas had and the checkered hat Petkas had been wearing. They were both wearing black pants, so at a distance moving quickly, Mark thought if he leaned down a little to compensate for the height difference, he could pass for Petkas for a short time at least.

Mark waited by the exit staircase on the other side of the large room packed with household goods for sale and held the door to the steps open about halfway. He was glad that there were not too many shoppers on the fourth floor of the department store. When the elevator opened and he noticed one of the men who had been following them come out and look around for them, Mark moved into the stairwell slowly enough to know that his back and the distinctive hat would be seen and that the door would close slowly on the spring hinge. Then he started down the steps rapidly making noise by letting his feet splat on the concrete.

He was two floors below when he heard the door fly open and the fast pounding steps of the man following him trying to keep up. When he got to the bottom he moved as fast as he thought was practical through the crowds into the street and rushed off. About two blocks away he saw reflected in one of the store windows that the man had slowed his run to a pace that kept him behind Mark by about a half block. Mark continued to go in and out of stores, past racks of coats, pants, shirts and counters covered with everything from clothing to kitchenware to children's toys.

Petkas had not heard anyone following him as he reached the foot of the stairs, rushed into the street and turned the corner where Maria Becket's housekeeper waited for him in Maria's old car that she kept in a garage and only used for trips to the country to gather farm produce. Petkas dropped the woman a few blocks away and checked that the rear seat held his backpack with the camera, tape measure, lights and other material he had asked Maria to put in the car. Although she was very curious, she had been through enough clandestine adventures in earlier years not to probe too much as to what Petkas and Mark were up to. She knew they would tell her at the appropriate time and that she would help them further if they asked her.

After he zigzagged around several blocks, down narrow alleys and through dense traffic until he was confident that no one was following, Petkas began the long drive to the narrow valley near Delphi. When he arrived, he pulled off the main road and the car climbed the gentle slopes of the valley to become hidden behind a rocky outcrop that blocked it from the road below. Petkas parked near to the landslide area behind one of the larger fallen rocks that had covered the passage into the cave so many years ago. He went back down to the narrow road and used a branch to sweep away the tracks where the car had entered the field so any casual passersby would not suspect anyone was there. Back at the cave site, it was a short climb carrying the backpack over some boulders to the place where he had covered the entrance. He was relieved to see that the area was undisturbed from the last time he had been there, and he let himself down by crawling over jagged rocks into the larger passage and then down into the full cave. A quick scan with the flashlight indicated there had not been any more falling debris from the ceiling and the interior of the cave looked intact.

Petkas sat for a moment in the dim glow, letting his eyes adjust and feeling the power of the place and its contents. He felt the honor of leading an effort to bring the statues back into the light of civilization after being housed so long in their underground purgatory. This visit renewed his confidence that he was doing the right thing, and he tried to imagine what it would feel like to walk among these glorious gods placed beside each other as intended by their makers in an imaginary Olympus. What would the world think when they saw them all together creating such perfection that any one of them would rival the best-known sculpture today?

He set up and adjusted the powerful glow of several battery-operated floodlights and measured all the pieces carefully for height, depth and width, and then readjusted the lights again and again to take photos of each piece which several years ago he had so carefully uncovered. Then he shot a close-up of the heads and shoulders, named each piece for the gods they represented and noted their location in the cave on the legal pad he was carrying. After that he adjusted the exposure settings on the camera and shot some time exposure photos of the cave interior from all angles so that when the photos were placed side by side, the viewer would have a panoramic view of the full interior.

After removing the equipment and re-covering the entrance, he climbed down off the rocks and walked into the field to take more photos of the area near the cave and up and down the valley. As he was preparing to leave, with a careful eye and ear out for traffic, he shot more photos of the entrance to the valley and up and down the narrow mountain road in both directions, and then swept the entrance again.

Later that night he met Mark and Maria with others from the campaign at a restaurant, and he gave Maria the car keys which she used to return home after the meal. Petkas caught a ride with a colleague to pick up his car at the office.

After their clothing switch in the department store, and once Petkas was away, Mark continued to meander his way through many Athens stores, going in one door, rushing through the racks of items, and out the other door for over two hours, and then in one crowded market, certain he had lost the follower, he ditched the hat and coat and ducked out a side door undetected and jumped into the first available taxi at random for a quick trip to the American Embassy.

Now was the beginning of his part of the plan. There was only one person Mark knew that he thought could help Petkas and had the clout to get the sculptures out of Greece. In an earlier campaign the year before in Panama, he had met a thoroughly despicable CIA agent named Bruce who though crude and unlikable, was very good at his job. He was thinking about that man and remembering how much he did not like him as he left his hotel that morning.

At the U.S. Embassy entry desk, he asked to speak to the intelligence officer who had been in a meeting with him and Maria earlier. After some back and forth with the lower level bureaucrats, he was ushered into a room and met the person he was seeking. It took some arguing but he finally got the man to place the call he wanted, and after spending more time alone in a small office, the man took him into another, smaller room that housed the embassy secure phone and dialed a number. He asked for Bruce and, when he was on the line, gave the phone to Mark and left the room.

"Hello, Boy Scout. Help any old ladies across the street recently?"

"Bruce, what I have to say is serious. We need to meet. I have something important that you will see the value of immediately. I can't talk about it on the phone, even on this secure gadget. You remember where we were the last time we met? Meet me at the same kind of place when I arrive in Paris in three days at about the same time of day when we last spoke. You need to take me to a safe place where we can talk."

"Hold up there, Road Runner, why should I do that? I cannot imagine what you have to tell me in some kind of amateurish cloak and dagger setting that you cannot tell me when you get back here in the states whenever that is. And you know, Mark, I kind of have a hard time imagining anything you would have to tell me that I'd want to hear under any circumstances."

"Okay, Bruce, you know me... sort of... and you know I don't really like you very much. You must also know that I would not be making this call unless it was absolutely necessary and you know that I'm doing the same job here I was doing when we last met. I'm involved in something very important. I would not be sucking up to you otherwise. You must know how much I wish there was someone else I could talk with. There are influential people here and in other countries who would love to know what I'm going tell you."

"Might help your case if you can tell me what the 'this' is?"

"When we meet and you hear it, you will understand. Remember you mentioned the Soviet ambassador here when we last met. I can't talk about this on the phone and we need to be in a secure place when we talk."

"Mmmm... okay. Your little request will cause me to pull in some chits and you better not be screwing around or have some bullshit story. We'll have the meet at the place in Frankfurt, not Paris. I have some resources nearby that I may need to use with you, but I need some time to set up the meet. Someone will find you at the place two weeks from this Friday at the same time of day we last saw each other and bring you to me."

After the call, Mark asked the station chief if he could leave the Embassy from an exit that he would not be observed by the people Mark had thought were following him. The man showed Mark out a side door that led him into a back street. He grabbed the first taxi he could and had it take him to the top of Mt. Lykavittus where he walked around the church and amphitheater for a few minutes and said hello to one of the guards and a priest he had seen there often to establish that he had been on the mountain hike. Then he walked back down the hill and went to the office as he often did when he and Petkas had their daily walks. Arriving at the office, he spotted one of the usual shadows leaning against a nearby building with one foot on the wall, who stood up straight and seemed startled to see him as he walked past and then tried to hide his surprise by looking away.

The next morning there was another anti-American political protest in the city. As Mark threaded his way over to the campaign office from the hotel, he could tell the march had been well organized and featured predictable signs in Greek and English, and there were march managers every 50 yards or so to keep the thick crowd moving along the roadway leading to the plaza near the Legislative buildings. The path of the crowd filled a narrow street and cut Mark off from the direction he needed to go to cross it and reach his office. Because of the anti-American nature of the protest, and calls and signs to remove the military bases from Greece, Mark did his best to look Greek. He quickly purchased a Greek language newspaper to carry in his hand from a nearby newsstand and kept his head down as he threaded along the side of the street, looking for a way to cross through the throng of protesters on the jammed street so he could get closer to his office.

He noticed just ahead on the other side of the packed street there was an alley that intersected with the narrow street that would move him in a perpendicular direction to another street a block away from the massive crowd. At almost the same time, one of his tails who seemed to be taking advantage of the opportunity, began to shout from about 20 yards back on the same sidewalk and point in Mark's direction. The man quickened his pace toward Mark and raised his voice louder as some of the throng being swept along on the path down the street began to notice him. Mark quickly assumed the man was pointing to him and saying that he was an American and as he became more anxious, he immediately and instinctively plunged into the throng and began to work his way at a diagonal to cross the street toward the alley. It was tough going as the marchers were thickly packed and forcefully headed in a different direction. Mark was bumped and jostled against them as he wormed his way and pushed to get to the other side of the street. His knees knocked with others, and several boots landed on his feet, throwing him off balance and into others who righted him as they pushed him into other marchers coming fast in the next wave of the crowd.

However, his move to blend him into the throng countered the watcher's ploy to out Mark as an American as everyone was moving along, and now that he was immersed in their midst, there was no way to determine who the man on the sidelines was shouting about. Then the birddog realized that Mark was making progress at moving away from him, and he too lunged into the crowd to cross the street. Mark had to be careful not to anger anyone in the mob as he almost clawed his way through them at a pace that would not call undue attention to himself. As he was swept along, the mouth of the alley got closer and he wondered if he was going to make it to the safety of the cavity, because the crowd momentum was moving him along with them quickly in a different direction.

As the mass of people pushed down the street crushing him along, he saw a gap where a fat man was moving slower than the rest and used that gap to charge forward through the mass, and still it was all Mark could do to shove himself into the alley just as the pack whisked past the opening. He put one hand on the wall and breathed for a moment. When he checked his back, the watcher was nowhere in sight, evidently having been carried along with the mob toward the plaza for the rally. He then quickly moved through the narrow passage to the next block where it was easy to adjust his route to the office.

As he moved toward the office he considered that the tactic to have him threatened by mob action was a new move and wondered if it was just an opportunity taken by that particular watcher or a new practice by the Greeks and Soviets. Whatever it was he'd have to be extra careful in the future, but he needed to go ahead with the trip concocted during his visit to the American Embassy. He was beginning to feel less enamored of being in Greece and more intimidated by the rising passion in the streets.

CHAPTER 31

The next day Mark met with Petkas in his office and got the rolls of 35mm film he had taken of the sculptures. Because the photos had to be shot with a flash or with a time exposure in the cave, they would not be sure of the quality of the images until the film was developed, but they hoped the sculptures could be seen clearly. Petkas also gave Mark several pages of an excellent narrative that included a summary of Greek history in the 400-300 BC period, the history of Alexander and the origin of the sculptures. He also had marked up some maps that pinpointed the location. Later Mark hid the rolls of film and documents inside the hand luggage in his room after cutting a small tear in the padding of one corner. He kept that bag in Maria's secure office until it was time for his trip.

Over the next few days, he and Petkas talked some more and practiced on a presentation so Mark could be comfortable in telling the back story of how Petkas found out about the sculpture and with enough detail so the CIA analysts could assess the truth of Mark's explanation. Petkas gave Mark his resume and a couple of names of people at Oxford and Stanford who could be contacted to verify that Petkas was a serious and honest academic historian and archeologist.

They talked about the watcher's attempt to get Mark in trouble with the crowd and decided it was just a spur of the moment opportunity by the spotter to harm Mark. They agreed he was likely connected to the campaign and did not have anything to do with the sculpture. They concluded too that if the Greek government or Russians wanted to hurt them, that could be done at any time. However, because they felt that the man shouting about Mark to the crowd was a legitimate attempt to cause Mark harm without any government fingerprints on it, they decided to stay away from large public gatherings in the future.

Mark went to see Maria Beckett at her home and they took a walk down a narrow side street that would pinch off any followers from overhearing them. She knew of their concern over surveillance and had lived in similar circumstances much of her life. "Maria, I know from your stories that you have had some interesting adventures. As you know I'm in a sort of an adventure now and need some advice. I have to make a trip and need to do it as quietly as possible. I'm worried if I purchase a ticket particularly on my credit card at a travel agency or at the airport, it will be noticed and attract the attention of the security people. Can you help me?"

"Well, yes I can. I suppose you will tell me what this is about at the right time; but if you need my help I will be there; and when you want to tell me more, I will be more than happy to listen. For now, I need to know your destination and travel schedule. I can get my housekeeper to purchase the ticket with cash at a suburban travel agency and you can pay me back. But I must tell you something based on the 'interesting adventures in my life' … once you start down the road to fight tyranny you can never turn back. It sets the hook into you and the other side will never forgive you.

In the security meeting, a bulky GRU intelligence man with a sheepish look on his face reported that the surveillance had lost both Petkas and Mark, yet again. Petkas for almost an entire day and Mark for several hours. Bokhan shook his head and stared at the large Russian. "These are amateurs… a damn college professor and an American campaign consultant. What is going on with you and the Greek surveillance teams? The ambassador had ordered you to increase coverage, not to have this cock up. What happened?"

The man squirmed, "Well, in both cases we were following them and then lost them in shopping areas where they went into and out of several stores and we think changed clothes to make it harder to keep up." Bokhan slapped the palms of both his hands down on the table, "So if they know you are following them, why keep such a distance? The reason to follow them is not to lose them. We want to know what they are doing and when they shake you on purpose it means they are doing something we

REALLY want to know about."

Looking at his report and then back up at Bokhan the man said, "We think they may have gotten some training or suggestions of how to make it hard to follow them. They seem to be smart and crafty."

Bokhan closed his eyes. "How many times have you lost them?"

"Several, but our teams lose them also because they don't know the territory or speak the language and get confused in these winding, narrow streets."

Bokhan shook his head. "From now on I want one of our Soviet team and one of the Greek security team paired together on the surveillance work. No more excuses! Get out! No, wait. What is happening with the Election Day celebration? Have we coordinated with PASOK to have large crowds demonstrate in support of a Papandreou victory? Do we have the communist party members lined up to join them so we show a large crowd of supporters?"

"Yes, sir. We have mobilized everyone we can and the PASOK people are planning on having a large turnout. They will have the people pour into a big wide street and march toward the legislative buildings plaza and have the stages set for the international press to cover the rally, and the television can record smiling faces and banners and many signs proclaiming the happiness at the victory of socialism and communism. We have identified people to speak on behalf of the government as normal citizens of Greece who will echo that message. The PASOK people are working hard to counter any loss of support the election results reflect."

"All right. Just stay on top of everything. We must have a backup plan to dominate the international media, as they will surely report any diminution of support for socialism and make that their main story. We must make the public outcry of happiness about the election loud enough to overcome any drop off in the vote. See to it."

As the meeting ended, Tito walked slowly down the hall to the office of the bulky man who had reported the security lapses. He entered without knocking and closed the door. The security officer looked surprised as Tito quickly crossed the three steps to his desk. Tito smiled and held out his hand, "Comrade, regarding the report on your surveillance of the capitalists...." the man reached out to shake the hand Tito offered, but Tito quickly grabbed the little finger of the offered hand and snapped it in a ninety-degree motion outward, breaking it at the joint. Before the man could scream, Tito moved in a flash to be just inches from the shocked man's face and growled, "Do better next time," stifling the officer's scream. He held the gaze of the frightened man's eyes for several seconds before letting go of the damaged hand, and then leaving without another word.

The story of this incident spread through the embassy, with the embellishments gossip usually attracts, and afterwards the staff paid much better attention to the surveillance of New Democracy and also kept as much distance from the 'humming man' as possible.

Two days later Bokhan found himself in the almost empty Embassy café with the mysterious Tito Petrovia who was sitting by himself. Tito seemed not only comfortable being alone but he seemed motivated by some invisible force, satisfied and self-assured as though he was untouched by the normal laws of man or nature in need of friendship or congenial associations. As Bokhan approached the table he saw Tito holding the knife to cut his meat with a full grip – four fingers around one side and the thumb wrapped around the other and overlapped onto the fingers like he was holding onto a rope. Bokhan had a strange impression that Tito was stabbing the meat as though he meant to kill it. Practice?

He stopped nearby, stood still until acknowledged, nodded and then sat down with the menacing Russian. "Excuse me, but we have not had much of a chance to talk since you arrived. We appreciate your help here. I'm just wondering, so we don't get crossed up by trying to do the same thing, and as the time to vote is fast approaching, do you have any plans toward affecting the election outcome?"

Tito looked at the number two man in the embassy and because he had done his research on the bureaucrat and knew that he had a good record, he leaned back and decided to treat him with more respect than the lightweight ambassador. "I did have a plan about two weeks ago that would have guaranteed a good result, but some nosy policemen got in the way. Anyway, the people I hired to do a job failed, and we will have the result we will have now."

Bokhan surprised, and now cautious, tilted his head sideways. "So, the thing over near Aeros Park and the National Archeological Museum you set up?"

Tito shrugged. "If those men could have removed the American in a messy and public way, it would have shown that the New Democracy people had to hire Americans to tell them how to have an election. That would have been a big embarrassment and turned many people away from the capitalists. But, unfortunately the plan failed. Got to try again in a crowd on the street a few days ago, but the lucky bugger slipped away before we could set the crowd on him." He smiled, put down the knife and fork and leaned further into the table.

Bokhan, being careful to cover his surprise and disgust at these brutal and ham-handed methods, nodded. "Brilliant! Too bad it did not work. It would have changed everything to our benefit. Any other ideas?" Bokhan suddenly felt nervous that he was prying too much into the mysterious man's business.

Tito shrugged, his shoulders stretching the tight coat. "The election is soon. I wanted to get him killed before the election so it would be a stink story and help our side by showing the Americans were here. Now, after the election, it is more important to look at the professor. Now I will look for the art."

Bokhan frowned. "Yes. But I think the Ambassador and the Greeks have a plan to work on him."

He shrugged again. "So. They can go first. I have to go back to Moscow for a week or so. If they are not successful by the time I return, I'll give it a try."

Bokhan, frowned, "But what can you do that the secret police of Greece and our security cannot do?"

Tito looked down at his hands and then scratched a place on his nose. "I find him alone and I tell him that he will give me the information where to find the statues or the next day one of his children will die." He paused, nodded and smiled to himself. "I have had success with this method and it has worked for me before."

Bokhan tried not to let Tito see him swallow. "That ought to do it." He tried to shrug his shoulders the same way that Tito had, but it was a pale imitation, almost embarrassing. "Oh, well, I need to get back to work. Good to have this little chat. Let me know if I can be of help."

Tito did not answer but nodded slightly at Bokhan and began to hum quietly. He picked up the knife in his thick fist and continued to assault the meat.

CHAPTER 32

As the Election Day approached, the New Democracy staff became more active with planned appearances in cities and towns where they thought they would do the most good. Their television message pointed out the poor trends of the economy under the Papandreou government and used charts and graphs to criticize increased government spending going in an upward track, and private sector jobs and government revenue going in a downward path. Testimonials similar to those of Mark's experience near the town of Arta, gave examples why the socialists' ideas sounded good but were actually misleading and bad policy. A few days before the election, Maria released the embarrassing radio commercial of Papandreou speaking off the cuff in Moscow of his intention to punish business in Greece. It had been edited as Angus had recommended and was placed as a breaking news release from a foreign news organization, run on business talk shows and the three highest rated news broadcasts. The word of mouth follow-up worked and people on the streets were talking about what Papandreou had said just before Election Day.

On the other side of the political spectrum, the last-minute marketing by the Papandreou campaign was all about his creating a positive change in Greece and having a more promising future as Greek citizens would get more holidays and more government services. The communist party tracked close to the PASOK's message of a world brotherhood of workers and concentrated on radio, posters and street demonstrations to distribute their message. It was hard to tell if any of these party promotions were getting through, although Maria and others in the New Democracy headquarters said they could feel more encouraging momentum and positive anecdotal reports from the far-flung areas of Greece. They heard from the rural areas that some people who had flirted with PASOK were becoming discouraged and were changing their allegiance to vote New Democracy.

Compared to U.S. elections and his recent experience in Panama, Mark thought the overall public response felt flat and observed there was limited signage or public displays for any candidate. People on the street, who had not been organized by the political parties, just did not seem to be very emotionally invested in the election. He did not know if the people of Greece were unfamiliar with mass advertising in campaigns, or maybe were just disaffected with all things political. Perhaps it was just that both Papandreou and Mitsotakis were fairly boring men.

The Greek parliamentary elections on June 3, 1985, made the public atmosphere more festive than on a normal day, but based on Mark's experience, still rather tame. Though Angus had moved on to another election three weeks earlier, Mark had stayed on because of his commitment to Petkas and to finish the campaign job by personally overseeing the details for the final rally. The complete results were slow to come into the headquarters and to be reported by the media. However, by midnight the news reports were of a PASOK victory and another term for Papandreou, but with his party winning the popular vote by only five percentage points, a considerable drop from earlier elections. The communist party also declined capturing less than 12 percent of the vote, which was a 3-point drop from their showing in the previous election.

The big news was that The New Democracy vastly improved its popularity from the previous election and gained eight points on Papandreou's party. This political surge by the business community was seen as a rejection of his policies by everyone except Papandreou.

Because New Democracy was within five points winning against Papandreou's socialist party, Maria Beckett felt confident that the poor economic direction of Greece and the false promises of future success under the socialist and communist influences would produce a victory for the business community in the next election. The problem for the New Democrats was that the common-sense measures that would be needed to put Greece on sound economic footing would be unpopular among people who had been told that no sacrifice would be needed to have a successful and prosperous nation.

Mark sat at his desk and looked at the *International Herald Tribune* newspaper from the day before that had covered the last big New Democracy rally in the capitol and had tried to handicap the election by putting a positive spin on the favorite candidate of the United States.

Papandreou's Race for Re-election Too Close to Call

June 02, 1985|By Ray Moseley, *Chicago Tribune*.
ATHENS — For a moment, Athens' Constitution Square looked and sounded like a battlefield.

Hundreds of powerful fireworks exploded in quick succession; flares lighted up the evening sky, and clouds of thick smoke billowed upward, obscuring the buildings surrounding the square and the Acropolis in the background.

The night before the election the smoke lifted and, as an army of New Democracy Party supporters caught sight of party leader Constantine Mitsotakis standing at an elaborate rostrum under a shower of blue confetti, they shouted, 'You are prime minister, you are prime minister.'

The rally, which wound up the center-right party's campaign for Sunday's national election, was one of the biggest and most spectacular Greece has seen.

The campaign has attracted wide attention abroad because of its implications for Greece's standing among Western nations. At stake is whether the country will continue to be governed by a man who says he wants to steer Greece toward neutralism, and who often acts in unpredictable and antagonistic ways toward the U.S., or whether leadership passes to Mitsotakis, a man committed to the Western alliance.

For Greece's allies, the major issues in the campaign are its membership in the North Atlantic Treaty Organization and the Common Market, and the question of whether the U.S. will be allowed to keep its four military bases and nuclear weapons in Greece after 1988 when an agreement on the bases comes up for renewal.

These subjects, however, were scarcely mentioned in the campaign. Pocketbook issues that are of much greater concern to the Greek voter dominated the debate.

Mitsotakis sought to exploit the fact that under Papandreou, who was first elected in 1981, Greece has inflation of 18 percent, almost triple the Common Market average, and unemployment of 9 percent.

Mitsotakis scored heavily with a promise to abolish the tax on imported automobiles and to establish a free-enterprise economy in contrast to Papandreou's socialism. Papandreou argued that his current economic policies will begin to produce results if he is given another term. He also promised a greater role for private enterprise.

Mark tossed the paper in the trash.

In the next staff meeting, Maria solicited comments from the full staff which collectively agreed that although Mitsotakis lost the recent election, the New Democracy party was likely to win the next one. The leadership of The New Democracy party felt as though they had made progress and the effort and expense had been worth it. Everyone thought that by the next election the younger members of The New Democracy party would make up the major group of candidates and bring in fresh faces and new ideas, and some of those younger party members were already starting to jockey for position the day after the election.

Mark had informed Angus that he would stick around to do some sight-seeing, but did not tell him that he was actually involved in helping Petkas with the treasure. He continued to regret that helping Petkas would keep him away longer from going back to Washington and to Vicki. She still had not answered any of his letters or his calls.

The day after the election Mark visited with Maria, Petkas and a few others and they talked about what they specifically needed to do over the next few years to improve their chances of winning the next election. Mark packed the documents he wanted to take home and slowly cleared out his desk. Though there was some celebration by the PASOK supporters, the organized crowds were more subdued than expected, Mark guessed because they could sense that their policies and politics were headed in the wrong direction. The slide in the productivity of the Greek economy and the poor government administration would continue to increase the debt and to push it inevitably toward the debacle that would come years later.

Inside the Soviet embassy, Igor continued to be uneasy that the new leadership in Moscow under Gorbachev would see the drop in public opinion in the elections as partially his fault. He had a very legitimate dread that the election results would make the Soviets more nervous and believe that their influence in Greece was waning. He began to look more intensely for scapegoats and other news to counter the PASOK political decline from the election.

Sergei Bokhan heard a disturbing story from the woman he had placed to spy on Igor's mistress. The day after the election when Igor was feeling vulnerable and like he might share some of the blame for the decrease in PASOK's vote, he took it out on the young Greek woman. He had gone to see her after many drinks at the election party and had continued to drink at the apartment. He had told the girl that her father's party was incompetent and that it was causing him problems. He had hit her several times over the next 12 hours. The woman had bruises on her face and had a cracked rib. After Igor had left the next day, the Russian woman who was watching over her ambassador's mistress panicked and took the injured Sophie for treatment at the Soviet embassy's clinic.

As the woman was getting Sophie settled in the emergency area of the embassy clinic, the wife of Ambassador Andropov who was there by chance, overheard a nurse talking about the treatment of the Greek woman. Tatiana Andropov walked into the emergency area and appeared in the doorway to the examining room. Her small son stood behind her looking amazed at the brightly lit room, medical implements and all the people he did not know.

Tatiana watched for a few moments as the doctor treated Sophie for her bruises. Then as the doctor touched Sophie's damaged rib it caused her to wince and start to roll her body away from him to protect the injury.

The Ambassador's wife walked slowly as she entered the emergency space, surprising both the woman who worked in the security department of the embassy and the doctor. They both pulled away from the table in the center of the room out of respect for the Ambassador's wife and also because her stately bearing demanded acknowledgement. She walked over to the table where the young Greek woman lay and, as if she were the consulting physician touched the girl's head, turning it towards her for a better look at the bruises. Then she allowed the same hand to trail down the girl's body slowly to the place where the doctor had inspected. She lay her hand flat and still over the area like she was a priest giving a blessing, and then pressed inward. The Greek girl cried out and her eyes flew open wide. Tatiana pulled her hand away quickly, and a slight smile appeared on her red lips.

She looked over at the doctor as though she were recognizing his presence for the first time. "Doctor, my son is here for his shot." The boy stayed at the doorway transfixed, fearful to enter, and with his eyes wide taking it all in. Tatiana turned and left, grabbing the boy by the hand as she walked out, and the doctor dutifully followed her.

The woman Bokhan had placed to look after Sophie was frightened by the look on the face of the ambassador's wife, which caused her to call Bokhan for advice. She told him that she realized she had made an error by taking the Greek woman to the Soviet Embassy. She was also afraid that Igor would learn who she was and punish her for taking care of the woman he had injured. On top of that, she was also frightened the ambassador's wife might punish her for looking after his mistress.

The medical treatment for the ambassador's girlfriend, and the distraught woman who had been looking after Sophie, were just more problems Bokhan now had to handle that had nothing to do with his real job. He'd have to cover up this beating for Igor with the embassy staff, and he knew that he could not tell his boss what he actually had done, because the embarrassment of the exposure would only make Igor's temper and violence worse. Sergei was becoming anxious about Igor's erratic behavior. He was also becoming more troubled that the family ties of Igor's mistress to a top Greek government official had the potential of an international incident if the woman's family learned what was going on. Now to complicate matters, Igor's wife knew about Sophie, and might get involved. He shook his head in disgust as he felt his life turning.

He needed to think of a way either to soften Igor from his excessive temper and drinking or get him to find another woman as his mistress. The pressure to manage the ambassador was becoming acute; Bokhan was having trouble sleeping. He decided he needed to talk to someone about the internal toll his job was taking and the direction he was headed. He had been depressed and struggled to maintain his usually efficient demeanor and focusing his concentration at work. His own wife sensed something was wrong, but for security reasons, he could not share his embassy worries with her. The only person he felt comfortable talking to was the priest at the church who was trained to give advice and was bound by church dogma not to reveal such conversations. He also knew with a dread and lump in his stomach that becoming attached to Igor Andropov had been a death sentence for his career. In the Soviet system, if the top manager or diplomat failed in his job, the number two man usually also got the blame. Moscow always found enough people to punish downstream so the system itself was held harmless. He was next.

Sophie Speros thanked the woman who lived down the hall for helping her with her injuries and for bringing her food, mail, and cosmetics. She had not wanted to go outside because the swelling was still noticeable under her eye. She did not like to use the ice packs as they made her face cold. This time it was taking longer for her to get better, but the makeup and medicine she got through the Soviet Embassy helped, although the pain in her side made it hard for her to take in deep breaths. The woman who lived down the hall was so nice to check in on her and to do little errands. She thumbed through the mail that her parents had forwarded to her. She had not seen them in several weeks, and her friends had almost stopped calling her. They seemed to tire of inviting her to events she no longer attended. Plus, Igor did not like her going out of the apartment on her own, and lately he became angry when she even suggested visiting her parents.

She began to wonder about the kind of attention he paid to her. She was tired of the rough treatment, and her feelings of being alone and neglected were growing. She wondered if he was ever going to change, divorce his wife and marry her and take her to accompany him to the embassy parties and live in the Soviet Embassy residence. Perhaps she had made a bad mistake and would have to endure the shame and embarrassment of her family to admit it. Her life was so confusing.

She checked the supply of cocaine that he had given her and planned her day watching television. Later she would experiment with the make-up on her eye and the other places. Now it was time for her to feel better, so she put an icepack on her sore ribs and laid out another line of cocaine.

Sophie did not know that Igor had a never-ending supply of drugs that he received once a month from a military attaché who stopped by the Greek Embassy on a flight back to the Soviet Union from Afghanistan. Igor took a small package for himself to use with Sophie, his wife, and others as needed. The attaché took a larger package on to Moscow where an old friend of his distributed it and split the proceeds with Igor, who had seen the potential for smuggling as an opportunity to make some extra money from his posting. One needed to find additional income when the advantage presented itself, and many others were doing the same thing. It was not his problem if people in Russia chose to destroy their lives with drugs, but he was pleased to make it his business to supply the drugs to them. The people in Russia were becoming more like the U.S. in that respect.

When Igor came home that afternoon, his wife gave him an account of her visit to the hospital and seeing his fragile mistress. She berated him for not having more control and knowing when to stop beating his girlfriend, and called him a fool for allowing his private indiscretions to be paraded all over the embassy medical center. She told him that he had better move quickly on getting her uncle the sculptures he wanted or she might have to let her uncle know about his sloppy behavior and lack of self-discipline. Igor could not answer her by smashing in her face as he wished but he had to suck up the insults. He'd let that stupid Sophie know about what his wife said and show her how he felt about her going to the embassy hospital over a little bruise the next time he was with her.

CHAPTER 33

The next day, Igor was still angry from the scolding he got from his wife the night before. He vented at Bokhan while pacing behind his desk, looking out a large window at the Athens skyline and toward the old city two miles south of the Soviet Embassy. "We have to do better. We can't keep losing these guys all the time and we must find the treasure. We need to have a maximum effort to find what is going on with the theft of Greek treasure by the New Democracy people and that American pig. I look bad because that stupid Papandreou did so poorly in the election he almost lost. If we can uncover this plot to steal Greek art treasures, it will give me credit in Moscow, get Tatiana's damn uncle off my back, give our government something to be glad about, and also take the heat off this stupid war in Afghanistan. We need to put together a good story about capturing an American and the Greek capitalist stealing Greek treasure so it will take public attention away from the economy here and these incompetent Greeks.

"I want to have updates daily. Work up a profile on all the people who may be involved. I want to see the reports from the people who are shadowing them and transcripts of the taped conversations. I want to interview whoever we had inside New Democracy campaign personally. We need to get the treasure that is in those photos, get the benefit of it from the Kremlin and get me out of this backwater posting and to someplace more important. This archeology thing may be a blessing in disguise for me. It will be how I show my worth and make my mark with the party bosses."

Sergei Bokhan grimaced and tried to think how to get his boss away from talking all the time about this fantasy of art and back on more reasonable footing. There were real and practical issues to handle, not this wild goose chase. But he nodded to the ambassador and said, "You are right, of course, and we will follow all the measures as you have suggested. But

I have seen this kind of thing before, and it might not turn out to be as significant as these bits of surveillance transcript indicate. Perhaps . . ."

"Perhaps nothing! I can smell the treasure is right out there. That is where we MUST put our energy. It is the only way I can see to gain positive attention and become known to the new leadership. You must see to this, Sergei. I am not going to spend my career as a bureaucrat reading cables in these dead-end assignments. Put together the dossiers on these people as I have asked and bring them to me. You and the others will see that I am my father's son and that I know how to handle these secret maters. I can flush out spies. Watch me and see how it is done."

Bokhan remained quiet and began to think that the assignment, which earlier he had assumed was a godsend, was fast turning into a real disaster from which he could not recover. He had an inexperienced boss who did not want to learn his job, who was cruel to women and subordinates, was sacrilegious, and only cared about his public image. He was beginning to believe this assignment would wreck his career, and it degraded him to have to prop up the ego of a spoiled megalomaniac. He was being pushed to act in a way he never would have thought possible. His options were fast being refined.

Mark did not realize his continued presence would make Igor Andropov all the more suspicious. He did wonder, however, why the watchers still seemed to be following him because he had assumed that the intrigue of surveillance was only used for the campaign. Now that the election was over and they were still trailing him, he started to worry that the Greek and Soviet governments had begun to suspect the secret plan he and Petkas shared. He also noticed some new faces following him, and it seemed that often there were now two people and not just one. He realized that he and Petkas needed to establish new patterns of movement.

CHAPTER 34

Maria thanked the kindly priest who worked in an administrative and political role for the Greek Orthodox Church. Maria and the man had shared confidences many times over the years for their mutual benefit. As soon as they had finished their conversation and he had left, Maria called Mark and Petkas to a lunch meeting outside the campaign offices at a seaside restaurant where she knew the owner who would seat them in a private, safe room. They watched through the large glass window facing the sea as a flurry of birds dive-bombed the nearby shore to grab restaurant leftovers tossed on the narrow, rocky beach.

Maria turned to look at the two men with her serious, dark eyes, "What I have to say is highly confidential. I got to know Archbishop Makarios very well when we worked together in politics before he died a few years ago. Through Makarios I met many of the other leaders of the Greek Orthodox Church. One of these associates recently told me something that I think we need to consider. Now, under normal circumstances, he should not have told me what he did, but I believe he thought it critical enough to break his vows to do so. He reported about a confessional, actually several conversations, with a high-ranking Soviet diplomat who is Russian Orthodox, but attends the Greek Orthodox Church while he is posted here with the Soviet Embassy. This man is disillusioned and morally torn by some of the activities of the Soviet Ambassador, Mr. Andropov.

"I did not get too many specific details, but apparently Mr. Andropov has some perverted sexual proclivities and, more importantly, a disdain for the Church. He evidently defiled some church icons and is causing his assistant, a Mr. Sergei Bokhan, considerable stress to the point that it could work to our benefit. I just wanted you to know what I have been doing and for now, just sit on it. It may play into whatever else you two are doing. But the potential of a defector also might be a crack in the armor of the Soviets and their socialist allies here in Greece."

Mark questioned, "How can that help us?"

Maria glanced around and then leaned in to Mark, "Knowledge of private and personal weaknesses and the disillusionment of highly placed Soviet diplomats is spy stuff. Someone in your intelligence agencies might choose to make an active case out of this news. People like Sergei Bokhan, the First Secretary and the deputy Athens station chief of the GRU, who is Andropov's chief aide, do not have these conversations randomly, but out of some deep moral outrage or personal vulnerability. I'm talking about a Soviet diplomat who has shown us a weakness. These people are trained not to do that. He has made a chess move and for him a risky one. He had to know it was likely his conversation with the priest would reach the intelligence services of the west.

I think we just need to see where things are headed a little longer before we decide how to use this information. I have ways to tell if what I learned is legitimate. If this person felt strongly enough to speak, even if it was in a confession to a priest, his dissatisfaction is eating at him enough to overcome his training and loyalty to the Soviet Union. That, gentlemen, is no small matter.

"What we have here is a rare gift and we would be fools not to exploit it, but it might be better to wait until the time is more propitious. I have found that in these diplomatic and political wars, the potential to embarrass and undermine your opponent can have the same effect as an air strike.

"Remember the man I mentioned to you named Gust Avrakotos in your intelligence services. For a time, years ago, he worked the Greek desk at the CIA, and of course, being Greek, he was good at it." She winked and smiled. "They moved him somewhere else, but he was the kind of man who would know how to exploit the potential of a disillusioned Russian. But again, we must use it at the right time. I will make discreet inquires and we can decide how to proceed when it is most appropriate."

Mark thought to himself, perhaps the disaffected Russian was the extra spice they needed to get the CIA interested enough to act on the sculpture.

Maria spoke to her old friend in the CIA who gave her some advice on the conversation she needed to have, and told her if the discussion was promising to get back to him and he would arrange for a current operative to assume the case going forward. She learned he was now working in Pakistan and Afghanistan and realized he must be involved against the Soviets there. Though using Maria to facilitate this communication was unorthodox, he knew her well and was confident that with her experience in espionage and being right there on the ground she would best know how to handle the initial encounter. As a local woman, she would also be less threatening to the Soviet diplomat.

Maria asked the priest to set up a meeting, and one afternoon a few days before Mark was to leave Greece to meet with Bruce, Sergei Bokhan came to the Greek Orthodox Church and met the priest, who led him back to his sparsely furnished office where they sometimes talked. A pleasant incense was burning on a side credenza that gave the room a calming atmosphere and there the priest introduced Maria Beckett and left. They moved quickly through the pleasantries and introductions. Each recognized the serious reason for their meeting.

Bokhan's embassy driver waited outside as he usually did. A very attractive young lady appeared nearby about the same time he parked the car in the visitor's area, and she got off her bicycle and proceeded to start general maintenance beginning with the tire, checking the facets and pumping up the tube. She happened to be positioned not too far in front of the embassy car where her efforts caused her to bend over several times in her tight stretch bicycle shorts. Somehow the driver was not monitoring Bokhan's time as closely as he otherwise might have.

Both Maria and Bokhan knew the risk and the uncertain outcome of the meeting, and she spoke quickly so their encounter would end before the driver became suspicions and perhaps came inside to look for Bokhan. She had told the young woman to work on the bicycle tire and other parts of the bike as long as was practical, but not to overdo it to the point where the driver would become suspicious.

Bokhan sat quietly and listened to Maria as she spoke to him in her passable Russian, which she calculated would put him more at ease than

Greek which she knew he understood fairly well. "I am speaking to you in the words from a friend who lives in another place that you can easily guess. Sergei, you are not appreciated. Your work is not appreciated. Your faith is not appreciated. Your family and children are not protected. Where I live we honor the commitment and dedication of men such as yourself. The world you knew and the country where you grew up is changing. The old, traditional honor that men like you have has been replaced by people like the untrained and underserving Igor Andropov. These young, brash, privileged people are like models from magazines and just as shallow. They know nothing of the sacrifices that made your country great. They do not remember the war with Germany. They are more corrupt than the worst capitalist industry leaders. They have no respect. They believe in nothing except themselves.

"Where I live, we have worked to make a large middle class of comfortable workers with schools, hospitals, jobs and comforts for all. The old fight is over, we won. Come and join us and help us build an even greater society in the West. When it is time for the Soviet Union to make its big change and become more equitable, you will be positioned to be one of the people to help it rebuild, but to continue down the path you are on with this man Andropov and others like him, will eat your soul and strangle your children. You know he will fail; and you know you will be blamed. When that happens, it will be too late to help your family. Your career and your well-being are at risk here.

"My friend can give you and your family a life of comfort and honor. If you make this choice, be prepared. You will be invited on short notice to collect your family and put what you can carry into suitcases and come to a place where you and your family will be safe. You know we do not need to have many of these conversations. If you decide to make a move, my friend will welcome you and provide for you. I believe that you would do the same for me if our roles were reversed. If you do decide to make a change, a transfer here in Athens will be the best place. We have facilities here and can have you and your family on your way in minutes. You will be in a safe place and in a new home the next day. Your children will be in a good school soon after that. You will have a good place to live and money for your family. Both you and your faith will be respected.

"However," she paused, "I must give you a friendly warning, Sergei, we have a narrow window and the window is already closing. The move should not be a hard decision for your family and your honor. Here." She handed him a small bag containing a cloth prominently featuring the image of the former Russian leader Vladimir Lenin. "Think about our conversation and if you agree, tie this red cloth on your balcony at home. You will get a notice to be back here with your family one morning soon after that, ready to go. Someone will meet you, honor your needs and take care of your family. You will receive diplomatic protection and be taken in secret to the U.S. base. You will be away from Greece within the hour and on the way to your new home. New schools for your children. Safety and comfort. Our churches will welcome you." Maria stopped and nodded at Bokhan.

Bokhan bowed his head as his eyes stared at the floor, "First, I know all about the American bases here, so I understand the extraction route you mentioned. I do understand what you have said and for many years have been concerned about the changes in my country that are not useful. We had a different honor in the earlier days. We did not get into foolish wars like Afghanistan. There was not so much public drinking, drugs, the shortages of food and everything else. Now there is a lack of respect for our former standards, but that is true for your side as well." He shook his head, "But I love my country and its history. There are some things I can...I will not say. I can't do that to my country."

Maria thought they were at the key moment when he was struggling with giving up his honor and she knew she needed to bring him along. To appeal to the ruse of saving his dignity she said, "Of course, you can't. That is the way you will play it with the Americans. Only give them what you must. You will know how to secure the things you must protect." Inside she thought 'of course he will tell them everything. He will have to, and although he is deluding himself now, to get through the guilt of betrayal, he knows it too.'

He shook his head again with disgust at what his life had become. "I will think about what you have said. In the interim I will continue to do my job and I will oppose you if that is called for." He looked up at her to punctuate holding on to his independence, then his eyes darted left and right as though they were looking for an escape from this small office. "I understand about the red cloth, but if I want to talk to you or anyone else about the subject again, I'll make the contact through the priest." He hesitated. "But regardless of whatever happens with me, you need to get that poor Greek girl, Sophie, away from him." His voice dropped. "He is a monster."

Bokhan stood, started moving to leave and then hesitated again. "I assume you know that if we ... or they catch the American who was involved in the election for the New Democracy party stealing the Greek historical artifacts, they will make it bad for him. There is a man, sent from Moscow, who has already tried to have him killed. They don't know about the artifacts for sure... what it is, just that something suspicious is going on, but that would be a big story and a boost for the Soviets and the socialists in Greece. It is not much of a secret anymore and it has the ambassador's full attention." He nodded and left. Maria assumed that unsolicited and helpful information was a sign that Mr. Bokhan had indeed decided to defect.

CHAPTER 35

The next day at their morning meeting, Igor leaned forward conspiratorially toward Sergei Bokhan. "Listen to what our people picked up on the surveillance. What you will hear is the professor talking." There was a click of the machine and a whispered voice said, 'My life's work has been in pursuit of this art, and they are so valuable that we must get them out of Greece to a major museum because I know they will not get proper care in Greece.' Igor clicked off the player and leaned back. "So, there you can hear it. There is no denying what the men are going to do or the value of the art. I have been right all along. I told you I have a feel for this kind of thing. I bet these are what we saw in the photos we got from the campaign office. It's been two weeks since the election, and there has been very little conversation from Moscow about the drop in Papandreou's support. I may have been a little too concerned about how that might affect me."

Now Igor leaned forward again toward Bokhan, both elbows on the table, showing his renewed interest, "Maybe we will choose not to make it a public story and embarrass the Americans. There may be a way for you and me to make a lot of money out of this Greek antique business. If we can catch the American and the Greek with some old Greek sculptures, there will be a market for them with people back in Russia who want to own such things, and also perhaps in the Middle East and Asia. Tatiana's uncle has the resources and the will to purchase what we find. He and his other wealthy friends are admirers of Greek culture, and when I saw him last week in Moscow he told me he would provide the resources for an operation to obtain these kinds of old statues and stuff. We can get them out of Greece on one of his ships or on one of his aircraft. After we expose the theft by the American, we can find a way to get some or all of that stuff out of here and make money for ourselves from it. We can give some to the Greeks to make them happy and keep them quiet, and then sell the rest. After we take the rest away from here they will not be able to complain to anyone.

"Then we can deny it ever existed and we can find another way to silence the American pig and the Greek traitor." He smiled and leaned forward, "Once the Spetsnaz soldiers have it, we will hold it in secret and then remove it later for safe keeping. The Greeks are too weak to protect it themselves, and even if they find out, we will have money set aside for the Greek minister Dedacus and his friends to cover any concerns they have or any injury to their national pride. Either way we win. We have good options. For your help, you will see that I can be generous. I can take you with me and improve your life as my career advances. So, Sergei, you see that I do have a mind that can see these things strategically."

Igor leaned back and felt a sense of relief for the first time in a long while that the pressure from his wife's uncle might finally pass. If he could get the ancient sculptures out, it would also put him in good standing with the others at the oil ministry and whoever else his wife's uncle planned to reward with the Greek sculptures.

Bokhan was trying not to look disgusted when Igor's secretary rushed in and shouted, "Turn on the television."

On the American worldwide news network, *CNN*, there was a live story about another airline hijacking. A very serious looking reporter was saying that Trans World Airlines Flight 847 had just begun a flight from Cairo to San Diego with scheduled stops in Athens, Rome, Boston, and Los Angeles. Shortly after the first stop in Athens, it was hijacked by members of Hezbollah and Islamic Jihad. It was reportedly headed to the Beirut International Airport in Lebanon while the negotiators tried to decide what to do. One of the hijackers had pulled the pin on a hand grenade and was threatening to explode the aircraft. Igor laughed, "Those Americans have themselves in a mess by supporting Israel. The Arab terrorists know they will get big headlines by capturing Americans. Those crazy Arab bastards are not only causing us problems in Afghanistan, now they are also fighting the capitalists in the West. I love it."

CHAPTER 36

That same day as the unfortunate passengers were loading onto TWA Flight 847 to depart Athens, three gates down, Mark was also in the Athens Airport boarding a flight to Frankfurt, Germany.

When Mark realized that he could not call Vicki to help him with a fake cover story of another romantic vacation in Paris, he started talking openly on the phone and around the office about visiting nearby Turkey while he was still working in Greece. He used his credit card at a travel office near his hotel to book his ticket to Istanbul's Atatürk Airport and reserved a hotel room near the Hagia Sophia.

For his real trip Mark had the additional ticket Maria had purchased for him through her housekeeper along with enough clothes in his carry-on bag for a three-day trip to Frankfurt, Germany. He was feeling nervous but optimistic as he left for the airport. He first checked in for the flight to Istanbul, stood in that line, and just before boarding, he went to the restroom and then moved over to the Frankfurt flight.

He watched as the other passengers boarded the flight to Germany and noted how European women dressed more provocatively with tight and revealing clothes than women in Washington, D.C. Several wore what looked like expensive clothes and jewelry and checked him out as he sat nervously in the middle of the economy section. Everything seemed to be going well, and he was beginning to relax when he spotted the familiar faces of two rough, suspicious-looking men he had suspected of recently following him. The two men rushed onboard just before the flight closed the doors and were given two of the last seats available in the rear of the aircraft. They did not act as though they were traveling together and took care not to look his way, but he was sure it was the same two men. Mark started to panic. He hoped they did not know enough about what he was doing on the trip to arrest him, because if they did, they would likely find the film of the sculptures in the cave and Petkas's story that he had with him, and then everything would come crashing down.

As he thought more about it, he suspected the men were following him as they always did, just to find out more about what he was doing. Then he started thinking that they must be there for more than just casual observation, and likely had been watching him with Petkas and following all his moves. He hoped that they had not been trailing Petkas when he had gone to Delphi, and now his fears increased that they were going to catch him with the evidence of the secret treasure. He began to feel felt claustrophobic as the flight moved through the skies toward his uncertain future in Frankfurt. He felt he had to shake these guys somehow or he would confirm their suspicions that he really was doing something clandestine, and they perhaps would arrest him or do worse.

He assumed the ruse about going to Istanbul must not have worked. He became distressed that these men might see him with Bruce or whoever Bruce sent to pick him up, and then the entire idea of getting the sculptures out safely would be squashed. As he continued to mull over his problem, he thought that if they had seen through his deception, they might try to get rid of him like Maria had warned.

He began to think that if there was a plan to kill him away from Greece, the Greeks and Soviets could have a cover story to inoculate them from suspicion for his death. He started to think of all the reasons he never should have gotten involved in helping Petkas. Finally, he started looking around the aircraft and thinking of how to get himself out of an impossible situation.

In the galley, there were two stewardesses who looked like sisters lost in the age above thirty when makeup can add or subtract ten years. Their makeup seemed to do both. They looked like the movie version of friendly hookers in a rundown hotel. Both had looked Mark over from the moment he rushed aboard out of breath, wild-eyed, and hair askew.

They brought around refreshments for the three-hour flight, and later one of the sisters stopped by to offer more coffee. He had noticed that stewardesses always seemed to do that when his mouth was full, and he gulped the remainder of his cookie while smiling.

She asked, "Where are you from?"

"USA."

"You're not Greek?"

"No, I...."

"She thinks you are Greek," pointing to the other sister.

"No, I'm American." Mark was pleased that the clothes he had worn to blend in had been successful.

"Your parents are not Greek?"

"No. I look Greek. It's the hair and eyes." Mark realized he was patting his head and face as he talked.

"That's why she spoke to you in Greek. She thought you were...."

"Yes, the dark hair and eyes."

During this awkward conversation, Mark got an idea. He had been sitting with his long legs twisted between his seat and the one in front, trying to get comfortable while he worried about his predicament with the followers. In this aircraft, the arm rests did not flip up.

"Sorry, but I'm not feeling well. I wonder if I ...."

"Why don't you try it this way?" She folded down the back of the empty seat in front of him to make both the seats together resemble a recliner.

"Thank you, I ...." He made a sick face.

"Here," she ripped open a blanket and proceeded to shrink-wrap his feet and legs on the top of the seats. He had his shoes off and remembered the pads of his feet showed where he had almost worn through his socks, but pretended not to notice that his exposed feet were embarrassing. "There." She left him with his fake illness like an octogenarian on a cruise ship deck chair taking the air. As he slumped there he considered all the possibilities, including more elaborate thoughts on the idea that these men could have a plan to assassinate him somewhere outside of Greece. He became convinced that they would try to grab him at the busy Frankfurt airport as soon as they arrived.

When the flight began its descent he quietly told the same stewardess that he was really feeling much worse and needed to leave the aircraft immediately upon landing, before the other passengers. His worry had given him a look of someone who really was sick, and as they landed the stewardess brought him and his carry-on bag to the exit door and let him get off first. She held the other passengers until he was away. Thankful for the head start he evaded the men onboard who had to work their way out from their rear seats. He rushed as fast as he could through customs and passport control feeling a little better and wondering if his very active imagination had been over-thinking the situation.

As he exited the customs area into the swirling crowd of people in the terminal lobby there were signs everywhere in multiple languages and throngs of hurried passengers. He was confused and feeling lost, facing a throng of people many of them holding signs with names on them, when out from the gaggle of people awaiting the arriving passengers a stranger stepped forward and greeted him like they were old friends. The man picked up his bag and led him laughing and pointing to the outside door. When they reached the exit of the airport, a car immediately pulled up to the curb and they both got in and sped off.

The man did not speak often; however, he did tell Mark that they were headed to a hotel in the old part of the city. Mark figured that whatever was going on, he was grateful that he had lost the two men from the flight, and he immediately felt better about the efficiency of the CIA operation. They traveled in heavy traffic for about 20 minutes and then the driver pulled into a modern hotel in what looked like the old downtown section of Frankfurt. The man sitting next to Mark gave him a key and told him to bypass the front desk and go directly to his room, and the car pulled away. Mark crossed the sprawling lobby to the elevators, and the door opened.

He entered the elevator with his carryon bag and noticed that a very attractive woman was already in the elevator, and she stood next to him. She smiled as the door closed and, almost so quickly Mark did not know it happened, switched the room key from his hand with the one in hers. She kept looking straight ahead and said nothing. He looked down at the new key, and somewhat bewildered, got off on that floor and went to his new room.

Bruce, the CIA agent he had met in Panama, sat by a large pane of glass in the spacious, modern room, blowing the smoke from his cigarette through a smaller side window vent into the Frankfurt air. He looked over at Mark. "Put the bag on the bed and have a seat over here." He gestured to a chair opposite him. The television was turned on to *CNN* where the news of the TWA hijacking dominated everything else. The latest report was that terrorists had killed an American sailor on the flight, and the commentator speculated about injuries or the deaths of other Americans or Jews onboard. Bruce picked up the remote and turned the volume up to a medium level. "Damn, that makes us look impotent." Then he tossed the remote onto the bed and looked at Mark. "We have gone to some trouble to set up this meeting, so I hope what you have to say will be worth it."

Somewhat bewildered by the past several hours of this spy stuff, Mark had practiced what he was going to say. He knew Bruce was not going to give him much time to get to the point. He noticed that since the first time he had met Bruce in Panama about a year before, his wardrobe had improved and he was wearing better shoes and clothes that fit. Had he lost a little weight? Maybe he had a better job in the CIA now or a girlfriend to advise him how to look better. He was, however, still a dumpy, unlikable guy. Not someone you would notice shopping at the mall.

"I needed someone as sneaky and devious and well connected as you to help with a problem."

"Thanks for the compliments. So, what is the gig?"

"It's not about the election or directly about Ambassador Andropov, although his surveillance is part of it. I'm here about ancient hidden treasure." For the next hour and a half Mark did most of the talking and gave Bruce the story from start to finish. Once he got to the valuable sculpture, Bruce perked up and began to show real interest. Near the end of his story he took the rolls of photos from his bag, along with the maps and the description of the sculptures from Petkas, and handed them to Bruce. During the conversation, they both pulled food and drinks from the mini bar and crunched on the fast food snacks and washed it down with fruit juices.

He also told Bruce about Sergei Bokhan, Andropov's aide, and his overtures to the priest. He let him know about Maria's conversation with Bokhan and her notification of another CIA officer who Bruce said he knew. Bruce was very interested in that bit of information.

When he finished, Bruce leaned back. "So, you say the strong man of Greece hired the most prestigious foundry with the best stone carvers in Greece to make the greatest commission of sculpture ever. He paid some of the cost up front and he likely planned to pay the balance with the proceeds from the war. They took almost 20 years and made the best carvings ever created." He laughed and slapped his leg. "This is good stuff. You were right to figure you were in over your head and give me a call. I'm going to need some time to think about your story and talk to some other people. I need to have a conversation with the guy who used to work the Greek desk and get his take on what you've told me about the Russian." He tossed the rolls of film on the bed and nodded at them. "I'll get the film developed. Hope your guy did a good job with the camera." Bruce put the Petkas documents and maps on the bed with the film and leaned back, thinking.

"Unfortunately, we need to come up with a plan while you are here since we can't take the risk to have much contact when you are back in Greece. The election result has kicked off a timetable we need to follow or they will get too suspicious of your staying in Greece much longer. The Russians are good at surveillance. They've got lots of people around Europe who do nothing but look for people in circumstances like yours, and they likely have a bunch of them searching for you all over Frankfurt right now. You were smart to do what you did on the airplane and at the airport, but they'll have many more people looking for you now that you're here. We're going to have to hide you for a couple of days until you go back. We've got ways to do that, but you need to be ready to do exactly what we tell you and move when we tell you. Mark, it's time to put on your big boy pants."

Bruce picked up the phone and dialed the number for room service. "I've decided to have the vichyssoise. When can I expect it?" He hesitated. "That will be fine." Bruce looked at his watch and turned to look at Mark. "Okay, use the restroom here now. Clean up, change, or do whatever you have to do. When you leave here you will leave your bag. We'll get you taken care of for tonight. You've got about 10 minutes and then we will be putting you into an environment where it will be hard to find you. When we meet again, I'll have checked everything out with the experts, and have something of a plan for you to follow. Any questions?"

"I don't know enough to have any questions."

"Good," said Bruce.

The man who met him in the airport and accompanied him to the hotel came to the door rolling a food cart and dressed as a room service waiter. He dressed Mark in a waiter's jacket that had been stuffed under the cart and took him down the freight elevator to the kitchen and then to a small office off the kitchen area, where Mark swapped clothes again and put on a dirty and smelly pair of coveralls, thick work gloves, a long blond wig, glasses, and a stocking cap, and then the man put a white bandage over Mark's right ear. Now that he was ready and in his disguise, along with his minder, they waited in the room for the next step. Even in the crowded back room of the noisy kitchen, the atmosphere of Germany felt so different from Greece – industrial metal compared to stone and wood. It was a shock to be in such a different environment. The ride from the airport and the intense discussion in the hotel room with Bruce did not give him time to appreciate the difference in the surroundings. But Frankfurt was a modern city with the noise, pulse, and grit of a modern city, and it was an adjustment after the leisurely, calm pace of Greece.

When it was time to move, he was led back in to the kitchen just as the trash service team was taking out refuse, and he became part of the detail. Mark kept his head down and rolled a can of trash outside the door to the garbage truck in the alley. He got on the back of the truck and made three additional similar stops to haul garbage out of other kitchens and service dock areas. In the kitchen at the fourth stop, a man wearing glasses who was a similar size to Mark and who had long blond hair and a white bandage on his right ear quickly took his place.

Mark was then taken into another small room to change clothes again, this time into a muted plaid shirt and also a bulky plaid jacket of a different pattern and a felt hat containing the name of some British soccer team. To top that, he was given eyeglasses with thick black rims but clear glass in the lenses. He was led by his babysitter, similarly dressed, into the lobby of that hotel to join a group of British tourists. He stayed on the tour for the afternoon and went with the British group to their hotel for the night. His guide stayed with him every step of the way, and he provided Mark with a small travel kit like one available in business or first class on most international airlines, with a toothbrush and basic grooming needs, but there was no change of clothes, and Mark wondered when his suitcase did not appear if that meant something was wrong. He and his minder stayed in the same double room together and they rejoined the sightseeing tour the next day.

By midafternoon the clothes he had worn for two days were feeling crusty. His shirt retained a stain from the dinner sauce the night before and his pants showed a smear from chocolate left undetected on the bus seat. Then, at one of the tourist stops for the group at the 80-year-old Frankfurt Festahalle, with photos of uniformed Nazis lined in rows for large chess tournaments on the walls, his minder led him away from the British group into a side hallway and down a long stone corridor into an office. Inside Bruce sat at a table with some papers and bottled water in front of him. He was watching a small television tuned to *CNN*'s coverage of the ongoing TWA high-jacking. The man waited outside. There was a change of clothes that fit him and Mark gratefully rid himself of the British tourist garb.

Bruce frowned and looked uncharacteristically uncertain as he got up and paced back and forth while Mark sat exhausted from the hectic British tour schedule and drank a bottle of water. "You've given me a three-bank pool shot. The extraction will be hard to pull off and will require too many people to know about it to be safe. Starting now, don't say anything to anybody else about what we are about to discuss. Timing will be critical. It would be catastrophic for us to try to undertake the heist and fail. We'd be embarrassed forever. No lawyer would recommend following through on what we've concocted. You couldn't get insurance on this scheme for any premium." Bruce then stopped pacing and allowed his lips to move into a slight smile.

"Our analysts agree on the value and importance of these sculptures. The photos turned out to be good and the narrative of the history was very helpful. It would be a big coup for us to get them out of Greece under the noses of the socialists and communists. But it will be tricky to do and there is some real danger involved. There will be personal risk for you, this Petkas guy, and whoever else is going to be in on the crazy plan we have. Your buddy Petkas can never go home again. We'll need to get his family out and anyone else involved who could be punished later. It didn't hurt that Maria Beckett has given us a cherry on the top with this Bokhan guy. He could be a great get for us, and could really embarrass the Russians. So, we've got a twofer.

"If we are successful, the short-term problem we will have is what to do with the sculptures. We can't just put them in a big museum like the Smithsonian because the Greek government and Russians will know they were stolen and make a big stink internationally. What you've brought us is such a big story we have got to figure out how to break it. But we can figure that out later. First, we've got to get them out. That's all we will concentrate on for now. You're under the risk of international legal charges, and you will need to get your ass out of Greece and soon. After your little visit here, they are going to be very suspicious and will ramp up the surveillance on you. Because they are watching you, we are on a short fuse and we need to move on the deal now. If we wait for any length of time, they will grab you, Petkas and the others and sweat the secret out of all of you. We don't need an international incident with no reward. The defector is more of a straight shot. We'll do him at the same time."

Mark said, "But can't we work your plan through the embassy in Athens? They've got resources and are right there."

Bruce sneered, "Well, if your goal is to have them make this scheme public and start doing deals to trade the statues for some diplomatic bullshit, then go ahead. Those guys are trained not to take risks. They will never agree to removing a national treasure from a country. They are incapable of thinking outside the box. They built the box. And they can't keep a secret.

"Let me give you the fully blown plan we've cooked up. It's not sanctioned as yet, which will be difficult, and we have very little time to pull a team together and get them trained for this... insanity. So, none of what I'm about to tell you may come off, but sit down and listen." Bruce talked and Mark asked questions for two hours. They set up systems for communications and timing for all the events to come. Bruce grilled Mark to make sure he could remember the plan and the various sequences that needed to happen to make the timing work for each of the various tasks. He cautioned Mark not to write anything down. Starting at that moment they were on a clock that was quickly running down. Bruce made a call and said goodbye to Mark.

As Mark walked through the large plaza and back across the street from the Festhalle and into the lobby of his original hotel, he noticed that it had begun to rain and he got wet crossing the wide plaza. As he entered the elevator, he saw that the same woman was on it again, and she handed him his original room key. He found his luggage and all his clothes in the hotel room but noticed that his room was messy as though he had been there overnight. Toilet items scattered in the bathroom, some of his clothes were on the floor and others in the closet. A damp towel was hanging on the shower rail and he was impressed with all the attention that had been paid to the details of faking his having been in the room.

He was glad to at least have an opportunity to freshen up and change into his own clothes even though he had not slept well the night before, and turning on the television to *CNN*, he saw that some of the TWA hijackers' demands were being met and others rejected. The Greek government had released one of the hijacker's accomplices, and in exchange the hijackers had released eight Greek citizens including a Greek pop singer. He switched off the TV, picked up the ticket on the top of the bureau and headed to the airport. It was raining harder as he left the hotel to get into the taxi and his fresh clothes became wet on his shoulders and back.

As the taxi rumbled along, with wipers splashing the rain back and forth on the autobahn toward the airport, Mark wondered what Vicki was doing now. It was Sunday morning in Washington, and he imagined the *New York Times* and *Washington Post* piled around the condo and Vicki with her coffee in that old robe from her college days she always wore when she was puttering.

The exciting prospect of being a father was building in him and he wanted to share it with her as well as learn more about what impending motherhood meant to her. He didn't even know if she and the baby were healthy. He worried about how angry and hurt she had been in Paris and wondered if she still loved him. Nothing made any sense, and he was so caught up in this spy stuff he had to force himself not to think of his very real life back in Washington.

As they drove on through the thick traffic, the rain blurred everything happening outside of the car, and as Mark listened to the steady metronome sound of the wipers his mind wandered back to Vicki. He remembered hearing the phone ring several months before and the sound of her voice.

Vicki had called Mark in his office with the news that it was going to rain that afternoon. She concluded, "You need to leave the office. We've got to try Great Falls today."

"Isn't it too cold?"

"No. It will be perfect. It'll be an experience that we will both love and it will make us feel closer to each other."

"Well I don't know . . ."

She interrupted. "We've talked about this. Remember, we both said it would be wonderful to do and so much fun."

"Well . . ."

"No one's going to catch you. Do I have to start to make clucking sounds to shame you into doing this?"

"I'll meet you at the condo at two."

During their many walks moving west away from Washington along the C&O canal tow path they had explored the woods and rocks between the canal and the Potomac River. They found in the many nooks and crannies past the water filtration plant where there was a place among the rocks few people ever went. There were enormous boulders, some as big as houses and others the size of small cars, which lay in random piles between the two strips of water.

That afternoon like school kids playing hooky they made it onto the trail just as the rain was starting. They put on their ponchos and felt the humidity warm them under the plastic as they walked briskly down the trail to the place where they cut into the woods. After watching carefully for a full 15 minutes after they saw the last person scurrying off the trail seeking shelter, and as the rain's intensity picked up, they found the special place in the rocks.

There in the rain they took off all their clothes and bagged them in the plastic to keep them dry. They lay down together side by side on a sight incline midway up one of the larger boulders and let the rain splash over them and roll down their bodies. It came trickling down from the higher places in the rocks onto their heads and shoulders and formed small streams around their sides as gravity took it further down to the ground. At first, they felt the movements and tingle as grains of sand and small leaves swept past them down off the rocks, but those were quickly dispersed and then the place felt clean and welcoming. In the distant brush, there was the sound of the scurrying of a few small creatures, but mostly the rain dominated everything and was the only thing that could be heard or was in motion as they faced the sky.

In the dim afternoon, quiet except for the sound of the rain, it felt as though they were the only people on earth. They had been planning this outing since they had moved in together and were determined to do it before Mark left for Greece. As they lay face up and let the drops splat on their faces, they became used to the surprising sting of the drops and it soon felt welcoming. Large beads that landed on the rocks by them exploded giving secondary splatters that tickled their ears. Looking up they could see the thousands of drops coming individually down that eventually hurt their eyes too much to watch.

So, they closed their eyes and one hand found the other as they lay side by side, and even though they were naked and alone together, the feeling was not sexual, but purely and completely sensuous. They had both speculated on how it would be, but for now they just enjoyed the free feeling like Adam and Eve or whatever primitive beings must have felt in that first rainstorm before the world evolved.

After a while, with the cumulative dampness on their skin, and with the temperature dropping they rolled into each other, holding on and allowing their body heat to warm them. The rain gradually stopped and they lay there, not talking but just looking at each other as the drops rolled off leaving them almost dry.

Mark looked at Vicki and said, "Wow. That was wonderful. What a great idea I had."

"You had!" She playfully slapped him on the arm.

As the taxi approached the airport for his Lufthansa flight, he sensed that the damp from the rain and the odor from his wet clothes was the same smell he remembered from being with Vicki at Great Falls.

CHAPTER 37

Igor was pacing the floor while he talked to his staff during a security meeting at the Soviet Embassy. "The American went to Frankfurt and lost our trackers. We did not pick him up again for two days when he was returning to Athens. You're telling me that we don't know what he was doing or who he met with? I've had enough of this incompetence. We need to find some excuse to get the Greek police to pick him up and sweat him, slap him around some. Those Americans are so soft he'll crack like an egg."

The senior security man with a cast on his finger, demurred, "But Mister Ambassador, because he is an American, that is very risky. If we pick him up, his embassy will get involved, and they may uncover our enterprise and also begin to follow him. Also, it is likely they will put security around him or just send him home. Then his plans for the theft of the sculptures with the professor will be in jeopardy. We may never find out what we wanted to know about the treasure unless we keep him here." Realizing he needed to give something back to assuage Igor's ego, he now said, "We did what you suggested and listened to the phone of the woman in Washington. She and the American person have not spoken in weeks although he has tried to call her several times.

"Before he went to Frankfurt, we found that he had made plans to go to Istanbul. On that day, we followed him to the airport, and we had people waiting for him on his Turkey flight and in Istanbul to meet his flight when he arrived. We bribed the hotel person and had video and audio set up in his hotel room, but that morning someone called and cancelled the room and the flight. We had no way of knowing that though, and we almost lost him at the airport here because we had our people already on board for the Istanbul flight. Somehow, he had gotten a ticket to Frankfurt. We had to rush two more men after him who barely made that flight, but because they had to take seats far away from him, we lost him in the Frankfurt Airport. We did everything we could have done. Perhaps… perhaps if you had told us more about what you wanted us to do and we had known of this plot to steal Greek treasure earlier… well we are doing all we can now."

Igor nodded and ignored the implied criticism, "Maybe so, but I fear we are getting behind on what is happening here. And I feel certain he knows he is being followed. NOT losing him is what is important. Maybe it is time to get the Greek leaders involved. We will need to do it eventually, and perhaps they will be of assistance in getting to the American spy or the Greek professor. Start with the Greek professor. I want the Greek security service to grab him and work on him. Brief them on our suspicions about stealing treasure, but don't give them too much. Have them make him fear for his family."

Still nervous the security man said, "I have already had discussions with the Greek security people, and their bosses say this man is a respected professor. He has a good record and is well-liked. They believe if they pick him up for questioning, then the university will protest and that will give the government and PASOK bad publicity. I spoke to them again right after the election, and they are even more concerned now that they seem to be losing public support because of the drop in the voting. They do not know what we heard on the tapes, or if they know somehow, they do not consider it a cause for concern."

Igor nodded, and at the same time frowned at the security officer. "As you will. Call the First Secretary to the Prime Minister and the Interior Minister. Have them come to see me here tomorrow at 10 a.m. I will deal with this problem myself."

After the meeting, Igor ranted at Bokhan about the pace of the investigation of the American and the professor and how it might affect his career. When he had calmed down he told Bokhan, "Tomorrow, pick me up at the home of the woman where you did before. I feel like some excitement tonight."

The next morning the First Secretary of the Greek Prime Minister and the Interior Minister of Greece came to the embassy as requested to see Igor in his office. "Gentlemen, you may thank me later for what I am about to do. I have saved you and your country great embarrassment from thieves and traitors." The two men collectively gasped, "What?"

Igor calmed himself and summoned as much charm as he could muster to lead the Greek political and government officials where he wanted them. "Please, my comrades, be quiet and listen. I wish to share with you how we are working to protect your country and uphold your honor and ours as well. Because I and my Soviet staff are diligent and care about treachery in your country, we have been watchful for problems. We have uncovered a plot to steal some of your national treasures from antiquity."

"What? Who is this? We must . . ."

Igor held up his hand, "Please, gentlemen. Listen as I have asked you to do. The best part of our discovery is that the villains are your political enemies. When the time is right, and it is fast approaching, we will catch some high-ranking members of the New Democracy party stealing Greek artifacts to sell to the West." Igor could tell from the looks on their faces that these blockheads were not going to be compliant and he needed to be firmer in his discussion. He had to get them under his control to manage what needed to happen to the sculptures.

The Greeks stammered. "But, how can what you are telling us be true? We must know."

"You must know what I decide to tell you! And you will know it when I am ready to tell you. If it were not for me and my Soviet staff you would be sipping tea and ouzo and be blissfully unaware that a big theft is going on under your noses."

"But what … why did you bring us here to tell us these fantasies. This is our country. We demand to know."

"You will demand nothing! If you want to be in on this capture of these traitors and the very big international press attention the apprehension of these thieves will generate, here is what you will do. First, you can tell the Prime Minister that something is going on that will be a great benefit to him, but you must not tell him too much. He might mistakenly give up the secret, and the thieves will get away. Second, you must have a group of police you absolutely trust to be on the alert and ready for several raids on the homes and offices and hotels that I will tell you about when the time is right.

"Now, third, I want you to break into the home of this professor, Stanos Petkas, who works at the New Democracy party. Grab him and his family. Threaten them. Make him choose between his family and his secret. Make it messy and public. Embarrass him in public when you pick him up."

The two men leaned back at the audacity of the Soviet ambassador. "We cannot just do that based only on your suspicions. We have laws here that prevent that kind of activity. We can pick him up for questioning, but we will not shame him and his family. He is a respected academic at our university and a world authority on Greek history and antiquities. What proof do you have that Professor Petkas is involved in some plot? You can't just come in to our country and make these wild claims."

Igor looked at them with disgust and shook his head. "Very well. But you should know that I am making a note of your timidity. We will find the stolen treasure as I have predicted, and you will be ashamed that you did not act sooner with this professor. At the right time, I will give you the dates and times of these raids, and the names of those who are to be detained, and what to look for in the raids. However, no one, and I must emphasize this at the risk of your damaging your relations with the Soviet Union, no one will say anything or do any investigating until I tell you to do it. The theft of your historic artifacts is in a delicate stage. If you try to interject yourselves without me, you will scare them off. I have spoken to you in good faith today. I expect you to return the respect and confidence I have shown. Am I clear?"

The Secretary of the Interior shook his head, "Ambassador, you are not giving us anything to make us understand or fully appreciate the wild story you have told us. We will look foolish with these highly irregular directions. You must give us more details of this proposal of yours. We must be able to tell our Prime Minister and our police or soldiers more. You cannot tell us what to do in our own country. You either come up with proof of what you are saying or stand down with these charges."

"That is exactly what I will not do. I am doing you and your government a favor to bring you in for the publicity photos so you can get some credit. I will not have your incompetent police or military foul up my plans. This is my operation. If you do not want some of the credit, I will be glad to take it all. When you interrogate this Professor Petkas you will find out the truth in what I'm talking about. Confirm your suspicions and then I will share more information."

The men looked at each other and back at Igor. "No. We will start with what you have told us, but we must be informed as these events evolve. We will talk to Professor Petkas, but we must have warning to mobilize forces for these arrests and searches, and we must have proof for a reason to act. You cannot act with this aggression in our country without our approval. Do not think you can exceed your authority on our soil."

"That is precisely why I am telling you to get ready. I know it may take your people time to prepare. You are alerted to be ready! Is that so hard?"

When they left, the angry Minister of the Interior was so offended at Igor's dismissal of them, that he put a 24-hour surveillance team on him and demanded to see daily the transcripts of the tap on the Ambassador's phone. He contemplated bugging every phone in the Soviet Embassy, but thought he would wait until they found out more about the plot to steal some Greek artifacts and see what Professor Petkas had to say.

CHAPTER 38

Mark lay awake in his bed at 3 a.m. remembering everything that had happened earlier as he looked out the window at the Parthenon in the distance, lights shining on it and perched over Athens like a space ship that had landed in the rocky hills. A strange thought to have, but not so much considering everything else that had happened. He recalled the first the attempt to assassinate him, then the move to get the crowd to attack him, now tonight's kidnapping of Stanos Petkas. The danger and threats were all getting too close. He felt like he was in a narrow street with a car driving fast toward him, with the lights on bright blinding him in the night. This constant danger needed to end soon or he would leave and the hell with the sculptures.

Maria had gotten the call from him not long after he was released, then even though it was almost midnight she picked up Mark on a side street a few blocks from his hotel and they drove to convene in a neighborhood park near the home of Stanos Petkas at a set of benches where they could see if anyone approached. When they arrived and found him, Maria was shocked to see her friend looking so rumpled and uncomfortable. He had a swollen bruise on his lip and she could see dried blood on his shirt collar even under the dim lights of the city park. Concerned, she and Mark approached Petkas as he slumped on a bench and sat down beside him.

As they sat quietly, Petkas recapped what had happened much earlier that evening. He spoke looking at the ground, trying to remember the details as best he could and his voice had taken on a detached manner in a monotone as though what had happened was about someone else, someone other than him who had been frightened and abused.

Earlier that afternoon he had finished clearing out the last of the papers in his desk and stacked them with some supplies he wanted to keep from the New Democracy campaign office and began to take the material out to his car in the parking lot. As he walked to his car struggling with the cumbersome box, a large man quickly walked in front of him and from behind he felt a meaty hand wrap all the way around one of his elbows. As he looked, he saw that he actually was surrounded by three large men. They told Petkas that they were from the state security services and that he had to come with them for a meeting. They did not give him any options, and one of the men put the box in Petkas's car and drove it, following the car containing the other two men and Petkas.

The two men who drove him across Athens were quiet and gave him no answers to his repeated questions of where were they going, what was the urgency, why he was needed, and what was going on. They continued for over 30 minutes until they finally left the traffic and drove into an area on the outskirts of Athens where Petkas had never been, and that had a rundown, industrial look.

Petkas was taken into an ugly four-story building with no markings on the outside and few windows. Inside, the place smelled musty and stale and he was quickly led down a dimly lit hallway with several metal doors on either side and ushered into a windowless room that was furnished with a small metal table and several metal chairs and featured a slightly slanted floor with a drain in the low end. The walls were spare concrete and looked like they had never been painted, and there was a pile of trash including some rumpled clothing in one corner. On one wall a faucet poked out of the wall and a hose hung draped over the spout. He was seated in a hard metal chair facing the door, across a sturdy metal table with two chairs on the other side, and his hands were then cuffed to a metal ring on the table-top that was secured through the top to the underside of the table. One of the men shook the chain to make sure it was fastened. Then the men who had led him into the small, dank room and had locked him to the table left, and a few seconds later the overhead light which had a thick wire screen protecting the bulb, went out. He heard a latch turn in the door and then everything got very quiet.

He sat there for what seemed like a very long time when suddenly the light came on again, blinding him, and two of the men who had picked him up when he left his office then came in, and unfastened him from the table and stood him up. They changed the position of the handcuffs to pin his arms behind his back. One man went behind him and the other got close to his face. The man's breath was rotten with garlic, cigarettes, and stale food. He looked at Petkas with disgust. He nodded at the man behind Petkas who suddenly pulled on the chain connecting the handcuffs to Petkas's wrists which jerked his arms upward, wrenched his shoulders, bent him over at his waist and caused such pain that Petkas cried out.

He was held at that position which had raised him awkwardly on his toes to try to escape the pull of the chain. Then the man behind dropped him, and Petkas, off balance and in shock from the torment, crashed down on the hard metal table, bruising his lip which began to bleed.

Without warning he was lifted again in the painful position, and he was afraid his shoulders were being ripped out of their joints and he felt vomit rising in his throat. The man in the front who must have been the alpha dog said, "You should stand with respect when you are with us. You remember this position for next time." Then the man who spoke nodded at the other who dropped Petkas again on the desktop, unfastened the handcuffs and put them on the front again, pulling his arms roughly to renew the pain as he snapped them shut and reattached them to the desk. He then leaned down again to look at Petkas close to his face, and the smell from the man's mouth coupled with the pain made Petkas gag and struggle to avoid throwing up. He whispered, "Soon someone will come in here to talk to you. You will give him the answers he wishes or we will be back."

The man smiled at Petkas's discomfort. "You remember when you talk to the man, what will happen if you do not tell him what we want. I actually hope you do not tell him, because I would like to smash up a smart man like you. You think you are better than us with your books and your college. I will teach you the lessons of life. I will teach you how to beg for mercy and to crawl on the floor. I will stick that hose up your ass and turn it on. So, I ask you, just for me, do not tell the man what he wants. Do not prevent me from my pleasure. I wish to spend a lot of time with you in this room." He smiled leaning close to the face of Petkas, and as he said these things his eyes deliberately looked over the face of Petkas as if searching for a place to injure him next time. He then pulled away slowly and the two men deserted the room, leaving Petkas slumped over the table. The light switched off. They had moved the chair back when they got him up, and it was too far away to reach it with his leg to pull it close enough to sit down so he was forced to lean over the table in a position that pained his back and left his legs quivering.

At a point when he was not sure he could take the pain and discomfort anymore, the door opened, the light came on, and a man came in. He brought the chair under Petkas who immediately collapsed into it. He breathed deeply as the pain in his back began to subside and the dizziness from the stress lessened so he could focus again. The new man was of a normal size and not muscular like the others, but trim and neat. He carried some papers in a folder and sat down in one of the chairs on the opposite side of the table from Petkas and smiled at him. "Dr. Petkas, before we have our little talk, I want to make sure you know what is at stake." He then pulled out photos of the Petkas household, his children at play in the neighborhood and his wife in their car taking the children to school. "There are so many innocent people who could be harmed if you do not decide the correct thing to do. So many accidents can happen. I want you to think about what could happen to your family for a few minutes and then I will return."

"Please, I need to go to the bathroom."

"Certainly. You have my permission. There is a drain in the back end of this room so whatever you do will flow down in that direction. Please rest assured you will not do any harm to our facility. Go ahead whenever you feel like it. And, thank you for asking first. It is so polite." The man left, the light went off again, and Petkas felt the warmth down his leg into his shoe, fill it over the top and onto the floor.

He sat for a long time in the dark with the smell of his urine mingling with the other smells of cement, metal and the faint odor of vomit in the room. He did not have any idea if it was the same day or the next, and it gave him time to remember stories he had heard of how this treatment was not uncommon with political prisoners, and was designed to disorient interrogation subjects and cause them to bring what they were hiding to the front of their consciousness. This kind of mental torture was supposed to make it harder for them to conceal their secrets and easier to question. In spite of this knowledge, Petkas could feel the fear building in him.

He thought, I am a smart person and I know what they are doing, so I'm not going to give in to this stupid and childish game of anticipating what they might do to me or let my imagination conjure up the ghosts and monsters that these people wish for me to fear. I am going to use my intelligence against these scare tactics. Petkas concentrated, but the quiet and the dark persisted, and it began to annoy him, and he wished he had an idea how long he had been there with no sound or light to give him a touchstone to reality and help him with his effort not to be afraid. Occasionally he could hear in the distance a clang like a banging against metal or a thump as though something big had fallen over.

In the dark with no other stimulus, he could sense the primal functions of his body, the path of the blood, the soft thump of his heart, and he could hear his breathing. His legs in the damp pants and his foot soaking in the shoe were now cool. He felt the pain in his shoulders and back gradually subside and tried to calm his body and concentrated on slow breathing exercises to soothe the pain as well as his nervous heart. He wondered if they would interrupt this rather pleasant and unusual reverie with a sudden rush into the room with more physical threats or actual pain. He had heard stores of torture and how no one could stand it. He knew that his threshold for pain was very low, and he wondered how he could avoid telling them what they were after. He had thought about a counter story to any sculpture that was somewhat believable involving potshards and coins buried north of Athens. If they hurt him too much he would give them that. He continued to try to control his breathing in order to calm down, and finally he felt his body relax.

Just as he was getting sleepy from the quiet and the dark, the door opened and the light flashed on to almost blind him once again. Petkas blinked to adjust his eyes and squinted to adjust his vision. One of the men who had hurt him earlier entered, checked to see that his restraints were firm and then left. Then the man with the photos came back for another round. He still carried the same folder and sat down again opposite Petkas. Stanos Petkas realized he had to get his act together now for his sake and that of his family. He focused his not inconsiderable brain on what he had to say and how he had to act.

"Doctor Petkas, why don't you tell me why you are here?"

"I have no idea. You have made some sort of mistake. I do work for the New Democracy party in my political life, but I thought we stopped abusing political opponents like the way you are treating me many years ago. Besides you won the election. I am guessing that Premier Papandreou does not know about our little meeting, and I doubt he would approve."

The man looked down at his papers and then back up at Petkas. "Oh, he would be most enthusiastic, Professor. Although he is a kind man, he dislikes traitors and thieves. You have been an honorable man in the past, Professor. Why would you risk your career and all the work you have done to make yourself one of the great experts in the world on Greek history and archeology? Why risk losing all that, to say nothing of what will happen to your family? Those cute little boys and your lovely wife will miss their daddy, their husband. It is a sad path you have chosen." The man thumbed through the papers and then sat silently looking off onto a blank corner of the back wall.

Petkas knew the man was using a ploy to get him to speak and reveal something damaging, but he also was worried that an innocent man would be asking his accuser what the man was talking about and proclaiming innocence. So, he said, "I don't know what you are talking about. I do not know why I am here." "Professor, it has come to the attention of our security services that you and the American spy, who has been working at the New Democracy campaign, are conspiring to steal valuable artifacts from the Greek government and from the Greek people. You are involved in a conspiracy that is disloyal to your country and which is against our laws and the laws of all international governments written to prevent the theft of national treasures. You of all people should know that."

Petkas felt his anxiety rising and tried to control his blood pressure by breathing evenly and telling himself to remain calm. He made an effort to control his voice and speak slowly. "Mister, I do not know what you are talking about. I love my country and I love its archeological treasures. I have spent my whole life understanding their history and teaching their value to the students at two of our major universities. No one has more respect for our antiquities and culture than I do."

The man thumbed through the folder and moved a couple of pieces of paper around. He smiled at one reference, made a note with his pen, and then put the folder down. The man then crossed his arms and rested them on the table. "You are not as clever as you think. We know of your plans and those of the American. If you work with us now, we will spare you and your family. You can go on teaching and living your life as you wish. We really just want the American. You can help us to catch him and actually come out of this cell looking like a hero instead of the traitor that you are. Your choices are quite starkly opposed, considering the alternative. We just need you to confirm what we already have. We want to hear it from you. Be careful, because we will know when you are lying.

"Tell us what the treasure is, where it is, what your plans are to steal it, and about the involvement of this American and who else is helping you. Do this and you can live your life untarnished. If you lie or refuse to help your government, you and your family are finished. You will be in jail forever and your family will be disgraced and thrown into the cold streets to fend for themselves with the curse and the stigma of your treachery hung around their necks for the rest of their miserable lives."

Calmer now with his breathing exercises, Petkas was better prepared to respond. "You do paint a bleak picture. But I still have no idea what you are talking about."

Now the man leaned forward on his forearms halfway across the small table and turned up the temperature. "Do you or do you not know the American, Mark Young?"

"Of course, I know him. We work together in the campaign, or did work there before the election."

The man nodded. "And have you been talking about the theft of Greek archeological treasure as you walk around town?"

A light went on in his mind and Petkas now felt that this interrogation session was caused by some conversations that had been overheard by the watchers on the walks he had with Mark. He remembered the times when he had been so frightened and Mark had to calm him down. He tried to remember what he was rambling about when he had the panic attacks, and suspected that they did not have any really specific information, or at least enough to arrest him. He now felt somewhat relieved that this inquisition was to find out information not to confront him with a complete legal case. "We do take walks around Athens for exercise and I have been telling him about Greek history, and that includes telling him how sculpture and other archeological art and treasures were made, where and when. I've been giving him bits and pieces from my classroom lectures as we walked about. We have walked into museums and historic sites where I have shown him our culture. There is nothing wrong with that."

"Professor, we know you are planning to steal art and treasure. You were overheard talking about the theft. There are recordings."

"No. That makes no sense. Whoever told you that has made up a story that has wasted your time and mine." He paused calculatingly. "Well, I guess if someone overheard only part of a conversation, and had an active imagination, they might make a false assumption, but they would be wrong. I've talked about appreciating our art history and seeing it in museums, not stealing it. I'm a professor not a thief. Now, we have just shared an interesting experience, but I'm ready for you to let me go. Let me leave now and I will not press charges, but if you keep me here any longer, when I get out, I will call a press conference and I'll have you and whoever talked you into this inquisition put in jail." Petkas stared at the man who stared back for a few moments, broke eye contact and then got up and left the room. The light stayed on.

About 10 minutes later one of the big men came back in, unshackled Petkas from the table and led him back to the street, where in the dim light from the street lamps he could see where his car was parked. He tossed Petkas' keys onto the sidewalk and went back inside.

Petkas let out a sigh as he finished his story and looked up at Maria and Mark as if he was coming out of a dream. His shoulders slumped.

Mark could tell that Maria was forcing herself to remain calm and kept her voice free of emotion as she responded, "Although you have not told me everything, I suspect you have discovered something from Greek antiquity and you and Mark here are plotting to smuggle it out to protect it from the incompetent Papandreou government and the greedy Soviets."

Both men remained silent.

Maria snorted, "So that is the intrigue I have been feeling around the office." She looked at Petkas. "I do caution you for removing the treasures of your homeland. I trust you have good reasons and your plan is to bring whatever it is back when it is safe to do so."

Petkas nodded.

"I may be able to help with some of my contacts and resources. Come to me as your circumstances require. There is a woman who is a secretary in the finance office who I have known for some time is a spy for the Soviets. I can let her overhear or find information for her to pass on that will send them on a false trail. We will have the office open for two more weeks to prepare for the next election and store our materials for another time. I'll make sure she is kept around to spy on us. We can use her as our connection to them when it will do the most good. I hope you both know how dangerous the game is that you are playing?" She smiled and looked at Petkas, "Over the past couple of weeks I've met with a Russian diplomat who you remind me of, Stanos. I spoke of him when we had lunch down by the sea."

"How do you mean?

"You are something like this Russian, Sergei Bokhan. Similar ages, successful in your fields, both married with two kids, and you both have struggled with ethical questions and in the end decided to do the moral thing over loyalty to your country. That can't be easy."

Petkas looked back at the ground. "It's not. But if he is our enemy, I don't see how I can identify with him or have much compassion for him when I think of what he has been doing for all these years and for whom."

Maria patted him on the knee. "I'm sure he thought he was supporting the honor of his country as you do yours. Anyway, it's likely you both will end up in the U.S., at least for a little while. By the way, he mentioned the sculptures to me, so it is widely known. You guys are not great spies."

Petkas shuffled his feet in the dirt in front of the bench to keep warm. "Mmmmm. Can't help what they know now. I understand what you say about the similarities, but I want to avoid him. I have to keep myself and my family first in my mind."

"I understand. And you," she turned to Mark, "you seem to have gotten into something here in Greece that is not your responsibility. Not to be insulting, but I know you are not sophisticated in the intrigues we are more accustomed to in Europe. I just want you to be careful and remember that being an American can protect you only so far. Americans disappear and Americans die abroad. Catching you doing something illegal would be a coup for the security people here and at the Soviet Embassy. Do not be foolish with your life and safety."

She looked over at the car park and back at her colleagues. "Stanos Petkas." He looked at her, surprised at her addressing him so formally. "Given what has happened to you and may likely happen again at any time, now is the time for you to go into hiding. You need to put some ice on that lip and wherever else you are hurt. Get your family ready to leave as soon as possible. I'll send someone over to your house soon, tonight, to collect your family and send them somewhere out of the country as though they were going on a vacation. Do whatever you have to do quickly. You yourself need to disappear. Tomorrow get some cash and go to a small hotel on the edge of town or someplace you cannot be found. I'll send someone to help you when you are settled. Here." She gave him a phone number, "Call this number once a day and I will have a way that Mark can keep you up to speed with information."

Petkas frowned and his brow wrinkled, "This is . . ."

Maria quickly responded, "You have gotten yourself and your family in this mess and I am giving you advice on how to stay alive and out of prison. They know about whatever you and Mark here are doing! Whatever you two have planned better happen soon or you are done."

She turned to Mark. "And you better be prepared to leave very soon as well. They may give you a few days of grace because you are an American, but that will soon disappear." She breathed out a sigh. "That is the best advice I can give you two, not knowing what you have planned.

"It's time for you to execute whatever it is you have cooked up. I can see over there under the street light that the watchers have caught up with us and are making their way over here to try to listen to what we say. Time to go."

Igor Andropov fidgeted as he watched the video of the Petkas interrogation by the Greek security forces and then he began a running commentary on the proceedings. "What was that? Who was the idiot who was asking the questions? He applied no pressure. He did not hit him once! What happened to those two big guys? They need to have beat him more. What kind of place do they run? That was pathetic. My grandmother could have been harder."

Bokhan calmly said to Igor, "Mr. Ambassador, I spoke directly to the head of Greek security, and the Greeks felt that because they did not have solid proof of this man's guilt or even specifics of the crime, they were limited in how far they could go. The man in these pictures is an honored professor and an internationally known scholar. They did not feel they could beat him up on the speculation from the transcripts of the tapes we obtained from our surveillance."

Igor squeezed his hands on either side of his head. "My God! These Greeks are all incompetents. Double the surveillance! I want all the phones tapped. I want daily reports. FIND what we need to know to catch them. Do I have to do everything?"

He then turned to Bokhan, "Send in my chief security officer. Not the man with the broken finger, the new one, and find Tito Petrovia. You can leave. Now is the time for men with balls. You are too cautious. I'm ready for action and your advice is that of an old woman. But before you go, are the Spetsnaz solders here in Greece and in hiding as I requested?"

"Yes, Mr. Ambassador. They arrived yesterday and are in hiding"

"Good. Now send in my security people. I can handle it from here. I had hoped you would be more of an asset to me Mr. Bokhan, but you have disappointed me when the time came for bold action. After I capture these traitors and spies, we may have to reassess our relationship. Send in the 'hummer'."

Igor was calculating all of his options and now believed he had arrived at a solution that would satisfy everyone and leave him in a significantly enhanced position. Once he had secured the sculptures and other artifacts that the Greek professor and American spy had been hiding, he would throw the Greeks a bone and give some of it to them. The larger portion he would get to his wife's uncle, but he would bargain with the uncle for a significant fee. At that point in his musings, Igor once again let his imagination take over.

He could see how the sculptures transaction would enhance his reputation with the uncle and others at the oil ministry, which should secure for him a posting in Paris or London. He would find a way to blame his assistant Bokhan for the delay in obtaining the sculptures and the decline in the Greek election. With Bokhan as the scapegoat for any troubles in Greece, he could find a new assistant with more experience to the new posting in whichever better country he was assigned. He'd make sure his son knew and saw that his father was an important man, and he'd find a way to keep that bitch of a wife away on travel and out of his hair. His new plan would work; he knew it.

The next morning as Petkas left his house, a car pulled in front of him blocking his car on one of the lightly traveled streets near his home. A man of average size but with muscles showing through tight clothing got out and walked slowly to the side window and put both of his thick hands on the door frame.

Petkas nervously rolled down the window halfway and asked what the man wanted. A slow smile came over the man's face and he stared at Petkas with cold dark eyes for a moment before speaking. "Mr. Stanos Petkas?"

"Yes. What do you want?"

"Pro-fes-sor," he dragged out the word, highlighting all the syllables. "Professor, what I want is the sculpture you and the American are planning to steal."

"I don't know what you are talking about, I . . ."

The man cut him off and leaned in closer. "No more bullshit."

Petkas was now scared. "You people tried to intimidate me in that prison yesterday and I told you that I . . ."

"That is not me! Those men yesterday were weak men who must live in the polite society and obey the laws of the government. That is not me. You will tell me what I want to know or one of your children will disappear tomorrow. And then the other one the next day. And then your wife. Then I will start to take things from your body. You will tell me."

A car belonging to one of his neighbors drove around them and had to use the shoulder of the street to pass the two cars and slowed to a crawl. The woman driving looked at the configuration of the two vehicles, with one blocking the other and taking up most of the two-lane road. Something which was highly unusual in this residential area. Tito waved the car on, but it continued to pass slowly and then stopped about twenty yards on and the woman and two children in the car looked back at them and did not move further. Tito smiled at the car and turned back to Petkas. "You can thank your neighbors. I give you till tomorrow morning, but no more time." He then slowly got back into his car and pulled off, leaving Petkas sweating and tightly gripping the steering wheel of his car.

CHAPTER 39

Maria Beckett sat down in the elaborately decorated office of Marcellus Dedacus, the PASOK official who was the Undersecretary of the Interior, the officer in charge of much of Greek internal security. She had confirmed her earlier suspicions and now had firmly in her mind what she needed to say. He greeted her warmly but with a note of caution in his voice, "My old friend, I'm not sure if I should be meeting with you. There are rumors that one of your distinguished political associates may be in trouble. Have you come here on behalf of Professor Petkas?"

Maria smiled wanly and shook her head, "Secretary Dedacus, I am sure whatever the rumors are concerning Dr. Petkas are untrue and will be sorted out by you and your excellent staff to a just conclusion." She looked over at the window where a large vase of flowers was tastefully arranged. "Oh, my, are those from your wife's lovely garden? I've always admired your fabulous lawn and beautiful horticulture. She is so gifted."

"Yes." He said proudly. "In the season, she brings in a fresh arrangement every week to brighten my office, which otherwise is occupied with more solemn matters. She makes this place more cheerful." He looked around the office and smiled.

Marisa bowed her head in acknowledgement and was pleased that she had moved the discussion onto a friendlier turf. "Unfortunately, I am here regarding another, different rumor that I hope in my heart is as untrue as the one about Dr. Petkas. But as a good Greek citizen I feel obligated to report such things to your office as is requested by law."

Dedacus nodded with a serious look on his face and spread his hands apart in an accepting gesture.

Maria hesitated, "Coming here for me is embarrassing and I beg your forgiveness if I am being indiscreet, but we have been friends for many years and I thought you should be informed." She patted her hair nervously and wiggled to settle a bit more into the chair. "Well, you know how all of us women like to talk... and sometimes we are overly protective of our families." She paused. "You have a beautiful niece, I think her name is Sophia Speros, who I have seen at many of the embassy parties over the past few years. She is charming and so full of life and has such a youthful spirit. Although..." here Maria wrung her hands, "I have heard from some of my lady friends, who also have young daughters, that she has become very friendly with the Soviet Ambassador.

"That in itself is nothing to even consider, but I hear that he can be very controlling and may be keeping her under circumstances that could pose somewhat of a disadvantage for her. Now, I'm sure if her immediate family is in close and constant contact with her, that rumor is entirely untrue, as I hope it is." She wrung her hands again. "I came here today based on our long-standing friendship, because I did not want to let my suspicions and those of the other ladies in my circle pass unreported just in the remote case that she is not receiving the absolute respect, honor ... and s...safety she deserves. You have my word I will never speak of our conversation again as it has been most unpleasant for me even to come here and whisper about what I trust is an unlikely circumstance, but I know from my own unfortunate experience that sometimes the loving family is the last to know in these kinds of...misfortunes." Maria bowed her head again and gathered her purse to leave.

Dedacus rocked back and forth in his chair uncomfortably and waved one of his hands in a small circle. "Well, I am honored that you feel close enough to me to share this confidence. I feel certain that what you have implied is absolutely just a rumor, and untrue, but now that I think of it, I have not seen her out at the embassy functions in the past several months. In fact, when I have called her to come with me as she used to do, she has made excuses. I seem to remember that started not too long after she began to see more of Mr. Andropov. That is not like her... contrary to her nature." He paused and looked over at some photos on his credenza of his family that included the beautiful Sophia. "I will look into your suggestion with my family and appreciate your confidence and promise that our conversation will not leave this room."

"You have my word of honor and my enduring respect for your service to our country and for your family that I have admired for many years." Maria left assured that, like most men, Dedacus would see the issue of Sophie's well-being as the undue concern of helpless women that once he made inquiries, only needed the firm hand of a man to resolve easily.

Not long after she received the new message from the priest, Maria sat down in the Greek Orthodox Church pew next to Sergei Bokhan. She needed to confirm the plans that she had received from the CIA and get an affirmative reaction from the disgruntled Russian diplomat before notifying the Americans. As she gave him a side glance, she could see that he was even more morose today than she remembered from the earlier meeting. She had known other staff people trapped in a disastrous political situation, where ironically the loss of face and defection were their only path forward to any kind of a future. She felt sorry for Bokhan, but was glad that through the help of her Greek Orthodox Church friends, she had encouraged his decision to move to the West.

He was glancing around the chapel at the church icons, symbols and tapestries on the walls, fingering a rosary, and he looked like a man who appreciated tradition. The smell of the frankincense from the incense burners gave off an odor in the nave that Maria knew had begun centuries earlier to obscure the stink of the hard-working and unwashed parishioners packed together, standing on the stone floors of ancient Greek Orthodox Churches. She slid over closer to him on the bench, whispered to him the upcoming date, and gave him a note from Bruce with instructions and a more precise timetable and meeting location.

In an almost inaudible whisper he said, "I do not know what happened to our dream. Communism was to create equality for all and brotherhood of the workers. Do you remember when you were young and all the ideals coalesced of how you were going to make the world you knew a better place? I worked so hard. I believed so much in what we were trying to do to equalize wealth and opportunity."

He looked down toward his hands holding the beads in his lap and a great sadness came over him as he let go of everything he had worked to achieve for his entire life. "It was a wonderful dream, but we tried to manage equality, and the managers first became the bosses and then the capitalists." He looked up then turned his head toward Maria, and it bounced once in a slow nod. She quietly got up and left out of a side door held open for her by her friend who was the church official.

When the phone rang, Maria silenced the music she had been playing. When she picked up, it was Petkas who whispered, "Thank you for the referral to find the diggers. We have contacted them and they will leave with us in the morning to do the job."

Maria sounded worried, "Do you think it is safe?" She looked around and wondered where the other recently placed devices were installed in addition to the tap on her phone.

Petkas spoke in a rushed and worried whisper, "As safe as anything can be. We will know better when they return with the goods. Our plan to get the material will bring glory to the New Democratic party and give us something to show the people of Greece why we should be in charge."

Maria challenged, "Will we be ready when these things are found? What do you have anyway?"

Petkas again, in an exaggerated whisper, "We won't know until we open it all up, but it will be a great embarrassment to the Papandreou administration and likely the Soviets as well. The sculptures we expect to bring back alone are magnificent."

Maria said in a slightly louder voice of conviction, "Then it is worth the risk. Let's shame those smug bastards. Let us not speak of what you are about to do again until it is done. I wish you and Mark good luck."

Petkas said eagerly, "I can't wait until you can see some of it! I hope to be back in Athens tomorrow night with the goods."

Maria hung up and remembered the note she had left only half folded on the top of her trash reflecting the need Petkas had expressed to her of finding competent Greek diggers who would keep their mouths shut for a project to retrieve some artifacts he had located. She had put it in her office wastebasket toward the end of the day and then left with her door open to run out for an errand. When she returned as the office was closing, she noticed the note had been removed from the other trash in her basket, and the woman who worked in the finance office had on her coat and was leaving the building. She hoped the paper in the trash was not overkill, but assumed they were so anxious to catch Mark and Petkas, that the note and this phone call she had just finished with Petkas would reinforce each other to confirm their suspicions.

Later that evening, Tito Petrovia was in a foul mood. He was not used to failure and as he was reporting to the ambassador, whom he considered a lightweight, it made his shame all the more embarrassing. "I must report that I cannot find the traitor professor. I've been into his house and it seems he and his family have gone. It is strange, and I believe they may have left Greece. They took photos off the wall and I could see in the dust where small boxes and other things had been removed, but they left behind many of the items a family would normally take with them even on a long vacation, like the kid's toys. I'm suspicious because they also left things to make it look like they were coming back soon like food in the refrigerator and a calendar on the kitchen counter listing things they were going to do next week. I have searched other places where he frequented and found nothing. I have plans to get the American away from his hotel and break something to make him talk, but wanted to tell you first."

Andropov nodded and felt a rush of pride, as he was ahead of this clod who he considered just the muscle for Tatiana's uncle. Because he was still afraid of the man, he decided to be cautious in his response. "Well, maybe the professor will show himself. Hold off on the American for a day or two. It may be that you can have your fun with him, but I've got some things going with the Greeks that must play out first. You deserve a few days to relax and I will be in touch soon. You have done well and if we find what we are seeking you can accompany it on the ship where you are staying and take it to our mutual friend, Mr. Valentine Gubanov."

After the burly, humming, man left, Igor called the commander of the Spetsnaz team on the phone to execute his plan. "Get your men together and be ready to go. It is going to be tomorrow morning. Likely it will start early. Our people here are monitoring them and will watch the way they leave Athens. We will call you and then you and your team can proceed. We will have them followed and the chase car will give you updated reports and directions on the radiophone where to intercept them. Are you armed and do you have your snipers ready?"

"We are armed and ready Mr. Ambassador, but what you have asked for us to do is highly… this is an unusual assignment."

"Just be ready! When you get the notice to move in, go and capture them. I want a report immediately on what you find. You will soon see a result that will be a good thing for your career and for mine. You will have your photo in *Pravda* and the Moscow girls will throw flowers at you.

"I will be following in a car about two or three hours behind. We need to give them time to expose the treasure before we swoop in. When we get the call, I'll be with some Greek officials and a photographer. We will have to turn over the prisoners to them, but you will get full credit for the capture. Once the chase starts and we are on the road, we will not be able to communicate with you from my car, so do your best and honor our country. I do want the American and the Greek Petkas in handcuffs or bound by rope for the photos. Get some of the old Greek treasure dusted off and prepared. Set up the treasure and the captives together so it will make a good photo with me and the Greek officials. And when the treasure is secured, you are to bring it all directly to me at our embassy, understand?"

"Yes, comrade Ambassador."

CHAPTER 40

The day before Petkas and Maria spoke on the phone about the diggers, a group of campers moved into the valley where the Anatos family had lived 2400 years earlier and set up their tents and campfires. They had shopped for groceries locally and spoke German and a little Greek so as not to arouse suspicion of what was going on, and told the locals they were hiking every day into a different local valley in celebration of a holiday from their work at an automotive factory near Stuttgart, Germany. However, these were not normal hikers, but U.S. Navy SEALs and U.S. Special Service personnel. As some of the campers were visibly hiking and camping to cover the actual operation, others hidden further up the valley worked around the larger boulders and removed the smaller pieces of rubble from the landslide, entered the cave, and began to prepare the statues.

First, they carefully removed the dust and debris from the remains of the original crates gathered over many centuries and also any rocks that had held them in place. Then they repackaged each sculpture by hand, wrapping them into a soft plastic that when pressed carefully molded into the smallest tips and curves of the stone. Next, they surrounded each piece with a slightly firmer but still pliable padded covering. Any loose bits from each piece that had fallen off during the two and a half millennia were also wrapped and carefully included in the packaging with the larger piece of stone. The preparation took two days, and after they had fortified the sculpture to be moved, they began to carefully dislodge more of the debris from the rockslide to form a path to extract the sculptures when the time was right.

Normally, clandestine military exercises were held in a waning moon for maximum darkness. Because that was the time of the month when Mark was in Frankfurt earlier and the planners needed some time to assemble and train personnel, they decided to do the exfiltration two weeks later when the moon was almost full. They thought the brighter moonlight on the ground, just after summer Solstice, would provide better visuals for the extraction and eliminate the chance of an accident. They did not think they could afford the time to wait until another month for dark skies, so in the small valley, boulders and obstacles stood out clearly in the full moon.

On the night before the exfiltration, about sunset, a medium sized delivery truck rumbled into the valley, drove up past an outcropping that would hide its presence and finally parked further along the valley near the upper camp site. A dozen hard cases were moved from the truck and taken into the cave with other supplies and then the vehicle quickly left the area. Each invaluable sculpture in its padded wrapping was placed inside one of the hard-plastic cases specially configured to hold and protect the pieces from any penetration while in transport. Inside the hard cases, special protection supported the footing of the statues and its overall weight. Each case also had pliable filler and straps in the interiors to give every container a snug fit. Then they inserted into each case through several strategically placed vents a foam material that expanded and hardened to fill out every nook and cranny of the inside of the cases and hold the sculptures firm and immovable. Once all of them were sealed in the cases and the foam hardened, the cases were secured firmly and were ready to be moved.

By this time each container now weighed over 3000 pounds and it was almost midnight. The hard cartons had many handles and hooks on the exterior to enable the boxes to be lifted straight up to keep the sculpture vertical with the statue heads upright during transport. Then one, then another and then yet another of the new U.S. Marine Corps CH-53 Super Stallion helicopters specially outfitted for heavy lifting came in and landed. Two well-used tractors that had been made in Greece were unloaded with special accessories that would enable them to move the larger boulders from the path and away from the cave entrance.

After the large rocks were moved aside and a trail was made into the cave, the tractors were then reconfigured with a forklift-type attachment and special hooks to fit into the handles on the crates to hoist each container and move it to the waiting choppers. The helicopters had been stripped down to carry the heavy freight and outfitted with metal hooks and straps to hold each carton securely in place. At the choppers, a team of soldiers straining carefully with specially configured dollies, moved the heavy cases into preselected positions and attached them so the cases would stand in the stations where they were placed, balanced and secured: two on each interior side of the three choppers.

By four a.m. all 12 containers were transported into the field away from the cave by the steep hillside and placed inside the three large transport helicopters. Their effort was only possible with the help of all the Special Forces and the other personnel who had done the packing. It was done carefully but also in haste since they had practiced the maneuver several times before. Then they policed the area for any trash, debris, excess packing materials and parked the tractors with their specially configured tines and fittings in the cave and finally they covered the entrance back up as well as they could with rocks and brush and the debris of the rockslide. By five a.m. the choppers and all the military personnel on site were ready to head back to the naval communications base northeast of Athens where they would soon be loaded onto a large C-141 Starlifter cargo transport aircraft. As the choppers rose in the cool morning air one of the seals pressed a button that set off a charge, not a big or loud charge, but one significant enough to dislodge a new slide of boulders and rocks that crumbled a further portion of the hillside down onto the cave entrance.

Earlier that same night in an Athens suburb, Mark and Stanos Petkas drove in Petkas's car and met with a team of diggers hired with their equipment of picks, shovels and ladders that the diggers loaded into two pickup trucks. Petkas, in his car, led the group out of Athens. They left after midnight and drove in a motorcade just under the speed limit for almost four hours following each other to a place north of Athens, East of Thebes, and across a bridge onto the island of Euboea. They continued eastward almost to the Aegean Sea just to the west of the town of Kymi at the foot of a mountainous area at a place called Choneftiko. There they parked one of the trucks.

At Choneftiko, following a map and directions given to them by Petkas, the workmen staked out a large square on the ground at a specific location. They used string to mark the sides of the square and set up their plans to dig. Then the group of men left one truck parked and locked with their equipment and piled into the other truck to follow Petkas and Mark for breakfast in the nearby town of Kymi. After they had finished eating by about 7:30 a.m., the truck with the 6 laborers and the foreman went back to Choneftiko to start the dig.

CHAPTER 41

The competent and handsome Captain Demetros Panos felt his star was on the rise. Today he had been selected to be the liaison with the American military for this NATO sanctioned exercise. More importantly, he had been given the orders to manage the exercise so the American presence over Greek airspace would not be noticed, and the operation would be over and forgotten as soon as possible. He checked his freshly pressed uniform and recently trimmed moustache in the mirror and was pleased to see that his military bearing and posture were excellent. Panos assumed the main reason he had been picked for this mission was because he spoke very good English with the correct idioms and expressions gained from often visiting his relatives who lived in Chicago and had a restaurant there. He had been given this honor and important chance, and he planned to produce shining results for his superiors.

His job was to go onto the U.S. Hellenikon air base to observe an approved but hastily arranged nighttime training exercise designed for the U.S. to provide support to Greece and remove injured civilians just after a disaster. During the maneuver, he would be the equal to any of those U.S. military officers as he was to be the on-site person overseeing and approving the exercise that would take place in his country. There on the base, he would make contacts that might be useful in future international military exercises, and he would report back to his superiors how he had taken the measure of these soldiers who were supposed to be so much better equipped and trained than the Greek military.

Prior to his mission, he had heard in the briefings that his Greek military superiors did not like the idea, but it was petitioned by NATO, which provided much of their budgeting needs, and his superiors had requested, no demanded back to NATO, that as a requirement of their cooperation, a Greek liaison officer be made available to observe the training. The U.S.

military agreed to the demand saying the maneuver would show they were a good partner to NATO and to Greece. But as the U.S. military was not popular, the exercise was designed to be executed away from any population, beginning late at night and ending by early morning.

The Americans had promised to conduct the training in an unoccupied and remote area of Greece with special attention given so that the noise from the helicopters would not disturb Greek citizens and not fly over any major roads or areas of dense population. The agreement was seen as a compromise that would lessen any potential civilian criticism and not risk the much-needed NATO funding for the Greek military. The job of Captain Panos was to get it over as quickly as possible and in a way that the public did not realize the exercise was happening on Greek soil. He also had to make sure they did not disturb any Greek citizens or tie up any traffic on the nearby road. Panos knew that his orders made him the key Greek citizen on site and, in effect, in charge of the operation.

When he arrived on the American base, he was greeted warmly and with respect and then taken into a dark room filled with radar equipment and scopes set to show a 150-mile radius of Athens. About half of the radar over land showed ground clutter near the base and out toward the mountains in the west and north west. The other half of the radar over water showed several patches of a blank screen except for a blip representing a late flight coming in from Turkey. For the exercise, a portion of the Greek airspace was outlined on an overlay map covering the dim screen to track where a flight of helicopters was to land and load several injured people. As he sat with the weak American coffee, he was reminded of what his colonel had demanded of him in harsh terms the day before, that he was to call in the Greek military if the Americans dawdled or did not keep to the script of the exercise. His commanding officer had said, "I have given you specific orders. If the exercise turns out to be a mess for us, you will be held responsible. You must keep it quiet and get it over quickly. Your job is to make the Americans seem invisible and I want you to impress me."

In an unexpected spirit of accommodation, the Americans had asked the Greek military to assign a jeep or two on the highway near the fake disaster to take care of any road traffic, and simulate actual conditions in a disaster to block off and secure the scene of the tragedy from further civilian injury. The soldiers on the jeeps would send away any locals or curious onlookers attracted by lights or motion from the exercise or anyone else who drove into the area who might see that the rescue choppers were from the U.S. and were not Greek. Although the exercise was to be at night and the likelihood of anyone entering the exercise area was small, the Greek military felt that they had covered every aspect of supporting NATO and would remind the NATO commanders of their cooperation when the next budget cycle occurred.

As Demetros watched on the radar screens in the darkened tent he could hear the ground controllers give orders to the rescue aircraft. He noticed from the map that was overlaid on the radar that the activity was to be in an area to the west of Delphi and was pleased as that was a truly remote location and he thought maybe no one would see it after all.

As the exercise slowly proceeded through the middle of the night, he heard the Americans on the ground tell the control officer next to where Demetros was sitting in observation, as each stretcher was loaded onto the flight. The scenario was explained to Demetros that these civilians had been injured in a disaster from an earthquake and rubble had to be cleared to reach the injured, then they had to be carefully prepared and triaged of their injuries before being strapped onto stretchers and loaded onto the choppers. Practicing these medical proceedings and complicated logistics were why the exercise took some time.

Captain Panos checked his watch. He had to make his report later that morning and needed time to make sure he did a good job. He would note in his logbook as each element of the exercise was completed. He also felt he had to make himself seem important for his dispatch, so he went over to the U.S. Colonel in charge and told him that the exercise was taking too long and they needed to speed it up. Dawn was coming and he wanted the helicopters off Greek land. He tapped his wrist watch and looked over at the radar screens. The American Colonel said he would see to Panos' wishes. The conversation with the colonel would look good in the narrative he planned for his report and show that he had pushed the Americans. He was responsible that the mission went off without a hitch, and the honor of Greece was upheld.

He listened to the mission chatter on the loudspeaker in the room that came from the radios, "Rescue Bravo 01, we have three aboard now and expect more soon. Alert the trauma unit on base we have extensive internal injuries." Finally, the last of the exercise victims was on the helicopters, and they all left for the US base. He had been told that all the choppers would fly out at one time together to lessen the potential of bothering Greek civilians or being seen. He watched on the radar as the yellow blips representing the helicopters appeared and he could see that the flight path had been carefully planned to fly over water as much as possible and not over populated areas and not become in any way a distraction to Greek military or civilian air traffic. He made a note of that for his report.

"Rescue Bravo 01, 02, 03. Feet Dry. Approaching Athens airspace and ETA to base of 5 mikes." The message meant the choppers would land not far from him in a few minutes and now his part in the exercise was almost over.

Panos started to leave and then stopped and turned to the Colonel. "I believe it would make my evaluation more compete if I were to observe the helicopters as they arrive here and see the job they did first hand. I want to find out what took so long. Can you please direct me to the place on the flight line where I may observe the return of the helicopters?" The Colonel looked surprised and made a call. He talked for a few minutes with his hand over the speaker part of the phone.

The colonel came back to Panos and smiled thinly. "Captain, as part of the exercise we took the more serious injuries directly to the hospital which is on the other side of the base. However, I can show you part of our exercise of the injuries that landed on the flight line near here for further triage and later medevac." The colonel pointed to the door, "If you will please come with me." They walked from the radar control tent past some Quonset huts and tin metal storage houses for about 200 yards over to the flight line. Although the area was washed by flood lights from the hangers, Panos could see the beginning of the light of dawn in the distance.

At the edge of the flight line, Captain Panos observed a large helicopter and nearby where there were people standing wrapped in bandages and on stretchers lying on the ground, with an ambulance standing by to complete the simulation and ruse. This scenario had been in preparation for two hours. The "show" chopper was prepared in case there was a need for a demonstration and included elaborate splints, bandages, lots of fake blood from fake injuries, and hanging bottles of blood plasma and fluid. The soldiers dressed as civilians being removed from the chopper had been coached to be moaning and begging for help. As they approached the scene, one of the wounded reached up from a stretcher to Captain Panos, pleading for comfort with bloody hands which caused him to step backward so as not to soil his uniform. The floor of the chopper was covered in fake blood, and an ambulance nearby was loading the "wounded" on their stretchers. An assembled group of other soldiers wearing Red Cross arm bands were being trained in the exercise and were grouped to the side receiving instructions from a doctor in a white coat with a stethoscope around his neck. The colonel explained to Panos that part of the exercise was to show the group of young medical technicians standing nearby how treatments in a disaster should be handled. Impressed by all the theatrics, Panos thanked the Colonel and left to return to his office and begin his report. Across the flight line the CH-53 Super Stallion helicopters were cooling down in another hanger with the doors closed.

Standing inside the hanger with the personnel access door opened only a crack to hide the real helicopters containing the cases of sculpture, Bruce smiled and lit a cigarette as he watched the theatrics with the Greek captain across the way. He checked his watch and saw that his schedule indicated that he was to meet the Soviet diplomat, Bokhan, in about 20 minutes. He had to interview the Russian face to face to ensure the defection would be useful and that Bokhan was not a plot to give the CIA disinformation. For this task, he needed to ask probing questions to produce the correct answers that would prove Bokhan had truly and completely cut the cord. Bruce needed to have the feeling that he had Bokhan's balls in his hand to approve the Soviet's departure on the flight. Bokhan was so far out on the limb he had only Bruce's highly selective generosity as a lifeline to safety, which for the proud career Soviet diplomat must have been truly frightening and emasculating.

As Bruce prepared to go to the meeting with the Soviet diplomat, he recalled what Maria had told him and with that and the surveillance they had employed after Bokhan had met with Maria, he could smell that Sergei Bokhan was a legitimate runner, even though he still had to go through the required procedures.

He told the Air Force major standing nearby to go ahead with moving the containers to the C-141 transport that would be taking off in the next few hours.

Two hours later, after breakfast and a short debrief on the mission, the SEALs and other personnel on the removal team readied themselves to board the same transport aircraft.

About an hour after that, as the last of the heavy luggage was being stored, Mark and Petkas arrived and boarded. The last passengers Bruce ushered aboard, with a young male CIA minder hovering nearby, were a family of four with two small children who looked very uncomfortable as they settled in with several bulky bags of luggage.

CHAPTER 42

The Greek workmen arrived at the dig site after their breakfast in the village and started with their picks and shovels inside the area bordered by the stakes and string. An hour later the Spetsnaz commander and his team arrived after following the directions relayed from the car which had tailed the motorcade of diggers from Athens. The Soviet soldiers stayed out of sight and the commander quickly put his men in several key places to observe the excavation. Some of his men who were in camouflage gear moved from the other side up the hill, across its higher ridges to position themselves just above the diggers and what was starting to be a sizeable hole. The major leading the larger group of Russian soldiers were all hidden around the edge of the hill but close enough to rush the burrowing quickly. Through his 8x30 USSR military binoculars he could see several men working and shoveling in a large pit surrounded by stakes in the ground connected by string. They were piling up a considerable mound of dirt on two sides of the hole. He wished he had a way to communicate with the ambassador to give him status updates, but he would have to wait until the ambassador and the Greek officials arrived.

The commander had been told only some of what was happening, but he knew that one of the main people he was after was the head of archeology at the National Technical University of Athens, and who also taught at the Aristotle University of Thessaloniki. He had his photo and one of an American who was supposed to be with the Greek professor. Thessaloniki was north of Athens by an over six-hour drive, and this hillside was about halfway between in a very isolated area and not near any telephones.

He did not see the faces of either of the two men he was supposed to find at the dig. So, after the soldiers got into their places, he dispatched the car with the radiophone carrying the men from the embassy who had been following the team of diggers and told them to go snoop around the seaside village. Perhaps the men in the car could find some sign of the American and the Greek professor. He assumed they would return with the two missing men from the village near the coast and have some new orders for him.

By midmorning, as the hole continued to grow, the heat was starting to rise and the bugs were out in droves. The commander was thinking the surveillance job was turning into a task that could be handled by a few local policemen and had not been important enough for him to come all this way with his men into another sovereign country without the permission from the locals or even telling them they were here. That worried him, but he assumed the ambassador knew best. It was not his place to question orders. Then he saw one of his men motion for him to come to the jeep. A call had come in for him over the radio. A relay from the embassy said to go ahead and proceed with the arrests on the timetable agreed upon earlier.

About thirty minutes later, as the digging became more intense and piles of dirt were growing higher on both sides of the deep hole, the fore-man of the diggers looked up to see a military truck rush up to the site, and several well-armed men, wearing the identification of the Special Purpose Forces of the Armed Forces of the Soviet Union, descended on the pit and surrounded the team of Greek diggers. On the hillside above the dig several other soldiers stood, also holding automatic weapons, in camouflage clothes and wearing outer garments around them of strange netting covered in small sticks and leaves. These armed men walked down the hill to converge on the surprised diggers and gave them orders to drop the picks and shovels and gather together in a bunch. They were searched, their identities recorded, and their hands were secured. A man with more marking on his shoulders than the others asked them questions about who they were, why they were digging there, what they were looking for, and where was the American and Stanos Petkas.

Frightened at first, then confused, then glad for a break from the toil of digging, the foreman turned over the papers he had been given which showed that Petkas had hired them for the dig and paid for all the costs of the truck rental and their salaries for the day. He showed them the running clock that he was told to use to time how long it took them to dig a hole in the ground fifteen feet deep and fifteen feet square. The foreman's instructions were very specific and he showed the tall Major where the second phase of this project was to take place over to one side. His instructions read that the fill dirt would be "suitable for shaking in fine meshed screens to look for potential artifacts and antiquities before it was replaced into the ground." Over on the side there were two of these fine-meshed screens constructed with wooden frames about three feet square for this purpose. They were to remove any ancient architectural treasures found in the dirt and take them back to Athens.

He explained that the two men who had led them here had stayed in the town over by the sea after breakfast and had not yet returned to the site. The foreman was unsure why the military men seemed so upset, and he did not understand why the man with more markings on the collar of his uniform walked back and forth slapping his leg as he looked several times first into the hole and then down toward the town of Kymi. The man then gave an order and the soldiers, much to the diggers' relief, stopped pointing the guns at them.

Several hours earlier in the town, after the men had piled into the truck and left to return to the site of the dig, Petkas returned to the restaurant where he met and paid one of his former students he had hired two days before to take his car back to Athens. The man was to take another route back to the bridge that led to the mainland of Greece and then to use the regular road back to Athens. He was to park the car near a busy street, leave the window rolled down, the keys in the ignition with the door unlocked. The young man thought everything was in place except a sign saying "steal me." He had been instructed to wear gloves for his entire trip to leave no fingerprints. Petkas was glad that two days before his wife and two daughters had left for a family visit to Turkey and from Istanbul boarded flights to Frankfurt, Germany, where they were met and driven down to the U.S. military base at Rhein-Main, West Germany.

According to Bruce they were surely to be followed to the area of the dig and watched carefully. Knowing they would be followed by the Russians, they planned to start the men digging in the early morning soon after breakfast. By the time the dirt began to fly, Mark and Stanos Petkas had moved a mile down from the village to the bay and harbor east of Kymi and were getting onto a small but fast US Navy shore boat they met down by one of the more remote boat docks, that took them to a larger Navy craft anchored outside the harbor. A helicopter on that ship took them speeding fast toward the south along the shoreline of Greece over the Aegean Sea to the US Hellenikon Air Base operations for Air Transport Command flights.

At the same time the Spetsnaz major was standing in the dirt and slapping his leg, a large C-141 transport aircraft with Mark and Petkas on board was taking off on the way to the U.S. Air base at Rhein-Main, West Germany, southwest of Frankfurt and thirty miles west of Mannheim, Germany. As Mark and Petkas settled in the meshed web seats, to top off what had already been a bizarre day, they noticed on the enormous cargo plane many large crates, a dozen men who were obviously soldiers in civilian clothes but wore their hair longer than normal, and they recognized from his photos a Soviet diplomat clustered together with his family. Over in the corner toward the front of the cargo hold, Mark saw his old nemesis, Bruce, fidgeting in great discomfort and looking like he would give just about anything to be able to light a cigarette. The young soldiers were drinking beer and laughing among themselves.

Petkas remembered the similarities Maria Beckett had mentioned between him and Bokhan, and he watched the Russian huddled with his family while being monitored by a fit young man in a suit who occasionally looked around him as if he was uncertain about everything going on. The young man was one of those newly minted agents who spoke college Russian and who had been ordered to accompany this defector, first to check in at the Rhein-Main Air Base, and then on to Virginia. His only job was not to lose them.

The young agent had little background on his Soviet defector and his agency career had not yet taught the man the social graces designed to give comfort or a sense of safety to his charge. There was no warmth coming from this American who followed a well-established system designed to process people. Nurturing the asset and beginning to encourage the willingness to divulge information useful to his new host nation was far down the list of what the young man currently knew how to do. That might come later, but for now the Russian and his family were treated like pieces of freight.

Petkas could see that the Soviet diplomat and his family were frightened. They folded into each other, whispering and looking down at the metal floor of the enormous cargo aircraft. He noticed that the kids, shivering with pinched and worried faces, were of similar ages as his kids, and he walked over to introduce himself. He did feel an affinity for the situation they were all in and hoped that this transport portion of their exile would be over soon, and they all could find some comfortable place to renew family life in exile.

Using his limited Russian in what began as a brief conversation he assured them that they would be well treated and implied that he and his family were in similar circumstances. The eyes of the wife and children melted in gratitude at his act of kindness. The father, however, held in his eyes a look of professional pride and maintained his posture leaning back with a tinge of honor, however false, that he was still in some control of his destiny. Petkas recognized the feeling in himself, and nodded politely to Bokhan.

Bokhan now remembered the face of Petkas from security photos and the interrogation video as well his voice from the recordings. He thought to himself, 'So both this Greek man and I have come to this embarrassment and disgrace,' and nodded back to Petkas.

In the front of the aircraft, Bruce checked his watch as the C-141 cruised through the sky above Greece. He smiled at how good he was at timing these things. He thought how ironic that this C-141 was headed to the same airfield in Rhein-Main where the remaining U.S. hostages from the hijacked TWA flight had been taken the day before to be met by Vice President George H. W. Bush, and then on to the U.S. It worked out perfectly that those hijacked people after an almost two-week ordeal would get the media attention, and this flight when it landed on the same base would be cloaked in the disguise of the back-end clean-up for the TWA crisis. All eyes would still be looking toward the ghost of the hijacked aircraft, the glitter of the news coverage on the base, the lingering smell of danger and redemption. It was the magnet that would draw people's awareness away from this C141 and its cargo. He felt confident that no unauthorized personnel would notice most of the military men offloading here, with a few staying on board to cross the Atlantic on the long haul after refueling and the boarding of the anxious members of the Petkas family to reconnect with their husband and father.

He also thought how good it would be to have a glass of single malt 20-year old scotch and a cigarette. Then he noticed Mark making his way over to him past some large crates strapped down in the cargo hold.

As Mark sat down, Bruce handed him an Alfa Greek beer from a small cooler and resumed the conversation from where he had left off in Frankfurt. "All these statues and the defector add up to quite a stunt you got me into." He nodded at the cases and then over at Bokhan, "Could be a career-maker."

Mark first looked toward the rear of the cargo hold, nodded back at Bruce, and took off the cap on the beer, "Bruce, don't you know in the forefront of my thoughts, I've always had your career's best interest at heart?"

"Well, smart ass, it's not every day we grunts in the back basement at Langley get to screw the Soviets, steal what may be the most valuable art on the planet, and get a valuable defector as a bonus. All that shit is here together on this one aircraft, and I'm getting the credit for it... at least at my workplace. You and Petkas over there did most of the work and deserve some thanks, along with Maria Beckett, but they don't know you two back at my office. We've come a long way from our hotel meeting in

Frankfurt. Anyway... thanks."

"You're welcome. So, is all this little game of yours going to have a happy ending for Petkas and that Russian guy?"

Bruce nodded to the back of the aircraft. "We'll get them both resettled with their families. Petkas will be easier because those Greeks don't know what he did, at least not as yet. They just know he's disappeared. He'll get a good job at a university and will be just fine. That other one we'll have to debrief for a while and then relocate and hide him and his family somewhere. He'll probably be all right too. Probably end up a cowboy in Montana or a barista in Sand Point, Idaho. Did you know him?"

"Never saw him before we got on the airplane."

"Yeah, that was a slick job by your friend, Maria Beckett. She just hand delivered him. It was beautiful. She is a real piece of work. They damn sure don't make 'em like her anymore."

"From the little I know of her and I've only been around her just for a few months, I'd have to agree. Have you heard the stories about her from back in the junta days?"

"They talk about her in the training classes in Langley and at the Farm. She's one of those living treasures. We're lucky she works for the West and not the other side."

"Well, from getting to know her, I'd say she will always be on the side of what is right. She's got a pure heart and . . ."

"Mark, let's not over-do the piety and noble sensitivity here. I don't want to get all weepy."

Mark gave Bruce a hard look and shook his head. "Little chance of that. You always have a way of reminding me why I don't like you almost every time I see you. So, Bruce, just to be clear, what you think of as beautiful is Maria getting a dejected Russian to leave his country and defect, and we've also gotten a world class expert on Greek history and culture to steal his country's greatest art treasure. Both acts of treachery and deceit. You've got an interesting set of values. Thanks for the beer. See you around."

Bruce grabbed Mark's arm and pointed to the rear of the aircraft. "Hold up, smart ass. We're gonna get good intel from that Russian guy, and that information may help to save American lives in the future. So, yeah, I think that is beautiful, and if you don't, maybe you need to rethink a little more about whose side you are on."

"Nice speech, Bruce, but you seemed a lot more genuine and enthusiastic when you were talking about how this airplane flight would help your career." Mark stood and went back to his seat where he noticed that Petkas was still talking to the Russian family and giving them words of encouragement, showing them photos of his kids. As he sat back in his seat, he thought to himself what a thoroughly decent man Stanos Petkas was, likely the finest human being on the aircraft. That brought him to thoughts of his homecoming. He found himself imagining the scene of introducing Vicki to Petkas and his family, before remembering the dilemma he and Vicky were in and hoping it was just a temporary aberration. What would he say to her when he saw her next, and more importantly how was their child? 'My God' he thought, 'I'm going to be a father.' He replayed the long night and morning he and Petkas had experienced and as he felt the lull from the steady droning of the lumbering cargo aircraft, he leaned back and let his body relax into the netting of the bucket web seat, crossed his arms and was soon asleep.

It had been over an hour since the Russian major had captured the suspects with their digging equipment splayed all over this desolate hillside far off the main highway. His orders were to hold them and examine what they had found once they had gotten well into their digging. Now that it was lunchtime, this whole day and the surprise he was supposed to find were looking like a total bust.

The men who had gone into the nearby town in the car that had followed the diggers from Athens had returned with no trace of the American, the professor, or the car they had driven to Kymi. To make matters worse, the communications in their car were not working this far from any booster signal.

As the Soviet major paced in the dirt around the unfinished pit, he wished that he had a way to contact Ambassador Andropov, who was headed to the site in a two-car convoy, along with the Greek ministers of Culture and Interior, but the cars had no phone or two-way radio. He was not privy to the full intent of this raid, but he suspected the result of this hole in the ground was not what Andropov wanted. He had been led to believe that he and his team were stopping a significant theft of Greek antiquity by an American agent and a renegade Greek professor. Now he was concerned how this farce would play out once the Soviet ambassador found out the truth. It was illegal for him to be here in another country uninvited, and he worried about the consequences.

The major suspected that the chance of catching an American who had been involved in the Greek election and in stealing Greek archeological goods was too irresistible a story for the ambassador. Igor Andropov and the members of the Papandreou government were supposed to arrive soon to supervise the arrest themselves and pose for photos. It was now apparent to the major, however, that nothing was going on except the digging of a large hole and that the leaders of this bogus project were missing. He suspected that his superiors back in Russia would be very disappointed, and wished he had a way to take his men with their weapons and disappear in a puff of air from the sovereign territory of Greece which he was now violating.

A short time later, the Interior Minister of Greece, after being lectured to for several hours by Igor Andropov on their drive here about being an ignorant rube, had something of a pleasurable feeling as they stood near the piles of dirt surrounded by a number of armed Soviet soldiers illegally occupying this bit of ground in his country. Andropov at first shouted at the workmen and then the Soviet soldiers, and then his voice waned when he realized he was on a phony mission, he had wasted everyone's time, and he was responsible for an unauthorized intrusion into Greece, of armed soldiers from another country.

The major watched the Ambassador walk back and forth with his head down. He seemed to be muttering to himself but no noise came from his lips which were moving as though making words. The man was handsome and well dressed in his mid-forties but today, on the dirt of this barren plane, he looked like a lost little boy.

Andropov tried to sort it out as he reviewed all the facts. What could be happening here? What was this hole in the ground? Where were the statues and other old trinkets? He had the intelligence reports. He had the tapes. He knew being in this exact spot at this time was the result of a progression of the facts of a story he had been hearing for many weeks. Could all the messages about the sculptures have been just a trick? No. It had to be about real treasure. How could he have been so wrong? He felt the bottom drop from his stomach.

He needed to keep moving to walk back and forth to make them all think he had a plan. He needed something to hold onto. Look at those smug Greeks over by the car. He felt embarrassed for the respectful Spetsnaz officer and all these soldiers standing around with their weapons. Look at those stupid Greek peasant diggers. What the hell was digging this hole about?

He felt the late summer heat on his head and he began to feel faint as the sweat trickled down to dampen his shirt collar. The fear was on him. He could see in the spotlight of his foolish actions the betrayal he felt was surely somewhere back in Athens. Somewhere hiding. He could not be this wrong. There must be some answer to save his career, to give him the medals for his mother to see and send him to Paris or London. The promise of his career could not end here on this patch of dirt in the middle of nowhere. What would his son think of him?

The Interior Minister and the other officials of the Greek government had the photographer document the scene with photos and took the names of the workers for interrogation later. They told the diggers to fill the hole back up and return to Athens. Then they got photos of the soldiers and copied their documents and identification for what would be an extensive report. They also took photos of the Soviet Ambassador standing with a forlorn look on his face near the pit. Soon after that, they left for Athens in their cars, leaving Andropov with his storm troopers milling about in the field. It was not until they had returned to their offices the following day that they received the memorandum, filled with calendar references and evidence, distributed just before he left by Sergei Bokhan, stating that Ambassador Andropov had beaten and abused the daughter of Marcellus Dedacus, the Undersecretary of the Interior and in charge of much of the internal security in Greece.

Interestingly, the detailed communique and other records of Andropov's actions, including documentation on unauthorized inspection of the homes, as well as the wiretapping and surveillance of Greek citizens, was provided by this unimpeachable source of Andropov's deputy, who was now somehow strangely unavailable. It was with great pleasure that Dedacus, with Papandreou's agreement, now wove all these personal excesses and disrespect for a Soviet ally into his comprehensive dispatch.

Earlier he had received a call from his sister who, on his urging, had taken the injured Sophie from the apartment where she had been kept by Igor to her personal doctor for treatment. His sister had told him that in addition to the physical injuries, his niece was suffering from an extended overindulgence of cocaine use and needed hospitalization and long-term therapy.

Dedacus now paced in his office, gesturing with one hand while he read from the draft of his report held in the other. "... and on numerous occasions, desiring for the best of friendship between our counties, I deferred to the rather demanding rhetoric of Ambassador Andropov. Even when he told me, and I quote, 'We Greeks lack the sophistication to understand how devious international plots are hatched right under our more than ample noses.' I hope that this rhetoric and behavior is not the standard practice of how the government of the Soviet Union manages its international relations, comrade." He smiled and dropped the legal pad onto the table. He turned to his secretary and said, "I'd love to be there when Mikhail Gorbachev reads my report."

Dedacus worked on the document to emphasize the most damning points in such a way that they were irrefutable Much of it was a review of Andropov's delusional treasure hunt for Greek sculpture and the unauthorized intrusion of Soviet troops into Greece. He referred to witness accounts as back-up to his brief.

He ended with the information he had received from Bokhan about the damage of Greek and Russian Orthodox Church historical materials that gave him the greatest pleasure to report. He expounded in his description how after the private ceremony, Igor had ridiculed the priests who had welcomed him to the embassy and had offered such glowing prayers for his success. Andropov rejected the gifts of antique icons, symbols of the traditional churches of both Greece and Russia used as tokens of the common bond and similarities between the two countries. He embellished Bokhan's description of how one of these ancient icons was shown a lack of respect by Igor when he threw it against a wall. He closed that section by using Bokhan's own words as a key reason that had driven him to defect to the Americans. Dedacus read with pleasure directly from Bokhan's report, "What Igor Andropov did to the religious relics was the last straw. His destructive act confirmed his disdain for the long-standing diplomatic traditions of both Greece and the Soviet Union. I had the duty to put my family and my faith first. Something must matter more than your job."

The complete report with the photos from the dig near the Choneftiko hill was sent to the Greek Ambassador in Moscow to hand deliver personally to the new First Secretary, Mikhail Gorbachev.

Dedacus received a separate message from Bokhan indicating that a recently arrived man from the Soviet Union was responsible for hiring the team that had been involved in a gun battle with police on May 15. He soon dispatched a SWAT team comprised of fellow officers from the unit of the fallen policemen and used the information he had received from Bokhan to track down a bulky Russian man, Tito Petrovia, as he left one of the Soviet oil tankers. The heavily armed team surrounded and captured the man just after he left the shipyards en route to the airport for a trip to Moscow.

Dedacus felt a deep satisfaction that the one responsible for the deaths of three policemen could be captured and brought to justice. However, fearing interference from Moscow on behalf of one of their citizens, he ordered the man to be taken to a maximum-security facility far from Athens and held incognito. There was no record of the arrest. He gave orders that any inquiries by anyone into the whereabouts of this Russian be answered that the Greek authorities had never heard of him. He then gave the responsibility for Tito Petrovia's long-term care to the detachment of police officers where the three dead policemen had worked.

When the Greek authorities called for Sergei Bokhan to come to a meeting and give his first-hand account about the recent events, they were told he was nowhere to be found. He was not in his office and the phone at his house did not answer. The staff at the Soviet Embassy, which were now much more accommodating to the Greek government's inquiries, had no idea where he was, and his personal effects as well as sensitive documents in his office were also missing. When they sent someone to the house to look for him, the family was gone and much of their clothing and personal effects such as family photos, were no longer in the house. It was curious that a red cloth containing the image of Vladimir Lenin was stretched across the dining room table in the Bokhan home, like a banner welcoming the visitor.

In the fall, an article appeared in one of the major newspapers in Athens and the international press in Europe.

ATHENS, Greece -- Soviet Ambassador Igor Andropov, son of the late Soviet President Yuri Andropov, will be replaced because of rumors of scandal in his private life and the defection of a key Russian operative in Greece, diplomats said Monday.

The Foreign Ministry sources said Andropov, already recalled to Moscow, will be replaced as the chief envoy to Greece by Victor Fyodorovic Stukalin, a government undersecretary.

Andropov was summoned home one month after the defection of First Secretary Sergei Bokhan, described as the deputy Athens station chief of GRU, or military intelligence, and Andropov's chief aide.

Bokhan reportedly gave the CIA the names of Greek agents working for the Soviet Union and described intelligence work by the Soviet Union in Greece, which is a key NATO-member,

U.S. diplomats said. 'As a result, two Greek civilians and a naval officer have been arrested,' the diplomats said.

A history graduate from Moscow University, the younger Andropov had worked from 1970-74 at the prestigious Institute for U.S-Canadian Studies at the Academy of Sciences.

Rumors that Moscow decided to pull Andropov back to Moscow because of scandals about his private life also have not been denied by the Soviet Embassy or the government spokesman. The son of the late Soviet leader Yuri Andropov has been named an ambassador-at-large and will work with Foreign Minister Eduard Shevardnadze, a ministry official said Thursday.

When Andropov first arrived in Athens with his wife Tatiana, the couple became the focus of social columnists. Andropov, 44, who unlike his predecessor, Vladimir Kaboshkin, wore Western-style suits and spoke foreign languages, was the unchallenged 'star of the Athens diplomatic corps.'

His wife, an attractive, blue-eyed blonde, captured the hearts of women's fashion magazine editors, was the guest at many fashion shows, and wore trendy fashions.

Andropov was named ambassador to Greece eight months after the death of his father in February 1984. His appointment came at a time when Prime Minister Andreas Papandreou's government was sharply attacking U.S. foreign policy and wooing the Soviet Union.

CHAPTER 43

Mark saw the lights shining through the windows of the condominium he and Vicki shared. He felt the urge to rush in but stopped at the door, uncertain after weeks without communication, if she really had ended their relationship. He had finally stopped trying to reach her over the past two weeks. He sensed again the pain he felt from the exile she had imposed on them and it was with a mixture of confusion, hurt, and love that he reached for the door, knocked first and then used his key to enter.

Inside the entrance hall eucalyptus incense burned, and leaning against the wall by the door lay a cloth bag with the name of a Lamaze class. He smiled as it was so like Vicki to research and prepare for everything long before it was needed. As he entered the living room he saw her lying back, propped against several cushions on the same couch from which he had started this long journey, when he had gotten the call from Angus about working the Greek election. On her lap was a nutrition book she was reading about having a healthy pregnancy. When she saw him, she froze, and looked at him with surprise. Then her face turned to the look she always got before she cried.

He remained standing by the door, unsure of how familiar to be or how welcome he was. Then everything just came out in a flood. "I tried to find you in Paris and called you and wrote to you. I wanted to tell you that I was overwhelmed by the news, but you ran off before I could explain. I wanted to tell you that I would have married you then, and I want to now. I love you and want to share our child. Well, to be perfectly honest, I'm not too excited about changing the diapers, but with the rest of it I'm thrilled. And, I'll likely get used to the diaper thing."

By now Vicki had tears rolling down her cheeks. As she put the book down, she shook her head as if to clear away bad memoires and bring herself into the present. "You must think I've turned into a helpless, sen-

293

timental ninny. In Paris, I was still coming to grips with the pregnancy, and being there with you was so emotional and mostly so wonderful, it all just overwhelmed me. It made what I was going to tell you all the more important, and all that anticipation kept building up in me. I just wanted things to turn out like I had imagined them on the flight over, and when your plans changed and it seemed you wavered, I thought that meant you didn't want to be with me, to be married, and to have our child. I crashed. I could not relive what happened to me when my father left after the endless arguing with my mother. I cannot do that same thing to my child."

"Vicki, it's our child, and you are not your mother and I'm not your father. You know I don't have a conventional job. Neither do you. How many people from your high school or college could pull together the information that helps to decide the direction of our country?"

He walked over and sat down by her. "Who I am has evolved from holding my cards close to the vest. I can't divulge what I'm feeling to my clients, colleagues, or candidates. I believe that I've got to stay strong and be analytical as much as I can. I've got to at least look like the person who will not panic in a crisis. I think it gives them and me confidence. I've tried to be like those dumb ass tough guys in the movies, and that behavior has spilled over into my personal life. I try not to show my emotions. I get some of that from my parents and my upbringing. I know that is wrong and I'll try to work on it. But there is nothing more I want in life than to come home and see you at the end of the day. Your problems, fears, joys . . . and all of them are mine as well as yours. I want to be here with you and to hold and love our child. The rest doesn't matter." He leaned closer to her. "I want to tell you that since we met, whenever I've been with you, even from the start before we dated, no matter what the circumstances, it always felt so natural being with you. You are my home and my family.

"Vic, you are not weak. You're strong. You were willing to go through the pregnancy alone because you thought I had failed you after you chose to deliver our child, even if it meant doing it by yourself. I failed you. Your choice was the brave one. And yeah, you caught me by surprise at a difficult moment, but that doesn't excuse me."

Vicki wiped her eyes and frowned at him. "Well, I hope you are not a man who will always choose career satisfaction over family."

"I can promise you, I'm not going to be like that."

She shook her head from side to side. "We both made awkward choices in Paris, but you had already made that career choice over our relationship once when you went to Greece."

"I'm sorry that I didn't know everything and if we had had more time, and if you hadn't left...."

"Mark, you did know somewhere inside you and you still made the choice. Just like the choice I made rather than trusting you and being willing to let you know how vulnerable I was...am." Vicki took in a deep breath, and rubbed her face with both her hands. "When you hesitated, I panicked. I was also afraid to admit to myself and to you that I needed you. I've always tried to be stoic like you were saying about yourself. My parents' divorce really affected me and made me feel like I need an extra layer of toughness, particularly in this town that eats people alive. With the pregnancy, over the past few weeks, it's just been hard to stay strong and I have been mostly hibernating. So, I'm no wonder woman after all. Damn, I just hate to be so needy."

"Big deal," he said. "Nobody is that strong. We need each other. Will you marry me?"

"Oh, my God, yes! But you've got to promise not to leave me hanging like that ever again. And let's both agree to talk things out when anything comes up that we..."

He leaned into what she was saying and interrupted, "Yes. I agree. I'd agree to whatever crazy thing you have to say right now. However," he took in a deep breath, "we've got some quick planning to do, for a wedding and all of that. You may need to wear one of those tent dresses."

"Shut up and kiss me."

"When is the next Lamaze class?"

Vicki smiled but had a serous face as he leaned closer, "That's not for a while yet. But, you know Mark, you need to think about that part of you that stayed in Europe; that part of you that did not come home then or did not come the next day. You are a wonderful man who has great instincts and character, but there is this place in you that is closed. That is the part of you that I am afraid will never choose me first and will always be able to hurt me. I guess all couples have priorities that sometimes shift, but let's always try to be at least open and honest about ours. I think we will be better if we do." Three days later Mark and Vicki attended the July 4th fireworks on the South Lawn of the White House. Under the glow of the awesome, colorful explosions, they sat on blankets and shared wine, bottled water, and snacks with other young political operatives, and Vicki showed off her engagement ring and passed out the invitations to their upcoming wedding.

Stanos Petkas and his family were temporarily resettled near Washington, and Mark visited him often, sometimes with Vicki. She loved how the Petkas family incorporated the kids into all of their activities, and how almost everything they did included a teachable moment. Petkas was a part time professor at American University and had an occasional guest teaching professorship at the University of Virginia. But now it had been six weeks since Vicki and Mark last visited. She was advised to limit her movements in the last month of her pregnancy.

Today, when Mark walked into the house he saw brochures and a children's book that showed signs of the Petkas family's recent trip to visit the Civil War battlefield near Frederiksberg, Virginia. On the carpet in the den next to a recently arrived crate containing more of their old household items sent by Maria there were the remains of the boys' efforts to learn to make tomahawks. On the nearby dining room table, there was a large half-finished puzzle of a thousand pieces that, when finished, would show the Washington mall with the Smithsonian museums and monuments along the sides. They had found a school to help with the learning disorder of their son and, at least on the surface, everything looked stable and happy.

Mark and Petkas took a walk in the backyard of the house near Reston, Virginia, where there was evidence of a spirited effort to make a rather short split rail fence. Mark could see that he had lost some weight, and he looked drawn and nervous. It took Mark a few minutes to notice that Petkas also had shaved his trademark moustache that had given him so much distinction. He started the conversation on safe ground, "So are you all settled here and the kids are in school?"

"Yes. Everything has been taken care of and we have been treated well. I've started to write a long paper on the statues, how I found them, and all that went into this incredible adventure of ours."

"Well, I hope you will be able to publish it. I have not heard any update on our getting them out of Greece and how that might affect international relations… and all of that. It seems everyone over there assumed the story of a theft of sculpture was a crazy idea of the Russian Ambassador and not true, so publically no one knows what we did. Not to say that the rumor might have an effect on your going back for a visit."

"Yes. I assume there is still an issue with that guy Bruce, but my writing gives me something to do, and it is best to do these kinds of things while the material is still fresh." Petkas seemed jumpy and continued to look around the yard.

"But you have begun a new teaching job …is that right?"

"Yes. I now have a new and better job, a permanent job. So, we will be moving to Boston in the summer so the kids can start the school year there in the fall. I will be at Harvard, and to start I will give guest lectures. It will be good for me to use that time to work into the professorship." Petkas looked up and around at nothing in the sky, seemingly searching for something to do. He then rubbed one foot in the dirt near the split rail fence.

Mark could see that he still looked dejected. "Are you bothered that you cannot go back home?"

"I'm sort of … I know Greece is governed by very bad men just now. I hope that the conditions will change and my country can once again be a place of pride and prosperity. I don't want to be hated by my countrymen for my actions. Just because I haven't heard that they found out what we did, doesn't mean they won't. It's just a matter of time. I hope that we can take it all back there to be in a great museum someday."

Mark tried to say what he could to give Petkas a lift, but he knew it all sounded shallow. "Once all this story about the sculptures comes out and is understood, I know you will be seen as a hero. Those idiots would have likely auctioned the statues off or split them up. I can just see little plastic models of them in the Athens airport, can't you?" They both laughed.

"Yes, I know you are right. I just I wish it could be over. My Greek friends here are amazed I waited this long to leave and work in the West. I will have a good life in Boston, but perhaps an incomplete one. I want the importance of the gods of Olympus to be seen and understood. They are needed to fill in many blanks in the artistic history of Greece and the world. I guess I am just frustrated that it's taking so long."

"It will work out. Come on, we have an appointment to go see them. Maybe there is more news about when they can be unveiled to the world."

Mark drove Petkas back toward Washington onto the George Washington Memorial Parkway and 25 minutes later into the entrance of the CIA headquarters. On the drive they talked of Maria Beckett and how she now planned to split her time between Greece and her apartment in London. She was under no suspicion by the Greek government of having anything to do with Bokhan or the sculpture and she was coming to New York in four months for a visit where they planned to meet and spend the weekend together. Mark was happy that finally Vicki would meet the woman he had talked about so much.

They both gave the gate guard their credentials and were directed to the visitors' central parking lot. At the entrance to the bland building, they were met by a young staff person, given visitors' credentials and taken on a tour of parts of the facility that had been arranged by Bruce. The tour guide told them, speaking with some respect about him, that Bruce had recently been promoted to a new and more important job in the agency.

The tour led them finally to a room where they found Bruce and met several of the people who had helped in their escape, either in the planning, or in the field, or with the execution. Some of these people had no idea that the others in the room had also participated in the project since the CIA kept these things compartmentalized for security. Both Mark Young and Stanos Petkas appreciated the opportunity to thank everyone for their help.

After the gathering and refreshments, Bruce took Mark and Petkas to the central courtyard patio where many CIA staff secretaries as well as agents ate their sandwiches and salads at lunch. In the large, pleasant terrace covered by a massive Plexiglas and steel roof to keep out the elements, there were shade trees, shrubs and a fountain mixed into the center and a greenspace spreading out to the edges of the area that felt like a huge, well-groomed garden.

Also, carefully placed on sturdy platforms were the gods of Olympus, now conversing with each other in the casual and fluid setting intended by their creators almost 2500 years before. The employees were forbidden to take photos of the sculptures, though many were sorely tempted. Here they would remain, protected and probably under-appreciated until the circumstances in Greece were favorable enough for them to be returned there. Or perhaps they would finally be displayed in one of the major museums of the world. Bruce shook his head, "I'm sorry, Dr. Petkas. that we have to show them here for now. We are still working on a story to explain how we got them, but we don't want to cause an international incident. Once that is done they will find a place where the public can enjoy them. That is how it should be, and they will then to be appreciated by everyone on earth."

They stayed there for a while walking among the statues and looking at them from different angles. Mark was astonished at how lifelike they were and how accurately Petkas had described them in Greece many months ago. After a while, Petkas started to walk away from the area towards the building entrance and then looked back. His eyes scanned each sculpture again, taking in the details of their incredible beauty. Mark saw his face drop, and a sad look come into his eyes. He turned and did not look back as he left.

As Mark turned to follow Petkas to the car for their return trip, Bruce stopped him, "Here." Bruce handed Mark a folded piece of paper. "Call me at that number Monday afternoon after lunch. We need to get together, there is something I want to talk to you about."

"What is it?"

"A real job."

Mark stopped with surprise, "As much as I'd relish working with you on a regular basis, I'm not a Yale smarty pants, and I'm sure I don't want to become one of those dark personalities with buzz cut hair who works out of beltway offices with no name on the door."

Bruce smiled, "It's not actually like that. But, let's just talk. What can it hurt?"

In the many years since that time, the agency has had its good days and bad, but the sculptures stayed, and flowers and shrubs grew up in the corners of the garden around them and became a home and resting place for the butterflies, birds and insects. The restrictions for photography of the stone gods and penalties for mentioning them are still there on an old, faded sign in the corner. Over time the sculptures have become accepted as part of the space and decor. The young CIA staff leaning over their electronic gadgets while absent-mindedly eating their sandwiches notice them only as a curiosity left behind by the agents who came before them.

AFTERWORD

A Note on the Greek Economy

The Greek economy has continued to live on borrowed time and borrowed money. From when I was there it has declined for over 30 years into increasing debt and found one Band-Aid after the other to put over its self-inflicted financial wounds. Many Greeks continued to live to excess and enjoy the largesse of the government until now almost half of the population in one form or the other are receiving direct benefits from the government and unemployment reached a high of 30 percent in 2013. That was the same year Greece became the first nation to be re-classified from a developed market to an emerging market.

From the time the Greeks invented democracy, people living in that system have been reluctant to give up the benefits it offered them. As the Greek economy declined, the public expectation and appreciation for government benefits did not decrease, creating a divergent financial impasse and unemployment averaging almost 25 percent.

Although still a maritime force, the business atrophy of the Greek ship owners' exodus to London or New York continued and the shipping lines which had traditionally hired Greek sailors turned to other crews. The shift in localized Greek business investment and employment further destabilized the middle class which included that significant population of Greek sailors who had received good salaries under ships of the Greek flag and who now had difficulty finding work anywhere in their homeland.

It was five more years before the party of Mitsotakis had a clear win, but the efforts to reform the socialist government was too little and too late. As New Democracy took over, the Soviet Union fell in 1989, sending shock waves through Europe. By this time in Greece the economic hook was set, sliding the country toward the embarrassment we see today.

Each Greek citizen carries a national debt level of 30,000 euros per person. Recently there have been signs of the economy improving through the government's painful efforts toward austerity. Although there are many plans to develop new sources of revenue for Greece, today two of its main sources of income are from tourism and the export of yogurt.

In the United States, our national debt per person is approximately twice that of Greece.

END

ABOUT THE AUTHOR

"Casting Stones" is a continuation into the fascinating world of political consultant, Mark Young, and the intrigue that began with *Panama's Rusty Lock*. The third novel in this trilogy will be released in 2019.

For more on the novels and stories written by Jay Beck, see
Jay Beck.net
or look up *Panama's Rusty Lock*
on Amazon or Barnes and Noble Books.

Beck has had 50 years of experience in politics, from stuffing envelopes, to working in the White House, to consulting on international campaigns.

If you like this book he would be grateful if you gave it a good rating (5 stars = the best) on Amazon. Just pull up the book on Amazon and follow the prompts to the Customer Reviews. Once you are there, next to other ratings is an invitation to share your thoughts and write a customer review. Reviews help to reach a larger audience. You can also recommend the book to your friends on Facebook and other social media.

Jay Beck at the Acropolis

View of the Acropolis from my hotel room

Jay Beck with Maria Beckett in 1992 at the home of "Angus Whelan"

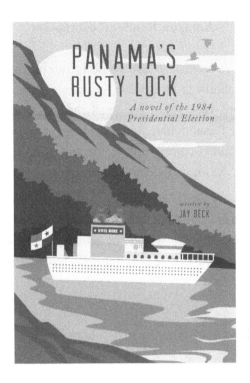

Here is what some readers said about the previous Mark Young book "Panama's Rusty Lock" which hit #2 on Amazon's Central American bestseller list.

Amazon Readers' comments

Page turning! *Panama's Rusty Lock* is interesting and intriguing. Jay Beck really is an insider that can communicate a story. Descriptions are very vivid - a must read. Thank you, Jay, for showcasing the Panamanian story that has not been told in such a lively fashion and is compelling to me and everyone else I know that has read it. Modern history well written.

As a history major in college, this book was impressive in its scope. The author's personal knowledge of actually being involved in the history as it was being made is an incredible read. Five stars seems inadequate. I give it 10.

Best book I have read in many years. Don't miss it!

As someone who has never given Panama much thought at all, I didn't expect to be very engaged here. Jay Beck managed to yank me out of the comfort of my home and into a climate of political unrest and corruption. The unsettling account of the drug trade in the area was by far my favorite part and I will be seeking out books on that subject in the future. *Panama's Rusty Lock* will appeal to those who love their drama mixed with politics.

I absolutely love historical fiction and non-fiction books and it seems like they have come together in *Panama's Rusty Lock: A Novel.*

I would highly recommend it, especially to lovers of historical fiction.

CPSIA information can be obtained
at www.ICGtesting.com
Printed in the USA
FFHW011046150119
50053633-54863FF